P9-DJL-212

Praise for *Never Let You Go*

"Stevens's taut writing and chilling depiction of love twisted beyond recognition makes this a compelling read from the first page to the last."   —*Publishers Weekly* (starred review)

"A fast-paced thriller with a surprise twist."
                                        —*Kirkus Reviews*

"The gripping, often terrifying story follows Lindsey as she endures the roller coaster that is survival and in the end finds an outcome that she never expected. . . . Stevens's portrayal is spot-on."   —*Booklist*

"A nicely managed puzzler."   —*Toronto Star*

Praise for *Those Girls*

"Tense, believable, and action-packed, made more vibrant by Stevens's sense of place."   —*Kirkus Reviews*

"Stevens skillfully builds suspense . . . this fast-paced nail-biter will keep readers up late—and may evoke a few tears."
                                        —*Publishers Weekly*

"Stevens's fifth novel has echoes of her blockbuster debut (*Still Missing*, 2010). . . . For the author's following or for those who like a frothy mix of suspense and melodrama."   —*Booklist*

"Hold on tight. This is a terrifying and terrific book."
                        —*Star-Telegram* (Fort Worth)

om

"If you are looking for a riveting mix of survival, redemption, and sheer terror, *Those Girls* is not to be missed."

—*Bookreporter*

"A pulse-pounding thriller."　　　　　　　　—*BookPage*

Praise for *That Night*

"Fast-paced and thought-provoking, *That Night* is a taut psychological thriller that skillfully explores bullying in its most terrifying forms. From the high school parking lot to the prison yard to a family's own living room, *That Night* shows just how fast those closest to us can become our most brutal enemies."　　　—Kimberly McCreight, *New York Times* bestselling author of *Reconstructing Amelia*

"Intense and disturbing—a terrific psychological thriller."

—Lee Child

"Chevy Stevens has done it again, crafting a story fraught with suspense that weaves back and forth through time and keeps you guessing. A gripping tale of secrets, betrayal, heartbreak, and ultimately, redemption, *That Night* is an emotional rollercoaster you'll be sorry to get off of when you finish the last page."　　　　　　—Jennifer McMahon, *New York Times* bestselling author of *The One I Left Behind*

"The writing is crisp and the dialogue realistic . . . Stevens has woven a warped psychological drama, a melancholy tale that comes to an existential and yet hopeful conclusion."

—*Kirkus Reviews*

"A compelling, exceptional read."

—*Library Journal* (starred review)

Praise for *Always Watching*

"In *Always Watching*, Chevy Stevens begins with a shivery premise—a family ensnared by a religious cult led by a madman. Stevens lights that fuse and lets it burn all the way to an explosive ending. A chilling, compelling read."

—William Landay, author of *Defending Jacob*

"*Always Watching* is a riveting examination of the power of childhood secrets over our past and our present selves. I couldn't put it down." —Alafair Burke, author of *If You Were Here*

"Chevy Stevens is in top form. *Always Watching* is a tense and twisty exploration of dark memories, hidden pasts, and a place that seems like heaven but might be hell. This is a deep and exciting novel, as unsettling as it is gripping."

—Lisa Unger, author of *Heartbroken*

"Haunting and harrowing, *Always Watching* is a stunner, offering not only consuming suspense but also a moving tale of mothers and daughters, the lingering echoes of the past that never stop reverberating." —Megan Abbott, author of *Dare Me*

"*Always Watching* grabbed me from page one. Its story of power, murder, and family secrets is seductive and sinister. Dr. Nadine Lavoie is a tenacious, compassionate heroine."

—Meg Gardiner, author of *Ransom River*

ALSO BY CHEVY STEVENS

Those Girls

That Night

Always Watching

Never Knowing

Still Missing

NEVER LET YOU GO

CHEVY STEVENS

ST. MARTIN'S GRIFFIN ☆ NEW YORK

This is a work of fiction. All of the characters, organizations, and events portrayed in this novel are either products of the author's imagination or are used fictitiously.

NEVER LET YOU GO. Copyright © 2017 by Chevy Stevens Holdings, Ltd. All rights reserved. Printed in the United States of America. For information, address St. Martin's Press, 175 Fifth Avenue, New York, N.Y. 10010.

www.stmartins.com

The Library of Congress has cataloged the hardcover edition as follows:

Names: Stevens, Chevy, author.
Title: Never let you go / Chevy Stevens.
Description: First Edition. | New York : St. Martin's Press, 2017.
Identifiers: LCCN 2016043109 | ISBN 9781250034564 (hardcover) |
    ISBN 9781250137173 (Canadian edition) | ISBN 9781250034571 (ebook)
Subjects: | BISAC: FICTION / Thrillers. | FICTION / Contemporary
    Women. | GSAFD: Suspense fiction.
Classification: LCC PR9199.4.S739 N49 2017 | DDC 813/.6—dc23
LC record available at https://lccn.loc.gov/2016043109

ISBN 978-1-250-13716-6 (trade paperback)

Our books may be purchased in bulk for promotional, educational, or business use. Please contact your local bookseller or the Macmillan Corporate and Premium Sales Department at 1-800-221-7945, extension 5442, or by email at MacmillanSpecialMarkets@macmillan.com.

First St. Martin's Griffin Edition: March 2018

10 9 8 7 6 5 4 3 2 1

For Carla, who never gives up

AUTHOR'S NOTE

The towns of Lions Lake and Dogwood Bay are fictional.
All other locations are real.

PART ONE

CHAPTER ONE

Lindsey

November 2005

I didn't have long. He was waiting at the beach—and he'd be counting every minute. I splashed cold water on my face, let the rivulets run down my neck and onto my shirt. I stared into the mirror. Tried to remember how to arrange my lips so I didn't look so scared, softened the muscles around my eyes, rubbed at the smeared mascara. It didn't matter how many ways I told him I hadn't been flirting with that man, I might as well have been shouting into the ocean.

The concrete floor of the bathroom was covered with sand and bits of paper that stuck to my flip-flops. Beside me a little girl struggled with her tap. I reached over and turned it on for her, then moved to the side, avoiding the curious look from her mother as she exited a stall.

They walked out hand in hand, the little girl chatting about Santa—would he find them at the resort? Christmas was a month away. I thought of Sophie with a sharp ache in my chest. Each day she added something new to her list. I had one thing on my wish list, just one.

This vacation was supposed to be an early Christmas gift from Andrew, but that was an excuse. He knew he'd gone too far last time. I came up with reasons we couldn't go to Mexico, but he'd overridden every one and booked a room at the resort where we stayed on our honeymoon. Our suite was even bigger this time, the view panoramic. As though white sand and sparkling turquoise water could make up for everything.

I had been careful to wear the pink one-piece when we went down to the beach that morning, layered with my tunic cover-up, the one with the high neckline and hem almost to my knees. Then I put on my straw hat and large sunglasses. As we left the room, he smiled his approval, drew me close for a kiss. I tensed, but I couldn't smell any alcohol on his breath or taste it on his lips. I wanted to pull away, but he had to end the kiss first.

We set up on the beach under one of the grass umbrellas for the next couple of hours as Sophie played in the sand. Andrew's hand held mine across our chairs, his thumb stroking lazy circles. A woman walked past and I caught her giving Andrew an admiring look. He was handsome in his white shorts, his stomach muscles clearly defined, his skin bronzed after only a few days in the sun, but none of this had any effect on me anymore. I was careful not to look around, but I imagined how we must seem to others. Just another happy couple with their child.

I pretended to doze, but I was watching Sophie behind my glasses. She was building an elaborate sand castle with turrets and a moat, and using a stick to draw designs in the side, where she carefully placed shells. She'd be seven in January, was already leaving the little girl behind, her limbs thinning out, her pale blond hair darkening to rich honey like her father's.

She picked up her pail and walked back to us. "I'm hungry, Mommy."

We flagged down the waiter, who'd been bringing Andrew Coronas all morning. "Una cerveza, por favor," Andrew would say, while I sipped on a lime margarita, and tried to ignore the growing knot in my stomach. We put in our order, chicken salad for me, burger and fries for them. Our waiter was handsome, with black hair and eyes, white teeth that flashed in quick smiles, and a cheeky expression. I avoided looking at him, but then I made the mistake. When I passed him my empty glass, his fingers lingered a moment against mine. It was an accident. He'd been distracted by some noise behind us, but I knew it wouldn't matter. Our hands had touched.

The waiter set down a fresh margarita in front of me and walked away. Andrew was wearing sunglasses, but I could still see his angry expression, the pinched look around his mouth, and my thoughts careened and slid around, trying to find purchase. I had to distract him.

I motioned to the beach, the palm trees. "The scenery is gorgeous."

"Yes, you looked like you were appreciating it."

"It's so relaxing." I molded my face into a pleasant smile. As if I didn't know what he was getting at. As if we hadn't been down this road so many times before.

Sophie, perched on the end of my beach chair with her towel wrapped around her waist, was watching our faces, her green eyes worried. She twirled a strand of wet hair around her finger. Ever since she was a baby, she'd twirl her hair when she was tired or anxious.

"Why don't you go collect more shells, sweetie?" I said. "They look beautiful on the turrets. I'll wave when lunch gets here." She got up, grabbed her blow-up dolphin, and walked back to the beach but looked over her shoulder at me a couple of times. I kept smiling.

"You must think I'm stupid," Andrew said when she was out of earshot.

"Of course not."

He focused back on his book, turning each page with a jerk. My breath was fast and tight in my throat. I took a sip of my drink, but the lime was no longer refreshing, the acid curling in my stomach. I rubbed at my breastbone, but it didn't ease the pressure.

Our meals arrived and the waiter asked if he could get us anything else, but Andrew wasn't speaking to him and I was forced to answer for both of us while Andrew stared at me. I could feel his rage from across the chairs, hear the rant he was rehearsing.

Sophie was now making her way back. I leaned closer to Andrew. "Please don't do this. Please don't turn this into something. He touched my hand by *accident*."

"I saw the way you looked at him, Lindsey."

"No, you *didn't*." This was when I should've been reassuring him, telling him he was my one and only, but the margarita had made me brave. It made me stupid.

"You're imagining things," I said.

It was as though his entire face broke apart and then rearranged itself into someone else. The real Andrew. The man no one saw except me.

Sophie ran up to us, sat beside me on the beach chair. Her skin was cold and wet against mine. She reached for a french fry. "Did you see all my shells, Mommy?"

"Yes, baby." I glanced at her castle. "They're perfect."

Andrew dumped ketchup onto his plate, smeared a french fry around. "Eat your lunch, darling."

"I just need to go and wash my hands." I could feel Andrew watching me all the way to the restrooms. I kept my head down and didn't look at anyone.

I threw my paper towel into the garbage, slid my sunglasses on. I had to get back to the beach. Sophie would want to swim again and I didn't want Andrew to let her when she'd just eaten. I thought of the Coronas he'd had. How many? I didn't even know. I used to keep count.

They weren't on the beach chairs. My salad was still on the side table, the lettuce wilting in the heat. My drink was empty. Andrew's burger and fries were gone, Sophie's half eaten. I looked around. They weren't at her sand castle. Maybe they went back to our room? I walked closer to Sophie's sand castle. Her towel was spread on the other side, her lime-green plastic sandals kicked off.

Her dolphin float was missing.

I took a few steps into the water, my hand covering my eyes. The waves rose and fell, an undulating mass of blue. Swimmers bobbed up and down. I squinted, tried to focus on their faces. Where was she? Where was Andrew? I spun around and scanned the people on the beach, the throngs of resort guests, clusters of kids running and chasing waves. I turned back and gazed out over the water again, looking for Sophie's small head, her red bathing suit.

Then I saw her blow-up dolphin moving up and down in the waves—with no one on it. I walked through the water as fast as I could, the current tugging against my legs, my feet sinking into the soft sand. When I was in deeper water I swam hard strokes to the toy and latched on. They had to be out there. Sophie never let that dolphin out of her sight.

I couldn't see her bright pink snorkel, but there were so many people in the water. I thought again of the food she had eaten, the beers Andrew had drunk. He was a strong swimmer, but Sophie was still learning, and tired easily. I plunged my head under the water.

I saw legs coming closer—masculine legs. I rose to the surface sucking in the air in big gasps. An older man a few feet away took his snorkel out of his mouth.

"You okay?" he yelled.

"I can't find my daughter!" More people were swimming

over. *What's she wearing? Did you see her go under? Someone get the lifeguard!*

I was treading water, my torso supported by the dolphin. "I didn't see her go in. She's only six. She's wearing a red bathing suit." A speedboat roared past and fresh waves sent us all bobbing up and down, salt splashing in my face. The horizon appeared and disappeared.

Someone from the resort on a Jet Ski radioed in her description. People were diving down, then rising to the surface with wet hair and foggy goggles.

None of them found her. I kept sticking my head under the water, but all I saw now were pale thrashing legs that stirred up the sand and made the water murky. I popped back up, looked out over the breakwater. Could they have been swept out to sea?

One of the resort boats was circling outside the roped-off swimming area. The staff in their white shirts and orange shorts, binoculars pressed to their eyes, searched the horizon. I waited for a yell, something, but the beach had gone curiously silent. People stood at the shore.

I didn't know how long I'd been in the water. My teeth were chattering and I was frantic, confused by all the people speaking to me. I explained that she was with my husband, that he could be missing too. The lifeguard wanted me to return to shore, tugged at my arm until I finally went with him. We swam to the beach and I lurched onto the sand, still clutching the dolphin float. My cover-up was clinging to my skin, wrapping around my thighs. My legs gave out and I collapsed onto my knees. The sun beat down on me, blinded my eyes as I stared out at the water.

Beside me the lifeguard urged me to drink water from a plastic bottle, then talked into his radio, Spanish phrases I couldn't understand. Jet Skis searched the water.

I felt something, an awareness that made me turn my head and look down the beach. It was them, walking toward us. Sophie in her red bathing suit with the white polka dots that we'd picked out together. Andrew, his long muscular legs taking those familiar loping steps. They were clutching drinks. Sophie looked like she was wondering what all the fuss was about.

I jumped to my feet, sprinted to them, almost losing my balance in the soft sand, but I was unstoppable. I lifted Sophie into my arms. I was crying into her neck.

"Mom, what's wrong?"

"What's going on, Lindsey?"

The lifeguard came over. "Is this your daughter, senora?"

"Yes, yes!" I lowered her down, pressed my hands to the sides of her face, and kissed her cheeks, her lips, her suntan-lotion-scented nose, her hair that had dried into salty ropes.

Andrew was talking with the lifeguard. "I'm sorry my wife put you all through this. She has an overactive imagination." He smiled and made little circles by his head.

The lifeguard gave him a confused smile, dropped a hand onto my shoulder, and peered into my face. "Drink some more water, senora. The sun, it's very hot, sí?"

He left us alone. The crowd was dispersing, but I could feel their judgment, the whispers. I didn't care. I had Sophie. She was solid and real and standing in front of me.

"I was so scared," I told her. "I saw your dolphin in the water."

"Daddy and I were playing and it floated away. He said we could get it later."

Andrew was staring out at the water. I tried to read his expression but he was wearing sunglasses. How angry was he that I'd made a fuss?

"It just kept floating away," he said. "Thought we might never see it again." Then he grabbed Sophie's hand. "Come on. Let's get out of the sun."

———

We were sitting under the umbrella. I was still shaking, though the sun was aiming directly at us and I'd wrapped a towel around myself—I'd noticed Andrew glancing at my wet cover-up clinging to my breasts and thighs. Sophie was sitting near me, her hand in mine. She kept giving me little pats. "I'm okay, Mommy. I'm okay. I'm sorry you got scared."

Andrew was watching me. I could feel his gaze burning into the side of my face. I wanted to ignore him, but I knew he was trying to get me to look at him. I turned. There was a look in his eye, something mean. Something smug.

"That was embarrassing," he said.

"Why didn't you wait for me?"

"You were taking too long." He shrugged.

"You did it on purpose. You were trying to scare me."

"Don't be silly," he said, rising to his feet. "You did that to yourself." He held his hand out for Sophie. "Come on, sweetie. I'll help you build another sand castle."

I watched them walk away. Sophie looked over her shoulder at me, her little face concerned. I smiled reassuringly. The lifeguard came over. "Is everything okay now, senora?"

"Yes, yes, it's fine." I didn't want him to linger. He turned away and I saw something in his face. Pity? Or did he think I was just a stupid blond woman who overreacted? I remembered how I had thrashed around in the water, how desperate I'd felt. How had I become this way? How had I turned into this woman who couldn't go to the bathroom without being afraid?

Andrew was filling a pail with sand. Sophie and he had the same determined expression. He felt me watching, gave a small wave and a friendly smile.

You're imagining things. That's what I'd told him, and then he made me pay.

But he hadn't just wanted me to be scared. He wanted me to

know he could take her from me. In the blink of an eye. One day I might be in the bathroom, or maybe I'd step outside for a moment, or go to the store, and they'd be gone. I would never see her again.

I had to leave him when we got home. There was no more time to plan. No matter what it took, no matter how risky it was, I had to get Sophie away from him.

I slowly lifted my hand, gave my palm a kiss, and blew it in his direction.

CHAPTER TWO

December 2016

The house is quiet when I wake, the floorboards cold under my feet as I push myself out of bed. "Sophie?" She doesn't answer. Sometimes she gets up early to work on a project, or goes for a walk. She likes to study the patterns in the snow and ice. It worries me when she goes off into the woods by herself, but she wears hiking boots and carries a whistle, and trying to keep her home when she's feeling inspired is like trying to capture lightning in a bottle.

Shivering, I wrap my flannel robe tight around my body and shuffle into the kitchen. Sophie's put a pod in the coffeemaker for me, left a note stuck to the machine.

Sorry, Mom. The snow was calling . . . XO

My baby, the artist. I pin the note onto the bulletin board, on top of the others I've saved, then check that she's locked the door and reset the alarm. She's always forgetting, says we have nothing worth stealing anyway. I remind her that's not the point.

I let the shower run hot as I can stand it, steam filling the room, soap swirling around my feet and down the drain. My hair is long again and the wet tendrils lay flat against my breasts. My mind drifts as I think about my plan for the upcoming week, which clients might need more help before Christmas, whether I should place an ad for another cleaner. Maybe I can expand and take on some janitorial work next year when Sophie goes away to school. I enjoy this feeling of accomplishment. In the beginning it was just me, a beat-up car, and a box of cleaning supplies. Now I have four full-time employees and nothing holding me back.

After I'm dressed, I unplug my phone from the charger and notice I've gotten a text from Marcus. *You still want to skip this week? Let me know.* Marcus teaches a self-defense class for my domestic violence support group and sometimes gives me private lessons.

I text him back. *Yeah, just busy, but I'll see you at the meeting.* I make a second cup of coffee—the first is for sanity, the second is pure pleasure—and prop my phone up against the bowl of fruit on our kitchen table. I sign in to Skype and wait for Jenny to answer my call.

She comes into view, her blond hair still messy from sleep, her face pale without makeup, but she has an ethereal kind of beauty that makes her look angelic—and much younger than her forty-five years. I always tell her that if she wasn't my best friend, I'd have to kill her.

"God," she says. "What a morning."

"Yeah?"

"Teen girls." She shakes her head. "Enough about that. What are you doing today?"

"I have one cleaning job. Then maybe some Christmas shopping."

"I thought Saturdays were your day off."

"One of the new girls I hired just quit—she's back with her boyfriend." Most of the girls I hire are from my support group.

Women starting over with the shreds of their lives stuffed into suitcases, garbage bags, or the backseat of their cars. Unfortunately, they aren't always ready to move on. "She says he's changed, but you know . . ."

"Right." We're both quiet. She doesn't need to tell me that she's thinking about her ex-husband, just like she knows I'm thinking about Andrew. Jenny and I also met in group.

"How's Sophie?" she says. We talk about Christmas gift ideas, anything and everything that crosses our minds. For the last couple of years we've done all our shopping together— Jenny can actually turn Christmas chaos at the mall into a fun adventure. Since she moved to Vancouver a few months ago, I miss her terribly, but we try to talk often.

"I'm not sure about Greg," I say. "What do you get someone you've only been dating for a few months?"

"How about a nice dinner? Or cologne? The Gap has sweaters on sale."

"I don't think he's the Gap type." I smile, trying to imagine Greg, with his colorful tattoos and tight-shaved head, wearing a preppy sweater. I've only ever seen him in his UPS uniform, or shirts and dark jeans when he's dressing up. He looks intimidating, but when you speak to him, you notice his warm brown eyes and happy-go-lucky laugh. Maybe cologne is a good idea. Then I realize I don't even know what cologne he wears.

"I'll have to think about it," I say. "I was wondering about inviting him over to help decorate the tree with Sophie and me, but that's always been our tradition."

"You should probably ask her how she feels about it."

"Good idea." I glance at the clock. "I better get going."

It's started to rain, the snow on the side of the roads turning to mush that grabs at my tires. Winter in Dogwood Bay means you never know whether to expect rain or snow, or sometimes both. I'm a half hour late, but it won't matter. Mrs. Carlson, a nice old lady who lives with her cat and bird, always leaves in the morning to visit her sister on cleaning days. I follow the garden path around the side of the house. The rain is melting snow off the shrubs and trees, chunks hitting the ground with a muffled thud. I squeal as one almost hits me.

When I unlock the door, the house is freezing cold. I fiddle with the thermostat, bumping it up a couple of levels, then set my boots on the mat, slide on my slippers, and put my tray down on the kitchen counter. Something smells burnt, like toast. The dish rack holds one plate and teacup, and a knife. A small plastic Christmas tree sits in the corner of the living room, hung with a few brightly colored ornaments. There's already a stack of presents underneath.

I start on the kitchen, scrub the counters and sink until they gleam, then mop the floor. I hum Christmas carols as I work and think about when Sophie and I should put up our own tree. We always get a fresh one, then decorate while watching *Elf* and drinking hot chocolate.

I move into the living room, wipe every surface with lemon-scented cleaner, fold a knitted blanket, fluff the pillows, vacuum the cat fur off the back of the couch and from under the cushions. I haven't seen Gatsby, but he's probably sleeping under the bed. Next I vacuum the carpet so the lines are all in the same direction, backing up as I go, careful not to leave a single footprint. I grab my tray and move down the hall, then pause halfway when I hear a noise behind me. I turn quickly, my body stiffening. A streak of white. Gatsby.

I make a kissing noise and call his name, but he doesn't come running like usual. He must be chasing a spider.

When I'm finished in the master bedroom, I make my way to the spare room at the other end of the house. Mrs. Carlson rarely has guests, but the room always needs dusting because of her budgie, Atticus. It's my least favorite room—the dander from his feathers makes me sneeze and Atticus screams the whole time I'm cleaning, but today he is remarkably silent.

As I push open the door, a cold draft whistles toward me. The window is open. I hurry over and slide it down. So that's why the house is so cold. When I turn around, rubbing my arms to get warm, I spot Atticus hunched into a ball at the bottom of his cage. He's always perched on his wooden branch, screeching at me or ringing his bell. I frown, take a tentative step. "Atticus?" He doesn't move. I take another step. His eyes are closed, his tiny chest unmoving. I look back at the window. How long had it been left open? Mrs. Carlson's going to be devastated.

Back in the kitchen, I rummage through my purse on the counter for my phone, knocking it over in the process. My lip gloss rolls out. I don't stop to retrieve it. Mrs. Carlson's sister answers and I have to repeat my name. Finally she puts her on the phone.

"Mrs. Carlson, I'm so sorry, but Atticus . . ." I pause. How do I put this? "Atticus has passed away. I'm so sorry," I repeat.

"Oh, no!" she says, her voice quavering. "Whatever happened?"

"I think he might have gotten too cold."

"The window! I was sure I closed it—I always let him have some fresh air in the mornings so he can sing to the birds outside." I don't know why she had the window pushed all the way up at this time of year, but I'm not going to make her feel worse by asking questions.

"Poor Atticus," she says. "I'll have to take care of him when I get home." Her voice is starting to break and I can tell she's near tears. "Perhaps I should bury him outside under the lilac bushes. They're so pretty in the summer. Do you think that's a nice place?"

"It's a perfect place." I can't just leave her to take care of it on her own. "Would you like me to do it?"

She pauses, and I hear her blowing her nose. "I couldn't ask you to do that."

"I wouldn't mind."

"Oh. That's very kind. I'd like that." She catches her breath, a hiccup of sound. "I'm going to miss him terribly. The house will be so quiet without his beautiful singing."

"He was a lovely bird." She sounds so shaken. I'm glad she's with her sister. I'll bring her flowers this week, stop by and have tea with her.

"Thank you, dear." She blows her nose again. "Can you say a prayer for him?"

"Of course."

I grab a small box and newspaper from the recycling and create a makeshift coffin for Atticus's body, which I place in the garage. I finish the rest of the cleaning, vacuuming Atticus's cage and pulling a sheet over it. Then I get Atticus's body from the garage. When I crouch down to pick up the box, I catch the scent of something masculine in the air, something woodsy. I stand quickly and look around. The garage is neat and tidy, only her dead husband's old Buick filling the space. She must have an air freshener.

I'm still thinking about Mrs. Carlson as I walk into the kitchen. Her animals have meant the world to her since she lost her husband three years ago. I set the shoe box down, look for my keys on the counter, then pause. They're gone. My purse is upright. I'd knocked it over earlier, and my keys and lip gloss had tumbled out. I left them lying there. I stare at the beige fake leather bag I'd found on sale at Walmart that looks like a Chanel, according to my daughter anyway. I peek inside. My keys and gloss have been carefully placed on top of my wallet.

I stumble back. I don't stop for my boots or my coat. I just run out of the house, noticing in a quick flash that the door is unlocked. He went out that way. He could be waiting.

I sprint for my car, lock the doors, and press the numbers

on my cell. I rummage through my glove box for my pepper spray, remove the safety, and hook my thumb on the trigger. While I'm waiting for the police, I stare at the house and the path, watch for any movement.

It's been three months since my brother called to tell me Andrew had been released from prison and that someone saw him on Vancouver Island. I can still remember the sound of Chris's voice when he phoned, the hesitation and tightness. I knew before he even said anything. This was the call I'd been waiting for. Andrew was a free man and he was going to find me.

But days passed. Then weeks, months. Nothing happened, and I thought we were safe.

My gaze travels from the door to each window, up to the second floor, then down again. The whole time I was inside, cleaning, singing, and vacuuming, he was in there too. He might have been standing so close he could have touched me. Why didn't he make his move? Then I realize why he didn't. It wouldn't have been enough for him. He needs me to suffer.

He's going to make me pay for every year he spent behind bars.

CHAPTER THREE

DECEMBER 1997

"Watch out!" Andrew shouted, and I ducked as a snowball hit my boots. "That's it!" He tackled my brother to the ground. I laughed as they wrestled in the snow, trying to shove handfuls down each other's necks. My dad jumped out of the back of the moving truck and started lobbing snowballs at them. It was good to see him with a smile on his face.

I wished my mom could have been there. Maybe we could bring her over later. I worked my way through the snow, carrying the heavy box, and walked carefully up the icy steps. The hallway still smelled of fresh paint, a welcoming sage-green. Andrew had the painters come back twice because of drip marks, but now it was perfect. We'd stacked boxes everywhere. Most of them came from Andrew's house, others were wedding gifts.

I slid the box onto the counter. I should have gone outside for the next one, but I couldn't help wandering into the dining room to stroke my fingers across the silky surface of the pine table we'd picked out last week. I imagined my family over for dinner Sunday nights, plates heaped full, everyone talking and laughing. Mom could rest on the couch while I cleaned up. She seemed so tired lately and I was sure her MS was getting worse, but she wouldn't talk about it. I'd send them home with leftovers so she wouldn't have to cook for days. Andrew and my father would talk about houses they were building, rolling plans out on the table. Chris would hang on to their every word, counting the days until he graduated so he could work for Andrew too.

I walked to the front bay window, where ice bloomed in the corners of the glass like beautifully frosted spiderwebs. The house was freezing—the utilities had been hooked up that morning—and we'd been taking sips from the flask Andrew had brought with him. "That doesn't taste like hot chocolate," I teased.

He laughed. "It's my special recipe."

I spun in a circle. Where should we put the Christmas tree? Maybe right in front of the window. We'd get one that reached to the ceiling, and cover it with so many lights and ornaments the branches would bend. We'd had a heavy snowfall, early for Lions Lake, and it was looking like we'd have a white Christmas. I couldn't remember the last time that had happened.

When I walked back outside, Andrew was unloading a wardrobe box, his leg braced, his face determined and flushed from exertion. He'd removed his coat and was wearing a white knit shirt, sleeves pushed up. His work trucks were all immaculate white, same with his crew's shirts and caps. His construction company's dark green and black logo stood out in crisp contrast.

My dad and Chris were in the back of the rented moving truck. Andrew had wanted to hire a company and didn't think it was fair to ask my family. "Your dad works hard all week." I explained it was the kind of family we were. We helped each other.

I came up beside Andrew. "So who won the snowball fight?"

"Me, of course." He smiled. "You okay?"

"I'm absolutely completely beyond happy."

He threw his head back and laughed. I felt that little hiccup in my chest, the same one I'd had the summer day he came into the hardware store where I worked, asking to speak to our manager. I hadn't seen him around before, and I knew everyone who worked construction in our small town. After he left I made a beeline to the back and found out his name was Andrew Nash, he was from Victoria, and he was developing a parcel of raw land at the end of the lake.

The next time he came in, I helped him find everything he needed, chatting about Lions Lake, all the fun things we did in the summer, how hot it had been lately, thinking the whole time that I really needed to shut up and let him say something, but I couldn't stop my runaway mouth. I even pulled out a map and showed him the best swimming spots around the lake. As if he couldn't find them himself. While he waited for me to ring up his order, he kept pushing back his dark blond hair with one hand. It was streaked lighter in spots and fell to his shoulders.

"You need a haircut," I said, then blushed. What a thing to say.

"I do," he said with a laugh. "I've just been too busy." The light was shining through the side window and hitting his eyes—green, the color of glacier water.

"Is your dad Ian Finnegan?" he said.

I passed him his receipt. "You know him?"

"I heard he might be looking for work."

"My dad's a great carpenter, has lots of experience." I held my breath. I didn't want to say too much, but I couldn't help thinking of my dad, sitting at home and making call after call. He'd had a good job but was fired because he had to take so much time off to help Mom.

"Tell him to drop by the site."

After that I'd see Andrew on the days I brought lunches for my dad. He rarely stopped to eat with the crew, but almost always paused to say hello to me and ask how I was doing. "He never quits," my dad told us at dinner, his admiration clear in his face. "He's there before we are with coffee and donuts for the guys, and he's the last one to go home."

One day I brought him a roast beef sandwich and he looked so surprised, just stared at it in his hand while I waited in humiliation. Then his face broke into a huge smile and he said roast beef was his favorite. We sat and talked, and he invited me to see some land he was thinking of buying. We hiked that entire property together, climbed under and over logs, slid down hills, laughing as we both almost fell on our butts, sharing a bottle of water and cursing ourselves for not bringing more. From that day on, we saw each other as much as possible.

We hadn't actually lived together yet, but I wasn't worried. We understood each other's every thought and mood—he knew when I was getting hungry and tired, or when something had upset me. And I knew *him*, just like I knew marrying him was the best decision I'd ever made.

Now Andrew stopped as he walked past, kissed me on the cheek. "Welcome home, Mrs. Nash."

I was unpacking a box in Andrew's new office, carefully placing files in his desk drawer, when I heard his footsteps behind me. I turned and smiled, but faltered when I saw the look on his face. He almost seemed upset, but then his expression smoothed out.

"You don't have to do that," he said.

"I don't mind." I wondered if it was the sight of his desk that bothered him. It was one of the few things he had from his father. We'd found it when we were cleaning out his storage unit. He wasn't sure about bringing it to the house, said it was too old and scratched and that it wasn't really his style, but I told him the oak was gorgeous and we could refinish it as a winter project.

He came over, took the files out of my hands, and set them down. "I have my own system. If you put something in the wrong place, I'll have a hard time finding it."

"Right, sure. Of course."

"Dinner smells good." I could tell he was trying to ease the sting of his rebuff, but I still felt bad. I should've asked. I was just so used to helping around at my parents' house. Nothing had been off-limits since Mom was diagnosed with MS. I even did their banking.

"I'm making Yorkshire pudding."

"Hmm. Perfect," he said against my neck.

"Your nose is cold!"

"I was shoveling the driveway." My dad and Chris had gone home hours ago and we'd been unpacking ever since. "Looks like it's going to snow again tonight."

"I hope they clear the roads. Josh asked me to come into work tomorrow."

He lifted his head. "I thought you were taking the day off so you could finish up here."

I sighed. "Someone called in sick again." It seemed this time of year someone was always calling in sick after too much Christmas cheer.

"I was going to talk to you about this over dinner, but I'm going to offer your dad the foreman job. It will mean he has to travel a fair bit."

"Oh, that won't work with my mom." I felt disappointed for my dad. They could really use the money and I knew he was excited about some of the projects they were bidding on.

"If you quit the hardware store and work with me, you'll be around to help her. I need someone to stage the houses and the display suites, picking out fixtures, things like that."

"I don't know. . . . Josh was saying they might promote me to work in the office." I didn't want people thinking I was a spoiled rich housewife who had everything because of her husband. When Andrew's mom died, he inherited the trust from his grandfather's stock market fortune, but he only got small payments—he wasn't wealthy like my friends seemed to think. Besides, I liked working at the hardware store, seeing my regular customers, helping people find things.

"Honey, Josh is talking out his ass. He's never going to promote you."

"I've been working there for years." I'd started when I was still in high school and went full-time last year after I graduated. I'd thought about going to college or taking some classes, but I wasn't sure what I wanted to do. I admired how focused Andrew was at only twenty-seven.

"Yeah, you're the cute girl who works behind the counter. I knew about you before I even stepped foot in there. I'm sorry, Lindsey, but I heard they were going to promote Mike."

"Josh sounded really sincere." I felt hot and angry, but mostly hurt.

"I'm not trying to make you feel bad. I'm just saying how other people look at you. They only see a pretty blonde." He tugged on the end of my ponytail. "They don't appreciate you the way I do, they don't see how intelligent you are, how creative."

Maybe he was right. Maybe the hardware store was a dead end, but how many hours a day could I spend choosing paint colors? "Maybe I could help with the bookkeeping?"

"It's probably better if I take care of the finances. But you have a great eye. I love what you've done with this house already."

"I haven't done much." He'd picked out all the colors, said they had to be neutral earth tones so the house would be easier to sell in a year, but I tried to add some personality with our bedding and curtains and plants. We hung our wedding portrait over the fireplace.

"You've made this feel like a home. You know how much that means to me." His hands were sliding under my shirt, up my shoulder blades, and to the nape of my neck as he gently pushed me against the desk. In one quick motion, he lifted me up, sat me down on the top of the desk, and nudged my knees apart. I almost lost my balance, but he held me steady with his large hands on my hips and gave me a mischievous look. "Think about it, okay?"

Then he was pulling me closer and spreading hot kisses from my collarbone to my mouth, and I was grabbing at his shoulders and I wasn't thinking about anything.

The idea for the perfect Christmas gift came to me the night we moved in. We were relaxing on the couch when I realized we had lots of photos of my family on the mantel, and only one of his mother. He didn't have any pictures of his father because he lost a box of photos when he moved years ago, but I knew how I might find some. His father had been in the Navy. Surely there was an association for former members. I just needed to do a little research.

Andrew never talked about his family much and I'd never pressed, but his face shifted if he mentioned his mother. Sometimes his expression was sad, other times his lips would lift in a fond smile as he shared a happy memory. She died when he was twenty, and then he was on his own—his father had already been gone for years. He'd left on a Navy trip when Andrew was twelve and never came back. "He couldn't adjust to family life after being out at sea for months," Andrew said. "It was too much for him." He didn't sound sad or angry, just matter-of-fact. And when his dad died a few years ago, Andrew paid for the funeral.

I went online and found a list of ships that were in operation on the West Coast during the years Andrew's father served in the Navy. Then it was a matter of searching through the archives for names and photos of crew members. Within two days I found a photo of Edward Nash, standing on the bow of a ship with some other men. I blew up the grainy black-and-white photo on my computer screen and studied Edward. He looked stiff in his uniform, and very young, but his features were so familiar it was startling. I wondered if they shared more than their looks. It was too bad they never had a chance to reconnect. I would've liked to meet him. I leaned closer, imagined telling him about Andrew.

Your son is wonderful. Everyone loves him. He does all kinds of things for the community, builds park benches, belongs to a charity baseball team, and he even helped my dad build my mom a wheelchair ramp so she can get around better. You'd be so proud.

I sent an e-mail to the photo lab and asked if they could clean the pictures up, then browsed online for the perfect frame. Andrew was going to be so surprised.

It was Christmas Eve, and Andrew and I had decided to open one present each. In the morning we'd go to my parents' and have a pancake breakfast. It was the first year I wouldn't wake up with my family and I felt a little sad, but also thrilled to celebrate with my new husband.

Later we were going to finish wrapping the presents we bought for my parents and brother. I'd been excited to go around the mall with Andrew and heap our cart full of gifts. When I worried we were spending too much money, Andrew said he wanted to spoil them because they'd been so welcoming. "I just want them to be happy."

"Maybe this one?" Andrew had chosen the frame I'd carefully wrapped in glimmering pale blue paper, the silver ribbon shaped into spirals like cascading icicles.

"Sure." My stomach fluttered with excitement and I wished I hadn't drunk so much eggnog. His large hands carefully eased the paper off. He was taking his time, giving me a wink, teasing out the moment. I was almost ready to snatch it out of his hands and unwrap it for him.

He removed the last piece of paper, then stared down at it. "What's this?" His voice sounded hollow. I was confused. Was he overcome with emotion?

"It's a photo of your dad." I'd chosen one where his father looked the least stern, his gaze focused on something in the distance.

"I know what it is. How did you get it?" He was glaring at me, and now I saw it. That same expression as his father's. I didn't know his face could go like that. I fumbled for my words.

"You told me his name before, so I found a Navy Web site." I reached out a hand, rested it on his forearm. The muscles flexed and bunched under my fingers. I slowly pulled my hand away. "We have all these photos of my family, and I thought—"

"That you would make me feel like shit? My father walked out on my family. I don't need to see his face to remember that. I can't believe you did this."

My embarrassment was turning to hurt and my eyes stung. "I was trying to do something nice. I didn't know you're angry at him—I barely know anything about your childhood."

"Is that why you looked online? So you could dig up dirt on me?"

"Of course not. I don't understand why you're so upset."

"You want to know about my father? He was an asshole,

okay? He treated me like crap, and he treated my mother like crap. He came back two days after she died, said he wanted to get to know me, but he just wanted money from the trust fund. I kicked him out." He dropped the frame onto the floor, shattering the glass. "That's what you've done to our Christmas."

He walked away, and a moment later his office door closed with a thud.

I sat on the couch, staring at the tree through blurred eyes. How could I have been so stupid? Of course he didn't want a reminder of his father. Just because I loved mine so much didn't mean everyone felt the same way. But I couldn't stop replaying Andrew's words—the way he looked at me. We'd never fought before. There was only one time on our honeymoon when he snapped at me, then took off for a long walk by himself, and left me waiting in the room. Later he said that he didn't like how the tour operator was speaking to me, which was totally my fault. I was definitely being too friendly and didn't think about how someone could misread that.

Maybe Andrew was just tired, still recovering from our trip and the move. I glanced down the hall, wondered if I should apologize, then decided to give him some space.

I picked up the broken glass, swept up the tiny fragments, hid the frame in a closet, then turned on the TV. The distraction helped, but when Andrew still hadn't come out for over an hour, I softly knocked on his door. He didn't answer. I rested my hand on the wood.

"Andrew, I'm really sorry."

Silence.

It was almost midnight. My eyelids were drooping and I needed to go to bed soon, but I was in the living room, wrapping the last few presents for my family. Finally I heard Andrew's office door open, then his weight settling on the couch behind me. I held my breath.

"I'm sorry, Lindsey," he said. "I behaved like an ass."

I spun around. "No. I'm sorry. I should have known."

"How could you? You're right. I didn't tell you about him. I've never talked about it with anyone, none of my friends, not even Melissa, and we lived together for three years." I tried not to wince at the name of his ex-girlfriend, who cheated on him and then stole half his stuff.

"I'm not her," I said. "I love you."

"I know." He let his breath out in a sigh. "I don't deserve you."

"Don't say that. Of course you do. I just wish you'd share more about your life with me." I moved to sit beside him on the couch. "I just want to *know* you."

"There's not much to tell." He swallowed. "Let's just say my father made it pretty clear I wasn't wanted. He shoved me down the stairs a couple of times, knocked me around a bit, and was handy with the belt. I spent most of my childhood being afraid of him whenever he was home from the ships. He was always yelling at my mom—and I saw bruises on her arms. I was glad when he finally left, but then a few years later my mom found the first lump. I tried to take care of her the best I could until she died, but I was still a kid, you know?"

I wanted to cry, thinking about everything he had been through. He'd grown up so fast. "You have my family now." I leaned over and wrapped my arms around him, squeezing hard.

"You all mean so much to me," he said. "It's like I was floating along for years and now I've finally found somewhere to land. I never want to lose you." He rested his warm cheek against mine, his arms holding me tight. My body relaxed, and I felt a surge of relief. This was the Andrew I knew and loved. "I'm really sorry I broke your gift," he said. "I hate to think that you spent all that time trying to make it special for me, and then I go and wreck everything. I don't know why I get like that sometimes. It's like I just see red and then I can't think straight. I don't want to be like that with you." He sounded so confused, so unsure of himself, so ashamed.

I pulled away, looked him in the face. "It's not that big of a deal, okay? We have lots of Christmases ahead of us. Next year I'll knit you a tacky scarf or something."

He cupped the side of my face. "You're too good. How did I get so lucky?"

"You might not think you're so lucky when you deal with my family chaos tomorrow."

"Let's go to bed. I want to hold you and show you how much I love you." He was looking at me in the way that usually made me crave his touch, but something held me back.

I picked up a red bow. "Not yet! We have to finish wrapping these gifts!"

I watched him carefully place the bow in the center of a large package. I was still unsettled but pushing off the lingering negative feelings. This was what made a *real* marriage—arguments, misunderstandings, then talking things out and becoming even closer.

It was okay that we didn't wrap the presents together. We finished them together.

CHAPTER FOUR

DECEMBER 2016

The officer's name is Corporal D. Parker. She looks to be in her late thirties, with auburn hair pulled back into a bun, pale blue eyes, and a friendly smile that I know is meant to make me relax, but I can't stop shivering and stumbling over my words. I'm holding her card tight in my palm and keep glancing at it as though the RCMP logo and official letters will somehow make me feel safe. I can't remember what the *D* stands for, the introductions a blur. I was so relieved when I saw her car pull in behind me. She went inside first and made sure no one was lurking, but I already knew Andrew would be long gone. He's too smart to linger.

We're standing in the kitchen now and I'm trying to explain why I'm so sure it was my ex-husband. "He put my keys on top of my purse—he used to get mad at me for losing them."

"Anything missing from your wallet?"

"I don't know. He put my lip gloss back in my purse too." I stare at it, and know I'll never use that gloss again as long as I live. "He must have come in through the window."

"Okay, show me where."

I take her to the spare room, point at the window, and she looks outside. I think about how much it's rained in the last hour, how the snow has melted all around the house.

"Do you know if she has any valuables in the house?"

"Maybe a few pieces of jewelry—but Andrew wouldn't have taken anything. He just wanted me to know he was in the house. I think he was hiding in the front closet and snuck out when I was cleaning the bedrooms. Gatsby spooked at the end of the hall."

"Gatsby?"

"The cat."

"I should probably talk to him too." I blink at her, and she smiles and gives a shrug. "Cop humor." She glances at the window frame, leans over like she's looking for something on the sill. "I'll dust for prints, and I'll need the number for the home owner."

I wait on the couch while she works upstairs. I can hear the low murmur of her voice on the phone, her footsteps. It was obvious she didn't want to talk to Mrs. Carlson when I was in the room—she asked me to stay downstairs because she might have more questions.

The officer (I remember now her first name is Dana) comes downstairs with her fingerprint kit. She's already taken mine so she can compare them and has dusted my purse and the closet door, but she wasn't able to get anything. She sits on the other side of the couch.

"I got a few off the windowsill. I'll do some comparisons at the station later." I already know, if she didn't find anything in the rest of the house, she won't find anything on the window.

"Did you talk to Mrs. Carlson? She must be so worried." And scared. I hate thinking that Andrew caused her beautiful bird to die. What will she think of me now?

"She's on her way back and will let me know if anything's missing." She glances at her watch. "I'll meet her here in a couple of hours."

"Can I leave now?"

"Just a few more questions, if you don't mind." Her voice is still casual, but her eyes are intent. "You said your ex-husband was released from prison recently. What was he in for?"

"Impaired driving causing death." The officer is still watching me, her eyes narrowed like she's waiting for me to get to the point, but I'm having a hard time speaking, all the memories flooding back. "He hit another driver and she died. They found a gun in his truck. He told the cops he wanted to kill me." He'd been given ten years, the maximum sentence. Many offenders only serve two-thirds, but finally his temper worked in my favor. He refused to join any programs, never showed remorse, and got in so many fights he kept getting denied parole. After seven years, he would have been eligible for statutory release, but then he stabbed a man in prison, nearly killing him. He claimed self-defense, so he wasn't charged, but he ended up having to serve his whole sentence.

"Have you heard from him since he was released?"

"No, but you don't understand. He plays mind games. He would do this to scare me." My body is breaking out in a sweat and I feel cold all over. I want a thick blanket, a hot bath.

"I'll check into his whereabouts."

"I'm not making this up." I hear the defensive tone in my voice and know I sound hostile, but her expression doesn't change. "He was here. I *know* he was."

"I understand you're afraid of him," she says. "But, unfortunately, without evidence of an actual crime or proof he was in the house, I can't do anything." Her face is sincere, and I get the feeling she actually does believe me, but it's not bringing me much comfort at the moment.

"Then what can I do? How can I protect myself?"

"You could apply for a section 810 peace bond, but the Crown will want more evidence that he's a threat to your safety. If your ex-husband is the one who moved your keys, it's creepy, but not necessarily threatening."

"Is that a restraining order?"

"Similar, yes. If you want a protection order, that's usually granted in family court at the time of your divorce. The peace bond is more of a preventive order. He has to agree to the terms in court and he could fight it. Then it will fall on you to prove why it's necessary."

"So I have to wait until he does something really bad."

"If you do feel he's becoming a definite threat, give me a call and I'll help you through the process." She writes something on the back of another business card, passes it to me. "And if you remember anything else about today, please call me. My cell number is on the back."

As she walks me to the door I realize that Atticus's box is sitting on the counter. "I was supposed to bury her bird."

"It's raining pretty hard out there now."

"I said I would do it." I pick up the box and hold it tight against my chest.

"How about you leave him with me?"

Right. So she can toss him out the window of her car as she drives down the highway? "Thanks, but I know that Mrs. Carlson would feel more comfortable knowing I took care of this for her." I grab my purse and walk toward the door before she can stop me.

She watches from the back porch as I march to the garden shed and drag the shovel toward the lilac bushes. I stab at the ground, use my foot to jam the shovel into the hard earth. The cold rain is blowing into my face and my hair is getting soaked, icy rivulets dripping down my neck, but I can't stop. My breath heaves out of me. *Come on, come on.* I get a chunk of dirt up and toss it to the side. Footsteps come up beside me.

"Are you sure you don't—"

A clod lands near her feet and she neatly sidesteps, doesn't say anything else while I dig the hole and place the box inside, scraping dirt back over with my hands.

I stand straight and take some breaths. I don't look at the officer. I close my eyes, bow my head, and say a prayer for Atticus. Then I say a prayer for Sophie and me.

CHAPTER FIVE

November 1998

She was kicking again. I stopped in the middle of the hardware store, ran my hands over my belly. There was a foot, her tiny bum, or maybe the curve of her shoulder. Andrew was so thrilled when the doctor told us we were having a girl, he bought her a pink fishing rod. I pressed gently on my stomach, smiled as I felt her push back and imagined her doing somersaults. A baby ballerina, an acrobat. I hadn't planned on getting pregnant five months into our marriage, but when Andrew told me how he wanted to have children young so we'd have the energy to keep up with them, then enjoy our retirement, it made sense. I could always focus on my career later.

I sighed, looked back up at the wall. I'd been staring at this display of kitchen faucets for twenty minutes and still couldn't remember if Andrew wanted brushed nickel or stainless steel. He'd said, "Just get the ones we talked about," but he'd been in and out of the house so much lately, giving me instructions in passing, and it seemed like most of it leaked out of my head the minute he was gone. He'd been so patient with me. Twice he'd had to come home from the job site to bring me his spare keys. Later he found my set in the freezer. I couldn't for the life of me think why I'd put them there. Now he puts them on top of my purse every morning.

When he gave me a concerned look and said, "Maybe you should see the doctor. These pregnancy hormones seem to be making you confused," I said I was just tired.

He'd been tired too. This new project was taking up so much of his time, but he still fussed over me, always making sure I was eating healthy and going for long walks. I was surprised when he came with me to pick out maternity clothes—most men didn't seem to care about those things. My friend Samantha teased me that I was starting to dress like a forty-year-old soccer mom, but she *liked* to show off her body. I didn't need to do that anymore. Andrew's taste was more grown-up, mature. What man wanted everyone looking at his wife's cleavage?

The price labels blurred. I blinked a few times, widened my eyes, and tried to force myself to concentrate, but my eyelids still felt so heavy and I couldn't stop yawning. I thought of our bed, the chicken stew in the Crock-Pot. Maybe I should give up on the faucets.

I ran for my car, one hand holding my coat tight around my stomach, and kept my head down, but the rain still blew hard into my face. The November sky was dark and dreary, rust-colored leaves spinning and floating down the stream rapidly forming beside the road. My feet were soaked, my toes cold. I should've worn boots, but I'd thought it would be a quick trip.

Wrenching open the door, I climbed in and huddled behind the wheel. When I turned the key, the starter made a clicking sound. I tried a few times, feeling more desperate with each attempt. Finally I gave up and reached into my purse for my cell, which I now realized I'd left at home. I huddled in my damp coat and tried to think what I should do. We didn't have roadside service and my mom couldn't drive. I was going to have to use the phone inside to call Andrew. But I hated that he'd have to leave work to pick me up.

I slogged back through the puddles. My hair was drenched, and I was cold through to the bone. "Do you mind if I use your phone?" I asked one of the clerks. "My car won't start."

"Need a ride?" the man standing behind me in line said.

I turned around—it was Bob Irvine, who ran another construction company in town. Thank God. Now I didn't have to bother Andrew. I'd known Bob for years. His daughter went to school with my brother. He'd always been nice.

"Sure," I said. "That would be great."

I was stepping out of a hot shower and drying off my hair, luxuriating in the steamy warmth of the bathroom, when I heard Andrew's truck in the driveway. He must have decided to come home early. I pulled on yoga pants and a long sweatshirt, made sure to hang the towel, and straightened the blankets on our bed so there wasn't one wrinkle. As I passed through the house I did a quick scan, and shoved my shoes into the closet. I liked our house to be tidy even though it was getting harder now that my belly was so heavy that sometimes it felt as though I were going to topple over. My favorite aisle at the grocery store was the one with all the household cleaners. Andrew was always teasing me that I was addicted, but in a way, it was true. If there was a new wax or polish or scrub brush on the market, I had to try it. I liked to stand at the end of a room I'd just cleaned and take in the gleaming wood surfaces, the perfectly vacuumed carpet, the sparkling windows, the lemon-scented air. There was nothing as satisfying.

Andrew was coming in the front door, the rain blowing in after him. I caught a glimpse of the trees outside, bending and swaying wildly. The storm had picked up.

"Hi, honey!" I said. "Do you want some chicken stew and biscuits?" I'd popped some biscuits into the oven before my shower and I could smell the buttery scent through the house.

I leaned up and gave him a kiss. He turned at the last moment. His face was ruddy, almost looked windburned, his cheeks cold under my lips. I stepped back, startled.

"Where's your car?" he said.

"It broke down. I tried to call you. Bob Irvine drove me home."

"You should've called a cab."

"I didn't think about it. He offered, and—"

"You're my wife, carrying *my* child. Do you know how this looks?"

I didn't understand what was wrong. I thought he liked Bob Irvine. "I was careful. I didn't stress out the baby or anything."

"God, for a smart girl you can be so stupid sometimes, Lindsey."

My mouth opened, the pain so quick and sharp under my ribs it was as though the baby had kicked me, but she hadn't moved. "That's really mean." My cheeks felt hot as I remembered all the mistakes I'd made lately. Was this what he actually thought of me?

He pushed past me in the hallway, almost knocking me into the wall, and I caught the smell of whiskey. But that couldn't be right—he was working all day. I hesitated, then followed him into the kitchen, watched as he took a beer out of the fridge. His balance was unsteady.

"Have you been drinking?" He liked to go to the pub after work with his crew if they'd had a hard day—and he'd had a lot of them recently—but he didn't have more than two beers and always called and checked that I was okay first.

He turned around, opened the can. "I never want to see you getting out of another man's truck again. I saw the way you smiled at him, your flirty little good-bye."

"Were you *watching* me?" I hadn't seen his truck in the driveway or on the road. Maybe he'd come home early, then left again. But why would he do that?

"You've had too many kilometers on your car. Where have you been going every day?"

"Sometimes I just drive around. I get bored." Andrew had asked me about my day before, liked to hear everything I did and who I saw, but I thought he was just interested. I had no idea he'd been checking my kilometers. I wanted to tell him it wasn't right, but the look on his face was scaring me, the way he was leaning against the counter, his hands gripping the edge.

"You had lunch with Samantha at the pub yesterday."

He looked so angry, almost accusing. I was starting to get upset too. I didn't like being spoken to this way, didn't like feeling as if I was in trouble—and didn't even know why.

"I told you we had lunch." I rarely saw my friends anymore. Most of them were in college, or had moved away with boyfriends, and Andrew didn't seem to like the ones who'd stayed in town. When Samantha called, I'd jumped at the chance to meet with a girlfriend and chat.

"You didn't mention it was at a bar, Lindsey. You're about to be a mother."

"I wasn't *drinking*. I don't understand why you're so angry."

"Peter's wife used to go to the pub too." He was holding my gaze steady. "You remember what happened to her." Peter was one of his workers. One I didn't particularly like. I usually avoided him when I came to the job site. He'd caught his wife cheating and divorced her, got the kids and the house. I couldn't believe Andrew didn't trust me. How could he threaten me like this?

"I would never cheat on you, Andrew."

"You better not." He took a long swallow of his beer, still holding eye contact.

"What's that supposed to mean?"

"It means you don't get rides with other men."

My pulse was racing. I'd seen Andrew get frustrated, seen him come home in bad moods where he went into his office for hours or sat and stared at the TV, but he'd never been cruel or vindictive. I felt as though a stranger had walked into our house.

"Maybe I should stay at my parents' tonight."

"You're not going anywhere. The roads are bad."

The baby was shifting and rolling. I imagined my heartbeat, how loud it must be. Stress was bad. I had to stay calm. I curved my hand over my belly. *Shush, little baby. Shush.*

Andrew's gaze was focused on my stomach. "That's what I'm trying to tell you, Lindsey. You need to be more careful. I don't want anything to happen to the baby, understand?"

No. That wasn't what he was saying at all. I saw it in his face. The warning. He wasn't just threatening that he might divorce me. This was a threat of something far more serious. Something I couldn't even fathom, but it was thick and dark and dangerous.

"I understand."

He drained his beer, grabbed another from the fridge. "Then I guess we don't have anything to worry about, do we?" He walked into the living room and collapsed onto the couch, reached for the remote. I didn't know if we were done talking, and I was scared to move. I slowly walked to the doorway and waited for a moment, but he was staring at the TV. I watched as he brought the beer to his mouth, his throat muscles flexing as he gulped it. Could it be the booze? Some men got really mean when they drank. Andrew would never normally say these things.

The stew was bubbling on the stove behind me in the kitchen. Food. I needed to get him to eat. My mom always told my dad not to drink on an empty stomach.

When I came back into the living room, Andrew didn't look up. I placed the bowl on the coffee table in front of him. He was watching a hockey game, their red uniforms reflecting in his eyes. I slowly sat on the couch, my breath tight in my chest. His hand suddenly reached out and I flinched, but he just rested it on my stomach. His palm was hot.

"We should get a security system in the house," he said. "Been a lot of break-ins lately. We can hook it up so I can check the cameras in my office at the site."

I stared at his profile, thought about cameras watching me all day, following me around. His hand pressed harder against my stomach, and I winced at the sudden pressure.

"Okay," I said. "If that's what you want."

CHAPTER SIX

December 2016

When I get home Sophie is sprawled on the living room floor drawing. As a child, she was obsessed with painting and would stand in front of the easel Andrew made for her, chubby cheeks smeared with paint, hands gripping a paintbrush she splashed against the paper in bold purple streaks. "Look, Mommy! It's you!"

Since she started high school her chosen medium is ink. She can work on one sketch for weeks, her face grimly determined or full of blissful contentment. I find her doodles on the papers by the phone, on our mail, the newspaper, magazine pages. I started tucking them away into a box. Sometimes I take them out and study the lines, the curves of each pen stroke. I love this glimpse into her mind, her imagination. A world where fairies can morph into trees and fish into birds and boxes become flowers and wings and gnomes and dragons.

Sometimes I worry about what I see: a skull with a broken heart, a tire with flames, devil's horns, sad clown faces, rivers of tears. When I ask her what they mean, she shrugs.

"I don't think about it. They come out of my fingers that way."

Everything about Sophie is expressive, her words, her face, the way she moves her hands when she's talking. She looks more like Andrew than me, but her style is all her own. She wears tunics, patterned leggings, and scarves, colors her hair pink and blue and turquoise. This week it's violet, makes her green eyes huge. She has my shape. Small, but we're strong. We run fast.

When I told her Andrew was out of prison, she went silent, then said, "So? He told his lawyer he was going to leave us alone, right?" His lawyer called my lawyer after the divorce went through: *Andrew wishes Lindsey well and won't bother her anymore.* He also sent a large check for Sophie's support. I never used any of it and put it in a savings account for her.

"We still need to be extra-careful from now on," I said.

"We don't matter to him anymore," she insisted.

"You matter to *me*. So be careful, okay? Tell me if you see him."

"I don't even know what he looks like anymore." She was annoyed, frustrated with my anxiety, and I hoped that she was right and my worry was for nothing.

Now I know Andrew had just been waiting.

I grab a pillow from the couch and lie beside her. "How was your walk?"

"It was okay." She glances at me. "How was work? Is your back sore again?"

"I took an Advil."

"You need to do yoga. It will help." Sometimes she pours me a bath or massages my feet with lavender oil, nags at me that I need a different job. She doesn't understand that I enjoy cleaning. I let my mind drift as I scrub and wash and sort. Everything calms down inside me and I feel content and satisfied, proud as I close my client's door behind me. I like that I have my own business, that I'm independent and can support myself and my daughter.

I tried to tell Sophie that cleaning gives me the same feeling she has when she's painting, but she just said, "What are you going to do when you're old? You need to think about retirement, Mom." I told her that she was my retirement plan and she just laughed, then gave me a hug. Some people would probably say we are too involved in each other's lives, too enmeshed, that we lack boundaries, but to hell with them. I need it this way.

"I have to tell you something," I say. We've had a lot of hard conversations, more than any child should have had to endure, but I don't know how to start this one.

She glances at me. "Did you and Greg break up?"

"What? No." I notice she looks upset about the idea and tuck it away for another time. I can tell she likes him, but Greg and I are only casual. I hope she isn't getting too attached.

"Something happened today," I say.

Now I have Sophie's full attention. "What?"

"I had to call the police because someone broke into Mrs. Carlson's house, but it doesn't seem like anything was stolen." I take a breath. "I'm pretty sure it was your dad."

She looks shocked. The pen rolls out of her hand. "Why would he go there?" Then she meets my eyes and I see the awareness settle in. "You think he wanted to hurt you?"

"I don't know what he wants." *Yes. Yes, I do.* "Did you notice anything out of the ordinary today? See any cars driving by our house or parked nearby?"

She shrugs. "Everything was normal." She stares down at her drawing, notices where there's an ink splotch, blots at it with her finger.

Normal. Such a simple word, and something our lives will never be. I get up and look out our front window, check the shadows under the maple tree. I turn around, pause for a moment to take in the comforting sight of our cozy living room, the sagging couch we found at a garage sale and covered with a multicolored afghan, the coffee table we made out of driftwood we dragged home from the beach, the paintings we collect from secondhand shops, our choices based solely on whether they make us smile—from a bright bouquet of paper flowers to a group of whimsical owls perched on a snow-covered branch.

After Sophie and I ran away, we waited in hiding for a year before Andrew's case went to trial. We lived in cheap hotels all over BC, surviving on loans from Chris and some money I earned doing cash jobs. I couldn't risk him finding us while he was still out on bail. We even stayed on the border of Alberta for a few weeks. I'd wanted to cry every time Sophie packed her little suitcase and asked, "We're moving again?" It was even harder when she stopped asking and packed silently.

When Andrew was finally convicted, we took the ferry from Horseshoe Bay up the coast until we reached Dogwood Bay, a tight-knit community built on a hill facing the ocean. I fell in love with the quaint shops and pubs down in the city center where you can see the dark blue ocean and coastal mountains stretching for miles, taste the salty mist in the air, then order crab pulled up from the water and watch the float planes land, white froth spraying out from behind.

Sophie and I needed a home, needed to be close to the ocean, and a couple of hours from my family. The only way to Dogwood Bay was by float plane from the island or an hour-and-a-half ferry ride from the mainland. We could be happy here, I thought. We could be safe.

I come back to sit beside Sophie on the floor. She's drawing, her face still. She has that ability, same as Andrew, to tuck everything far in behind her eyes and disappear for hours. The difference is she'll come dancing out again, with the right touch or question, blinking as though she's emerged from a dark cave and wondrous about where all the time has gone.

"What are you thinking?" I say.

"Dad. The night of the accident. Do you really think he would have killed you if he found us?" She turns to look at me, her eyes searching my face.

"I think he would have tried, yes."

"But why would he want to hurt you now? You said he's stopped drinking. He didn't hurt you when he was sober." I thought I was doing the right thing by sharing everything Chris had heard through the grapevine about Andrew's life, but now I have serious regrets.

"He didn't hurt me *physically* when he was sober, and I know this is hard to understand, honey, but it's like drinking was just an excuse for him. Even when he was sober, he was jealous and cruel and threatened to hurt me if I ever left him. I was terrified."

I remember how hard it was to explain to her that her father had gotten into a car accident when he'd been drinking and someone died so he had to go to jail. She would still ask to visit, no matter how many times I told her it wasn't a safe place for a little girl. I'd shielded her so well from his drinking, his anger. She only knew him as a loving father and she missed him. Finally I told her she could write letters and draw pictures and give them to him when he was released.

When she was old enough, I told her more about our marriage, how jealous and controlling he'd been, how many chances I'd given him, but that he was an alcoholic and violent and nearly killed me. That's why running away was the only option—because I was scared. She stopped asking about him. When I was putting clothes away in her closet one day, I found the box with her letters pushed all the way to the back. I hated how relieved it made me feel.

"It's been so many years, though," she says.

"He's still dangerous."

"What if he's changed?" Something about the way she says it stops me cold. It's the hope in her voice, maybe even a little doubt, as though she's not sure my concerns are real.

I think for a moment. She knows what prison he was in, so she could have written—or even gone to see him. It had never occurred to me that she would do something so important without telling me. But she's a teenager now and might have been curious.

"Have you talked to him? If you have, it's okay to tell me. I won't be upset." I'll be furious, but if I share that, she won't tell me anything.

She shakes her head. "I just feel bad you're so scared of him." Meaning she isn't. My heart is twisting and turning on the end of a sword. I don't want her reassurances. That's my job. But she's not afraid. I can see it in her face, and that means she could make a mistake. I need her to be careful. If Andrew sees that there's a crack, he'll turn it into a window.

"I don't believe a person can change who they are at their core," I say. "It doesn't matter how many years it's been—he hasn't forgiven me for divorcing him. He's angry, and probably dealing with a lot of problems and emotions now that he's out of prison. That means he's unstable." I think of him sending that message through his lawyer, how he must have sat in his cell so smug and satisfied, knowing that he'd yet again managed to fool me.

"I know you're upset," she says, fiddling with her pens. "It just seems like if he was really mad at you, he'd do something else. Not, like, stalk you or whatever."

"Sophie, look at me."

She raises her head, meets my eyes.

"Your dad loved to scare me. It wasn't just about him hurting me. Making me afraid is exciting for him. It gives him a powerful feeling. I'm hoping that he'll go away now that he's made his point, but we need to keep an eye out. You'll tell me if you ever see him, right?"

She nods. "Yeah." Then picks up her pen and starts to draw. I watch her fingers. They seem hesitant, unsure, but I don't know if I'm imagining it. Her strokes become more confident, her expression smoothing out, her body relaxing. I sink down onto the pillow.

It's going to be okay. We'll get through this together, just like we always have.

CHAPTER SEVEN

September 2003

"Daddy parked the truck in the mailbox again." Sophie was standing by the front window, still dressed in her pink Barbie nightgown, her hands and face pressed to the glass.

I stood beside her. The wooden post was sticking out from under Andrew's front tire, the wood splintered, our cheerful red metal mailbox knocked partway across the lawn. The first time it happened, he told me he just took the corner too sharp. The second time it was because I parked in the wrong spot in the driveway, didn't give him enough room.

"Come on, baby. I'll turn on the TV, okay?"

"When's Daddy getting up?"

"Soon." I glanced at the clock. I couldn't let him sleep too long—he liked to spend Sunday mornings with Sophie, but I liked the peace and quiet. It had been a hard week. He lost a couple of workers, had problems getting permits, got outbid on another project.

Sophie jumped onto the couch, burrowed under her blanket. "Can I have milk, please, Mommy?" The word came out

"Mulk," which always made me smile. Andrew thought we should correct her when she mispronounced words, but when it was just the two of us, I never said anything, wanted to keep my baby a little longer. She'd started preschool that week, only half days, but I missed her terribly, would watch the clock until it was time to get her.

I brought her milk, set it on the coffee table. Sophie was digging around in the couch cushions, pulled out my silver charm bracelet.

"Oh, no, Mommy! It's broken!"

"It's okay, baby. It just fell off." I kept my smile in place, my tone upbeat. "Thank you for finding it." I took the bracelet from her, tucked it into my housecoat pocket. The bruise wasn't too bad, should fade in a few days, but I'd have to wear long sleeves. I should have known better, should have remembered to text him in the afternoon to let him know we were okay. I'd just gotten so busy, taking Sophie to a birthday party, making all those cupcakes.

I poured coffee into the mug Sophie had made Andrew for Father's Day, a dark blue painted disaster, and carried it down the hall. As I passed Sophie's room, I caught a glimpse of her white antique rocker, remembered how when she was born Andrew would sit and rock her for hours, change diapers without even making a face, gaze at her with adoration when she made her soft little grunts and coos. He'd come home from work with milkshakes or fresh bread from the bakery, slather it in butter and feed me pieces. He was so happy back then.

I padded into our bedroom, set the coffee on the night table. He didn't stir, so I went into the bathroom and brushed my teeth with the water running slowly. I flicked my gaze around, checked where my makeup bag was on the counter. A few times I came home after errands and found my bag in the wrong place, the contents out of order, my clothes shifted around in the drawer as though he'd been searching for something. When I cautiously asked if it was him doing this, he'd accused me of being paranoid. Now I kept careful track of everything.

"Lindsey?" His voice startled me. I dropped my toothbrush, splashing water onto the mirror. I grabbed a cloth, wiped at it.

"Yeah," I said. "Coffee is on the night table."

"Where's Sophie?"

"Watching TV." I walked out, let him tug me down beside him in bed. His body was warm, his chest muscles hard under my cheek. He pressed his lips against my forehead and slid his hand down my arm, gently circled my wrist, stroking the tender skin.

"Your wrist okay?"

"Yeah. Sophie found my bracelet."

"You shouldn't have pulled away so fast like that. I could have really hurt you." His voice is raspy from sleep, but there's another tone. One I know well. Remorse.

"I know. I'll be more careful." He hadn't meant to grab me that hard when I started walking away, but that didn't make it hurt any less. Just like when he knocked over the hand-blown glass vase my grandmother had given me for our wedding, or dropped the ceramic owl I'd had since I was a little girl and always kept perched on my dresser. He glued it all back together, piece by piece, spent hours with a magnifying glass and tweezers, but I could still see every crack.

The sound of Sophie's cartoons drifted through the open door. She was watching *Caillou*, would be absorbed for a little while longer before she came looking for us.

"I'm worried about you," I said. "You're drinking a lot lately."

"I'm fine. I'm just under a lot of stress because of the north island project."

"Maybe you can slow down a little and not take on so much at once."

"How can I do that when I'm supporting you and your family? Your parents are carrying a lot of debt and I promised your dad I'd have work for him for years."

I looked up at him, surprised. He'd encouraged my parents to buy a new car and renovate their house. "I didn't know you felt that way."

"Of course. I mean, we'd be all right if I shut down the company. I have my trust payments, but what about your dad and brother? There's not much work out there. . . ."

I felt unsettled, panicky. He'd never spoken about shutting down the company before. I thought he could pick smaller projects, lay off some of the new guys. My father was almost fifty and had a bad shoulder. No one else would give him a job as a foreman.

"Maybe you can hire someone to help you. Then you'll have more free time."

"That'll ruin my business. People in the industry have always thought I was just some rich kid who had everything easy. If I hire someone, I'll be proving them right." He looked upset, and I felt like I'd let him down. Of course he didn't want to risk his reputation.

He tugged on my hair, tilted my head. "You're worrying about nothing, I swear." He held my gaze, his expression serious. "I'll cut back, okay?"

"You always say that, but—"

"I *will*, Lindsey. This time I will."

I rested my head against his side. He hummed a few bars of a tune, his deep voice vibrating his chest. *You know our love was meant to be* . . . I recognized the song by Chicago. It was on our wedding CD. Andrew had an uncanny knack for remembering lyrics, could quote a verse for every occasion. He knew what song was playing in the restaurant on our first date, what songs we made love to, what was playing in his truck when he picked me up.

He stopped singing. I tensed, waiting. What was wrong now?

"It must be hard for you, now that Sophie's at school," he said.

"The house is really quiet." I wanted to say more, but it was too hard to talk, all my emotions building in my throat, the relief of having my best friend back—the sweet Andrew, the loving Andrew. *This* was my husband. Not the man who gripped my wrist like he wanted to snap it.

"Remember how I said we were working near a farm this week? The owner has a border collie with a litter of puppies. We should get one."

I sat up straight, stared down at him. "You're serious?" I'd wanted a dog for years. We'd had one when I was little, a spaniel named Hurricane because he destroyed everything, but after he died my parents didn't want another. I borrowed all the neighbors' dogs and played with them. Andrew and I had talked a few times about getting a dog, but he wanted to wait until Sophie was older and we'd settled in one house and didn't have to worry about damage.

"I just want you to be happy, Lindsey." He stroked the side of my face, so much tenderness in his eyes I wanted to cry. "We'll pick one out tomorrow."

His name was Blaze, a roly-poly ball of black fluff with floppy ears and a white star on his forehead. We visited him a few times over the next couple of weeks—he wasn't old enough to take home yet. Sophie and I usually went together, but sometimes Andrew would meet me while Sophie was at preschool and we'd have lunch in the barn with the puppies. I laughed, watching him throw small sticks for Blaze, talking about all the things they were going to do together. "We'll go camping, buddy. You'll like that. I bet you're a good fishing partner."

In the evenings, I read puppy books, researched the best food and training methods for border collies. Andrew bought the puppy a leather collar and leash, got him an engraved silver name tag. I was thrilled that Andrew had kept his word—I hadn't seen him drink once.

The day we were supposed to pick up Blaze, Andrew didn't come home at five like he promised. I called his cell. No answer. We waited until six. Then seven. Sophie was getting more upset, more impatient. "Why can't we get the puppy, Mommy? Where is Daddy?"

Finally I loaded her in the car and we went and got Blaze by ourselves. When we came home, Andrew's truck was in the driveway. Sophie, holding Blaze tightly in her arms, ran inside. "Daddy! Daddy!" I followed her into the house, started putting the dog food and treats into the cupboard. I was so angry at Andrew, I didn't think I could talk to him without revealing my fury.

Sophie came into the kitchen. "He's sleeping." She sounded so confused, so disappointed. This was my fault. I should have known he'd do this. I'd been talking about the puppy too much. Not giving him enough attention. Why didn't I see it building?

"That's okay, honey. He's probably having a nap. Why don't you show Blaze the backyard?" While she went outside, I checked on Andrew. I could smell the whiskey as soon as I walked into the bedroom, saw the empty glass on the floor where it had slipped from his hand.

I cleaned up the mess, blotted the wet spot on the carpet, and went to make dinner. Andrew didn't come out of the bedroom. I put a covered plate for him in the fridge.

Sophie wanted to sleep with Blaze in her room, but I told her it wasn't a good idea. Andrew and I had agreed we would crate-train Blaze in the laundry room. Not my wishes.

After I set up the dog bed inside the metal pen, with newspaper all around, I tucked Blaze in with a teddy bear for comfort. Then I eased into bed with Andrew, listened to the rain outside. It was a miserable night, fall just around the corner. I was going to miss the long warm days. I closed my eyes, tried to go to sleep, but I could hear pitiful whimpers from Blaze.

I sat up, swung my legs around the side of the bed. Andrew's arm latched around my middle. I gasped in surprise as he pulled me backward onto the bed.

"Leave him. He has to learn." He rolled over, yawned. "Can you get me some water?"

Water. He wanted water? No explanation, no excuses even for coming home drunk. I gritted my teeth. This wasn't a good time to get into it. I'd wait until tomorrow.

I filled up a glass in the bathroom, brought it to the side of the bed.

He took a sip, his watch flashing in the dim light. "This is warm. I want ice."

Of course he did. I slipped out to the kitchen, the floor cold on my feet. Blaze was howling now, pitiful high-pitched whimpers. Sophie was going to wake up.

I left the glass on the counter, snuck down the hallway to the laundry room. "Shush," I whispered. "It's okay." Blaze was wiggling and grunting, trying to get out of the pen.

"What are you doing?" Andrew, standing in the doorway. "I told you to let him be."

"I was just checking on him."

Blaze was barking now, clambering up on the side of the pen, rattling the metal.

"Fucking dog." Andrew reached into the pen, grabbed him by the scruff of his neck.

I stood up, snatched at his arm, trying to pull Blaze back toward me, but Andrew was holding him up high in the air. "What are you doing?" I said.

He didn't answer, just spun around and walked out of the

laundry room. Blaze was crying, his legs kicking in the air. I followed them down the hall, hissing, "Andrew, stop!"

Andrew opened the back door. Wind and rain swept inside, blew my nightgown against my legs. "You can't put him outside!"

Andrew looked over his shoulder at me—and dropped the puppy. Blaze landed with a small thud, a yelp, and rolled onto his side. I squeezed past Andrew, reached for the dog. My fingers were on his fur. Andrew grabbed me around the waist, yanked me back, and shut the door.

I pushed against Andrew's chest, hit him without thinking. He shoved me against the wall, grabbed my shoulders, and shook me hard. My teeth bit into my cheek.

He leaned closer, breathed whiskey into my face. "If you go out there, I'm going to smash his head in with a shovel. Got it?"

We stared at each other in the dark hallway until I nodded. He let go of my arms. I slumped against the wall. "Come on," he said. "I'm tired."

I followed him back to the room. I couldn't breathe, wanted to cry. Made myself put one foot in front of the other. I'd wait until he fell asleep. I'd go get the puppy.

I tried twice to sneak out of the bed, but he heard me move each time, held me down with his leg, his arm across my chest like an iron band. The hours ticked past. I stared at the ceiling, tears rolling down my face. I wanted to be stronger, to shove him away from me and fight for the dog, but I was too scared that he'd make good on his threat. I couldn't forget the look in his eye, like he was daring me. Like he wanted me to make one false step so he could kill the puppy.

Finally it was morning and he got up for work. I pretended to be asleep. The moment I heard his truck leave, I went outside and found the puppy hiding under the front deck, shivering and sodden. I fed him warm food, tucked him against my chest in a towel, crooned my apologies, and swore that he'd never be hurt again. I'd make sure of it. When Sophie woke I gently told her that the puppy was sick and had to go back to his mommy. She was heartbroken.

I cried when I drove Blaze back to the farm and explained to the owners that my daughter had allergies we hadn't known about. I didn't know if they believed me, but the wife looked sympathetic and promised she would find him a great home. I gave them all of his belongings, the food, his dishes, even the collar. Every last item. I couldn't look at any of it.

When Andrew came home, I told him that I realized I didn't have enough time to care for a puppy right now. I wanted to focus on Sophie. He never asked about him again.

I watched as my mom poured hot water into the teapot with a trembling hand. I wondered how much longer she'd be able to do this. The doctors said she might manage for years, but no one really knew. The October sun streamed through the window, lighting up her blond hair and pale skin, so fair I could see the faint blue veins in her neck.

"Let me get the tea, Mom."

"Stop. I'm not completely useless." She smiled, and I made myself smile back, but my thoughts were all over the place, my nerves raw. I glanced at my watch. I couldn't be long. He might come home at lunch. I mentally scanned through the items in our fridge, trying to decide what I could make quickly. He didn't like me to drop anything off at his job site anymore. He said it wasn't safe, that a beam could fall on me, but that wasn't true. He didn't like how the men looked at me. I saw it in his face, felt it in the way he'd hurry me to the car.

A few days after I gave Blaze back, Andrew told me he'd listed the house with a real estate agent. It sold quickly. It had been a week since we'd moved into our brand-new house, even bigger than our last one. Our third in as many years. I'd wanted Sophie to grow up in the same home for all her childhood like I had. Everything in my parents' house was familiar. I gazed around at the pretty yellow curtains, the cow cream-and-sugar containers, the chicken salt-and-pepper shakers. My mother loved anything country, and for years we bought her the most obnoxiously cute things we could find for birthdays and Christmas. She cherished every one of them. She poured my tea from a pig-shaped teapot, gave my hand a pat as she sat across from me.

"Do you need me to do anything while I'm here?" I said. "I could help with the laundry."

"Thanks, sweetie, but your father took care of it last night before I even got a chance. You two are so much alike." She blew steam off her tea.

I thought of my father, coming home after a long day's work and taking care of my mother. I wished life was easier for them.

"Your windows need to be washed. I'll come on the weekend."

"Stop," she said. "They're fine."

"I like cleaning."

"That's true. When you were a little girl you'd pretend to be Cinderella and go around the house dusting and wiping everything." She laughed.

"I wish I could say the same for Sophie."

"How's our little princess? Does she like her new room?"

"She loves it. We picked out some owl stencils, and she insisted on putting them up all by herself. Most of them are crooked but she says they're just flying upside down."

She reached over and brushed my bangs off my forehead like she did when I was a child. "I can't get over this new hairstyle of yours. You look so grown up."

Andrew had kept at me about my hair—I looked like a high

school girl, or long hair was too sexy, it gave men the wrong idea. When I came home with a pixie cut, he said, "What did you do that for?"

"I'm not sure if Andrew likes it."

"You could shave it all off and he'd still think you're the most beautiful girl in the world. He adores you."

"It hasn't felt like it lately. He's been so busy." I opened the door a crack, hoping she would ask me to explain more, hoping she'd seen that something was wrong between us.

"He's just focused. He dropped your father off yesterday, then went straight back to the job site." She shook her head. "He's a hard worker, that husband of yours."

I heard the respect in her voice, felt it sinking through my body. She hadn't noticed anything. The truth was pushing at my tongue. I couldn't keep this all inside anymore, couldn't bear the weight of all this worry and fear, but I felt a wild panic at the idea of telling my mom. I imagined the look on Andrew's face if he found out I had talked about him. I thought about the hunting rifle he kept in the gun safe—even though he rarely hunted. I thought about how he kept Sophie's passport in his bank security deposit box and was the only one who had a key.

Mom slid a plate of cookies toward me.

"I'm not hungry, thanks."

"You okay?"

His drinking is out of control, Mom. He gets so angry when he's drunk. I think he might really hurt me. You don't know what he's like. I can't breathe. He's so jealous. He spies on me and goes through my things. He wants another child but I'm taking birth control. I keep it hidden in my tampon box. I want to leave him but I'm terrified he'll take Sophie away from me somehow. I don't have anything of my own. What should I do? How can I get out of this? I don't have a credit card or bank account. Everything is in his name. I'm trapped.

I imagined how shocked and confused and upset my mom

would be. How much my having hidden the truth for so long would hurt her. How worried she'd be about Sophie and me.

"I ate before I came over." I took another sip of my tea. I wanted to stay in this moment a little longer. "Is Dad's shoulder getting any better?"

She shook her head. "He tried the exercises the doctor prescribed, but they haven't helped. Surgery would be the next step, but it's risky. Thank God Andrew gave him that job."

"Does he still like working for him?"

She tilted her head. "Of course. Why?"

I swallowed a couple of times, trying to dislodge the tight, desperate feeling in my throat that was always there lately. "I just wonder sometimes if it might be strange for him, working for his son-in-law. If he wanted to do something else, it would be okay with me."

"Your dad knows that." She rested her hand on mine. She was looking straight into my eyes with a concerned expression. This was my chance.

"You and Dad are so important to me, and—"

My mom's eyes widened. "Oh! I want to show you the catalogue Andrew dropped off."

"Catalogue?"

"He's sending your father and me on a cruise—for an anniversary present, but he's calling it a bonus, you know, for tax reasons. He hasn't told you? I hope it wasn't a surprise. Maybe he's taking you too!" She got up, talking excitedly about where they would go. "You'll have to help me pick out some cruise wear. You know, we've never been on a real holiday before."

She sat back down with the catalogue, pushed it toward me, but I couldn't make my arms move, could only stare at the shiny cover with the smiling couple.

"Lindsey?"

"Sorry. I was thinking about something." I straightened my chair, pulled it closer.

She was still looking at me. "You sure you're okay?"

"I'm fine, just a little tired. I probably need a vitamin B shot."

"That's a good idea. Having a toddler is exhausting." She flipped the catalogue opened to a marked page. "What do you think about this one?"

I sat in the car and stared back at my parents' house, the flower boxes, the wooden swing where my dad and mom would sit in the evenings while my brother and I ran around in the front yard, where my mom would snuggle with me while she pushed gently against the porch railing with her foot until I fell asleep against her warm body. My mom was going to wonder why I hadn't driven away, but I needed a moment to think, to brace myself before I went home. The seat belt was too tight around my waist. I tried to tug it looser, but the locking mechanism wouldn't let me. I pulled and yanked while tears rolled down my face. Finally I gave up and slapped my hands down hard on my steering wheel. "Damn it, damn it, damn it!"

There was noise beside me, a bird chirping in one of the apple trees. I rolled down my window, inhaled the crisp fall air. The days would get colder soon, Andrew would come home earlier, and maybe his work would slow down. Maybe he wouldn't need to drink so much and things would get better. He loved Christmas. I clung to that thought, remembered how he always got up at the crack of dawn like a little kid and made waffles for us, how he couldn't wait for Sophie to open her presents. Last year he'd built her a dollhouse, even all the little furniture inside, and given me a maple jewelry box he made in my dad's workshop. He told me that those hours spent with my dad were some of the best times he'd had in his life.

I looked back up at the house, thought about my parents re-laxing on a cruise, everything taken care of, and how much fun they'd have. They needed this. They'd done everything for me, sacrificed so much. I had to stay with Andrew. Leaving wasn't an option. Not right now.

I put the car in gear and drove home. I'd make soup and roast beef sandwiches. He liked those.

CHAPTER EIGHT

SOPHIE

DECEMBER 2016

May 19, 2016

To Andrew Nash,
C/O Rockland Prison

Hi, my name is Sophie and you're my father, but you probably
already figured that out. Right now you're probably wondering why I'm writing you, so I'll get to the point. My English
teacher gave us an assignment and we're supposed to contact
someone who had the biggest impact on our lives and tell them
what they meant to us, or how they changed us. I think it's
supposed to be someone we admire, or like our hero, and I
guess you used to be that for me when I was kid, but I chose
you for this project because you changed a lot of people's lives.
Not just mine. And hey, maybe I can get an "A" for having a
dad in prison. Okay, stupid joke.

So, for this part I'm supposed to tell you how I feel when I
think about you. Sometimes I feel sad, but I'm mostly still
really angry at you for drinking and driving that night. I

think about that woman all the time. She was trying to get home to her family and now she's dead. After you were arrested, we had to move all over the place and Mom worked two jobs. I hardly ever saw her and I didn't have a dad anymore. Now it's been so long. Eleven years. That's more than half my life. You've missed everything. I don't even know who you are now.

I don't know what else to say.

Sophie

That's how it started. I got that assignment and I couldn't stop thinking about how much I wanted to tell my dad how he ruined our lives. I talked it over with Delaney, the only one who knows about my dad. It's bad enough that everyone knows my mom has a cleaning business. She cleans for some of their parents. I mean, how weird is that? My mom makes their *beds* and scrubs their *toilets*. I helped her clean in the summer and it was disgusting. I hated how some owners stuck around while we worked and went about their lives, giving us apologetic smiles, like they're just too busy or too important to clean up their own messes. I want her to get a different job, like in an office or something, but she says she prefers working for herself.

Delaney thought it was a cool idea to write my dad and agreed that she'd be my drop-off point. She mailed the letter for me, and I used her address in case he wanted to write back.

Two weeks later I got a letter.

May 29, 2016

Dear Sophie,

The best day of my life since I've been in prison is when I got your letter. I must have read it six times already. You have every reason to hate me, but I hope you can find it in your heart to give me another chance. I'm not the same person.

You're right, I have missed everything. I can't believe you're almost eighteen.

Your mom didn't want you to visit me until I got myself together, and she was right, but I want you to know that I never stopped thinking about you. It's taken me a long time to accept responsibility for my actions and I'm sorry I haven't been a good father to you. I was just so full of anger for so long, I couldn't see my way clear of it all. But then something happened in here and I hurt someone again. He jumped me and I was defending myself, but it didn't matter. I realized if I didn't straighten up, I might never get to see you again.

I go to AA meetings and I've been working the twelve steps and trying to make amends to all the people I hurt. I'm truly sorry for the pain I've caused everybody, and I know I let you down. I wish a million times over that I'd never driven drunk that night. I can't go back in time, but I'm trying really hard to make a positive difference with the rest of my life.

I go to a support group in here. They teach us anger management and how to talk about our emotions so they don't build up inside. For years I couldn't handle all my bad feelings because of what happened to me when I was a kid. I guess I never really got over my dad leaving and my mom dying. So then I was always scared your mom would leave me too. But I screwed up and lost you both. I'm not making excuses. I'm just hoping you can maybe understand a little.

Do you remember the boat we built together? I know I messed that up too and I'm really sorry. I remember every single time I screwed up and I know it would take me a lifetime to make it all up to you, but I'm willing to give it a try. Sometimes when I can't sleep at night because it's so noisy in here, I work out plans for a new boat and think about how we could build it together and take it out on the lake when I get released. I never got to teach you how to fish.

Maybe that doesn't seem like much, but when you were

*born, it was one of the things I really wanted to do with you,
but then I was drinking too much for all those years and it
just never happened. I forgot about a lot of things, but I never
stopped loving you.*

*I've got to get to work now. I have a job in here, managing
the tool room. It passes the time and some of the men are okay.
I also read a lot and I've taken some classes, but I'm looking
forward to getting out soon. I know you might not want to
write me back, but it would mean a lot to me if you did. I
want to hear about you. Do you still like to draw?*

Your dad

By the time I was done reading the letter, my throat was tight
and my face hot. I felt empty and headachy. It was too much.
I hadn't thought about that boat in years. We'd sanded and
painted for days, but then it sat with a tarp over it for months.
Now I remembered how it felt standing beside him while we
worked, learning how to use the different grains of sanding paper, our hands grimy and rough, the oily smell of the paint. I
tucked the letter under my dresser.

That night after Mom was in bed, I went to my room and
started sketching. I began with an enchanted forest, trees with
leaves and flowers twining around, but then in the middle I
drew a pond with our boat and there was a little girl and her
father sitting together with fishing poles and frogs jumping all
around them. I folded it up and stuffed it in an envelope and
gave it to Delaney the next morning so she could mail it to him.
After that, we started writing weekly.

Today he's flying over to Dogwood Bay from the island to
see me. Our first visit in eleven years. I'm going to see my *father*.
Which is so crazy I barely slept last night and I have big dark
shadows under my eyes that I had to layer makeup over and
then use more eyeliner than normal, so I can pretend I'm going

for the smoky look. Maybe Mom will be so distracted by my new style she won't notice that I'm way too excited for school.

I shove the bundle of letters into my backpack—I've been taking them with me every day. Mom would never search my room and she always asks before she vacuums or cleans anything, but I'm not taking any chances. I tiptoe out to the kitchen, hoping that she's still sleeping. Crap. She's already sitting at the table and eating toast. I smell peanut butter.

She glances at me. "You're up early. Want something to eat?"

"I'll eat at school, thanks." For a wild moment I imagine what it might be like to tell her that I've talked to my dad on the phone a few times. It was strange at first. I didn't know what to say, but his voice was so familiar and then I started having all these memories of sitting in his work truck, listening to him on the phone, feeling proud of how smart he sounded, how his workers always checked with him about everything. I could even smell the coconut air freshener he used. Then I remembered his metal lunch kit and how he brought little packages of Oreos for me and kept crayons in his glove box. I want to ask Mom if she remembers that too. How come we never talk about those things? How come we only talk about the bad stuff?

Well, darling daughter, because he threatened to kill me, remember that?

I do remember. I remember perfectly. That's why I asked him about it during our second phone call. And if you think writing my dad in prison took a lot of guts, asking him about the time he threatened to kill my mother just about ripped them out. What if he had shot my mom that night? When I think about it everything gets all shaky, and I feel like I have to sit down.

"There's something I need to ask you," I said. "It's important."

"You can ask me anything."

"Were you really going to kill Mom the night of the accident? You had a gun."

He was quiet for a long moment—long enough for me to think that he might have hung up, but then he said, "She tell you about the gun?"

"It was in the newspapers." Mom told me when I got older, but I already knew pretty much everything from the papers. I'd read them all online, everything I could find, any mention of his name. It had felt like reading about someone else's life, someone else's father.

"It's a fair question. But I feel like a real asshole that you even have to ask. You know? You were just a kid. You shouldn't have had to read that. I'd never have really hurt her. I was drunk and upset and not thinking straight. The gun wasn't even loaded."

I wanted to ask Mom if that was true, but there was no way I could bring it up casually. It would be suicidal. Even if I told her how he asks about my school and grades and what classes I want to take at university, and how we talk about job statistics and whether I should try to intern at a graphic art studio— they're going all digital these days. And how it's like how I imagine it is for my friends when they talk to their fathers. She would still completely flip out and ground me for the rest of my life. She doesn't understand. She doesn't know how he's changed.

I get my lunch out of the fridge and open my backpack, but I'm moving too fast, fumbling with all my art supplies, and the bundle of letters falls out—right near my mom's feet.

"What are those?" she says, her body shifting as though she's going to lean down. I quickly pick them up and press them against my stomach so she can't see the return address.

"Just a project."

She looks confused. "With letters?"

"It's hard to explain." God. I'm such an idiot. My face is burning now. "I have to go. I'm meeting Delaney."

"Okay, tell her to drive safe." She always says this and I guess most moms probably do, but it's different for her. It's more like her superstition, sort of a verbal knocking on wood, like if she forgets just one time something terrible will happen. It's because of my dad's accident.

I don't remember much about his drinking. I've tried to think back, but I was only six. Sometimes I think I can remember the smell of beer on his breath, or how Mom would be nervous when he came home, how he would sleep on the couch, but I'm not sure if those are my memories or pieces of things Mom told me. She tried to keep most of it away from me when I was little—she says she made sure I was asleep or watching TV if Dad was really drunk. She still flinches when she talks about him. I don't know if she even realizes. Once I get to know him again and make sure he's changed, I'll tell her so she doesn't have to be afraid anymore.

She looks back down at her cell phone, checking her Facebook page.

"See you." I bolt out the door.

The day passes so slowly that I feel like I'm going to explode by the time the bell rings. For the last hour I've been glancing up at the clock every few minutes, wondering if his float plane has landed on time, if he's driving to the coffee shop. Delaney meets me by my locker, wishes me good luck. "Tell me everything!" she says. "I wish I could come with you."

"It would be too weird."

"I know. Just text me later."

My stomach is churning as I ride fast away from the school and head downtown, where we agreed to meet at the Muddy Bean. My hood is pulled over my head and I'm wearing a wool scarf wrapped around my neck. Mom doesn't usually go downtown, but I'm worried she will finish cleaning her last house early and decide to go Christmas shopping.

I stop outside the coffee shop, chain my bike to a lamp pole, take a deep breath, then push the door open. I scan the people, feeling an anxious tug in my chest each time my gaze stops on a man, looking for something familiar, then moving on. What if I can't find him? What if he's changed so much that I walk right past him? What if he decided not to come?

I almost don't recognize him at first. I look past, then back again. He's sitting at a small table in the corner, reading a newspaper, and he's kind of frowning as though he doesn't like what he's reading, or maybe he needs glasses. He's holding the paper with one hand and his other is wrapped around a large mug. I see a flash of gold. His wedding ring?

There's a plate with crumbs on it. He's already eaten and I worry that I'm late. He's a big man, his arm muscles all bunched up, and it makes the table look even smaller. I wonder if he lifted weights in prison. His hair is short, almost a crew cut, and going gray. He has a beard. I don't remember him having a beard and I'm panicking now. What if he's always had one and it's something else I've forgotten? It feels like I've been watching him for five minutes. People keep bumping into me. I should walk over but I can't make my feet move.

He glances up. I can tell he doesn't recognize me, the way his eyes skim past without any expression in them, then he takes another look, and smiles, but it's kind of crooked, like he's embarrassed or something, and his cheeks are turning pink.

He stands, wipes his hands on his jeans. He's not as tall as I thought, but his shoulders are large in his brown knit sweater.

I walk over and stand in front of him. "Hi." My hands are clutching the straps of my backpack, like it's a parachute and I can leap out of here anytime I want.

"Your hair," he says. "I didn't expect that."

"Yeah, sorry. Forgot to warn you." I didn't think about how he would react to my choppy cut, shaved over my ear on one side, long on the other, and the violet color.

"I like it." He pauses, just staring at me for a moment. "I can't believe how much you've grown up. I mean, I know it's been years, but wow. You're not a kid anymore."

I don't know what to say, the mood is so intense. I need to lighten it up. "I didn't recognize you at first either. I thought maybe my father was that bald guy over by the door."

He laughs. "I've been looking at every teenage girl walking in here. I kept thinking the staff were going to ask me to leave."

"Yeah, that's kind of creepy."

"My bad," he says, and smiles at my look. "Hey, I learned a few expressions in prison. We had TV. Not much else to do!" He sits back down in the chair.

I glance around the room. I don't see anyone we know so I shrug my backpack off my shoulders and sit down, but I leave my scarf and hoodie on.

"I didn't order for you," he says. "I didn't know what you'd want."

"I'm not hungry." Mom would have dinner ready in an hour. We often eat in the living room, watch TV and talk about our day. It feels like rubber bands are around my body, snapping and pulling. *What are you doing?* I hear my mom say in my mind. *How could you lie to me?*

I just want to know what he's like, I remind myself. I have a right to know my own father. I feel a surprising stab of anger at my mom. If she had let me visit him in prison, I wouldn't have to sneak around. I know she was trying to protect me when I was a little kid, but I'm older now. I can make up my own mind about people.

"What about a tea or coffee?" He spins his coffee cup and I remember how he used to make me hot chocolate after we'd been playing in the snow and how he'd spin the cup around so the marshmallows swirled and say it was for good luck. I'd forgotten all about that.

"Hot chocolate," I say. "I want a hot chocolate."

We drink slowly. It's raining outside now and people dash into the coffee shop, their coats slick and shiny, shaking their wet hair, giving that laugh people have when they've escaped something. I think about Mom and wonder if she's feeling better. I wish she didn't have to work today. I know she's still upset about what happened when she was cleaning Mrs. Carlson's. I wish I could tell her it couldn't have been Dad—he was working at a job site on the weekend.

I think about taking her something home from the shop, maybe some soup and a fresh-baked bun, or those spicy chicken sausage rolls she likes, but then she'll ask questions, and I'll have to lie about who I was with and what I was doing and I might mess up somehow.

He's been talking about his job. He's working as a construction foreman for a company so he can get back into the swing of things, then he's going out on his own again. I can tell that he's picking his words so he sounds upbeat and positive, but I don't think he really likes his boss.

"I knocked off early. Didn't want to be late." He points to his coffee. "I've already had two of these." I study his face. He looks honest, almost a little shy. "How's your mom?"

"I don't think we should talk about her." He's never asked about her on the phone or in any of his letters and I was glad about that. Now I feel uncomfortable. I glance at his ring again. It definitely looks like he's still wearing his wedding band. Mom would hate that so much.

He notices my look, touches the ring. "I know I screwed

things up," he says, "but it doesn't mean I've stopped loving her."

"She's happy now."

My dad pauses and I think about my mom, wondering if what I said is true. I think she has fun with Greg—he's really nice and has a good sense of humor, always teasing Mom about something, like how she lines up all the sponges on the sink according to color. He's perpetually happy. I mean, who wouldn't be when you get to wear shorts to work most of the year? But she doesn't talk about him much. Maybe it's because there's not much to talk about. He's just Greg.

"I'm glad she's happy," my dad says. "Is she seeing anyone?"

"Dad." I stop; the word feels unfamiliar and strange and thick in my mouth.

"You don't have to call me that," he says. "You can call me Andrew."

"Andrew." That feels even weirder but I don't know what to say. Maybe I won't call him anything.

"She must have a boyfriend. She's too pretty to stay single for long." He's smiling like he's trying to joke around, as though this isn't a big deal, this question, but the coffee shop feels too busy now, the voices too loud, and the hot chocolate is making me feel sick.

"No," I say. "She's not seeing anyone." I don't want to have this conversation. I told him that I didn't want to talk about her but it's like he didn't even hear me.

"That's too bad. I really hoped she'd found someone who would make her happy." He looks sincere but I don't know his expressions. I don't know *him*.

"How's AA?"

"It's going well." He nods. "I have a sponsor."

"Are you going to all your meetings?"

"You're starting to sound like my lawyer." He smiles but I'm unsure again, nervous again about upsetting him. Is this how it felt for Mom? I think about telling him that I have to leave, but I also want this. To sit here and have coffee with my dad. Like a normal kid.

"You don't have to tell me," I say. "I just don't know what to talk about."

"Me neither," he says. "Let's start over."

"Okay."

"I brought you something." He reaches into a bag down by his feet, pulls out a long rectangular box, and hands it across the table. I know this box. Prismacolor Premier color pencils. I've stood in the art store and stared at them, but then I bought the cheaper set. I run my hands over the surface. One hundred and fifty shades. How did he know how much I wanted these?

"Thanks. These are great." I feel like I should say something else, but I can't find the words, can't explain how much I want to draw with them right now, how my mind is swirling with all the colors. I want to spread them out on the floor and touch each one.

"Did you bring your sketch pad?"

"Yeah."

"Can I see what you're working on?"

I pull my pad out of my backpack and pass it over to him. My face feels hot as he flips through the pages and makes comments. I hate how much I like this moment, the proud look on his face. How much I wanted to show him. I realize now that I drew some of them for him, and I didn't even know it. *This is okay*, I think. *Mom would understand.*

CHAPTER NINE

LINDSEY

JUNE 2004

He was home. His boots lay by the front door, dust tracks and clods of dirt all over the foyer. Sophie's pink running shoes were under his boots. I pulled them out. He was drunker than normal, had barely looked at me as he stumbled in and collapsed onto the couch.

I stared down at him, watching the way his mouth parted as he snored. One arm was thrown above his head. His hair was long again, falling into his eyes like it did when we met. It was only the first week of June but he was already tanned on his neck, his biceps, which I used to love to wrap my hand around, and where his shirt rode up at his waist. His other hand rested across his stomach. I could lift it and it would flop back down. He'd dripped something onto his shirt, ketchup, maybe pizza sauce or spaghetti. I studied the marks. I'd have to use stain remover.

My mom kept bottles of the stuff in the bathroom cabinet. She was always dabbing at a spill, on my dad's shirt, one of my dresses when I was little and in my mud pie phase. She said cleaning up after my brother alone kept the company in business and they should send her free samples. She and my dad had gone for their cruise in January, came back tanned and happy. The months had staggered on. Sophie was five and a half already. She got up on her own in the mornings, helped herself to cereal, and watched cartoons. She was going to see him like this.

I should go into her room, pack her things, and drive away. We could move in with my parents and I'd find a job. Something, anything. I felt another jolt of anger when I remembered the interior design class I'd loved so much. Then Andrew kept having to work late, or couldn't pick up Sophie from school, or needed me to bring something to the job site. What was the point? I dropped out.

He mumbled something, smacked his lips, and scratched at his stomach with lazy fingers. He'd wake up in the middle of the night and stumble to bed, his arm pulling me closer. The heat of his body would surround me so tightly I wouldn't be able to breath. I'd stay awake for hours.

"What's wrong with Daddy?"

I startled. I hadn't heard Sophie sneak out of her bedroom. She was wearing pink pajamas, her hair mussed. She twirled one strand around and around.

"He's just tired."

She walked closer, leaned over him, and sniffed. Then she looked up at me and whispered, "He smells icky." Her face was so innocent, but I could see the beginnings of awareness, the faint tone of accusation. How soon before she started to recognize the smell of beer? Would she challenge him about his drinking? How would he react?

I moved closer, pulled her away. "Come on, Sophie. Back to bed."

Andrew's eyes opened, and he swung his arm wildly, narrowly missing Sophie, and instead knocked me off balance. I fell backward onto the coffee table, then rolled off the edge. I lay stunned on the floor, sucking at the air. Sophie was beside me, hugging me tight. "Mommy!"

"It's okay, baby," I said when I could finally speak, but each word made my ribs hurt and my back felt as though it had been snapped in half. I looked over my shoulder.

Andrew was on his feet, his body swaying. "What the hell are you doing?"

"Daddy, stop!" Sophie cried. "You pushed Mommy!"

He stared at us for a moment, his eyes blinking slowly. "Sophie?" He reached out, and she cringed against me. His face pulled into a frown, and he took a couple of steps forward.

"Andrew," I said. "Andrew, please go to bed."

He focused on me, and I held my breath. Finally he spun around and lurched toward the bedroom. His hands fumbled for support against the wall. The bedroom door slammed shut.

I slept in Sophie's room, curled around her body, and smoothed her hair every time she woke. I'd gone to the bathroom, examined the damage in the mirror, wincing as I pressed a cold cloth to the upper right side of my back. That long red mark would turn to a bruise.

When I climbed into bed with Sophie, I eased onto my stomach, keeping my back straight and holding my breath so I didn't moan in pain. She reached over and tenderly touched my shoulder blade, her small hand drifting down my spine. "Does it hurt, Mommy?"

"A little bit."

"It was an accident," she said. "He didn't mean to. He'll say he's sorry tomorrow."

I choked back tears. My daughter, already making excuses for him. She'd learned that from me, I suddenly realized. She'd learned to forgive him. She wasn't even six.

———

In the morning I snuck out of bed while she was still asleep. He wasn't in our room. I found him in the kitchen pouring a cup of coffee. He lifted the carafe. "Want one?"

"No, thanks." I sat at one of the barstools around the kitchen island. The black leather stools he'd picked out, which I hated because they felt cold and were too masculine-looking. "We need to talk." I was jittery, had to brace my legs on the stool.

He turned around with a heavy sigh. "Sorry about last night. I didn't eat dinner, and the booze hit me too hard. We finished a job and I wanted to celebrate with the guys. You know how it is. They kept buying me drinks." I thought of the food spills on his shirt. More lies.

"You pushed me. I hit the coffee table."

He looked shocked, his head jerking back. "No, I would remember that."

Of course he would deny it, but I was surprised at how convincing he sounded. He was a much better actor than I realized. If I didn't know how he always remembered every single time I'd failed one of his rules, even when he was drinking, I might have believed him.

"Sophie saw everything. She was terrified."

Now he scrunched up his forehead like he was thinking over the night, trying to remember. His expression turned ashamed, and he sat down on one of the barstools. "I hurt you?" I nodded, and he rubbed his hands through his hair, his eyes wet as though he was going to cry. "I'll take the day off, okay? We'll talk about it, and we can take Sophie to the park."

"The park isn't going to fix this."

"You're right. I'm an idiot. How can I make it up to you?" He grabbed my hand. "I love you so much. You're my heart and soul. I hate thinking that I scared you like that. Can you forgive me?" He looked so serious, so upset, that I found my-self faltering for a moment.

"I don't know," I said. "What you did? It's abuse."

His eyes widened. "Hey, I'm not one of those guys. Don't even talk like that, okay? I got too drunk and made a mistake, but I didn't do it on purpose."

"It doesn't matter if it was on purpose, it still happened."

"I'm sorry. I'll tell you I'm sorry a million times. I'll spend the rest of our lives making it up to you. We'll stay in the same house until Sophie leaves for university. Whatever you want. I'll do it."

"Your drinking is getting worse. I can't deal with it any-more."

"What are you saying, Lindsey?" He looked nervous now, more scared than I'd ever seen him. "You want me to slow down? I'll stop drinking after work, okay?"

I took a deep breath and pulled my hand free. Maybe I should wait until later, when he wasn't hungover. He hadn't even fin-ished his coffee. No, there was never going to be a good time. I had to do this now, while he was still remorseful, while I was still brave.

"Our marriage isn't working. I'm not happy. You're drink-ing all the time—and Sophie sees, she knows. You won't let me do *anything*. You're so controlling. I feel like I'm suffocating." I saw him flinch but the words were tumbling out of me. "I'm going to take Sophie and move in with my parents for a little while. If you get help, go to AA, maybe we can—"

"You can't leave."

"I've already decided."

As soon as I said the words, it was like someone pulled a mask over his face. Everything smoothed out, his cheeks, his fore-head, even his mouth straightened, and his eyes went blank.

"We'll talk about it tonight, okay?" He glanced at his watch.

"I've got to get to work." He sounded so calm now. It was like we were talking about what to cook for dinner. I'd expected him to go ballistic. I searched his face, confused. Didn't he understand what I was saying?

He walked over to the counter, grabbed his lunch box, and left without giving me a kiss. I stood at the window and watched his truck disappear.

I told myself that he just needed to think it over. He'd take some time today and then he'd understand that he needed professional help. He had to see that this was best for everyone.

I dropped Sophie off at junior kindergarten, watched her trudge inside, her Barbie backpack so full it was almost pulling her over. She'd been quiet, her coloring book on her lap. I wondered if she heard her father and me talking that morning. I rubbed at the bone under my breast, caught my breath at the sharp stab of pain when I thought about how her face lit up when he said he was going to take her to the job site or to the hardware store with him, how she did a little dance and ran to the door. It didn't matter where he took her, she was always thrilled.

Tonight. He said we could talk tonight. I had to prepare, steel myself for what was to come. I couldn't let myself weaken now. I shifted, winced at my sore back. I needed to find a lawyer.

There was no way I could use my cell—Andrew went over the bill every month and asked about any strange numbers. I found a pay phone near a coffee shop, flipped through a phone book, and made an appointment with a female lawyer for later in the week.

My cell chirped beside me. It was a text from Andrew.

Forgot my lunch. Can you bring it?

He wanted me to bring him lunch? Did he think pretending everything was okay was going to make it true? He didn't even like me visiting the job site and he could easily buy lunch somewhere or come home. My heart was racing fast, and my car felt too hot and small. I kept looking at my phone. I'd never ignored him before. My phone chirped again.

Lindsey?

I couldn't move. Couldn't pick it up.

Don't do this.

Nothing for a few minutes.

Maybe I'll take Sophie out for lunch.

He's never gotten her from school before. Not at lunch. He was planning something. I grabbed my phone with shaking hands. Damn it. *I'll be there in a half-hour.*

The job site was busy and loud with equipment and men moving back and forth. I searched through the workers, looking for Andrew's familiar shape. Finally I spotted him near a cement truck. My breath was tight in my throat again as I got closer. Was he going to want to have a talk in his office? He was with a man, their white hard hats reflecting the sun.

I walked up beside him. "Andrew?"

He glanced at me, shifted his hard hat, and wiped at some sweat on his brow. "Hi, babe. I'll just be a moment. They're pouring the foundation." The barrel of the cement truck spun around as the heavy gray wet mass flowed down the chute. He turned to the man. "Every time I see cement, I think of Jimmy Hoffa."

The guy laughed. "No shit. He's probably in an underground parkade somewhere."

"Makes you wonder how many bodies are buried on job sites." Andrew threw his arm around my shoulder. "That's how you can get rid of me, babe."

I couldn't move, my hand gripping Andrew's lunch bag. The

other man was smiling, but he looked confused. The man was watching me now. Should I make a joke? Brush it off?

"Don't be silly," I said. "I wouldn't want to get my hands dirty." Both men laughed, but I could hear the tension in Andrew's throat, the forced tone. He was furious.

"It would be simple," Andrew said. "You could toss me in here and the guys would backfill over me and no one would ever know." He grabbed me, held me over the edge. I clutched at him. If he let go, I'd fall.

"Andrew!" I screamed.

He pulled me back toward him and wrapped his arms around me in a tight hug, his cheek against mine. "Hey, relax. I'm just messing around."

The other man was still laughing. He thought this was all part of the joke—Andrew and I were having fun. Andrew pressed his lips against mine and I was forced to kiss him back, watching over his shoulder as the man turned away, his face red.

Andrew finally let go and took the lunch bag from my hand. "Thanks for bringing this." He pulled a sandwich out of the bag. "Roast beef. My favorite." He took a big bite and chewed methodically as he focused back on the cement truck. The other man had moved around the side and was talking to the truck driver. I looked up at Andrew. His face was a cold mask.

"See you at home, honey." He walked away.

CHAPTER TEN

December 2016

When I walk into my support group Monday night a few women are already sitting in their chairs and staring at their feet or hands in silence, while others are gathered around the coffee urn chatting about the weather. I grab a coffee and find a seat.

We start group the same way each time. We check in about our weeks, how we're coping. This room is so familiar to me, the brick walls of the church basement, the rain on the outside window, the sour musty smell mixed with coffee and damp hair. I feel the coil of tension in my stomach easing and I'm glad I forced myself out of my warm house.

There are a few new women tonight, the shock in their eyes still fresh, their bodies tense as they sit huddled into their coats. One of the new members is a young woman, obviously dyed black hair, maybe mid-twenties. I catch her glancing at the doorway as though she's going to bolt. I give her a reassuring smile and she flushes, but then settles back into her seat.

Jenny and I met at my first meeting when I moved to Dogwood Bay. I'd never been to a support group before and didn't know what to say. I sat in the corner, my face hot and stomach churning. Then a blond woman with wild curly hair, damp from the rain and smelling like lavender shampoo, plopped down beside me and handed me a cup of black coffee.

"It's terrible, but it does the trick," she said with a warm smile.

Startled, I mumbled my thanks and took the cup from her. I wasn't used to being in a social situation without Andrew, or having the freedom to talk to whomever I wanted—part of me wasn't sure I even belonged at this group—but I liked the mischievous glint in her eyes, the funky glasses that were almost a little big for her face, her bright blue rain boots.

I took a sip and made a face. "I might never sleep again."

"I don't think many of us sleep anyway." She looked down at her cup. "The only thing blacker than this coffee is my ex-husband's heart." I'd been surprised by her wry tone. She didn't sound wounded or ashamed. She sounded *angry*. I realized then that I was tired of holding my head down, tired of feeling like I had brought this all on myself somehow. I was angry too.

"The only thing stronger than this coffee is the grip my ex-husband had on my life," I said. "They should both be flushed down a toilet."

She shot me a surprised look, her mouth lifting in a smile. "This coffee is so bitter, it could be my divorce lawyer."

I'd started laughing hard and almost spilled my coffee, which then made Jenny howl with laughter. We had to step out of the meeting to get ourselves under control.

Jenny shops at Whole Foods biweekly, knows more things about kale than I ever will, e-mails me recipes for her latest hemp- or chia-seed protein smoothies, and sends daily inspirational quotes. When she was offered the job in Vancouver as a lifestyle consultant, I was thrilled she was following her dream, but she left a big hole in my life. It had been so long since I'd had a female friend, one who supported me completely. We Skyped yesterday and I told her what had happened at my client's house and she was almost angrier than me.

"Ten years wasn't enough," she said. "They should've locked him up and thrown away the key. If you need to get out of that town, you call me right away."

I don't want to leave Dogwood yet—then Andrew would win. But if push comes to shove, I'm glad to know we have a home with Jenny. Both my parents are gone—my mother succumbed to her MS a few years ago, and my dad had a stroke not long after. They were devastated they hadn't realized how Andrew had really been treating me when we were married, and disappointed I'd never confided in them, but they understood more once I explained how he'd threatened and hurt me. My mom insisted that I tell them the truth about everything from that moment on, and begged me not to worry about them. Then my father made me promise I wouldn't come back to the island until Andrew's trial was over and he was behind bars.

Chris and I are still close, but he has a live-in girlfriend now and they're expecting a baby this spring. When I called him Saturday and told him what had happened, he was upset and offered to come stay with me, but I told him to stay with Maddie. She needs him more right now.

I share with the group about my recent experience and that I think Andrew is stalking me. They're understanding and have good suggestions for how to deal with the police and the courts, but I see their fear, the worry in their faces, and I sit back down feeling even more rattled.

Marcus arrives at the end of our meeting and unloads his equipment from his SUV—floor mats, punching bags, boxing gloves. He's come a few times over the last year and we all look forward to his classes. He's the most centered person I've ever met. When I'm standing next to him I feel like the world could be on fire and the flames would just pass over him.

One stormy night I was the only one who stuck around for his class. He said, "You must have some story if you're willing to come out in this weather to learn how to throw punches."

We sat and talked and I told him about Andrew. After years in a support group, I'd become comfortable sharing my past with the other women, but I was surprised at how easy it was to talk to a man. He was so intuitive, guessing at some of the ways Andrew had controlled and demoralized me—and he was always bang-on. He really understands abusive behavior and how hard it was to break free. I had a feeling he had his own troubled past.

After that we started meeting once in a while on our own. When the weather was nice we practiced outside. I found him intriguing, was surprised at how much I enjoyed our workouts, and briefly wondered if it might grow into something more. He drove me home once after I had a flat tire, and lingered in the foyer while we talked. When I thanked him later with a bottle of wine, I thought he might invite me to enjoy it with him, but he never did, and we settled into a great friendship. Usually we have a coffee after we're finished. That's when I learned that he used to be a psychiatrist. He must have been a good one. I've probably told him more stories about my life with Andrew than anyone else. And he's shared about his daughter.

I'd seen photos of Katie at his house. She'd been a beautiful girl, with his straight nose, wide smile, and dark coloring. She'd fallen in love with an older man as soon as she graduated and spent the next couple of years embroiled in a volatile relationship. Marcus suspected her boyfriend abused her, but she denied everything and pulled away from her family. She'd called Marcus the night she died, saying she wanted to come home. He'd been on his way to pick her up when he heard the sirens. Her boyfriend had shot her, then himself. She was only twenty-two.

When his marriage dissolved a year later, he also decided to quit psychiatry—"I felt like a fraud. I couldn't help my own daughter, how could I help anyone else?" Marcus gave everything to his ex-wife, Kathryn, and spent the next few years traveling. I can't imagine how hard it was for him to lose his daughter, then his wife. They must have been very much in love at one time—he told me it was his idea to name Katie after Kathryn. But he seems at peace with his pain.

Tonight Marcus goes around the room and works with each woman until they get every move down perfectly, but I'm not myself, my punches are off, and I miss a few blocks.

"You okay?" Marcus says. I nod and he holds up the pads and I throw a few hooks. "Again," he says. I pause and his eyes meet mine. I'm always amazed at how quickly he senses my moods, good or bad. My daughter is the only other person who can do that.

I thump the pad a few more times until Marcus finally nods his approval and moves on to the next woman. After class I help Marcus take the equipment out.

"So you going to tell me what's on your mind?" he says.

"Stressful weekend." I'd called Mrs. Carlson on Sunday and she confirmed nothing was missing from her house. She's still shook up and is going to stay at her sister's for a couple of weeks. I'd called the officer myself and she told me she'd only been able to match my prints and Mrs. Carlson's. She hasn't been able to locate Andrew yet, but I don't think she's looking that hard. I mean, as far as she's concerned, Andrew hasn't done anything wrong.

"Andrew broke into my client's house. He was inside when I was cleaning. He did that thing with my keys—he left them on my purse."

"Shit." He stops in the middle of shoving a box into the corner. "You call the police?" It's started to snow softly, the flakes drifting down in the light from the open door and landing on his black hair and melting into his close-cropped beard. He brushes them off distractedly

"Right away, but they didn't find any fingerprints."

He shakes his head. "I had a bad feeling when you started skipping workouts. Guys like your ex-husband don't just go away. I should've said something."

"This isn't your fault. I let down my guard."

"Well, don't do that again. Make sure your alarm is set every night."

I nod. "I was hoping you still had time to work out this week?" Marcus has a home gym with top-of-the-line equipment. I'd become lazy when Andrew hadn't made any attempts to find me. That was my first mistake. One I didn't plan on repeating.

"Of course."

"It's all coming back, you know? The fear, the anger. I really thought it was over and he'd moved on. How could I have been so stupid?"

"You're far from stupid, but anger is good. We can use anger." I like the glint in his eye, the determination.

I nod and throw my shoulders back. He's right. I'm not going to let Andrew make me feel like a helpless victim. "See you Wednesday."

Greg comes over the next night, bringing a big bottle of local wine. He prides himself on finding ones with the most amusing names, like Red Monkey Velvet, or Purple Panda. It won't be expensive—Greg doesn't make much money as a driver—and I like that he's never trying to impress. I pour us each a glass while he builds me a fire, then we sprawl on the couch. The wine is good and I would love to finish the bottle, but I'm raw from not enough sleep the past few nights. Too much wine would wreck me.

I tell Greg about the weekend, downplaying the events, and switch subjects. I tell myself it's because I don't want him to worry, but it's more that I don't like the helpless feeling of stress and frustration that invoking Andrew's name creates inside my chest. Besides, that's not what this evening is about. I don't need Greg to be a consoling ear or a sympathetic sounding board.

We don't talk a lot. Our relationship has mostly been about having fun. When we get together it's always something simple, dinner and a movie at his house or mine, maybe a walk. He's a few years younger than me, in his early thirties, and doesn't seem to take anything too seriously. I still laugh when I think about how he literally landed on my doorstep after he tripped on a loose step. He was so embarrassed when I opened the door and found him hopping around and clutching his knee. The next time he came with a package—and a hammer.

My cell phone rings. "It's my brother." Greg pauses the movie.

"Just wanted to check on you," Chris says. "Everything all right?" His voice reminds me so much of our father's, but he has my mom's fair looks, and her upbeat everything-is-going-to-be-okay personality. When I'm with Chris, I feel like both my parents are still with me, which is comforting. I didn't expect to lose them so young and I miss them every day. Chris has been a great uncle to Sophie, protective and loyal, always coming to her recitals or soccer games, and every holiday dinner. Since Sophie's gotten older she travels over to the island and spends the weekend with him and his girlfriend. She can't wait to have a little baby cousin to spoil.

"So far, yeah. But can we talk tomorrow? Greg is over right now."

He pauses, and I know he's curious—I've told him about

Greg, but only that we're dating, not that he spends the night. "Okay, call me in the morning."

I set my phone down on the coffee table, and turn back to Greg. He shifts his weight so we're face-to-face.

"So when do I get to meet your brother?" he says. "We've been dating for nearly three months. He's probably starting to wonder what's wrong with me." He says it with a cheeky smile that shows off his dimples (one on his left cheek and a little divot in his chin), but there's a serious, almost shy tone to his voice. I'm surprised, hadn't thought he was all that concerned about meeting my brother.

"I haven't introduced Chris to a boyfriend for a long time." I laugh nervously and pick up the bowl. Greg made the popcorn, insisting the butter had to be layered right. He tossed it with a salad fork and spoon, the tattoos on his forearms flexing—a brightly colored phoenix, flames twisting high and disappearing under his sleeve, where I know they meet with a poker hand, the words KING OF HEARTS across his pectoral.

He smiles. "So I'm a boyfriend?"

"Do you *want* to be my boyfriend?" I don't want to have this conversation right now, when half of my mind is wondering where Andrew is tonight, if he might even be watching my house, but it's happening whether I like it or not.

"I don't know. Does it come with any perks?" His warm hand traces a circle on my thigh, moving upward, and my body tenses. I'm not in the mood and I'm about to suggest we just snuggle, but then I realize this is exactly what Andrew wants— to get inside my head and mess with my life. Greg and I have great sex. He's the only man I've slept with since Andrew, and it was strange at first, his mouth and body not as forceful, but he let me take the lead, which was exciting and new. I learned sex could be fun. I'm not going to let Andrew take that away.

"Let's go to bed and I'll show you."

While Greg heads to my room, I turn off the lights and text,

Goodnight, to Sophie, who's spending the night at Delaney's. I check the dead bolt on the front door and take a quick glance out the window to the road. I used to sense when Andrew was driving home before I even heard his truck, could feel that flutter in my stomach as he rounded the last curve.

I close my eyes, put my hand over my stomach. It's calm, but I know Andrew has something else planned. Will mind games be enough for him? Or is he going to try to hurt me? I remember his threats to kill me, how strong he is when he's angry, how nothing in this world can stop him. I touch my neck, feel the warm skin, my pulse. I'm alive, I'm still breathing.

I take one more look out the window, and follow Greg to the bedroom.

I wake at seven to the sound of rain. One of the gutters must be plugged, the water cascading in a loud waterfall outside my window. I'll have to call the landlord. I force myself out of bed and into the kitchen, switching on lights. Greg went home at midnight and the house is quiet. He rarely spends the night. I say it's because of Sophie, but the truth is I panic sometimes when I wake up with him in my bed, his heavy leg wrapped around mine suddenly too much.

Now I wish I had asked him to stay. I could have buried myself against his warm side, listened to the rumble of his deep voice, which always sounds rougher in the morning, like liquid gravel. I'd traced my finger over his scars: one from his appendix surgery, the long raised one down his leg from a chain saw, the jagged one on his collarbone from a motorbike accident when he was a teenager. I've never known a man with so many scars.

I put the coffee on, drink a cup while I make my lunch, then fill a thermos with the rest. I'm going to need the energy. Today

I have two houses to clean, then a training session with Marcus. My first client of the day is one of my oddest. Joe, a man in his fifties, who's had a head injury and suffers from short-term memory loss—his family hired me. Sometimes he forgets I'm in the house and visibly startles when he finds me scrubbing his bathtub. A couple of times I've been the one who's startled by the sight of Joe lounging in the living room in his striped boxer shorts, eating canned chicken or spaghetti, and once he was dancing to "Let It Go," from *Frozen*, wearing his tablecloth as a cape. He urged me to join in, calling me "Anna." I hesitated for a moment, then wielded my mop like a microphone and gave it my best shot.

After I'm finished cleaning for Joe, who spent most of the time watching *Matlock* reruns, I move on to my second job of the day, a large two-story house with four very busy, very messy kids all under the age of twelve. Today it's not too bad, though, and I finish a little early, so I decide to stop at the bank on the way to Marcus's house and get some cash. As I wait for the machine to spit out my money, I feel an odd sensation in my stomach, a flutter of nerves. I quickly glance behind me, but there's no one else in line.

I collect my receipt and tuck it and the cash inside my purse and turn around.

I see him standing by the corner of the bank. He's putting money into his wallet, sliding it into his back pocket. He looks different with short hair and a beard, but the way he moves is so familiar, the shape of his head, the shrug of his wide shoulders.

The cement walls of the bank are rushing toward me as though there are only inches standing between me and Andrew. I can smell his skin, his soap, see the edge of his mouth, the way it turns up. Sophie's smile. He's going to see me, then he's going to say my name with that tone that sounds loving and angry and scolding and disappointed all at once.

Run.

Legs. I have to move my legs. Some internal force spins me around. Too fast, I drop my keys. It seems as though they fall in slow motion, hitting the sidewalk with a metallic *clang* that echoes across the pavement. I lurch downward, clutch at my keys, and rise.

"Lindsey." He's moving forward, walking toward me. The distance narrows.

"Get away from me." I stand straight, holding my keys out in my hand like some sort of sword. They're nothing. Just tiny pieces of metal.

He stops with his palms in the air. "I was in the bank. I didn't know you were outside."

"Why are you here?" It doesn't matter. I know why he's here. I need to walk away, but my feet are rocks. I look around, hoping for people, for safety in numbers, but it's as though the earth has opened and sucked everyone down. Not a car on the street, not one pedestrian.

"The construction company I'm working for got a new subdivision contract in Dogwood Bay. I was looking around at some places to rent."

No. He knew we lived here. He planned this.

"I don't want you living here." I hate that my voice is trembling, hate how weak I feel. I want to sound powerful and authoritative, but I sound like a pleading child.

"I understand that, but I have to go where the work is. Times are tough." Times have never been tough for him. I'm glad he's talking. He's making me angrier.

"You can't see Sophie."

"She's eighteen next month."

"She doesn't want anything to do with you." But he's right. She's almost of age. I can't stop this. I can't do anything.

"She doesn't know me anymore."

"I want it to stay that way. She's a good kid. Don't mess her life up."

"I've changed, Lindsey. I'm not the same person you married. I got counseling in prison, and I go to AA now—I haven't touched a drop in eleven years."

I wish I could thrust the keys into his eyes and keep stabbing until he can't look at me anymore. "I don't believe you've changed for one minute."

"Let's not do this on the street. Can I buy you a coffee?"

"I'm not going anywhere with you." I shouldn't be shocked that he actually thinks I'd want to sit and have a coffee with him, but his ability to ignore reality is truly terrifying. It's like in his mind we're old friends. I turn away.

"Lindsey!" he calls out, but I keep walking. Then, his voice lowering an octave but loud enough for me to hear, he says, "I know what you did. I know you drugged me that night."

The words slam into my back and nearly knock me off my feet. I falter, the sidewalk looming in front of my eyes. I think I might faint, blink away the panic. *No, no, keep going.*

I make my legs move, glance over my shoulder. He's still watching. My car is parked on the street, which means he now knows I drive a blue Mazda. My hands are shaking as I try to fit the key into the lock. I stare down at them, force my fingers to get their shit together and get me in the car *now*. My anger helps, makes me feel stronger. I get in and drive away as fast as I can.

I'm ten minutes late, but Marcus still opens the door with a smile. "I was starting to wonder about you," he says. "Thought maybe you decided to stop at Dairy Queen."

I know it's a joke—he's teased me ever since the time I showed up with a Blizzard for each of us—but I can't make myself laugh today. "I'm sorry. Hope I haven't messed up your schedule."

"Nah. I was running late myself." Marcus is never late for

anything. He's just saying it to put me at ease. He widens the door and I follow him inside and collapse into one of his chairs.

"I saw Andrew in town. He was at the bank." It's so hard to say the words, to admit what just happened. My voice is breathless as though I've sprinted up a flight of stairs.

"He's *following* you?" He sinks down into the chair across from me, his dark eyebrows pulled together in an angry frown.

"He says he's moving here because of work, but that's bullshit. He wanted me to know he's changed." I give a bitter laugh. "He hasn't changed one bit." I wish I could tell Marcus everything—about the pills, what Andrew said—but I have to keep the terrifying truth to myself.

"Jesus, Lindsey." Marcus leans forward, grips my knee. "I'm really sorry." It's the first time he's touched me, outside of when we're training, and his hand feels solid, comforting.

"I called the cop. She says Andrew claims he was working the morning someone broke into my client's house. I know he's lying, but they don't have enough reason to check into it more, or any crime they can charge him with. They're not going to waste their time."

"Can you get a restraining order?"

"It takes more than seeing him once—and he didn't do anything threatening. Even with one, I can't do anything to stop him from moving to this town. He's a free man."

"I really hate this system sometimes. It protects all the wrong people." He looks out the window, his mouth tight, and I wonder if he's remembering Katie.

He turns back to me. "If you ever need to get out of town for a while, I have a lake house on the island. You and Sophie could stay there."

"You have a lake house?"

"It's been in my family for years. It's quiet, peaceful—a good place to get away from it all and reflect on life." He must have stayed there with his wife and daughter, so I'm honored at his offer, but the last place I want to be is at some remote lake on the island, where Andrew knows every inch like the back of his hand. Doesn't sound that peaceful to me.

"Thanks, but it won't matter where we stay. The only thing that would ever make me feel safe again is if he's back in jail." I crack a smile. "That should just be a matter of time."

He smiles back, but he still looks worried. "I'm serious."

"I know. I just need things to stay normal right now. I'll think about it, okay?"

He nods. "It's there if you need it."

We work out until I'm exhausted, my legs and arms throbbing. Finally we call it quits and I take a quick shower in the bathroom off his gym and get dressed in fresh clothes. The endorphin high from my workout is already fading. When I'd first arrived at Marcus's house, I was in shock, numb, not ready to face the truth. But now I feel every hard edge.

Andrew is moving to Dogwood Bay, and he wants to see Sophie.

As I walk up the stairs and through the living room, I pause at the window with its ocean view, winter waves kicking up in the distance, gray clouds, heavy and bloated with rain. I watch them for a moment, try to take some calming breaths. I can't walk out in tears. I think of Sophie: What am I going to tell her? The panic rises again. *It's going to be okay, just take a minute.*

I straighten the books on the side table, look at the titles. Marcus reads all kinds of genres, but seems to veer toward memoirs and biographies. I notice one on grief, flip through the first few pages, and think about him and his daughter. Then I carefully put the book back.

Marcus is in the kitchen, making coffee. He's showered too, his hair wet and tousled.

He holds up a mug. "Time for coffee?"

"Of course." I take the mug and sit down. "So how is your writing going?" He's working on a book about his travels around the world and how different cultures approach death and grief, and he's let me read a few chapters. It was fascinating and I hope he lets me read more. While he talks about his recent research, I try to focus, but I'm still thinking about Andrew's final words outside the bank. He's not going to leave it at that. He's known all these years and he's never done anything about it. Until now. My skin grows cold, ice snaking down my spine, making me shiver. For a moment it's like I can feel him sitting beside me, whispering into my ear.

I warned you, he's saying. *I warned you.*

CHAPTER ELEVEN

October 2005

He left while it was still dark that morning, brushed his lips against my cheek. I pretended to be asleep, but I'd been awake for most the night, listening to him breathe, the ticking of our clock.

I pushed myself out of bed, cleaned up the mess in the kitchen before Sophie could see the broken dishes in the sink, the left-over beef stew smeared on the floor. He'd been angry that I hadn't waited. As if I'd wanted to sit at the table with him and watch him eat like a sloppy old man, his head drooping, food falling off his fork before it could make it to his mouth.

He'd been going to work early for the last two weeks, and often came home after Sophie was in bed, his hair messy and his face haggard and drawn. After he was pulled over one night and given a twenty-four-hour driving suspension, he started chewing peppermint gum, as if that would mask the smell of beer. He told me that the cop was an overzealous asshole.

The kitchen clean, I made Sophie's lunch, then sang our wake-up song loudly as I walked down the hall toward her room. "I love you! You love me!"

Her little voice answered. "We're as happy as can be!"

I pushed open her door, snuggled in beside her under the warm blankets, tickled her until she squirmed out of her bed, giggling hysterically. "Mommy! Stop!"

I drove Sophie to school, watched her in the rearview window with a lump in my throat as she sang along with the radio. She met my eyes and smiled. "Today is going to be a good day, Mommy." She sounded so confident. She truly believed everything was good in the world. That her mommy and daddy loved her and she was safe. It was what I wanted. I wished I felt the same.

"Yes, it is, baby."

I parked behind one of the buses and let her out of her booster seat. "Learn lots, okay?" I gave her a tight hug, and watched her head into the building. Then I came home to cry in the shower. The sobs heaved out of me, a wild panicked wail. I leaned against the wet tiles, waited for the tears to subside, focused on my breath. In. Out. In. Out. I had to get it together. Today was too important to mess up.

I toweled off and blew my nose, tossed the Kleenex into the can. Andrew had thrown out my *People* magazines again. Having a long bath used to be my one indulgence, my only quiet time. The day he grabbed me at the job site, I'd gone home and sat in a warm bath trying to stop my body from shaking. Should I get Sophie and flee? Would he hunt me down? I thought about the cement, imagined it flowing over my body. He came home while I was still in the bath, startling me as he whipped open the door and sat on the side of the tub. I pulled my knees up to my chest, too terrified to scream. This was it. He was going to hold my head under the water.

"I thought about what you said this morning," he said. "You aren't going anywhere. I don't want to hurt you, but I might not be able to stop myself. I love you too much to let you go."

I tried to speak, thought about all the things I should say.

You can't force me to stay with you. Love doesn't work like that. The look in his eyes kept me mute.

"Just give me some time," he said. "Things will get better." He'd lowered himself onto his knees beside the bathtub, rubbed his hand across the nape of my neck. "Don't break my heart."

So I stayed. Not for him. I stayed for Sophie, because I couldn't stop thinking about that hole in the ground. I didn't want my daughter to grow up without a mother. To spend her life thinking I left her by choice. I would try harder. I would be a better wife. I would *make* it work.

That was over a year ago. Nothing had gotten better.

I glanced at the clock, felt an uneasy roll in my stomach as I stirred the cake batter. Three more hours until his lunch break. Would he be smiling when he walked in, or quiet and moody? I needed to finish his birthday cake and pick up groceries before he came home for lunch. Mentally I went over my checklist. The house was spotless, I'd hung the Halloween wreath on the front door, and the pumpkins were ready for carving when Sophie was home from school.

We usually went out for dinner on his birthday, but this year he'd said, "Let's stay home. Don't make a fuss." I didn't know if he meant it, or he actually did want me to make a fuss and would be angry that we were just having dinner here.

My fingers slipped on the metal spoon, slopping batter down the side of the cupboard. I wiped it up quickly. Then I sat back on my heels, pressed my fingertips against my temples, trying to ease the constant throbbing headache that followed me everywhere.

I thought of the small bit of money I'd hidden in a can in the garden under the maple tree, dollars I'd saved from returning items, cash I'd found in his pockets and squirreled away. It was the only area of the yard the video cameras couldn't see, but even so, I always took garden tools out with me. I'd been thinking of other things I could do for cash. Housecleaning for neighbors, babysitting, but I couldn't see how I could do them without getting caught.

I got to my feet and looked down at the orange batter, dipped my finger in for a taste. Four-layer pumpkin cake with cream cheese icing, like his mother used to make. I'd write his name on the icing, and wear the soft blue dress he bought me. But it still wouldn't be good enough.

The eerie Halloween music in the store set my teeth on edge and the skeleton decorations at the end of each aisle with their red glowing eyes seemed macabre, not fun. I tossed items into my cart, rushed through the till. When I walked out of the store, a fog had moved in, erasing the mountains that had been ablaze with golds and russets and plums. The fall air was moist on my face. It felt like tears. I had to drive home slowly, focusing on the center line.

Andrew's truck was in the driveway. I slammed the car into park so fast the seat belt cut into my stomach. He was thirty minutes earlier than usual.

When I got out I let my hand rest for a moment on his hood. It was cold. The truck was pristine white, not a trace of mud or dust from the job site, the tires oiled and the rims shimmering silver. When he was in his dark moods, he became obsessed with cleaning.

I jogged up the front steps, my arms full of groceries, and pushed open the door.

"Andrew?" No answer.

When I walked into the kitchen, he was sitting at the table, a bowl in front of him. The pot was still on the stove, an empty can of tomato soup beside the sink. He hated canned soup.

"I'm sorry," I said. "I should've been home sooner. The store was a madhouse. I can make you a sandwich. The bakery said the bread is fresh." I took out a loaf of sourdough and some slices of turkey cold cuts and quickly shoved the other groceries into the fridge. He was silent behind me. I risked a glance over my shoulder. He was staring at me, his eyes narrowed.

"You used too much nutmeg in the cake."

Now I saw the other plate on the table, empty except for a smear of white icing. I turned and looked at the clear Tupperware container on the counter. I could see the cake inside. He'd gouged off a corner.

I forced myself to make eye contact. "I'll make another one."

"You look like crap."

I touched my hair. "It's damp out. . . ." He sat back in his chair, still looking at me. "I'll fix myself up." I walked down the hallway, trying to think. He was pissed off about something. Was it because I wasn't home? Had I left something out? I'd been so careful to clean the kitchen.

I pushed open the bathroom door—and stopped. My cosmetics had been dumped everywhere, powders and blushes smashed onto the floor, the colors smeared on the white tile. The cupboard doors under the counter were wide open. Shampoo bottles, soaps, mouthwash, and lotions had all been tossed out. One of the bottles had broken open. Pale blue iridescent bubble bath leaked into the mess, and the scent, "Mountain Breeze," hung sickeningly sweet in the air.

I knelt down and dragged my tampon box toward me with shaking hands. *No, no, no.*

Boot steps behind me. They stopped at the doorway. He knocked on the frame. I closed my eyes, squeezed them tight before opening them, then slowly turned around.

He was holding the shiny silver packet of pills out in the air.

"I've been thinking," he said. "How come Lindsey got pregnant so easy the first time, but now it's so hard? The doctor says it isn't me."

I got to my feet, braced my back against the counter, the hard edge biting into my skin. "I wasn't ready for another child. I tried to tell you."

"You let me think it was me."

"No! I didn't mean—"

"You're a lying bitch."

My body recoiled at the hatred in his face. "You *made* me lie." My own anger was rising. The resentment I'd been stamping down for so long fighting to come loose. "Why would I want to have another baby with you when you treat me like this?"

"Treat you like what, Lindsey?"

His voice was so cold and I knew I was going too far and warning bells were going off in my head, but it felt good to finally strike back.

"Like I'm nothing. Like I'm just your maid, or some child who doesn't get to decide anything for herself. Like you don't really love me."

"It looks like you've decided a few things for yourself, doesn't it? But that's going to change." He moved toward me and I cringed against the counter, but he brushed past.

He stood over the toilet and popped the pills out of the package, dropping them into the water. Then he came closer, stood right in front of me, and braced his hands on the counter on either side of me. "You don't seem to realize how fucking good you have it. No one else would want you, Lindsey. You're not that smart, and not all that pretty anymore either."

"Then let me go," I said. "Divorce me. We can share joint custody."

"I'll never let that happen."

"It won't be up to you," I said, surprised by how strong I sounded. "The courts will decide."

"You think I'd sit around and wait for that? If you ever leave me, if you even *try* to leave me, Sophie will only have one parent, do you understand?"

I couldn't talk anymore. My heart was hammering so hard in my chest I thought I might pass out, but I forced myself to nod. He was inches from my face, his eyes staring into mine. He grabbed a hunk of my hair and tugged it back painfully, then whispered into my ear. "I'm going to get Sophie from school and we're going out for my birthday dinner. You're not invited."

He released me, and I sagged against the sink. His boots were loud as he walked back through the house. I followed after him, ran through the hall. He was already outside, down the stairs. I searched the counter for my keys, rifled through my purse, turned in a slow circle and scanned the room, searched the hook by the front door. They were gone.

Headlights streaked across the living room wall. I met them at the front door. Andrew came in first. I checked his face, noticed the flush to his cheeks and nose. From the cold? Or had he been drinking? God, please tell me he wasn't drinking with Sophie in the truck. Sophie trailed behind her father, dragging her school backpack. She was huddled in her pink winter coat and shivering slightly, but her eyes were bright and happy as she said, "Hi, Mommy!"

"Baby, I was getting worried." I dropped to my knees in front of her, rubbed her shoulders. "Why are you so cold?" Her braid was askew, and the baby-fine hairs around her forehead floated free. I smoothed some of them back. I searched her face again. She didn't seem upset, but she was twirling one strand of hair and looking up at her father. Lately she'd started to follow him around the house on the nights he came home drunk or she'd sit beside him on the couch, until I urged her to bed or bribed her away with a promise of a new bedtime story.

"I'm okay, Mommy."

"She's fine." Andrew's boots hit the wall behind me with a thud as he kicked them off. I tried not to flinch, aware of my daughter's gaze. I listened to his socked feet walking into the living room. I couldn't tell if he was stumbling.

"Where did you go?" I said to Sophie, trying to use a cheerful voice.

"Leave her alone," Andrew said from the living room. "She needs to go to bed."

Sophie's small white teeth were biting at her bottom lip. "I'm cold."

I unbuttoned her coat. "How about a bath to warm you up?" I glanced into the living room. Andrew was staring at the TV and flipping through channels.

"Stop babying her," he said.

Sophie startled, looked at me quickly. I gave her a hug. "I'll put an extra blanket on your bed," I said into her small, cold ear. "You can wear your fuzzy jammies."

I tucked her favorite Disney princess blanket tight around her, then cuddled beside her so she could feel my body heat, rubbed at her hands and feet, massaging her legs.

"Did you have a nice time?"

She nodded, her soft hair tickling my nose in the dark.

"Where did Daddy take you?"

"We went up the mountain and looked at all the stars. Daddy bought me new binoculars. They're pink. We had pizza. Daddy kept dropping his piece. He got cheese everywhere!" She giggled, then she rolled closer to me and touched my hand. "Do you feel better, Mommy?"

"What?"

"Daddy said you were sick?" She sounded confused. My stomach muscles clenched. Of course he lied to her. I was definitely sick. Sick and tired of living in fear like this.

"I'm all better now, baby. I'm glad you had fun."

She let out a big yawn, and her head lolled against my shoulder "Can I sleep now?"

I stayed with her as long as I dared, until her breath evened out. I knew he was waiting in the living room. What was he going to say? That I had to have a child or he'd do something terrible? What if I refused to have sex with him? If he was drinking he was never interested in sex. When he was sober and initiated anything sexual, I'd learned to go along with it whether I was in the mood or not. I disconnected from my body until it was over. Any excuses about my being tired were met with hostility and accusations of cheating. It was easier to just let it happen.

When I walked into the living room, I saw that Andrew had passed out on the couch, an empty whiskey bottle on the floor beside him. So he had been drinking tonight. He always liked to come home and finish his buzz off with a few whiskeys. I sat on the chair across from him, watched his sleeping form, and imagined him taking pulls from a beer as he drove my daughter up into the mountains on curvy roads. One wrong turn and I would have lost her forever.

I looked around the living room, so similar to those in all the other houses we'd lived in. Sophie's project was drying in front of the fireplace. She'd spent hours gluing leaves and pinecones onto the poster board and labeling everything with gold glitter glue. She couldn't wait to show him.

His wallet was on the coffee table. He rarely set it down anywhere. My key chain was beside it. Was this a trap? I watched his face, listened to his heavy breathing, then leaned forward and slowly picked up his wallet. I opened it and glanced down. Five one-hundred-dollar bills.

He shifted his weight and I froze, watching. He turned his face into the back of the couch. I waited until his breath slowed. I fingered the bills, carefully slipped them out. I couldn't believe what I was doing. I paused, then thought of my birth control pills down the toilet.

I picked up my keys, gripping them tight in my hand so they didn't jingle, and tiptoed out. I found my suitcase in the closet, packed my clothes, my toiletries, moving methodically around our bedroom. Then I went into Sophie's room, slid her drawers open, and packed her underwear, pajamas, jeans, and sweaters. Dresses. Right, I had to remember her princess dress.

"What are you doing, Mommy?"

I spun around, held my finger to my lips. "We're going on an adventure," I whispered.

She sat up. "Is Daddy coming?"

"No. He has to work tomorrow, so we have to be really, really quiet, okay?"

She nodded, her hair floating around her face, silvery blue in the moonlight. I lifted her in my arms and she wrapped her legs around my waist, tucked her head into the crook of my neck like when she was a toddler. I felt her body go limp and heavy. She'd fallen back asleep. I carried her to the car, eased the doors open, and placed her in her booster. Her head drooped. I turned her face to the side. Then I put her blanket around her and tossed our bags in the back.

I slid behind the wheel, flipped through my key chain. Something was wrong. I couldn't feel the shape of my car key. I glanced at the house, nervous about turning on the interior light. I dug my cell out of my purse, my fingers fumbling through everything. Finally I felt the cold plastic, aimed the light down. There was my mail key, the house key, but no car key.

A noise beside me, the rush of cold air, a hand gripping my arm. Andrew was pulling me out. I fought to hang on to the steering wheel, both hands clutching the rubber, but he was too strong and I fell onto the ground, my legs still inside the car. He dragged me the rest of the way out, sat astride my chest. I choked back my scream. Sophie. I couldn't wake Sophie.

I pushed at his chest, tried to squirm away. His body was outlined from the interior lights that had come on when he opened the door. I couldn't see his face. It was all black.

Hands were around my throat, squeezing. I couldn't breathe. I clawed at his hands, his wrists. My knees bumped into his back. Everything was slowing down.

"I warned you," he hissed.

Something felt like it was bursting in my eyes, blood roared into my head. I tried to gouge at his face, but he pulled away. My eyes were closing. My hands loosening.

"Mommy?"

Air, sudden sweet air. My head rolled to the side, cold dirt and gravel under my cheek. I had no strength, could only take gasping breaths. My throat felt as though it was broken.

"Mommy fell out of the car," Andrew said.

"Mommy?" Sophie's voice was tentative, worried. She was strapped into her booster seat, couldn't see me on the ground. Andrew shifted his weight and climbed off me, but his hand pressed down on my stomach—a warning.

"I'm okay," I gasped. After a moment, I rolled onto my side, eased to my knees. Andrew was getting Sophie out of the car, lifting her up into his arms. She was holding her blanket.

"I thought we were going on an adventure?" Sophie said.

"The adventure is over, sweetie," Andrew said.

He strode toward the house, Sophie still in his arms. She was watching me over his shoulder. I could just make out the shape of her small head bobbing with each of his steps.

CHAPTER TWELVE

Sophie

December 2016

I'm in the cafeteria, drawing in my sketchbook. Delaney has gone back to her locker already, but I'm holding off going to my next class. I'm trying to get the wings right on a crow—I keep messing up the feathers because I'm thinking about my dad. I'm scared I've opened a door to something and now I can't close it. He was asking so many questions about my mom. What if that's why he really wanted to meet me? What if Mom finds out I've been lying to her?

Jared McDowell sits down beside me. I keep working on my crow. I can feel him watching me, like he's waiting for me to look up or say something, but I'm not going to stop just because one of the popular kids is sitting beside me. He probably wants help with his homework or thinks I'm a dope dealer because I have purple hair. Least, that's my best guess based on nothing. We've never talked before, but I used to check him out sometimes when we had the same class last semester. There's something about his face that's interesting. His nose is long, and his lips are too big for his face, but he has nice eyes. Shiny black, almost like a crow's. Not that it matters. I'd never hook up with him. I don't think he's a jerk, but we don't hang out with the same kids or have anything in common. His family has a lot of money, a big house on the ocean, and he has a car. My mom cleans for his parents. So, there's that.

When I still haven't spoken for a couple of moments, he leans a little closer to me.

"I heard your mom had something creepy happen this weekend," he says. Some of the kids at the table next to ours turn around and look at us. I stare at them until they look away.

I meet his eyes. "How do you know about that?"

"She told my mom. She wanted to make sure someone was home when she was cleaning. Do the police know who it was yet? Does she think she's being followed or something?"

I don't know what to say. Mom didn't tell me she was nervous to go to work alone or that she was warning her clients. Did she tell them about my dad? Would she lose jobs?

"What do you care?"

He frowns. "What's your problem? I just wanted know if she's all right."

"She's fine," I say, too loud. It had to have been a robber who broke into Mrs. Carlson's house, not my dad, but I hate thinking about my mom being scared. Jared's holding a Starbucks coffee cup, his hands wrapped around it loosely. His nails are smooth and clean-looking, and he's wearing a silver thumb ring with this cool stitched pattern. I want to see it closer, but then I think about my dad's rough hands and how he was wearing his wedding ring. Mom told me that he tried to choke her once. How could he do that? I stare down at my drawing.

"You okay?" Jared says.

"I have to finish this before class." I shift my body to the side so my shoulder blocks his view of my face, and start working on the wings again, smudging them with my fingertip.

He's quiet for a moment. "Sorry I bothered you." He gets

up from the table, gathers his books, and walks out of the cafeteria. I keep working on the crow, but my face is hot. I take my pen and drag lines over and over the crow until it's obliterated. Problem solved.

Sunday afternoon Andrew and I are near the edge of the river. I'm still getting used to calling him Andrew. It feels awkward, like calling a teacher by their first name or something. He's been showing me how to cast, and I lost a couple of the lures, but he didn't seem to mind. He's made sandwiches. The bread is moist as though he took it out of the freezer that morning, and thick, with sliced roast beef and cheddar cheese. I'm pretty much a vegetarian (I'll eat fish and eggs), but I can tell it's important to him that I like mine. He keeps sneaking peeks at me. I choke one back, wash it down with the Dr Pepper he brought because he said he remembered I liked it. That was nice too. I don't tell him that I haven't drunk a Dr Pepper since I was probably thirteen.

"I'm still learning to cook," he says.

"They're good."

"Not really," he says with a laugh, and I smile. "The meat is dry. Your mom made the best roast beef."

He's circling back around again. Always back to her. I stare down at my sandwich.

"I wasn't sure if you would still meet me today," he says.

"Why not?" I glance at him, dancing my feet a little to keep warm. He's built a fire on the beach and we're sitting on a blanket on the log, but I'm still cold.

"Your mom was pretty pissed that I'm moving here." He gives me a look. "I didn't tell her we had coffee. I kind of got the idea she didn't know."

My legs stop moving. "What are you talking about?"

"She didn't tell you I saw her outside the bank on Wednesday? I was going to tell you the good news about my job today, but I thought maybe she already said something."

"You're moving here? Like you're going to be here all the time?" I don't know how I feel. I wanted to get to know him again, but what if we don't like each other? My mom must be so upset. I think back over the last couple of days. She has seemed stressed, but I thought it was because of her business. I was happy that she was distracted. Now I feel horrible.

"It's a good job opportunity and I've missed eleven years of your life. I want to be around more this year, before you go away for university."

"I didn't tell Mom I saw you. She's still really scared of you."

"I know." He looks sad, his mouth turning down. "I'm hoping that when she sees I'm not trying to mess up her life, she won't be scared anymore."

"You didn't treat her well," I say. "You hurt her." It's frightening to say the words out loud, but I feel daring and bold and reckless. I feel like she would be proud of me.

"I couldn't control the drinking," he says. "Every time it happened, I hated myself for days and I'd think I was never going to do it again, but the second I drank, I turned into someone else. It was like this big dark thing came in and took over and I couldn't stop."

"Do you think about the woman?" I almost whisper the question, can feel the dampness of the river and the winter air seeping into my bones. I shiver. I looked her up online, saw the photos of her car, the front all smashed in. Her name was Elizabeth Sanders and she was only twenty-eight years old. They used a photo of her from when she graduated nursing school, looking so happy and proud. I read all the comments underneath. Everyone hated my dad.

"All the time," he says. "I couldn't face it for years because I was in denial, but AA taught me about acceptance and forgiveness. One day I sat down and wrote her a letter."

"She had a family."

"I know. I wrote them a letter too."

"Did they answer?"

"No, but I understand. I ruined their lives." He looks at me. "I messed up yours too."

"It's been really hard."

"I missed you a lot. I didn't appreciate how good my life was. The stuff I used to get pissed off about . . ." He shakes his head. "I hate that I scared you and your mom."

"I don't remember being scared of you."

"Are you scared of me now?"

"I don't really know you anymore."

"I get that." He nods, picks up his rod, and walks to the shore. I wait on the log, not sure what to do. I watch him as he casts his fishing lure, and reels it in slowly. Then I push myself up and go over to stand beside him. He glances at me. "So tell me something I don't know. Your best friend is Delaney. Do you have a boyfriend?"

"No." I laugh, but the first image that pops into my head is Jared's face and I wonder why I'm thinking about his sleek black hair or how I might like to draw his crooked nose.

"What about you?" I say. "Do you date people now?" It's a strange concept, thinking of my father, *Andrew*, out having dinner with a woman. Would he talk about me? Would she want to meet me? Maybe she'd have kids and then it would be like I had siblings. Then I remember that Mom doesn't know about any of this. It's not like I can share Christmases.

"I had the love of my life already."

"You mean Mom?"

"Always."

I feel sick in my stomach, the roast beef in uproar. Maybe

it's time to tell him the truth. "She has a boyfriend. I didn't tell you last time because I didn't want to hurt your feelings."

He stares out at the river for a really long time. I can't read his expression. I thought it was better he knows about Greg so he can move on, but now I wish I hadn't said anything.

"That's good," he finally says. "I want her to be happy."

"You angry?"

"I'm disappointed, but I understand. She hasn't talked to me for a long time."

I have another horrible feeling that I've made a big mistake, that maybe he's doing all this for a different reason. "You can't come around her. She doesn't want to see you."

"Don't worry. I won't mess things up this time." Before I can say anything else, he glances at his watch. "We better get going or I'll miss the plane back to the island."

We pack up all our things and I walk him to his truck, where he tells me I owe him twenty dollars for tackle. I know he's joking because he has that sideways smile, so I laugh, but I'm thinking about how he said *this time*. As though he still has another chance with her. I'm scared he didn't hear anything I said about Mom. That he doesn't believe me.

CHAPTER THIRTEEN

LINDSEY

OCTOBER 2005

I was raking leaves in the front yard, and picking up walnuts that stained my fingers black, when my brother pulled into the driveway in his old blue pickup truck.

"Mom said you canceled Sunday dinner," he said.

I'd carefully applied makeup to my bruises, then wrapped a scarf around my neck. Sophie wanted to know why I was wearing it inside. I told her it was my new style. She wore one to school this morning as well, the ends trailing behind her.

Andrew had watched me while I made breakfast but he didn't say anything, just drank two cups of coffee back to back and swallowed some Tylenol. I turned around once and saw his eyes settle on my throat, then drift away, something dark coming into his face.

"I'm not feeling good." My voice still sounded raspy, from pain and fatigue. I'd barely slept all night, could only stare at the ceiling and replay the way Andrew's hands had felt around my throat, my lungs screaming for air, the certainty that if Sophie hadn't called out, he'd have kept going until I was dead. She'd saved my life. I used to be able to convince myself that he wouldn't really hurt me, he wouldn't go that far, something in him would make him stop. He loved me. I couldn't lie to myself now. It was going to keep happening.

Maybe next time it would be a shove into the furniture, or he'd knock me down the stairs—something he could blame on me. But how soon before he slapped or punched me? Or broke a bone? How soon before he lost all control and choked me again?

Chris came around the front of his truck, took the rake out of my hands, and started scraping it on the ground, adding leaves to my pile. I flashed to us doing this when we were children, seeing who could build the biggest pile. Hurricane would pounce in the middle and we'd have to start all over again. I thought about Blaze. How much I'd wanted Sophie to grow up with a dog.

I turned away, scrabbling with my hands at a walnut half buried in the dirt. I didn't want Chris to see me cry. I took some breaths, tossed the walnut into the wheelbarrow.

"The squirrels bury these everywhere," I said. "Crows drop them onto the roof and I can hear them rolling down all day and night. They clog the gutters. Drives Andrew crazy."

"I called him last night to wish him a happy birthday and see about stopping over. He said he was out with Sophie and that you had a headache. Must have been a pretty bad one."

I blinked a couple of times, fighting to keep calm. He knew something was going on. I glanced back at him over my shoulder. "It was a sinus headache. I took a couple of Advil and went straight to bed. Andrew was sweet about it."

"Good." He was looking into my eyes, not letting me break the hold. "I've been wondering if things are okay with you two."

"Of course." I wanted to tear away the scarf, wanted to show him the bruises and beg for his help, but I made myself smile. "Everything's great."

"You seem different when he's around. Like you're tense or stressed about something."

I stood up, brushed my hands off. "I'm probably just tired. We're okay, really."

"You know you can tell me what's going on, right? I won't say anything to Andrew."

"There's nothing to tell." I shrugged. "I'm happy."

"Don't bullshit me, Lindsey. You don't smile anymore, not the same way. And you don't do anything with your friends, or go anywhere. You used to have lots of goals. What happened to you going to school? It's like you've given up on everything and Andrew is your whole life."

"I have a child now. Things have changed."

"Come on. That's an excuse. Some of your friends have kids and I see them around. They ask about you. Samantha told me you never call anymore."

He wasn't going to believe that everything was perfect. I looked down the driveway, then back at him. "We're going through a rough patch, but we're working things out. Sophie needs him," I said. "He loves her so much, and he's good to her."

"You can't stay with him just for Sophie."

"There are other reasons. You don't understand."

"Other reasons? Like what?"

I grabbed the rake from his hands, scraped it hard against the dirt, and kept my head lowered. "I really need to finish this."

"You're worried about Dad? He can get disability because of his shoulder. He hasn't applied because Andrew told him that he needed him too much."

I spun around. "I can't leave, okay? I'm married. I made a *commitment*." I didn't realize I was touching my throat until I saw Chris watching, his eyes narrowed. I dropped my hand. "You should get back to work. Andrew will wonder where you've gone."

"Why are you so scared of him?"

I shook my head mutely. The tears were too close. I wanted to tell him I wasn't scared, I was fine, I didn't need his help, but I was afraid I'd break down if I tried to speak.

"Does he hurt you? Is that it?"

I dropped the rake and walked away, heading toward the house. I couldn't do this. I couldn't look him in the face and tell him that my husband had choked me. He grabbed my arm.

"Lindsey, stop. Talk to me."

The sobs were building in my throat, strangling me. I didn't want to cry. If I started, I might not be able to stop. I covered my face. He grabbed my shoulders, looked into my eyes.

"You have to tell me. You have to protect Sophie."

"Don't you get it?" I was almost yelling, the pain and grief desperate to come out. "That's what I'm trying to do! He'll take her away. He has all the money—everything."

"I'll help you find a lawyer. Someone good."

I laughed bitterly. "You still don't get it. He almost killed me last night." I grabbed the scarf, unwound it from my neck, and pointed to my bruises.

It took a second for him to react, then his whole body erupted with rage. His face reddened, his fists clenched, and all the tendons in his neck were sticking out like a bull about to charge.

"That fucking asshole. I'm going to beat the shit out of him."

Now I was the one grabbing his arm. "You can't tell him you know. He'll hurt me again."

"Jesus, Lindsey." He ran his hands through his hair, white-blond like mine. He looked older, suddenly—he was a man. Not my little brother anymore. "Maybe we should tell Dad."

"We can't. I'm scared he'll do something to them if they try to help."

"Okay." Chris looked calmer. Still upset, but not like he was going to attack Andrew at his job site, and I was relieved. His gaze flicked to his truck, then back to me. "There has to be a way. . . ."

"I'm trapped, Chris. He watches me constantly—there are cameras. He monitors everything I do, every single day. This corner of the yard is the one place he can't see on the cameras. The only time he's not watching me is when he's asleep."

His eyes met mine. "How does he sleep when he's drunk? Does he pass out?"

"Sometimes, but he's restless. He wakes up if I move an inch or even roll over onto my side. I'd be too scared to sneak out— and it would be hard to keep Sophie quiet."

"What if I have an idea?"

A few minutes later, I stood under the trees with my brother, while the wind blew leaves down around us and walnuts thumped onto the ground and my hands went cold, but I didn't feel any of it.

I was feeling hope. For the first time in years.

Andrew gave me a card after dinner, slid it across the table when Sophie had gone into the living room to watch cartoons. I stared down at the big red heart on the front, the shiny silver embossed words. *My Darling Wife.* I didn't want to open it, but he was watching me.

I read the romantic poem inside and tried not to flinch. There was a letter from a travel agent. He'd bought three tickets for Cancún, leaving mid-November. Two weeks from now.

He'd signed the card, *Love always, Andrew.*

"It will be good for me to take some time off," he said. "I need to focus on you and Sophie." He reached for my hand, held it across the table. "What do you think?"

I needed at least a month before Chris and I could put the

plan into motion. It was going to be hard enough to pretend everything was okay if we stayed home. I couldn't fake my way through a vacation. He was going to want to have sex every day. What was I going to do?

"Sophie has school."

"She can miss a week."

"I don't know. There's so much to do before Christmas."

"Christmas is almost two months away. Think about how much Sophie will love it. The ocean, the pool. She'll have a blast."

I stared at him over the table. He was using Sophie again, twisting the knife.

He leaned closer. "Lindsey, I'm really sorry about what happened, okay? Please let me make it up to you. We can spend the whole week relaxing. You can use the spa, get a massage every day, facials. Remember how much you liked those margaritas on our honeymoon? We can take one of those night cruises and watch the rhythm dancers on the beach. I'll even dance with you. Whatever your heart desires, it's yours." He smiled hopefully, his voice teasing, but I saw the fear in his eyes. He knew he was losing me. His fear didn't make me feel safe, though. It scared me even more. He would do anything to keep me from leaving.

"It sounds lovely." When he released me to reach for his beer, I rested my hand in my lap and dug my nails into my palm until the urge to scream had passed. It would be okay. Maybe it would even be better if he thought I was looking forward to a vacation with him. He'd feel more confident that everything was fine and might not watch me as closely. Soon. I'd be free soon.

CHAPTER FOURTEEN

December 2016

It's been a long day of cleaning. Wednesdays I have two houses, neither of which are small, and I'm looking forward to the weekend. Maybe Sophie and I can go to a movie or do some cross-country skiing. She doesn't love the skiing, prefers to sit in the lodge by the fire and draw, but I can usually get her out for a few hours. It would be nice to see Greg too. He was busy last weekend working on his truck—the transmission blew right in the middle of his Christmas rush. He'd joked about borrowing money. "Don't suppose you have a few thousand dollars lying around, do you?" But when I asked if he was serious he said, "No, I'll work it out."

When I told him I saw Andrew in town he was concerned and reassuring, which was nice. "Try not to let it worry you too much, but call the police next time." He offered to come over that night after his truck was fixed, but he sounded so tired, I said that I'd be okay. I figured he could use a break. Later, walking around my silent house, I wished I'd said yes.

When I arrived at Marcus's this morning for our workout,

he took one look at me and said, "That bad, hey? I'd hug you, but you look like you might burst into tears."

I nodded, held my mouth in a grim line. "I need to toughen up."

"No, you're great, but I am going to show you how to fight mean, okay?"

"What have we been doing all these months?"

"Baby steps. Now I'm going to turn you into a lethal weapon." He smiled, and I appreciated the humor so much, I almost did give him a hug, but he was probably right. I would cry. I took a step back, pretended to dance around and box the air, upper-cuts, jabs.

He watched me for a moment. "Okay, maybe I'll just show you how to kick a guy."

I drop my purse on the kitchen table, grab a water from the fridge, and lean on the door for a few moments, considering my dinner options. Quesadilla for one? Frozen pizza? Maybe leftover sausage and potato stew with toast—I burned enough calories today. Sophie texted me that she was going to Delaney's for dinner and would be home around eight. I pop the stew into the oven and make my way upstairs to do some online Christmas shopping.

My bedroom is cold and I shrug on a sweater and pull on my favorite fuzzy socks while I wait for my computer to boot up. I sit at my desk and check my e-mails, but nothing down-loads, which is strange—I always have a few e-mails, even if they're mostly junk. Then I realize some of the e-mails in my in-box are new—one is a potential client looking for an esti-mate, but the messages have already been opened, the subject headings no longer in boldface. I stare at the screen. Did So-phie come home at lunch? Why would she use my computer?

I scan down the list, check the time and date. A bunch were from the night before—e-mail flyers, Groupons, winter clothing discounts, Christmas sales. The inquiry about the cleaning was sent at six in the morning, just before I woke up. Then I check the time on the two other e-mails. They were sent while I was at work this afternoon, but they too are showing as read.

One is from Jenny about Christmas presents, chatter about what she's getting each of her daughters. The other is from Greg. I click on it, skim the content. He's sorry about the weekend, can't wait to see me, thinks I should spend a night at his house soon.

I'll make you breakfast and deliver it in bed.

I can't look away from the screen, my blinking cursor, the damning words. I'm anchored to my chair, but inside I'm moving everywhere at once. Fear heaves and smashes its way through my body, a giant lumbering beast. Was Andrew in my house? Did he read this e-mail?

It's impossible. We have an alarm. But then I remember Sophie dashing back into the house because she forgot something. She probably didn't set it again.

I glance down at my desk and see all the notes on my calendar, dates, times, appointments. Then I notice the mail beside my keyboard, bills I'd brought in this morning and dumped on my desk in a scattered pile. Each envelope has been sliced open cleanly and the bills carefully placed one on top of the other. Lined perfectly straight, every edge exact.

I stand up quickly, push my chair away from me, and step back.

I grab a nail file from my pencil holder, spin around, and scan my room. The bed. This morning I smoothed it flat, tucked all the corners in tight, but now there's an indentation on the edge as though someone had sat there. I look at the closet, the shadow under my bed. He could be anywhere. I fumble behind me, find my cell phone.

"Nine-one-one, what's your emergency?"
"I think someone's in my house."

While I wait for the police, I stay on the phone with the operator and make my way down the stairs, scanning for any movement. In the kitchen I pick up a butcher knife and my car keys, then head for the front door with the knife straight out in front of me. My senses are razor-sharp, the air so heavy I can feel it burning into my lungs. Finally I'm outside, sucking in the cold night air. I don't have my shoes or a coat. I wrap my arms around my body, run to my car, and climb inside. I lock the doors, blast the heater, and listen for the police sirens.

One officer searches the house while the other takes my statement. There's no sign of a forced entry and nothing seems to be missing. They don't dust my keyboard for fingerprints because apparently they need a smooth surface to get prints. It doesn't matter. He would have worn gloves. I think of his favorite leather pair that I'd picked out for his birthday one year.

I can feel the doubt in their polite voices as they make notes, the routine sound to the words. How many times do they get called by nervous ex-wives?

After they leave, I look around my house, conscious of every sound, the hum of the fridge, the gas furnace. There's a smell in the air, something burning, and I realize my stew is still in the oven. I pull it out. It's a dried brown mess, but I have no interest in food now anyway.

I text Sophie that I'm going to bed early and suggest she stay at Delaney's. She answers back right away: *Sure.* I go through the house, checking everything, pawing through my drawers, imagining things from his perspective. He would have hated seeing my lingerie, would have seethed thinking of my wearing it for another man. I go through my bathroom, imagine him checking every prescription, my makeup, my birth control pills.

A book has been placed open on the side of the bath with a few candles and a bottle of aromatic salts, which had been under the counter, now arranged nearby as though inviting me to take a long, relaxing soak. My celebrity gossip magazines have been tossed into the garbage.

Andrew hated when I read those in the bath.

He must have spent hours in my house. Even the fridge looks like it might have been rearranged, cream behind the milk. I'm sure it was on the side of the door this morning. I'm driving myself mad, thinking about everything he touched. Did he eat some food? Make himself a snack? Then I realize the dishwasher is empty and he's stacked wood in the fireplace.

I call Corporal Parker and ask if we can meet at the station first thing in the morning to talk about my options. She agrees and suggests I spend the night elsewhere if I think Andrew might come back, but I already tried to call Greg when the cops were here earlier, and he wasn't home, then I remembered it's his poker night. He didn't answer his cell either.

"I'll make sure the alarm is set this time," I say.

"Okay, I'll ask any patrol cars in the area to take some drives past tonight."

"Thanks. I appreciate that. See you in the morning." I disconnect my cell phone and sit down on the side of my bed. The sense of Andrew is overwhelming. I can feel his anger, his absolute fury. I've broken so many rules. I tuck my shaking hands under my legs.

Get out of my head. Get out. Get out.

The mantra brings me strength, reminds me that it's a different time, and I'm a different woman. He doesn't own me anymore. He only wins if I let him scare me. I make myself laugh, force the sound deep out of my belly, harsh and gloating. *This is the best you can do?*

The laughter dies in my throat.

I grab bedding, blow up our old air mattress, then drag it into the laundry room, near the back door. The floor is concrete, the window single-pane. I climb under my blanket still wearing my sweater, jogging pants, and socks, the knife clutched in my hand, phone under my pillow. Then I stare at the ceiling and wait for morning.

The roads are icy as I drive to the station. I take it slow, my hands tight on the wheel, my foot light on the brakes. I need to watch for black ice, but I keep glancing up at my rearview mirror. The air is cold and damp. The kind of West Coast cold that sinks into the marrow of your bones. The only cure is a hot bath and an even hotter drink, but none of the usual tricks will help me today. I can taste fear in my mouth, want to scrape my tongue to rid myself of it. *He was in my house, my goddamn house. He's probably watching me all the time. He knows about Greg.*

We're going to have to move, but how can we? We're so happy here. I've worked hard to build my business and Sophie loves her friends and her school. There has to be some other way.

The corporal reminds me to call her Parker. "It's easier," she says, and offers me a cup of coffee, which I gratefully accept. Her hands are freckled, and I find this comforting for some reason. While she gets the paperwork ready, I study her across the table. She looks athletic, healthy. She reminds me of someone I could've gone to school with. A small-town girl who played baseball, got into trouble on the weekend with her friends, but came out okay. I wonder why she wanted to be a cop. Her father was a cop? Maybe her brother? She probably has a husband and two ginger-haired kids. I bet they want to be just like her when they grow up.

"So tell me about your relationship with your ex-husband?"

"He was very possessive—he had cameras all over our house, I had to text him constantly, he controlled everything I wore, all our finances, and he was a mean drunk. But everyone else thought he was wonderful, including my own parents." My throat is tight and achy and my eyes sting. I have to stop and catch my breath. I wish she wouldn't look at me so kindly.

"It's okay," she says. "I know how difficult this is. Take your time."

She makes notes while I explain about Andrew's jealousy, his violent temper. "When I told him I wanted out of our marriage, he threatened to bury me in a hole at his job site. He said he wouldn't be able to stop himself from hurting me—he loved me too much to let me go. I'm *sure* he was in my house." I tell her about the book on the side of the tub and the magazines.

"Could anyone have seen him entering? Maybe a neighbor?"

"I don't think so. We're surrounded by trees." I'd loved the old farmhouse appeal of the house, the apple orchard on either side, the forest that stretched for miles.

"Has he mailed you any threatening letters?" Parker says. "Or left voice mails or e-mails?"

I shake my head. "Only time I've spoken to him was outside the bank on Wednesday."

"You said he was violent when he was drinking?"

"At first it was just shoving, or twisting my wrist. He liked to break my things. But then he . . . he choked me one night. I almost passed out. If my daughter hadn't woken up I think I would be dead." I touch my neck, rubbing at it as though that will take away the memory.

"You didn't press charges?"

"I was too scared."

"What about your daughter? Did he ever hurt her?"

"No—he was a great father. I tried to make sure she didn't witness any of our fights, but she saw him push me into a coffee table one night. I had some horrific bruises." I lean forward. "He made it clear over and over again what would happen if I ever left him. In his mind, he *owned* me. No one else could even look at me. If I smiled at someone, he was enraged. I'm dating someone and he knows about it and that's going to send him through the roof."

She looks down at her paperwork, her face thoughtful. Then she meets my eyes. "I'm going to forward this report to the Crown counsel and ask for the peace bond. If they agree there is a threat, they'll issue a summons for Andrew to appear in court."

"How long does it all take?"

"We have to find him first to deliver the summons, then it will depend on whether he tries to fight it or not. That will make things a lot more complicated."

Andrew would enjoy making me face him in court. I will have to be prepared for him to fight this. Even if this doesn't work, he needs to know I'm not going to look the other way.

"What will the peace bond cover?"

"He won't be able to have any contact directly or indirectly with you, he has to stay five hundred meters from your residence or workplace, and he has to surrender any weapons. We can't stop your daughter from interacting with him if she wants to see him, but he won't be allowed to try to communicate with you through her or go to your home."

"She doesn't want to see him." I have to tell Sophie when she gets home from school. I don't want to scare her, don't want her to even think about him, but she needs to know.

"The peace bond will give us more to work with, but we still have to catch him violating the bond before we can actually arrest him."

I nod again, trying to look calm, but inside I'm a mess of emotions—mostly terror. I've seen a few women from our group go through this process. One woman's ex-husband set her house on fire the day they walked out of court. Sure, he was arrested the next day, but she was almost killed, and lost everything she owned, including her two cats who died in the fire.

"He's going to be furious."

"If you ever feel like you're in immediate danger, call 911."

I nod, but I want to ask how long it takes 911 to respond. Five minutes? Ten? How long would it take Andrew to kill me? I watch Parker finish the paperwork, signing her name with a slash.

It's done. It's all been set into motion and I can't stop it now.

CHAPTER FIFTEEN

December 2005

His breathing had finally leveled, but his arm was still slung over my body. I watched the red glowing numbers change on the clock on the night table. The room was pitch-black except for a sliver of moonlight streaming through a crack in the curtain. If I were to pull it back, I'd see snow tumbling from the sky. It had been falling for hours and should be a peaceful image, the trees wearing their shrouds of white and hunched over like old men, the air quiet as though waiting to be told a secret. It should mean sled rides and winter walks, but I just thought of the roads.

Christmas was only a few days away. Andrew and Sophie had decorated the tree while I made hot chocolate and popcorn and brought it to them, my lips molded into a well-practiced smile. *It's the last one. The last time I'll have to do this with him.*

We stacked presents underneath the tree. Gifts from his associates, neighbors, garnished with ribbons and bows of silver, reds, greens, and blues that reflected the twinkling lights.

Sophie played with the tags, read the names out loud, shook the boxes, and guessed at their contents.

We wouldn't be there to unwrap any of them.

I eased my body to the side of the bed, held my breath as his arm slipped off my torso. For a moment his hand drifted across my breast and I shivered, but finally it slid off and landed on the mattress. I stayed still for a couple of minutes beside the bed, ready to make excuses—I was going to the bathroom, getting a glass of water, checking on Sophie—but he didn't move. I took shallow breaths, my eyes focused on the dark shadow of his face, the hollows of his eyes. I could smell the whiskey on his breath and skin. He'd been drinking it straight, hadn't even bothered with ice.

When he'd gotten too drunk to move from the couch, he asked me to pour him one. The moment I'd been waiting for. "Sure," I said. "I just have to go to the bathroom first."

I stood in the bathroom for what felt like hours with the bottle of pills in my hand, but it was probably only a couple of minutes. I kept reading the label with Chris's name on it. He hadn't had any problem getting his doctor to write him a prescription for sleeping pills.

This was the plan, I reminded myself. Andrew *had* to stay asleep. I carefully removed the cotton from inside the bottle, tapped three small blue pills out into my palm, and stared at them. How much had Andrew drunk? Would three kill him? If I didn't give him enough, he could wake up. Then he'd kill me. I needed to get back to the kitchen soon, but I still hesitated.

A noise in the other room, a soft thud. I flushed the toilet, put one pill back, and shoved the bottle into my housecoat pocket. Two would have to be enough.

I slipped down the hallway into the kitchen, glanced into the living room. Andrew was still on the couch, muttering something about the "fucking remote." I poured his drink. My hand hovered over the rim of the glass, then I dropped the pills, let them settle to the bottom, and stirred it until there wasn't a trace of power. I took a sip, testing. All I could taste was whiskey.

I went back to the living room, handed Andrew his drink, then sat down and waited. Twenty minutes later, he began to lean toward the edge of the couch, his eyes drooping. I suggested we go to bed and helped him walk down the hallway. It was done.

Now my feet padded across the floor and into the laundry room, where I stood on the stool and reached up into the ceiling panel. I took down the tote bags one by one, careful not to drop them. I'd packed the bare minimum over the last week. Not enough for him to notice. Sophie would be upset that we had to leave most of her toys behind, but we'd bring her favorite doll and stuffed elephant—she was sleeping with them now. I'd make it up to her somehow.

I placed the bags by the back door, peered through the side window to see if Chris was at the end of the driveway, and watched for the flashlight. Three blinks, that's what he'd said. Nothing but darkness.

I looked over my shoulder, listened for Andrew's heavy stumbling steps, but the house was quiet. The roads would be treacherous—the plows always cleaned the main streets first—and I prayed Chris wasn't stuck somewhere, wheels spinning. We wouldn't have a second chance at this. I wished I could take our car but it was in Andrew's name and he'd report it.

My fingers trailed against the hallway walls as I guided myself toward Sophie's room. She was sleeping on her side, one hand tucked under her round cheek, the other entwined with a lock of hair. The doll and elephant were on the pillow next to her head. I put them in her bag. Her face was warm and smelled apple-fresh as I leaned closer to whisper in her ear.

"Sophie, wake up."

142 · CHEVY STEVENS

She rolled over. I could just make out the whites of her eyes, her long lashes blinking slowly, then she sat up. Her hand touched the side of my face and she softly said, "Mommy?"

"You have to be very quiet," I whispered. "We're going on a trip, just you and me. Daddy is sleeping on the couch and we can't wake him up."

"Daddy said I couldn't go on adventures with you. He'll be mad."

Yes, yes, he will.

"I don't want to go." Her whisper was getting louder.

I leaned closer, said into her ear, "Sophie. Listen to me. We're going to a special place just for kids where you can color and pick out new crayons and markers, and paint all over the wall, but you have to be quiet like a mouse or we won't be able to go. It's all the way over in Vancouver—we're going to stay in a hotel, then take the ferry in the morning. You remember the ferryboat?"

"Can we sit at the front? Can we see the whales?"

"We can even go outside on the upper deck, okay?"

"Okay," she whispered, pushing back her covers.

"We're going to wear pajamas. Won't that be fun? Just like a slumber party." I'd gone to bed in fleece pants, dressed her in a warm pair of pajamas. I tugged her hand. She followed along.

We were at the back door. If he woke now, there'd be no excuses. He'd know. I held my finger to Sophie's lips, lifted our coats off the hook, and eased the door open, almost gasping at the rush of clean, snow-scented air, the cold biting at my skin. The bottom of the door made a soft scrape against the wood floor. I turned to look down the hall, then urged Sophie outside with my fingertips against her small shoulders and bundled her into her coat. Our boots were tucked under the wooden bench on the porch, the fabric stiff and cold as we slid our feet inside. I grabbed our bags, slung three across my back, and hooked Sophie's over her shoulders.

We stepped off the porch, lifted our legs high with every step through the snow that was already a foot deep. I had to help Sophie a couple of times, my own balance awkward with the heavy bags pulling my weight to the side. Adrenaline and exertion warmed me like a furnace from the inside out. Sophie kept glancing back at the house, her face worried.

"Daddy won't be upset at you," I whisper. "I promise."

I was staring straight ahead, searching the break in the trees for the flashlight beam. Then, finally, three quick flashes. We'd made it.

The truck was warm, the heater blasting a hot wave at us. Sophie was sitting in the middle. She cupped her hands over the vents while I rubbed her back. "You okay, baby?"

She nodded, but I could hear her teeth chattering.

"I brought hot chocolate in the thermos under the seat," my brother said, his face grim as he turned the truck around on the narrow road. I held my breath when the tires slid toward the ditch, the back end kicking out, but then the truck surged forward.

"Sorry I'm late," he said. "Had problems getting out of the driveway. Everything okay?"

"Yeah, I think so." I turned and looked out the rear window. The house was still dark. Sophie's gaze followed mine. "Have some hot chocolate," I said, tugging the thermos out.

"I'm not thirsty."

I looped my arms over her shoulders, pulled her closer. "Try to get some rest. I'll wake you up when we get to the hotel." It was the only choice. If Andrew did go searching for me, he'd check my parents' and Chris's house first. I didn't have friends anymore, and there weren't women's shelters in our area. Even if there were, Andrew would find some way to get to me.

Sophie settled her face into my shoulder, her nose cold, and I remembered when she was a toddler how she used to insist I lie beside her every night as she fell asleep, demanded that I rest my head on her tiny chest while she stroked my hair and sang "Twinkle, Twinkle, Little Star." After a few minutes, I heard her breathing deepen, felt her body lean heavier against mine. I nodded at Chris, letting him know it was okay to talk now.

"I checked you in earlier," he says. "Made sure you had one of the back rooms."

"Will he be able to make it through the snow?" Chris had arranged a ride for us a month ago with his friend Jackson. I'd wanted to leave Andrew as soon as we got back from Mexico, but Chris needed time to get a couple more paychecks and sell his motorbike—I'd only managed to save three hundred dollars; not nearly enough. Then this winter storm had blown through the coast. We'd come close to canceling the plan, maybe trying after Christmas, but then Andrew started drinking heavy again, switching back from beer to whiskey. He came home every night complaining about work, and I knew he was going to explode into another rage soon.

"No problem. You'll be on the first ferry over." He handed me an envelope. "It's four thousand. I can get you more next payday."

I wished we could get off the island that night, but the best I could do was a hotel near the ferry terminal, so we could catch the six-twenty boat in the morning while Andrew was still hopefully sleeping. I took the envelope and slid it into one of our bags. "I'll pay you back soon. I can clean houses or babysit. I'll figure something out."

"Don't worry about it."

"Are you going to be okay? If he realizes you helped—"

"He's not going to find out anything. I'm going to be as shocked as him when he tells me you ran away." He looked over at me. "I've got this, okay? I can handle him. Just get off the island and as far away as you can. Start over and don't look back." I saw the shimmer in his eyes, how hard he was trying not to cry. "I'll never say a word."

I knew he was remembering the time I caught him trying to put out the fire in the shop. He'd stolen our dad's cigarettes and was practicing blowing smoke rings, until he dropped one into a pile of sawdust. I grabbed a water bucket and helped him put out the flames, then bandaged his arm where he'd burned it. "Don't worry," I whispered. "I'll never say a word."

But this was different. This was so much more real and dangerous than two kids covering up a small fire. I had a flash of a thought, an image. The cotton from the pill bottle sitting on the bathroom counter. I couldn't remember if I put it in the trash. I must have. I still had the bottle with Chris's name on the label. I'd get rid of it in a Dumpster somewhere far away. *It's the only way*, I'd whispered. Chris had offered to help without a moment's hesitation. Since he was a baby I'd been taking care of him, protecting him, but now the tables had turned.

You're my sister, he said. *We're in this together.*

I'd been awake for hours already, peeking out the curtains. Turns out I'd been right and Jackson got stuck in the snow. We'd missed the first ferry while he'd dug out his driveway and were now waiting to catch the eight thirty boat. Andrew was probably searching all over Lions Lake for me, driving to my parents' house, then Chris's. I looked out again, checking for Jackson. I didn't want the hotel's housekeeping staff or anyone at the front desk to see us. We had to run for the truck quickly. Sophie was also awake now, grimly chewing on a granola bar and watching cartoons.

"Jackson will be here soon," I said.

She didn't answer. She'd barely spoken all morning, but I saw her eying the phone and had a terrifying thought that she might call her father. When she caught me looking, she said, "I was thinking about Grandma and Grandpa. I didn't get to say good-bye."

"We'll call them when we get to Vancouver, okay?"

"Can we call Daddy?"

"He's going to be working all day."

My new cell phone rang and we both stared at it. "It's Daddy!" she said.

"It's Uncle Chris," I said as I picked it up, relieved but also nervous when I saw his number.

"Something happened." Chris's voice was wild and high. I'd never heard him sound like this and I sat down on the side of the bed. Sophie was watching, her face intent.

"Good morning, Chris." I kept my voice calm, hoped Chris would understand that I couldn't talk freely in front of Sophie. "Is Jackson on his way?"

"Andrew was in an accident. I just heard about it this morning. He wasn't at the job site."

I snuck a glance at Sophie. She was watching cartoons now, her feet kicking up in the air, her hands under her chin. I walked toward the window and lowered my voice. "Is he all right?"

"He's in the hospital—he totaled his truck—but he's okay." There was something more. He sounded too shook up.

"When did it happen?"

"Last night—a couple of hours after you and Sophie left, I think."

"I don't understand how he could have been driving." Two pills. It should have been enough, but he must have woken up somehow and realized we were gone.

"I don't know either." He paused. "It's really bad, Lindsey. He ran through some red lights, hit a parked car, flipped the truck, then crashed into someone head-on."

"Are they okay?"

"It was a woman. His truck landed right on top of her and crushed her inside her car. She's dead."

"Oh, no, no." I had to sit down. I tried to get back to the bed, but the room tilted. I grabbed at the side table, knocking the lamp to the floor and shattering the bulb into tiny fragments. Sophie would step on them. I bent down and frantically gathered the pieces, and sliced my finger. I stared at the wound, my mind filling with images of mangled metal and blood in the snow. A woman. He'd killed a woman.

Sophie was clutching at my arm. "Mommy, Mommy!" she was saying, but I couldn't answer. I could only sob. On the other end of the phone I heard my brother crying too.

I'd drugged my husband and run away with his daughter, knowing he would chase after me. Now someone was dead. I would never be free.

PART TWO

CHAPTER SIXTEEN

December 2016

Sophie catches an errant string of melted cheese on her finger and sucks it into her mouth, laughs as some gets on her chin. I smile, glad for this moment. When she was a child, Andrew never let us eat in the living room, and there's no way he'd let me order takeout.

I'd picked up a vegetarian pizza from our favorite place for our Thursday night tradition of watching *The Bachelorette* together. We talk about the guys, the dresses, who we'd pick. She's been at Delaney's all day, while I cleaned the house, trying to erase Andrew's touch, his lingering essence, and rehearsed twenty different ways to have this conversation.

Sophie glances at me with a cheeky smile. "I saw the stew in the garbage. Were you trying to burn the house down?"

"Too bad for you I don't have any insurance money."

She laughs and takes a bite of her pizza, then leans back into the couch, pulling one of the pillows down under her shoulder. We both have our legs propped onto the coffee table. This would have been another unforgivable sin in Andrew's eyes and

I almost yank them away, can hear his voice in my mind. *Only men sit like that, Lindsey.* I force myself to hold still.

"There's something we need to talk about." I pick up the remote and turn down the volume. I can't wait any longer, can feel the words clawing to get out.

"What's going on?" Her eyes are wide, her mouth full of pizza. "Am I in trouble for something?"

"Should you be?"

"Of course not. I'm an angel."

"Right. Well, your halo is a little tarnished." Sophie is a good kid, but she's done the normal stuff, sneaking booze, missing her curfew.

She reaches up, pretends to straighten an imaginary halo, then stops and gives me a look. "Wait. You're not pregnant, are you?"

"No, no." I'm taking too long to explain. I have to spit this out before she leaps to any other conclusions. "Your father was in our house yesterday."

Her body jerks forward as if I had hit her. "What are you talking about?"

"When I came home, I noticed some e-mails were opened on my computer." I hesitate about telling her everything I found. I don't want to scare her too much.

"So you don't know if it was actually *him*. It could have been a computer glitch." She looks relieved, and I realize I made a mistake by holding back.

"I'm sorry, Sophie, it was definitely him. He opened all my bills and put a book beside my bathtub with some candles. There was no sign of a break-in, though."

I see the look in her eyes, the realization. "I forgot to set the alarm!"

I nod. "It's okay. I know it was an accident—but you *have* to be more careful. This morning I talked to the police and applied for a peace bond—it's like a restraining order. Andrew could fight it, but if it's approved, he can't come near me or he'll get sent back to jail."

She's staring at me, two red splotches on her cheeks. "What do you think he wants?"

"I'm not sure, but he read an e-mail from Greg. . . . It was personal." I'd called Jenny from my cell while I waited for the pizza and told her Andrew had been in my house. She invited me to Vancouver again, but I can't walk away from everything yet. Not when Sophie is so close to graduation and I've finally built my business up to a level where I'm not running in the red every month. This time of year is when I get extra bookings. I need that money to carry us through.

Sophie's staring up at the TV, the glow casting a blue light on her skin. She swallows a few times and I know she's trying not to cry.

"I saw him outside the bank a few days ago," I say. "I was careful, but he must've followed me home and that's how he found out where we live." I think again about what he'd said. *I know you drugged me.* For weeks after the accident, I'd waited to see if the police had done any sort of blood tests. When nothing ever happened, I assumed I was safe. Would he tell them now? Could I get in trouble? I remind myself that it's been over ten years and he can't prove anything.

She turns and looks at me. "You didn't tell me you saw him!"

"I didn't want to scare you."

"You should have told me." She's saying it almost desperately— and she sounds defensive, which doesn't make sense. I'm clearly missing something.

"Sophie, what's going on?"

She rubs at her face, presses the heels of her hands into her eyes, and sucks in a ragged breath. "You're going to hate me."

She's looking at me now, her eyes pleading with me to understand, to say the words she can't, but I *don't* understand. And then I do.

"You've talked to him. You've talked to him and didn't tell me."

Now she's crying, her face wet and her voice broken as she chokes out, "I didn't tell him where we live. I *never* told him!"

"Jesus Christ, Sophie." I'm up, pacing the room. "How could you do this?"

"He's my dad. I have a right to talk to him!"

"You *know*. You know what he put us through."

"He's changed."

"He was in our *house*. He's the same manipulative controlling son of a bitch as ever and now he's using you to get to me. What did you tell him? You must have said something, for him to find out we lived in Dogwood Bay. Did you tell him about me and Greg?"

"He was saying how he misses you, and I told him so he could move on." She's talking so fast I can barely understand her, but I get enough to know that I'm screwed. Truly screwed. This isn't just a stage-one disaster. This has gone into a nuclear meltdown too-late-to-run explosion.

"Your father doesn't move on, Sophie, and he sure as hell won't ever let *me* move on." I know I'm shouting, can see the stunned look on Sophie's face, but I can't believe she's betrayed me like this. "I *told* you that your father was insanely jealous."

"But that was years ago."

I stare at her, trying to remember that she's a teenager, too young to comprehend obsession and realize that years don't matter. I'd told her everything he'd done and thought that would be enough warning. I never considered that fear would have a time limit in her mind. Maybe I should have told her about the sleeping pills, maybe then she would have better understood his rage, but it's too late now. I sit down hard. "How did this happen? How did he contact you?"

"I wrote him. Then he wrote me back and sent it to Delaney."

"Of course. That project you said you were working on. You lied to me." I start laughing, a hysterical bitter laugh that I can't seem to stop. "*Of course.*"

"He told me that he doesn't drink anymore—and he's really sorry."

"It's not just about drinking, Sophie. It's about what is going on inside him. He'd need to be in counseling for years and I don't even know if that would help."

"He got counseling in prison."

"Your father can't handle his emotions, and that makes him dangerous. He's only been out a few months and look what's happening. You can't see him."

She looks away, her face flushing to a deep red.

"Oh, no. Tell me you haven't met with him."

"Only twice. I thought it would be okay. Then I could tell you that he was different so you didn't have to worry. He was nice. We went fishing. . . ."

His hands are around my throat again, choking. The thought of them sitting together. I don't want Andrew to have those precious moments with his daughter. He hasn't earned them. He doesn't deserve them. "You can't see him again. Not while you're living with me."

"You're *threatening* me?"

"He will kill me, do you understand?" I pause, holding her gaze, making sure that the words are connecting. "The only way your father will ever let me go is if I'm inside a coffin being lowered into the ground." I reach out, grab her hand. "I know he's your dad. I know how it must feel when all your friends have fathers and you don't. I know how much you want things to be different and how much you want to believe him. I felt the same way for years. I gave him *so many* chances, Sophie. So many. But he can't change. He just *can't.*"

"He's different, Mom. I can't explain it. Maybe it wasn't him in our house." I can see in her face how much she needs this to be true and I hate that I'm the one who has to break her heart.

"It's an act. It's a game to him. All of this. He's *using* you. I know that hurts to hear and maybe it makes you feel like you aren't enough or something, but it has nothing to do with you. You are *amazing*. I love you with all my being, but to your father, we are possessions."

She's silent for a long time, her gaze focused on her pizza. She's not crying anymore, just sniffling once in a while. I keep talking, trying to make her understand things that took me years of self-help books and joining a support group to finally realize, things I still don't truly grasp, how love can go so wrong, how I could have fallen so far off the path and lost myself so deeply. How he can be so sweet and wonderful and charming and so vicious and cruel a minute later.

"I don't feel very good," she finally says.

"Me neither."

"I'm never going to be able to eat pizza again."

"Something tells me that's not true." I pull her closer. "I'm really sorry, kid."

She lets out her breath in a sigh against my neck. "Do we have to move?"

"Not yet. We're going to be careful and see what happens, okay?"

"Okay." Her body sags into mine and I hold her close, crave the weight of her, and remember how she used to fill my arms. She's slight as a bird. "I just wanted a father," she says.

"I know, baby. I know." I think I've gotten through to her, but I'm still unsettled at how easily he'd crept back into our lives. I thought I'd had it all covered, hoped that if I gave Sophie enough love she wouldn't miss having a father. But she had. And he won't give up. Not now. Will she be strong enough to withstand him? Is she stronger than me? God. I hope so.

Friday afternoon Corporal Parker calls with news that the judge has issued a summons for Andrew to appear in court Monday morning.

"Now we have to track him down so we can deliver the summons. We aren't sure if he's in Victoria or Dogwood Bay. He's fallen off the radar."

"That's not comforting." Andrew has a plan, I can feel it. Even if I packed our bags tonight, I have no doubt he would find us. "He could be waiting in my bedroom with a shotgun."

"There are safe houses, and—"

"There are *no* houses safe from Andrew."

She's quiet for a moment. "I understand your fears, okay? I really do. And I want to help you. This is a step in the right direction. We're going to get him."

"I hope you're right."

When we pick up a tree from the mall on Saturday, I park where there are lots of people and hold my key between my fingers as I walk toward the entrance. At home we decorate the tree, then I clean up the fir needles, halting my vacuuming every few minutes to listen. Greg comes over after he's finished work and installs a dead bolt and suggests we sleep at his house for a while, but I don't think Sophie will like that. I'm grateful for his help but I feel distracted, and pull away when he tries to be affectionate—teasing him about smelling like his work truck.

"Never bothered you before," he says with a curious look, and I laugh it off, then lean in for a kiss so he doesn't worry, but he's right. I used to tell him he looked like a sexy grown-up Boy Scout in his UPS uniform, and I liked when he'd fix things around my house—but now it all reminds me of Andrew. He was always puttering around on the weekend, trying to make our house safer, which was ironic. I can't stop wondering when he is going to move to town. He could already be here. I could run into him at the store, the gas station, anywhere.

Greg leaves after dinner and Sophie and I wrap presents and stack them under the tree and watch *Elf* while eating popcorn, but I know she's forcing herself to smile and laugh for my sake. She didn't draw all day, just flipped through the channels on TV or played on her phone.

"We need to do something fun," I say.

"You're taking us to Mexico?" she says. "I can be packed in five minutes."

I feel the sting, but I know she didn't mean to hurt me. She doesn't know what happened in Mexico, how her father scared me. For years I told myself that I would take Sophie to Cancún again one day, just the two of us. We would do it right. Then, when I finally had enough money saved, I was too afraid of the memories. Something else I let him take away from me.

"Ha. But you're giving me an idea. . . ."

Greg usually watches hockey Sunday nights, so I invite Marcus over. I'd feel safer with some male company, but that's not what I tell him. I say, "You never let me pay anything for using your gym. Please let me do something nice?" He arrives with a case of Mexican beer and spicy dark chocolate for dessert. I roast corn and black beans and barbecue chicken for the quesadillas while Marcus makes salsa and guacamole. We work well together. Our shoulders brushing as we move around the kitchen, handing each other items from the fridge.

Marcus entertains us through the meal with stories of traveling in Europe and Africa, like the time he was nearly left behind on a safari. Sophie laughs hysterically when he shares that he ate termites and other local delicacies, wrinkles her nose when he describes how they crunched and their tiny legs caught in his teeth. I'm glad he came over. It's just what we needed.

After dinner, Sophie heads upstairs to do some homework.

Marcus and I have decaf coffee at the table, nibbling on the chocolate. I tell him Andrew was in my house and that the police are delivering a summons to him but I haven't heard whether they found him.

"Why didn't you call?" he says.

"I didn't want to drag you into my drama."

"Promise you'll call next time," he says in a firm voice.

"It might be hard if I'm running for my life." I smile.

"That's not funny."

I sigh. "I know. I'm just trying to deal with all this."

"Do you have a gun?"

"No. I've signed up to take my gun safety course, but then I have to apply for a firearms license. They probably won't approve it once they find out about Andrew." Canadian gun laws are strict, especially when it comes to domestic violence, which I used to appreciate. I'd never liked guns, even though my father had them when I was growing up, and I hated that Andrew had them when Sophie was little, but now I wished I had one stashed in every room of our house.

"Maybe I should try to get a gun, like from the black market," I say.

"Whoa. That's risky."

"What's risky is sitting around waiting for him to make a move."

"I'll put out some feelers, okay? I know people through my self-defense classes."

"Really? You'd do that for me?"

"I'd rather help than have you accidentally buy one from a cop."

"That would be just my luck." I flick a glance out the window, searching the shadows. "I hope they find him soon."

CHAPTER SEVENTEEN

SOPHIE

He's called three times but I haven't answered or listened to the voice mails. I have a twisty feeling in my stomach, like hunger and the flu mixed together. I rub at the knot, but it doesn't go away. We were supposed to meet today, but I texted him first thing and said I had too much homework, which is a lie because it's the last week before winter break and we're all coasting right now, except for Delaney, who failed a test and has to do a makeup project.

I'm sitting outside after school, waiting for her. I glance up, check the street. I keep getting this feeling that Andrew's going to look for me. This is what it must feel like for Mom. I was so stupid to let him back in our lives. I couldn't stop thinking about it all weekend, how he'd been in our house. This morning I woke up with a giant headache. Like Mondays aren't crappy enough with chemistry first period. Now I have to deal with trying to avoid my stalker dad. My cell chirps. This time it's a text from Delaney: *B a while. Have to finish this stupid project!*

I text back: *K, I'll catch the bus.* I walk down the street toward the public bus stop, wishing I had my bike. It's starting to snow and the road is covered with slush and my feet are getting wet. I wrap my scarf around my neck and face and hunch my shoulders in my coat. I feel a vehicle slow beside me, glance over, and catch a flash of white. I'm too scared to look all the way, but I'm pretty sure it's Andrew's truck. I walk faster. Shit. Shit. Shit. I should have stayed at the school. I fumble for my phone in my pocket. Who do I call? What do I say?

"Hey," he calls out. "I need to talk to you."

I shake my head. I'm not going to look at him. He pulls over in front of me, blocking part of the sidewalk. I can see him through his open passenger window. The back end of the truck is sticking out. Cars drive around him, one honks and the driver makes a gesture out the window.

"You shouldn't stop on the shoulder like that," I say. Is he going to grab me and force me to go somewhere with him? I take a couple of steps back.

"Why don't you get in the truck? You're getting soaking wet."

"I have to go home."

"Why are you avoiding me?" He's leaning across the front seat so he can see me through the window. More cars are driving past, but no one is stopping. No one is asking if I'm okay. I could be getting abducted right now and no one would give a crap.

"I have to go," I say again. "I'll miss the bus."

"Tell me what's wrong."

"You came into our house!" I yell over the noise of all the cars. I'm shocked at the anger coming out of my body. "I told you to stay away from her."

His face is blank, and then it's like all his features rearrange slowly like he's understanding something. "So that's why the cops are looking for me."

"You were supposed to go to court today. Mom's getting a restraining order."

"I haven't been near your place."

How would he know what was near or not? He must know where we live.

"You went through Mom's things. You read her e-mails."

He's not saying anything, but he doesn't look surprised anymore. It's like he's pulled inside himself and is just thinking. The traffic is whipping past. I wonder if someone will recognize me. I want to turn around and walk away, but I also want to hear what he says next.

"Sophie, I've been in Victoria all week—packing my stuff. I wouldn't scare you or your mom like that. What the hell would be the point? I'm trying to start over."

"I *know* you were in our house."

"Let's go for a coffee and talk about it. I'll tell you everything I did all week—every single day, hour by hour. And you can tell me why you're so sure it was me, okay?"

He sounds sincere, like he really doesn't understand what I'm talking about. I look at the road, the piles of snow starting to settle on the center line. I'd have to run to catch the bus, and if I miss it, the next one isn't for thirty minutes. Maybe it would be good to hear what he has to say. If it *was* him who broke in, I can scare him about getting caught and he'll stay away from Mom.

"If you take me anywhere else, I'll call the cops—I have my phone in my pocket."

He holds his hands up. "Okay."

I take one last look down the road, then climb inside.

We're quiet in the truck. He turns the heat up and I glance around, notice the big container of gum in the ashtray. I'm stabbed with another memory, the beer he used to drink at the job site, then he'd pop gum into his mouth before we drove home. He sees me looking.

"Want a piece?"

"It doesn't work, you know. Cops can still tell."

He glances at me and I think he's going to be mad, but he sounds calm as he says, "I'm not drinking, Sophie. I'm never touching a drop again. I missed it at first, but I don't think about it anymore. I was just using it as a way to cope with my emotions. I don't want you to worry."

"Doesn't matter to me." I turn away and stare out the window, see my reflection, my wet hair. I think about Mom and how angry she would be at me right now. I have to hear his explanation. She doesn't think I can see through him, but if he's lying, I'll figure it out.

The Muddy Bean is full and noisy, the air smells of damp clothes and coffee, and freshly buttered toast that makes my stomach growl. I order a cheese scone and coffee at the counter and pull out my wallet, but he insists on paying. It's strange, feeling him standing beside me, his arm brushing against mine. It seems like such a dad thing to do, paying for my lunch, but it also reminds me of how Mom was broke for so long. We rarely got to do things like going out for lunch together, unless you count a hot dog in the food court at the mall.

We sit down and I tear off a piece of my scone, shove it into my mouth. Partly from hunger, partly to buy myself some time before I have to speak.

"Good?" he says.

I nod. He's fiddling with the handle of his mug and leaning forward in his chair. He keeps looking at my face, waiting for me to talk.

"Why did you break into our house?" I say.

"If I did something stupid like that I could go back to prison." He leans forward even farther, his upper body almost on the table. "I spent ten *years* in there, Sophie. I know you can't imagine what that's like, but it's hell, okay? The prisons you see on TV and in movies? That *Lockup* show or whatever. Those are country clubs compared with the place I came from."

His explanation makes sense. Why would he risk his freedom? But who else would have broken in and not taken anything? "You were really angry Mom divorced you."

"I was pissed off for a long time, but I understand why she didn't want to be with me anymore. I was mostly mad at myself. I screwed things up, I told you that. But I'm not going to walk out of jail and start messing things up again. Are you sure anyone broke in?"

"What do you mean?"

"Listen, I know your mom is angry at me, and she has good reason, okay? But maybe she also wants to make sure *you* stay mad at me."

"She wouldn't lie. Someone opened all her bills too. And there was a book beside her bathtub, with candles. She was really scared."

He frowns, leans back in his chair with his head to the side like he's thinking. His eyebrows are pulled together. It makes him look tough, mean. "It sounds like someone is messing around with her. I don't like that, especially when you're living there. She needs to get an alarm."

"We have one. I forgot to set it." Maybe it wasn't him. Why would he tell us to get an alarm? I don't know what to think anymore. Could it be one of her creepy clients? Or that girl who used to work for her? She quit because Mom was giving her a hard time about getting back together with her loser boyfriend and missing work.

"Does she think I want to hurt her?"

We're holding gazes and I can feel the scone sticking in my throat and I have a gut cramp and want to run out the door and get far away from him. How can I look at him and say what I'm thinking? He doesn't seem angry, though, more like he's not really surprised. I don't answer.

"Right." He takes a breath and runs his hands through his wet hair. He has dark pouches under his eyes and I think he must be tired. "Did your mom ever tell you about my family?"

"A little."

"Well, I have what they call abandonment issues." He gives one of his sideways smiles and I think maybe I can understand why my mom loved him once. "Your mom was the most amazing thing that ever happened to me. She's so beautiful—I couldn't believe she was mine."

My mom is beautiful. She has white-blond hair like one of the elf queens in *Lord of the Rings*, and her eyes are big and blue, her lashes so dark she doesn't even have to wear mascara. She could date lots of guys if she wanted, but it took her a long time before she went out with Greg. I like how they are when they're around each other—they laugh a lot and she always seems relaxed. I can tell he's really into her, but I think maybe my mom is scared of that.

"You should have treated her better," I say.

"I know. I had it all backwards. I was so scared she would leave me that I turned into a jealous jerk and pushed her away."

"Why don't you meet someone else? Lots of people do online dating."

"Maybe someday, but right now I just want to get to know you again."

"You have to go to court and agree to leave Mom alone."

"I'll sort it out right away, okay? As soon as we're done here, I'll talk to the cops."

"You won't fight it? It means we can't talk about her either."

"Listen, I get that it might be too late for your mom and me, but I don't want it to be too late with you. You're the only family I have left. If you don't want to see me, okay. I'll just have to

hope you change your mind one day, but I'm not going to willingly give you up."

His words make me sad and frightened but also kind of happy.
He's trying to get me to look at him—I can feel his gaze—but
I'm staring into my coffee, studying the foam. It feels wrong
to feel sad for him, like I'm betraying Mom, but it's true. I'm
all he has left.

"You *have* to stay away from Mom," I say. "If anything else
happens, that's it."

He reaches his hand across the table. "Deal." As I shake his
hand, I feel someone watching and glance around. Across the
room I notice Jared with an older woman with black hair who
kind of looks like him. His mom. I've seen her around town,
driving a silver Lexus, always wearing sunglasses. He gives me
a smile and a small wave. I look away.

The next day at school, Jared comes by my locker. "You still
pissed at me for asking about your mom?" he says. "Sorry if I
said something stupid." He smiles. "Happens a lot."

"I was just in a bad mood. Sorry."

He leans against one of the lockers, his hands tucked into
his pocket and his shoulders hunched like he's cold, but then I
think maybe it's because he's tall and he's trying not to tower
over me. He's wearing black jeans, a maroon plaid scarf around
his neck, and a gray T-shirt with a picture of Jimmy Hendrix
on the front. Part of Jimmy's face is faded off. I wonder if the
shirt is vintage. He probably paid a hundred dollars for it or
something crazy like that.

"You were having an intense conversation with your dad at
the coffee shop," he says.

Jesus. How long was he watching? "That was my uncle. He's
going through some stuff."

He's quiet for a moment, and I tense, worried that he's going to ask a bunch of questions, but he just says, "You going anywhere for Christmas vacation?"

I laugh. In his world all his friends probably go skiing at their chalets or on expensive vacations to somewhere warm. "We've decided to vacation locally this year," I say in my pretend rich-girl voice. "The ski hills are just so *crowded* with poor people, you know?"

He looks confused at first, then smiles as he realizes I'm making fun of him. "I'm having some friends over this weekend. You should come."

"I don't think so."

"Why not?"

"We don't hang out with the same kind of people."

"I like that you're different. You're an artist, right?"

"Yeah."

"I saw your drawings in the yearbook. You're really good."

"Thanks." I don't know what else to say. My face feels warm and I want to make a smart-ass comment, but I can't think of anything. Why is he being so nice?

"You can bring Delaney," he says. Delaney has a crush on one of Jared's friends and would love to go to a party. She'd be totally pissed if I turned down an invite.

"Maybe," I say. His face breaks into a smile and I feel a weird tightening across my chest like someone is hugging me from behind and my whole body wants to relax.

"I'll see you Friday." He leans closer, the smell of spearmint strong on his breath. He must've been chewing gum. For a moment I wonder if he wanted to have nice breath for me, and the idea is confusing and exciting and a few other things that I can't think about right now.

"Don't worry," he says. "I won't tell anyone about you seeing your dad. I know he just got out of prison."

I stare at him, and all the noise in the hall disappears. I can only feel the thudding in my chest. How did he know? Has Delaney been talking to people? I feel so hurt I can't breathe.

His face changes, his smile dropping like he realizes he messed up. "I'm sorry. I could tell you were related and I've seen his photo online, so I knew who he was."

"So now you're going to tell everybody." I'm angry and upset, but also confused. How had he seen my dad's photo? There was a lot of press about it years ago, but I hadn't seen anything in the news about him getting out. Maybe there was an article in Victoria.

"I knew about it months ago, but I never told anyone."

"Why did you look me up?"

"I like you. I wanted to know more about you." He shrugs and gives me a smile. I've seen all his smiles. The ones he gives his friends, or the teacher. I've never seen this one. It's shy, but also hopeful and kind of sweet, maybe even a little embarrassed. But that can't be right.

"I don't want anyone to know about him."

"Don't worry. You can trust me." The bell rings and he glances down the hall. "I better get my books. See you Friday, okay?" He walks away.

CHAPTER EIGHTEEN

LINDSEY

It's loud in the shelter, a cacophony of barks and yelps as I walk down the concrete hallway looking at the dogs in their kennels. I don't like this feeling, their pleading, desperate eyes, the metal fencing, the smell of urine. I want to take them all home, but I can only afford one. I've thought about getting a dog for years, but always worried about the vet bills or food. Now I realize I was just scared that something could go wrong, that somehow Andrew would take it away from me, even from behind bars. I stop in front of a kennel with a German shepherd cross with a big head, big paws, and an even bigger smile. He has reddish brown fur and the hair down the middle of his back grows in the opposite direction like a Rhodesian ridgeback. His brown eyes are ringed with black and his muzzle and the tips of his ears, which flop at the ends, are also black. I make a kissing noise and he cocks his head, paws at the fence.

One of the shelter staff has been giving me the details of the dog in the kennel beside him—Buddy, a friendly black Lab with a full-body wiggle and a high-pitched bark.

"What this one's name?" I ask her.

"That's Angus."

I smile at his moniker, which suits him perfectly. His previous owner must have had a Scottish background or a good sense of humor. "I live alone with my daughter and we're looking for a family pet, but also a dog that will scare off strangers. Is he protective?"

"Angus is a real love and would probably just lick a burglar to death, but he has a loud bark." As though he heard the challenge, Angus stands up against the chain-link fence and woofs three times. Deep loud barks that echo against the concrete. He stands almost as tall as me and has to weigh close to a hundred pounds.

"Why did his owners give him up?"

"It was a divorce. The husband moved down to the States and the wife had to get a new job, so she didn't have time for him anymore. He's a good family dog. Loves women."

I touch my palm to his paw and he licks my hand. "Can I take him for a walk?"

We hike around the nearby trails and he nearly pulls my arm out of the socket, but I feel safer just having this big animal beside me, his shoulders brushing against my thigh. I'm trying to talk myself out of it, thinking about his food bills, how much he probably sheds. Every once in a while he turns back to look at me, his mouth open in a smile, his tongue lolling. We see a man in the distance running through the forest, and Angus pauses, body alert, tail high. He glances back at me. "It's okay, Angus," I say. "Good boy." He relaxes and we keep walking. For the first time in days, I feel myself relaxing too. Back at the shelter I fill out an application, confirm I have permission from my landlord and a fenced yard. I thought it would take a couple of days to hear anything, but the shelter calls me that night. I give Sophie the good news.

"For real? What kind of dog is he?" Her eyes are shining and it makes my stomach flip with relief. There isn't anything I wouldn't do to make her smile again.

"I'm not sure. He's a mix. Maybe a Labrador or rottweiler crossed with shepherd." I show her a few photos I've taken with my phone. "We can pick him up in the morning."

"God, Mom. He's a beast."

"I know. Now I have Beauty and the Beast."

She laughs, then her smile fades. "Did you get him for protection? You have the peace bond now. Are you still scared?" I was surprised at how easily Andrew had accepted the terms of the bond. I never thought he'd willingly sign anything that would keep him away from me. I want to be happy about this, but it's just given me something else to worry about.

"Partly for protection, and with you going away to school I'm going to need company."

"I'm being replaced by a big hairy monster!"

"He's probably cleaner than you."

She pretends to swat my arm. "Well, he better not sleep in my bed."

"No guarantees." I smile. "I'll probably keep him in my room. He'll help me sleep."

She's been scrolling through the photos of Angus on my phone, but now she pauses with a thoughtful expression on her face. "Do you still think it was my dad who was in the house?"

Alarm bells go off in my head, sudden and shrill. Why is she questioning this? And when did she start calling Andrew "my" dad? Maybe she's always done it, maybe it doesn't mean anything, but somehow it sounds possessive this time. It's as though she's claiming him.

"It was definitely him."

"But sometimes you forget things. Like where you put your keys, or when you gave away that box of your books and then you thought I had them all."

My keys. I stare at the side of her face. Does she remember

it was one of the things Andrew was always after me about? No. She wouldn't hurt me deliberately like that, but it scares me, this desperate grasping of hers. She still doesn't want to accept the facts.

"It was him," I say. "I know how he works."

She meets my gaze. "Don't you remember anything good about him?"

My breath catches in my throat. I lean over, take the phone back from her and flip through the pictures of Angus while I try to think how to answer. "Yes," I say. "But it doesn't take away from all the horrible things he did and all the pain he caused me—and others."

"It's the anniversary of the accident soon."

"I know."

"Do you ever think about that night?"

"What do you mean?"

"If we hadn't run away, he wouldn't have been driving. It's like the butterfly effect. You change one thing, it all changes. What would you do differently?"

I can see the pill bottle so clearly, the amber-colored plastic, the feel of those small blue pills in my hand. They should have felt heavier. They should have felt like the weight of the world.

"That's an impossible question." I stand up. "I'm really tired. I'm going to have a bath." I know she's watching me as I walk away and is probably confused by my abruptly ending the conversation, but I'm too close to tears, too close to telling her everything.

The butterfly effect.

CHAPTER NINETEEN

SOPHIE

Delaney drops me off at Andrew's new place in the south end
of town on Thursday. He's making me dinner. He offered to
pick me up at school, but I was worried about a teacher or someone who knows my mom seeing us together. Plus, it felt too
strange. I hate lying to my mom (she thinks I'm at Delaney's,
celebrating winter break), but I have to give him a chance.
Maybe she can't forget what he did, but he never hurt *me*, and
the more I think about it, the more I know she's wrong about
him breaking into our house. He never did tell me everything
he did that week, but he doesn't have to—I can feel the truth
in my bones. It's like some sort of genetic thing. If I tell Mom
it's not Andrew, she'll know I've talked to him again. She's so
sure it's him, she's not even considering anyone else. I'll have
to be extra-careful with setting the alarm.

I tug my backpack higher onto my shoulder as I walk down
his driveway. It's below freezing and the top of last night's snow
crunches under my feet. The house is nice, way bigger than
ours, but tucked in tight with all the neighbors like its shoulders

are squished up. The front yard is decorated with a snowman and a few plastic reindeer with lights. They look a little lost, like they don't belong there and aren't sure where they should stand.

Christmas is in a few days. I wandered the mall at lunch on Tuesday, doing the last of my shopping for Mom, Uncle Chris and his girlfriend, and Delaney. I thought about what it would be like to shop for my father. What would I even get him? I always know what to get Mom. I know the brand of coffee she buys, books she likes, what colors she looks the best in (blue and lavender), her favorite bubble bath and lotions (anything from Lush cosmetics), and all her shows, like *Outlander* or *Downton Abbey*. But Andrew is a total mystery.

Last night, with Angus snoring at my feet, I stenciled designs on the wrapping paper, and thought about what it might be like in the future if my dad stuck around. I laugh at the idea of Mom having him over for Christmas dinner—as if that would ever happen.

Angus woke up and yawned noisily. I wiggled my toes against his belly. It's fun having a dog in the house, even if he did chew up a couple of my pens already and wants to go outside every ten minutes and woofs at everything and tries to steal food off the counter. He's snuggly and always looks happy and bumps his head into my hand and flops down across my legs. During the night he took turns sleeping with me and Mom, like he isn't sure who he belongs with or where he was supposed to be, but it was his first night. I think he'll figure it out.

Andrew answers my knock with a smile and an overly cheerful, "Come in!"

I follow him inside, take off my boots at the door, placing them next to his work boots. The sight of them throws me for a moment. I remember his boots always sitting by our door at home, covered in dust or mud or snow and ice depending on the time of year. I'd forgotten about that, how I used to like wearing them around the house and he'd laugh.

I sit at the kitchen table, where I can see most of the upstairs living area. On the phone he sounded really excited because he'd lucked out and found this place at short notice and was able to move in by the middle of the month. It's all happening so fast that when I stop to think about it, my head spins. Then I remember how Mom and he got married in six months. Is this just what my dad is like? He makes quick decisions? I don't know if that's good or bad.

The kitchen is large, with modern appliances and granite counters, but he looks comfortable, like he was always meant to be in a kitchen like this.

"Can I get you something to drink?" he says, reaching into the fridge.

"Maybe just water, thanks."

He places a glass in front of me, then goes back to the stove. I take a sip of the water, noticing the geometric frosted design on the side of the glass. I imagine him at the department store, loading up his cart with whatever caught his eye. He's put a tablecloth on the kitchen table, but I can tell by the legs, dark espresso wood, that it must be expensive. In the living room he has a chocolate leather couch and a cedar-plank coffee table. There's no art yet. No framed photos or any of those things that make a house a home, but he's arranged a couple of big plants in the corner, look like fig trees. One of them has white Christmas lights strung around it.

"You like plants?" I say. He turns around from the stove, where he's stirring a pot of thick chili. The air smells spicy and sweet.

"My landlady gave them to me. I think she thought my decorating was depressing." He gives his crooked smile. He's showered and shaved, his hair still a little wet, and a few hairs are sticking up in the back. His jeans look clean and he's tucked in his shirt and is wearing a belt. I can tell he also cleaned the place—the cream throw blanket on the couch is perfectly straight and everything is set out nicely on the table, a cloth napkin folded beside my place mat, a knife, fork, and spoon all lined up on the napkin. In the center of the table he's arranged a few small bowls with cheddar cheese, sliced green onions, guacamole, and a big bowl full of tortilla chips. It makes me think of the Mexican dinner we had with Marcus and I feel another wave of guilt.

I get up from the table and wander into the living room, finger the leaves on the plant. No dust. The soil is wet. He has a flat-screen TV and a chrome stereo that looks sleek and expensive with blue glowing lights. It took Mom years before we could buy a flat-screen and we found our stereo at Walmart—a marked-down floor model with dents and scratches. A few books are stacked on the coffee table. I pick one up, flip through the pages. It's a Tom Clancy thriller.

"I read a lot in prison," he says from the kitchen. I come back and sit at the table, help myself to some of the chips, which make a loud crunching noise when I bite into them.

He glances over his shoulder with a smile. "Those are really good. They're a new flavor—garlic and black bean. Back in my day, they just had plain."

"Is it strange?" I say. "Going to stores and seeing new things?"

He nods as he takes a tub of sour cream out of the fridge, places it in the center of the table. "Yeah, but it's also like I get to live everything over again, which can be fun sometimes." He spoons chili into bowls and carries them over. "It's vegetarian."

I glance up at him. "How did you know I'm vegetarian?"

"When we were having coffee, you were wearing a T-shirt that said I DON'T EAT MY FRIENDS. I figured you either just liked the T-shirt or you were a vegetarian."

"Yeah, sorry."

He shrugs. "Nothing to be sorry about. It's good to have beliefs. Bet you really hated that roast beef sandwich I made you." He laughs as he sits down across from me.

"It wasn't that bad."

"Well, hopefully you like this better. Dig in."

I take a mouthful. "Yum. This is really good." This time I'm not lying. The chili is sweet and spicy, but not too hot, and he used big chunks of vegetables.

"I'm glad you like it," he says. "I missed vegetables when I was behind bars. The food they serve is crap. I wouldn't feed it to a pig."

We eat in silence for a few moments, then he says, "You excited about Christmas? When you were a kid you couldn't sleep for days."

"It's nice having a week off school." I don't want to talk about Mom or our traditions, how it is now that he's gone. "Are you doing anything for Christmas?"

"I'm going down to Victoria to stay with my sponsor. First Christmas out might be hard. I'll go to a few AA meetings when I'm there." He looks at me. "It means a lot, you being here tonight. I was going to get a tree but I didn't have time."

"It's okay. The plant is festive."

We both take another mouthful, blowing on the spoons at the exact same time to cool the chili off. I study his face.

"Do you look like your dad or your mom?" I say.

"Probably more like my dad." He takes a handful of chips and crunches them up on top of his bowl. "Try this." I can tell he wants to change the subject, so we talk about what TV shows he's been watching and what else he's been learning to cook.

After dinner we clean up the kitchen. I wash while he dries. I think back to when I was a kid, but I don't remember him ever cleaning up—he always left it for Mom.

"It's really nice having you here," he says. "The nights can be long. I'm used to having a lot of noise around me. I have to sleep with the TV on now."

"Maybe you could get a dog."

"I'll think about that. Might be nice to have the company."

"We adopted a dog," I say as I pass him another plate to dry. "His name's Angus."

"Yeah? What kind?"

"Don't know." I shrug. "He's just a big shaggy thing."

"That's great. Your mom always liked dogs."

I want to tell him more, want to say that Angus is really protective of Mom, and that he follows her around the house and sleeps with her at night, but he'll know why I'm telling him and I don't want to make him mad.

"You guys have anything else weird happen?" he says, reaching up to put a plate away.

"What do you mean?"

He picks up another dish. "Like someone going into your house. That's why she got the dog, right? What's her boyfriend like?" His questions are so fast, I don't have time to think.

"It's been okay. Greg is nice—he helped her put in a dog door."

He stops drying. "A dog *door*? Why the hell would she do that?"

I flinch, startled by his tone, like Mom is the stupidest woman on the planet or something.

"She had to because she works long hours and we figured it would be okay because no one could fit through it. If they did, Angus will bite their head off. He's really big."

His shoulders drop, but it's more like he's forcing them down, reminding himself to relax. "I'm sorry," he says. "I went all crazy protective dad there for a moment."

"Yeah. A little."

"Sounds like your mom has it covered. I'm glad she has someone who can help her out." He dries a few more dishes. "You trust this Greg guy?"

"He's super-harmless. He'd do anything for her. Like he's running around getting stuff for her Christmas party tomorrow." He glances at me and I realize that I said way more than

I should have. Mom would kill me. "She's having lots of people over. Lots."

"Good for her."

He actually does sound kind of relieved. I must have misunderstood the reason for the questions. He was making sure we were both okay. We wash the last few dishes in silence.

When we're finished, he says, "I know you can't stay long, but I've got something I want to give you. Go sit on the couch for a second and I'll grab it, okay?" He goes into his bedroom and comes out carrying a wrapped box. "I'm not very good at wrapping."

My face feels warm as I take the silver paper off. I can feel him watching me from the other end of the couch. I'm worried I won't like it and won't be able to hide my expression. When I get the last bit of paper off, I stare in surprise, reach out a finger to stroke the beautiful wooden box. It's about ten by ten, smells like fresh cedar, and gleams with a glossy golden stain.

"You made this?" My voice feels thick and scratchy.

"One of the guys I work with lent me his tools and shop. I'd forgotten how much I enjoy working with my hands. I thought you might want somewhere to keep your art supplies."

"This is really awesome," I say. "It must have taken you days." He has lots of money. He could have bought me anything, but he chose to make me something special.

"I have a lot of free time."

"Thank you so much. I love it." I look over at him and I can tell he's pleased at my reaction. "I didn't bring you anything."

"No." He's shaking his head. "You didn't have to. Next year, right?"

"I don't know. You still owe me for the last ten years. I mean, the box is nice and all, but you should keep the gifts coming if you want me to *really* like you." The second the smart-ass words are out of my mouth I cringe. Is he going to think I'm rude? Or looking for handouts?

"Wow," he says. "I just gave my long-lost daughter a gift from the heart and now I find out she probably would have been happier with an iPad." He smiles, making it clear that he's messing with me. "When did you become such a moment-killer?"

"When did you get funny?"

"It's a side effect of sobriety." He shrugs. "When your entire life goes to hell, you have to start laughing or you'll end up hanging yourself with your bedsheet in your cell." He picks up a piece of wrapping paper that has fallen onto the floor, smooths one edge over and over.

"Did you want to die?" I say in a hushed voice.

He nods. "I didn't know how I was going to get through ten years in there, and I hated myself for a long time for what I did to you and your mother. What I did to her. . . ."

For a moment I think he's still talking about Mom, then I realize he means the woman he killed. He can't even say her name.

"You mean Elizabeth."

He looks at me. "Yeah. Elizabeth Sanders." He gives his head a shake, fiddles with the paper. "But I couldn't go out without a fight. I had to prove to everyone that I could change."

"I think you've changed."

He meets my eyes and smiles. "Yeah?"

Now I feel shy, like I've admitted too much, and my face is hot. I want to say something to break the moment, to remind him that I'm still angry and he isn't forgiven yet, but I can't seem to bring those feelings back. I have to get out of here. I glance at my phone. "Delaney is picking me up in a couple of minutes. I should meet her at the end of the driveway."

"You guys doing anything fun this weekend?"

"We're going to a party tomorrow." It's weird that I can be so honest with him. Mom thinks I'm hanging out with Delaney because there's a Christmas movie we really want to see. She was okay with me missing her party, but she'd freak if she knew I was skipping it to go to a different one.

He raises his eyebrows. "A party? Will there be alcohol?"

"I don't know, maybe. But Delaney doesn't drink and drive." I realize what I said the instant the words are out of my mouth. How could I have been so stupid?

He gives me that crooked smile and says, "If you need a ride or the weather turns bad, give me a call. My truck is good in the snow."

"Okay. Thanks." When I stand up, he rises too, and we walk toward the door.

"Thanks for coming over," he says as I put on my boots.

"Thanks for dinner." He's standing close and I'm not sure if he wants to hug me, but I don't feel ready, so I quickly push the door open and step out.

"Sophie," he says. "Can I ask you something?"

I turn back. "Yeah?" I brace, worried he's going to say something about Mom.

"I'd like to buy you a car."

"You serious?"

"You're going to school soon, and you shouldn't have to ride your bike in bad weather or beg for rides from friends." I don't like how he's saying it, but a car would be amazing. Then I think about Mom, her old beat-up Mazda that she's been driving forever.

"I don't know. . . . I like riding my bike."

"I know it's a lot, but after everything I've done I just want to feel like I'm contributing to your future somehow."

"Can I think about it?" I wish Delaney would pull up so I could leap into her car. It's snowing again and flakes are landing on my eyelashes. I blink them away.

He nods, and stares up at the sky, watching the flakes come

down. Then he turns to me again. "Good night, kiddo." He gives a little wave and closes the door.

Delaney is so excited about going to Jared's, she changes her outfit three times while I wait on her bed, scrolling through my phone and trying not to be nervous. Finally she settles on denim skinny jeans and a light blue sweater, which looks really good with her brown hair and pale skin. I'm wearing my favorite patterned leggings—the ones with tiny fish—and a purple striped sweater tunic and green scarf. I don't usually like a lot of makeup, but tonight I've used lavender eye shadow and a neutral pink-toned lip gloss that works with my hair.

"You look pretty," Delaney says. "Are you excited about seeing Jared?" I had told her about our conversation, how he said he liked me.

"Not really. I'm only going for you."

She laughs. "Sure." I can feel my face getting hot, but I don't want to get into an argument. I can't really explain my feelings anyway. Part of me is excited, but the other part is still suspicious, wondering what this is all about and why he's being so nice all of a sudden.

When we arrive at Jared's and Delaney parks the car, we both sit still, just staring at the house. "Holy crap," I say. "It's huge." I've never been inside a house like this and I'm really curious, but I also have the urge to tell Delaney to drive us away, we don't belong here. Even Delaney, who's usually pretty brave, isn't making a move to get out of the car. We're both staring at the three-car garage, the huge cedar beams at the front, the circular driveway. I only see two other cars and recognize one of them from school. It belongs to Jared's friend Brandon.

"It's like Barbie's dream house," Delaney says, and we both start to laugh.

"Let's do this," I say.

Jared opens the front door with a smile and invites us inside. He seems happy to see me, and touches my arm when he introduces me to his friends, who are sitting on a big leather sectional in the living room watching a movie on an enormous flat-screen TV. There are only three guys and a couple of girls. I know that one of the girls is dating Brandon. Delaney settles on the couch beside Matthew, the guy she likes, and immediately starts talking to him.

"I thought you were having a party," I say. Jared's standing close enough that I can smell his skin and shampoo, something clean, like the ocean. I glance at his clothes: his black skinny jeans are designer label and I'm pretty sure his gray V-neck sweater is cashmere.

"It's a small party," he says with a grin. "Only special people allowed. Come on, let me show you around." He takes me through the house and I lose track of all the rooms. He's so casual, almost bored-sounding as he points things out, like the house doesn't mean that much to him. It's nice, lots of wood, big windows, fancy leather furniture, but it doesn't feel very warm or friendly. There's no personality. He glances at my face a couple of times and I wonder if he's checking to see if I'm impressed. He's probably used to girls flipping out when they get the tour.

We stop in the kitchen. "I'll make you a drink," he says. He's moving around like a bartender, tossing ice cubes into a glass, pouring rum, then adding Coke. His thumb ring clunks against the side of the glass. His hair is combed straight back like he used gel or something, but the front part flops into his eyes and he keeps pushing it back or tucking it behind his ears.

"Your house is really big," I say. "Where's your room?"

"Wow. That was fast."

My face burns. "That's not what I meant."

"I know." He laughs. "You don't like my house, do you?"

I think about how to answer. I could lie and say it's awesome, but I get the feeling he doesn't want me to like it, which is strange. "It's nice. Seems like it could be lonely, though."

Our eyes meet as he passes me the glass. "Yeah. Sometimes."

I take a sip of the rum and Coke. It's too strong, but I try not to make a face.

"Do you want to watch the movie? Or hang out in here?" he says.

"Don't you want to see it?"

"I can watch it anytime. I'd rather talk to you."

I glance into the living room. Delaney is laughing, looks like she's having fun. Some of the kids have set their drinks on the wood coffee table, no coasters, and a bag of chips is spilling onto the carpet. I think about my mom having to clean it all up.

"Do your parents know you have friends over?"

"Yeah, they're okay with it. My dad is working at his office tonight and my mom is away for the weekend with some of her friends."

"Your friends are making a mess."

"I'll clean it up." He gives me a curious look. "Just because we have a maid doesn't mean I'm a slob."

"My mom prefers to be called a housekeeper."

"Sorry. I didn't think." He looks embarrassed now and I feel bad for being snarky.

"It's okay. Sensitive subject, I guess."

"I think it's really cool that your mom has her own business."

"She works hard."

"She's a good cleaner. My mom likes her a lot." He says it so casually, rating my mom, and I want to tell him off, but I can tell he meant it as a compliment. I don't like thinking of my mom scrubbing their floors and bathrooms. I wonder if his parents know he invited me over. What must it be like to have a happy family? With a mom who gets to go away and have a weekend with her friends. My mom never gets to do stuff like that.

"She found my pot stash under my bed one day and left it on my pillow. I had to find a better hiding place." He laughs, showing a flash of white teeth. One of them is crooked and I wonder why he didn't get braces. I hope he never does. I like him not perfect.

He looks at my face. "You don't like weed?"

"It's okay." I'd actually only smoked it a few times with Delaney, whose older brother had some. I liked the way it made us giggle at everything, but we have just as much fun without it. I'm more surprised to hear about my mom. "You're lucky my mom didn't tell your parents."

Jared shrugs. "She's cool, I can tell." I'm still thinking about that—how can he tell anything about my mom? do they talk?—when he leans over, plucks a red hair off my shirt, and holds it up to the light. "You have a boyfriend I don't know about?"

"Yeah, his name is Angus. He's about a hundred and twenty pounds, snores, eats a lot."

"You got a dog. That's awesome."

"My mom wanted him for protection."

"From your dad?"

I give him a look. "What do you know about my dad?"

"Nothing, really. She just told my mom a few things, like about her support group."

I hate that my mom shared anything about our lives. She shouldn't go around telling people private stuff. I don't know why it bothers me so much that he knows my dad was abusive, but it makes me feel ashamed. Like if my dad is horrible, then part of me might be horrible too. Jared's dad probably adores his mom and buys her flowers because it's Friday or something.

"Maybe she should take the dog with her when she cleans. She does the big house at the end of Wakesiah on Thursdays. It has a really long driveway and is in the middle of nowhere."

"How do you know that?

"My mom tried to change her days around once." That

doesn't really explain how he knew about the driveway, but it's not far from their house, so maybe he knows the owners.

I glance into the living room again. "I should check on Delaney."

"Hang on. I want to show you something first." He comes around the counter and grabs my free hand, then tugs me down the hallway. I follow along, enjoying the sensation of our fingers wrapped together, his hand cool from his glass. He stops in front of a door.

"This is my room." He pushes it open.

We walk in and I look around, taking it all in. I can feel him watching my face. "It's nice," I say, and it is, but it's like something from a magazine, or the *Fifty Shades of Grey* movie, with all the black bedding and chrome, not a real bedroom.

"My mom hired a decorator," he says. His arm brushes against mine and we're still holding hands. I turn and look at him, see in his eyes that he doesn't like his room either.

"Is this what you want to show me?"

"No, it's over here." He leads me to a metal desk in the corner, releases my hand so he can turn on his computer, then nods for me to sit on the chair while he pulls a stool over. We're so close I can feel the whole length of him beside me, the heat from his arms, his leg. I peek at him from the side of my eye. He must have shaved tonight, his skin is so smooth, and he has really black eyelashes, even blacker than his hair. I like how his top lip is a little fuller on one side. He opens a folder on his computer, clicks on an image, and a photo fills the screen. It's a photo of our school, but like in a way I've never seen it before. It's taken from the ground up, capturing one of the corners and part of a window in an interesting way.

"That's so cool," I say.

He flips through more photos of the school, the trees in front of the gym, some areas around town, the coffee shop, an old woman at the park, and they're all fascinating, like little glimpses into a different world. It makes me see how he sees everything, how he *feels*.

He scrolls past another folder and says, "These are old," as though he doesn't want to show them to me, but I notice an album picture of a woman with blond hair piled on top of her head like how my mom wears it when she's working. "Wait, go back," I say.

He scrolls back. "This one?"

"Yeah. Is that my mom?" I look closer. She's standing by a large window with silver drapes, looks like his living room. She's turned away, so I can't really see her face.

"I forgot about that one," he says. "She was working."

"Why did you take her picture?" I look at him, confused.

"I didn't. She was in the way." He points to corner of the screen. "I was trying to catch the deer playing on the front lawn." Now I see the deer in the background.

"Check these ones out." He scrolls through more shots of people on a beach and walking downtown, and he explains how he makes up stories for each person. "Like in this one, I decided that this guy is a Google executive and he's taking time off so he can develop his new Web site that he's going to sell for a billion dollars, and he's secretly working for the government. This woman is a librarian, but she wants to be an actress and writes erotic poetry in her spare time."

I laugh. "That's crazy."

"It's more interesting than the truth. Most people are pretty boring."

"You think so?"

He meets my eyes, "Not all of them." He looks away and flips through a few more photos, but I'm not paying attention. I think he just he gave me a compliment, though I'm not really sure what he meant. I hear him take a breath beside me, then he clicks on another photo. It's me. I stare, stunned and trying to understand when he took the picture. I'm laughing about something in the shot—my head back and my mouth parted, my hair blowing across my eyes so you can just see parts of them. It's in black-and-white, but he's colored my hair violet.

"You have a great smile," he says beside me in a quiet voice. My cheeks feel really warm and I know I'm blushing. I pick up my drink and swallow the rest in two big gulps.

I turn and look at him. "When did you take this?"

"A while ago. You were outside with Delaney. Are you freaked out?"

"Should I be?"

"You might think it's weird." His gaze drops and I can feel him looking at my mouth. I want to rub at it, thinking that maybe my lipstick is on my teeth or something.

"You're staring," I say.

"I'm trying to figure out a way to kiss you."

"Why don't you just ask?"

"Can I kiss you?"

I nod, but now I'm unsure, thinking all kinds of crazy things, like I hope my breath is okay, and what if I'm a bad kisser— what if *he's* a bad kisser—but then his lips are touching mine and they're soft and warm and taste like spiced rum. We're getting more into it, our mouths mashing together and my face and body feels so warm and heavy, almost sleepy in a really good way. Someone turns the music up in the living room and the beat pulses through my body, and I realize I might be a little drunk and wonder how much rum he put in my drink, but I don't care. I wrap my arms around his shoulders and he pulls me closer so that I'm almost sliding off the chair and onto his lap. One of his hands is on my hip, under my shirt, and it's moving in slow circles and now it's sliding up over my rib cage and his thumb grazes under my breast. I try to pull back, but now his hand is coming over my nipple, rubbing through my bra, and it feels so good, but I also feel a jolt of fear. It's too much, too fast.

"Wait," I say, but he's kissing my neck now and his breath sounds fast in my ear and his hand is still rubbing circles around my nipple and I get this fluttery feeling in my stomach. "Hey, stop." This time he brings his head up, looks me in the face. His eyes are dark, the pupils huge.

"What's wrong?"

"I want to stop."

He slides his hand down to my waist. "Sorry. I didn't hear you over the music."

"I think I drank too much. I don't feel good."

"Oh, shit, really? I'll get you water." He grabs my hand and pulls me up off the chair. I follow him down the hallway, still holding hands. Delaney is in the kitchen, talking and laughing with his friend. She gives me a wink and I try to smile back. Jared passes me a glass of water and I gulp it down, but now my head is pounding and it feels like everyone is looking at me.

"I need to use the bathroom," I say to Jared.

He gives me a concerned look and leads me into the master bedroom. "Use this one, it's more private. Do you want me to get Delaney?"

"No, thanks. I'll meet you in the kitchen." I close the door.

I splash cold water on my face, the back of my neck, then look in the mirror. My lips are red and swollen, my cheeks pink from our faces rubbing together. I press my hand onto my stomach, trying to feel what he felt, my warm skin, the bumps and shapes of lower ribs. I can even feel my heart beating. I raise my hand, cover my breast, thinking about his hands, then lean forward and press my forehead into the cold glass mirror. I feel high, my mind floaty and dreamy like when I'm in the middle of painting and I can feel all the colors coming together perfectly.

Is this what love feels like? Am I falling in love with Jared? I keep staring into my eyes, waiting for the answer.

CHAPTER TWENTY

LINDSEY

"Can you take these?" I pass the last two hors d'oeuvres trays to Greg. "Mini-quiche on the coffee table, spanakopita on the sideboard."

"Got it." He walks out of the kitchen, balancing the glass plates carefully in his large hands. I double-check that all the food trays are out and the oven is off, then remove my apron and hang it up. I glance in the mirror by the back door, smooth my hair.

Maybe two days before Christmas isn't the best time to throw a staff party, but it's not like my employees are jetting off on tropical vacations or out of town for the holidays. For a couple of them, I suspect this is the most festive part of their season. And they all deserve a treat. God knows I do too.

Marcus's deep voice rumbles from the living room, followed by female laughter. Greg's saying something about napkins, tells everyone to "dig in." He sounds like the host, and it irks me for a moment. I take a breath, shake it off. He's only helping.

I glance at the phone, willing it to stay silent. When it first rang this afternoon, I assumed it was one of my guests. I've invited a few ladies from my group as well as my employees, and several of them have unlisted numbers. But when I answered, there was silence. It rang throughout the day, only stopping when Greg came over. He walked around the whole property and assured me that no one was lingering in the bushes, but I still can't shake my uneasy feeling.

At least Sophie didn't have to deal with the phone calls. She's been at Delaney's all day and they're going out for a movie and pizza tonight. They won't be home until late.

When I walk into the living room, Marcus and Greg are standing near the table. It's the first time they've met, and I'm glad to see that they seem to be having a good conversation. Greg was hoping to meet my brother but I told him that Chris decided to stay home because they're coming up for Christmas dinner. Truth is, I pretty much ordered Chris to stay home. He's been calling to check on me almost every day and I don't want him pacing my house, staring out the window, and making everyone, including his girlfriend, nervous. He very grudgingly agreed.

I say hello to a few of my guests, then loop my arm through Greg's. He looks great tonight in a pair of jeans and a soft brown sweater that makes his eyes turn to warm chocolate. He's letting his facial hair grown into a goatee, and I like the dark shadow on his jaw. Marcus also looks very nice, though more formal in a suit coat with a shirt underneath.

"What are you two talking about?"

"Marcus was telling me about his book," Greg says. "Don't you find all that research about death and grief kind of depressing?"

Marcus looks startled, like he doesn't know how to answer. I feel like kicking Greg. What kind of question is that? He's heard me talking about how Marcus lost his daughter.

"It's not depressing," I say. "It's about the triumph of the human spirit. How resilient we can be even in the face of terrible tragedy."

I smile at Marcus. "It's brilliant."

"You've read it?" Now Greg is the one who looks surprised.

"Just a few chapters, but enough to know it's amazing. When it's published, all the talk shows will want you, Marcus. You'll be on tour for years."

"I don't know about that." He laughs. "Maybe a few radio stations if I'm lucky."

"That could be fun. I'll call in and ask you all sorts of questions."

"I can just hear it now," Marcus says. "Dr. Copeland, were you smoking drugs when you wrote this? Dr. Copeland, can you autograph a copy for my cat? She's your biggest fan."

"Stop it," I laugh. "It's going to be a best seller."

"Well, when I'm finished you can be my first reader and give me feedback." He glances over at Greg. "Lindsey's a great editor. She doesn't pull any punches."

"That's my girl."

My *girl*? I guess technically I'm his girlfriend, but the way he said it made it clear that he wanted Marcus to know we are together. My face warm, I loosen my arm from Greg's, take a nibble of my cracker, glance at the table as though I'm planning my next snack.

"So you're a UPS driver, right?" Marcus says. "You must be busy this time of year."

"Yep, lots of packages." They lapse into silence.

Marcus wipes at his mouth with his napkin, says, "Excuse me for a moment," and walks over to a few of the ladies from the group, sits on the hearth beside one of them.

Greg looks at me. "The quiche is good."

Okay, so Marcus and Greg aren't going to be buddies. That's fine, but I wish Greg had tried a little harder. It's like he's actively avoiding Marcus now and keeps putting his arm around my waist and whispering in my ear whenever Marcus gets up to grab another plate of snacks or comes near me. I'm having unwelcome flashbacks to the parties I attended with Andrew, how it always turned into a game where he had to show everyone that I belonged to him. I've caught Marcus watching us a couple of times, an odd expression on his face, part amused, part curious. For the last half hour, I've been talking to Rachelle, one of my employees, and ignoring both men.

Greg is now sitting in one of the chairs, watching a hockey game on his phone. Marcus heads into the kitchen with his empty glass. I assume he's getting another drink, but when he hasn't returned after a couple of minutes, I excuse myself from the conversation and check on him. He's on the floor, playing tug with Angus, who's growling and pouncing happily on his toy, shaking it back and forth in his powerful mouth.

"I see you've made a new friend," I say.

"He's fun."

"He's a giant pain in the ass, but I'm crazy about him." I can't believe Angus has only been living with us a few days—it feels like we've had him forever. I love how he sleeps at the foot of my bed at night, cocking his ears at a strange noise, or raising his head and woofing if he thinks it's something I should investigate. I love how happy he is to see me every day, how his big melting brown eyes can somehow make me give him a sample of whatever I'm eating. Even his huge feet, which track in every bit of snow and mud, make me smile.

"You okay?" I say.

"Yeah, just thinking about Katie. This was her favorite time of year. She'd make everyone crafts, but she was terrible at it." He laughs. "I have a box full of ornaments with shredded ribbons and sparkles falling off of them. One year she tried to make Christmas candles and ended up with blobs of red and green wax all over our floor. It took us hours to scrape it all up."

"It sounds like she was a lot of fun."

He nods, but his smile is fading, and he looks tired now. "I think I'm going to take off," he says. "Can you say good-bye to everyone for me?"

"Of course." I walk him out and wave from the front door, feeling bad that he's going home to an empty house. Then I think of Andrew, how Sophie had thought he was lonely, and glance around the dark woods. Is he watching now? I close the door firmly. Then I head down the hall to the bathroom, and accidentally open the door on Greg, who is standing at the sink.

"Sorry," I say. "I didn't know you were in here." Then I realize his hand is on the medicine cabinet as though he was just closing it.

He gives me a sheepish smile. "I ate too much." He rubs his chest. "Heartburn."

"The Tums are in the kitchen." He waits for me in the living room and talks to Rachelle while I get him a glass of water and a few Tums, then we settle back on the couch in front of the fire. Now that I'm not watching the tension between Marcus and Greg, or scared that the phone is going to ring, I'm enjoying myself. Greg has also relaxed, and I'm not feeling as annoyed. It's natural to feel a little jealousy, I suppose. Eventually my guests begin to leave, and an hour later they've all gone home. Greg helps me clean the kitchen. When we're finished, he kisses me against the counter, his hands drifting down to my waist. "Want me to stay?"

"I would, but Delaney is sleeping over tonight and that might be awkward."

"You know you and Sophie can come to Vancouver with me. They'd love to meet you." Greg is visiting his family for Christmas and won't be home until after New Year's Eve. We've agreed not to exchange presents and instead go skiing for a day when he gets home.

"Maybe next year."

"Is there a next year?"

I hide my face in his sweater, unsure of my answer. The warm, cozy feeling the wine gave me earlier seems to have disappeared and left me with a tight, trapped sensation.

"Things are complicated right now," I say. "It's hard to think that far ahead."

"You mean because of Andrew."

"I don't know what's going to happen. We may have to move." I haven't seen Andrew since he agreed to the peace bond, but the phone calls were upsetting. It's like he knew I was having a party tonight and wanted to mess with my head.

"I wondered if you were getting ready to run." I feel him take a breath, his chest lifting under my cheek. "Promise you won't leave town without letting me know, okay?"

I hesitate. Is this a promise I can make? What if I have to leave in a hurry? I don't want to get into details right now and start an argument. Better to just agree and reassure him.

"Okay." I tilt my head back and look up at him. "See you when you get back?"

"I'll make dinner at my place."

"Sounds great."

He leans closer, whispers in my ear. "But I want to wake up next to you. No sneaking out with some lame excuse." He's using a teasing tone, but I know he's serious and I feel bad for how I've made him feel these last couple of months, always holding him at arm's length. I think about Marcus, going home alone. I don't want to be like that. I want a relationship—a *real* one.

"I'll bring my toothbrush."

The mall is going to be chaos, with everyone doing their last-minute shopping before Christmas tomorrow, but I still need a couple of things for Sophie. Last night she texted that she was staying at Delaney's because the roads were bad. I'm glad she's making good choices. I get up early and remove the snow and ice from my windshield while I wait for the car to warm up. My scraper bumps over something on my windshield. With my hand, I brush away the final bits of snow. A wrapped box is tied to my wiper. Greg must have left me a surprise. Smiling, I pull off my gloves, carefully untie the red ribbon, and open the box. It's a CD. I flip it over and look at the label on the back and suck in my breath when I recognize the songs. These are all from my wedding. One of them we used for our first dance. "Islands in the Stream," by Dolly Parton and Kenny Rogers.

I spin around, scanning the trees, the driveway. "Where are you, you bastard?" My voice sounds jarring to my ears. Angus is barking in the house. "Where *the fuck* are you?"

I stand still, daring him to come out, but nothing moves. The forest is quiet. Angus would have barked if a car pulled up last night. Andrew must have parked on the main road and crept in, so slowly we didn't hear his steps. I look for tracks, but there was too much snow during the night. I get in my car, tug off my gloves with my teeth, and call Corporal Parker.

"It's Lindsey. Andrew was at my house. He left me a CD. It was stuck to my car window!" My breath is cloud puffs and my whole body is shivering. I turn the heat up higher. I look around, expecting Andrew to lunge at my car and drive his fist through the window.

"Did he threaten you?"

"I never saw him, but the CD is full of love songs that he used to play for me."

"Do you recognize the handwriting?"

"The titles are typed out. He must have used a computer."

"Okay, put it in a plastic bag with the box and bring everything into the station."

I close my eyes, take a shuddering breath. "I hate this. I really hate this."

"I know." Her voice is kind, with a measured calm. I imagine that she must be good in a crisis. "I'll take a walk around your place and make sure everything is okay."

"Thanks." The ice is melting off my window in a circle. I can see the forest, my house. "I told you the peace bond won't work. He's never going to leave me alone."

"If he's left prints on the case, we can arrest him."

"He's not stupid. He knows exactly how far he can go."

"I still have his cell number from the last time. I'll give him a call and make it *clear* he needs to leave you alone." She sounds confident, even a little angry, which makes me feel better. "He needs a reminder of what will happen to him if he violates any conditions of the bond."

"He's not scared. That's the problem. He thinks he's invincible."

"Well, he's walking a very thin line—and he's going to find that out soon."

"Don't you get sick of it? This whole system is controlled by men. Why should we have to follow the law when people like Andrew get to do whatever they want?"

"Trust me, there are plenty of times when I wish I could take things into my own hands. I know what you're going through." She pauses, and I wonder if she's about to reveal something personal, but then she says, "I just have to believe I'm making a difference."

I let out my breath in a sigh. This isn't her fault. She's trying to help.

"I'm tired of talking about it," I say.

"What does that mean?" I hear the concern in her voice and realize how it sounded.

"It means I have to get to work. Thanks for listening." I end the call.

My brother and Maddie come for dinner and we gorge on turkey with all the fixings and polish off an entire pumpkin pie. Then we play some board games and a few rounds of cards, until Sophie and Maddie stumble off to bed, complaining of a turkey hangover. Chris and I stay up to talk by the fire like when we were kids. I tell him about the CD.

"This is getting out of hand." He's gripping his beer like he might throw it at something. "I should have put a bullet in his head when you first told me he hurt you."

"Jesus. Don't talk like that."

Chris looks down at his bottle. "Sorry." But something about the way he says it doesn't sound all that sorry. I know my brother, know that sometimes loyalty blinds reason.

"Hey, you won't do anything stupid, right? You're going to have your own baby." I give his arm a shake. "You need to be around for her."

He meets my eyes. "I know. I'm not going anywhere."

"Promise?" I hold my hand out and wiggle my pinkie finger.

"Promise." He hooks his finger in mine.

In the morning Sophie and I make breakfast for everyone—waffles with lots of whipped cream and strawberries—then we open our presents. Sophie's spoiled me with bath products, a beautiful new cream-colored throw blanket, and a pale blue knit cap and scarf. She also sketched me a funny drawing of Angus dragging me down the street. When she opens my gifts for her, art supplies, an iTunes card, and a leather portfolio for her drawings with her name engraved on it, she lets out a whoop and crushes me in a hug. "You're the best!"

Chris and Maddie love the quilt that Sophie and I made for their baby, and all the adorable toys we couldn't help purchasing. They've generously gifted us with a new latte machine, which we immediately put to good use. All too soon they have to leave and catch the ferry. I won't admit it to Chris, or in front of Sophie, but I felt safer with my brother at our house. I hug him hard at his car door and he says, "You need me, I'll be on the next ferry over."

After they're gone, I put on the cap and scarf Sophie gave me and we take Angus for a winter walk, then spend the rest of the day watching movies and eating all our stocking stuffers. Sophie seems distracted, though, lapsing into silence, checking her phone constantly. When I ask who she's texting, she says Delaney, but she doesn't meet my eyes and tucks her phone into her pocket. I haven't told her about the present her father left on my car. I will eventually, but I don't want to ruin Christmas for her. I keep wondering when Andrew left the CD. Was I sleeping? Walking around in the house in my bathrobe? Kissing Greg? How long was he outside?

Boxing Day morning, Sophie gets up early to go shopping with Delaney while I'm still in bed. I was hurt when she'd told me her plans last night—the two of us always go skating on Boxing Day—but I kept my thoughts to myself. I wake as I hear the front door close and Delaney's car drive off. I stay in bed for a while longer, staring at the ceiling until Angus whines that he wants to go outside. While I have my morning coffee, I flip through some flyers in the newspaper and consider whether I should check if Sophie actually went to the mall. She doesn't like shopping at the best of times and it will be packed today. Is she meeting Andrew again?

I get dressed and head down to the mall to browse around, telling myself that there is no harm in having a look. If I run into Sophie, great. If I don't, then I just have to trust her word.

After two hours at the mall, I've checked all Sophie's favorite stores but haven't spotted her yet. Finally I see a familiar head of violet-colored hair at the other end of the food court.

I'm a few feet away when I realize a boy is standing next to her, their heads close, his hand grazing her lower back. I freeze, caught off guard. The boy lifts his head and looks in my direction. Jared McDowell. When did *they* start spending time together?

Jared meets my eyes and nudges Sophie, says something to her. She turns and catches me watching. Her face flushes and she moves away from Jared a couple of steps.

I walk closer. "How's the shopping going?"

"Why are you here?"

Her abrupt tone stings. She's never rude like this, but I don't want to say anything in front of Jared. "I'm shopping," I say. "The Gap has some good deals."

"Hi, Lindsey," Jared says. It's not strange for him to call me Lindsey—it's what he calls me when I'm cleaning his house—but it feels odd in front of my daughter. She shoots him a look, like she's startled by his being so personal.

"Did you have a nice Christmas?" I say.

"It was great. You?"

"Lovely, thanks." We stand in awkward silence. "Where's Delaney?" I say.

"She's picking out shoes," Sophie says. "We have to meet her." I realize my daughter is brushing me off and feel another stab of hurt.

"Well, have fun. See you at home." I turn, then feel her hand on the back of my arm. I look over my shoulder at her.

"I'll make dinner tonight, okay?" she says.

"Sounds great." I know it's her way of apologizing, can see the conflicting emotions playing across her face, and understand that she doesn't know why she's embarrassed or how to deal with it. I force my face into a cheerful expression. "Nice to see you again, Jared."

"You too, Lindsey," he says.

As I walk away I have the sudden feeling that he used my name on purpose this time—like he was trying to make me uncomfortable, but I don't know why.

When Sophie gets home that night, I'm in my bedroom doing some bookkeeping on my computer while Angus lolls on the bed. I hear her footsteps come into the room, then mattress springs shifting and Angus's tail thumping on the duvet.

"Okay. I'm ready," she says.

I spin around. "Ready for what?" She's sprawled across the bed beside Angus, who rolls onto his back while she scratches his stomach.

"For you to give me the third degree."

"Now, why I would do that?"

"Because I was with Jared and I didn't tell you we're hanging out."

"Hanging out or dating?"

She shrugs, buries her face in Angus's neck. He whines and paws at her to keep scratching his belly. "I don't know what we're doing. He says he likes me."

"Do you like him?"

"Yeah, I guess. He's not like I thought."

"Why didn't you tell me?"

"It just happened recently and I wasn't sure how you'd feel about it. You know, because you work for them." She has a blank expression on her face, but I know she wants my approval. I remember how much it meant to me that my parents liked Andrew.

I choose my words carefully. "He seems like a nice kid, but I don't know him very well." He's always polite and friendly when I clean their house, but something about him has always struck me as a bit too . . . eager. I don't know if he's just lonely—I get the feeling his parents travel a lot—but most teen boys don't want to spend a lot of time chatting with their housekeeper, and yet he often comes into the room and asks me things or talks to me about the weather or whatever.

"It must take you a long time to clean their house," Sophie says.

"You've been there?" I feel another nervous flip in my stomach. Sophie has gone out with a few boys and we've had the sex talk, but I never worried about it because she never seemed really interested in anyone before. I knew it was something I'd have to deal with one day, but I hoped it would be when she was away at university.

"Delaney and I were there with some friends. Did you know he's a photographer?"

I think back over the last couple of weeks, wonder when she was at his house. She was starting to have so many secrets. "Oh, yeah? What does he photograph?"

"Just scenery, oceans, mountains." Her face is flushed and I know there's more to this, but I can't press, not without shutting her down completely. Jared doesn't strike me as the kind of kid who'd be interested in taking photos of tranquil ocean scenes. His bedroom with its black curtains, chrome desk and night tables, has always reminded me of a single man's apartment in the city. I don't know any teen boys who collect abstract black-and-white canvas paintings.

Sophie looks at me seriously. "Why did you really go to the mall?"

"I had a feeling you were hiding something and I was worried about you."

She turns to scratch Angus again, blocking her face from my view. "Well, now you know." She doesn't sound annoyed or defensive, or any of the things I expected, which is making me think she's hiding something else.

"I didn't want to tell you this at Christmas," I say, "but the morning after my party, I found a wrapped box on my windshield. Your father left me a CD."

She rolls over, sits up straight. "How do you know it was from him?"

"They're all songs that he picked for our wedding reception. I dropped it off at the police station." Corporal Parker hadn't noticed anything when she walked around the house—no signs of attempted entry, no footprints in the snow—just "a big hairy beast trying to tear me apart through the window." I explained about Angus and she said a dog was a great idea.

Sophie's eyes are wide, her mouth parted. She presses her hand to her heart for a moment like it's beating fast, then she meets my eyes and quickly pulls her hand away, but it's too late.

"You've seen him again," I say.

"No." She turns to Angus and strokes his back. He wiggles closer, paws at her leg.

"Please don't lie to me."

"You said you would kick me out."

"I said that because I was scared after he broke into our house. I was trying to protect you. I'm not going to kick you out, but I need to know if you've been speaking to him."

"He didn't break in. He was in Victoria packing his stuff."

"He's not going to admit it."

"But he agreed to the peace bond. Why would he risk going to jail?"

"People like him don't think of consequences. They act in the moment. I never called the police on him in all the years we were married, so he probably thinks I won't follow through."

I can see the truth settle into her mind, the disappointment that follows. Her shoulders slump. "I *really* thought he'd changed, Mom. He said he'd stay away from you."

"He can't help himself. He'll keep trying to find a way to get at me one way or another."

She looks so sad, her green eyes watery pools. "He made me a beautiful wooden box." I flinch as I remember the wooden jewelry box he'd made me one Christmas. Now he's playing the same games with my daughter. But I can't tell her that, can't hurt her more.

"It's still a beautiful box."

"I won't see him again." Her voice breaks, and I hate that she has to make this choice.

"We can talk about it when you're older," I say softly. "When he's been out longer."

"He lied to me," she says as she stands up. "I'm done giving him a chance."

"If he approaches you again, you need to be careful how you speak to him. He won't—"

"Mom, I can handle it."

Her phone chirps in her pocket and she glances at the screen. "It's Jared." She looks up at me. "I'm going to my room, okay?"

She walks out, her shoulders slumped and her arms wrapped around her body. Angus leaps off the bed with a thud, gives me a reproachful look, and trots after her. She didn't let me finish my warning. Fear slides in around my throat, thick and slimy. The one thing Andrew hates more than losing control is being confronted. When Sophie was a child she idolized him so much, he told me, "She makes me feel like I can do anything, like I'm a superhero." I don't know what he'll do when he realizes he's lost her forever.

CHAPTER TWENTY-ONE

SOPHIE

I'm sitting in my bed with my cell phone in my hand, my back against the headboard and the blankets pulled around me. I should get up and have a shower, make some breakfast, but the thought of food makes my stomach twitch and jump. I tuck my feet under Angus at the end of the bed and rub my cold toes on his belly. He grumbles and shifts his weight but doesn't move away. I look at the text from Andrew again. *How was Christmas? Want to visit this week?*

He texted on Christmas Day, wishing me a Merry Christmas, and I answered him, but that was before I knew about the present he left for Mom. I'd hoped I'd have more time to think about what I should text him back, but then he sent this message yesterday. I still haven't answered. I don't know how I'm going to tell him I don't want to see him anymore.

I scroll through my other texts, read the ones from Jared again. We've been texting nonstop since his party. When I met him at the mall on Boxing Day, he held my hand and gave me a kiss like we were boyfriend and girlfriend. At first I was embarrassed, but then I decided I liked it. Most boys leave you wondering and play stupid head games, but he's not like that.

What are you doing? I text him.

Editing photos. You?

I have to text my dad. He's going to be pissed.

Just call him.

What if he flips out? I'd spent most of the morning wishing I could ignore Andrew and pretend the last couple of months never happened. Then I could go back to the way life used to be—when I didn't have a father, which wasn't great, but it was okay. I had my mom. And back then I didn't have to worry that my dad was going to hurt her if I said one thing wrong.

Just talk to him, Jared texts. *Maybe he has a good reason.*

That thought scares me the most. What if he makes me believe in him again? No. He can't explain this one away—he left her a *present*. On her window. Like they're in high school! If I text him or try to ignore him, he'll probably call me anyway, and then it will be even worse.

OK, I'm going for it.

Good luck!

Andrew's phone rings a bunch of times and I'm about to end the call when he finally picks up. "Yeah?" His voice is a shout and I can hear noises in the background, like saws and machinery and hammers. He must be at the job site. I forgot it was Tuesday already.

"It's Sophie."

"Hey, kid, just let me hop into my truck." I can hear muffled crunching like he's walking on gravel, then the metal sound of a door closing. "That's better," he says. "What's going on? You okay?" The concern in his voice throws me and I almost chicken out, but then I think that if I really mattered to him, he wouldn't have screwed up everything.

"Why did you leave Mom that present?"

Silence, then a heavy sigh. "I was hoping it got buried in the snow."

I wasn't expecting him to admit anything and don't know what to say for a moment. "I told you to stay away from her, but you didn't listen. I don't want to see you anymore."

"Hey, slow down and hear me out for a minute." His voice is firm, a tight grip that holds me in place. "You'd been over at my house and I started thinking about how things could have been if your mom and I had stayed together. Then I found that CD and it reminded me of how good things used to be. I guess I thought maybe if I gave it to her . . ."

He found it? Could that be true? Maybe he really did have it from years ago. That's kind of less freaky than him making a new one. "You thought she'd want to get back together?"

"It was stupid, okay? I regretted it the next day, but it was too late."

"If I told the cops you admitted it was from you, they'd arrest you."

"You have to do what you feel is right. I just wanted to be honest with you."

I hate this, hate this impossible choice. I don't want him to go to jail. I don't want to be the one who put him there. I need to think.

"How did you know where we live?" I say.

"I followed you home from school." I'm silent, a looming feeling of terror coming up fast behind me. Mom was right all along and I ignored her. I led him right to her.

"I know how that sounds," Andrew says, "but I just wanted to make sure you were okay. I wanted to see where you live and I knew you couldn't show me."

I don't want him to say things like this, don't want to him to say things a father would say except that it's all twisted into knots. "We made a deal."

"Shit," he says. "My boss needs me. Come over this weekend, okay? We can talk."

"No. Mom is right. You can't help yourself."

"Is that what she told you?" He doesn't sound apologetic anymore. His voice is harsh and mean, like someone I've never heard before, except maybe I think I have.

"This is between you and me," I say. "This is *my* decision."

"I'm working the rest of the week," he says, "but I'm home all day Saturday—New Year's Eve. I'll stick around. Come over anytime. I'll explain." His tone has switched again. Now he's a friend sitting down at the table for coffee and conversation.

"You can't explain this!"

"I've loved her so long, Sophie. You're young and maybe you don't understand, but *real* love, like the way I love your mom, it's everything. It fills your head, your body, you can't breathe without thinking about them. I don't know how to move on yet, but I know I have to, okay? I know I have to let her go." His voice sounds thick and scratchy, like he's crying.

"Dad—"

"Just come see me," he says. "I'll make it right." He ends the call. I set my phone down on the bed, sink under my blankets, and press the heels of my palms into my eyes.

CHAPTER TWENTY-TWO

LINDSEY

I glance through Marcus's front window as I walk up his porch steps. His outdoor Christmas lights are already down and I can't see his tree through the window. I wonder if he's the type who always takes down his decorations before New Year's Eve, or if it has more to do with painful memories. He spent Christmas Eve with his parents on the island, then volunteered at a crisis center Christmas Day. "I have to keep busy," he said.

I ring the bell, glance up and down the street. The road is quiet, no trucks idling in the distance, but I'm still scared Andrew has been following me.

"Hi," Marcus says when he opens the door. "I pigged out over the holidays, so I'm going to be hitting the weights hard today. You up for it?" He gives me a cheeky smile.

"Hmm. Doesn't sound like much fun. Never mind." I pretend to spin around and he grabs my arm with a laugh.

"Get your butt in here."

When we walk through the living room and head downstairs to the gym, I notice there's no sign it was even Christmas a few days ago, not one tissue, ribbon, or shred of wrapping paper anywhere in sight. We exercise hard, the only noise the clanging of the weight machine that Marcus is using and the hum of the treadmill that I'm on. I turn up the incline and run until my calf muscles quiver and my lungs burn. Then he spots me as I lift weights, his face focused.

We sit after and have a coffee. He bought a new one for us to try—dark and rich with a caramel sweetness. I like thinking of him picking it out in the store.

"It's nice to take a break," he says. "I've been writing all day."

"How's it going?"

"Ask me tomorrow after I've deleted everything."

I laugh. "Did you have a good Christmas?" I say, then feel foolish for the question. I can't imagine that it would ever be possible to have a good Christmas after you've lost a child.

"It was productive," he says as he busies himself with pouring another cup of coffee. I can tell he doesn't want to talk about it. "How was yours?"

"Interesting. Turns out Sophie has a boyfriend. He's the son of one my clients."

"Does that bother you?"

"I'm not sure how I feel about him. He makes me a little uneasy."

"Mother's instincts?"

"Or maybe paranoia." I smile. "I'm sure he's fine. I'm just not used to Sophie dating, and they're texting constantly. It feels so fast."

"Young love," he says. "It's usually very obsessive." He glances at my face. "Don't worry. It's normal teen behavior. Just give her space. I tried too hard to warn Katie and ended up pushing her away."

"She asked if she could go to a New Year's Eve party at his house. I checked with his parents and they're chaperoning, so I agreed, but I think she's getting in over her head." Normally

Sophie comes with me to my support group's New Year's Eve party. I can understand her wanting to be with her boyfriend, but it feels like one more step in her moving away from me.

"How so?"

"Jared comes from a wealthy family. Their lifestyle is very different than ours."

"You're worried she won't fit into his world?"

"More that she might like that world and it will change her. And I'm worried that he has more life experiences than her. He's very grown-up." I know it isn't fair to compare him to Andrew, but I can't help thinking how I'd been dazzled—and then blinded.

"Sophie seems to have a good head on her shoulders."

"I know, but she leads with her heart." I fiddle with my mug. "She saw her father again—and he left a present on my windshield, a CD with love songs. She said she won't see him anymore, but I don't know what's going to happen when she shuts him out."

He looks alarmed. "Did you tell the police?"

"Yes, right away, but I can't prove it was from Andrew, so they can't arrest him. It's so stupid. Who else could it be from?" Parker had sounded frustrated when she told me there were no prints on the CD case, but sympathy doesn't change the facts.

"My offer still stands—you and Sophie are welcome to stay at my lake house, or if you don't want to leave town, I have a couple of spare rooms."

"I really appreciate the offer, but Greg is coming back Sunday."

"Right. Are you looking forward to seeing him?"

"Of course." I'm puzzled by the question. Truth is, I haven't thought about Greg much at all the last couple of days, but I don't want to admit that.

"You don't sound enthusiastic."

I shrug, stir my coffee. "I'm just distracted."

"Okay." But he doesn't sound like he believes me.

"What?"

"It's nothing. I just get the feeling he's pretty serious about you, but you already have one foot out the door."

"Not at all. I like Greg a lot." I'm flustered, my face hot. I hadn't realized Marcus was studying my relationship, or how it might look from the outside. Maybe it is true and Greg's feelings have grown faster and stronger than mine, but that's not a bad thing. I'll catch up. What we have is relaxing. "I don't have to worry about him," I say. "It's easy."

"Okay." He reaches for his coffee.

"There's that word again."

"I'm sorry," he says with a laugh. "I shouldn't have said anything."

"It's a little late now. You might as well go all the way." I'm joking like this is all in fun, just two good friends having a heart-to-heart. "You don't like Greg?"

"It's not that I don't like him."

"But you didn't say that you do."

"I just didn't think he was your type."

"So what's my type?"

Our eyes meet, and hold. My chest muscles tighten, squeezing the air out of my lungs.

He glances down at his mug. "Hey, what do I know? It's been years since I dated anyone," he says. "I should have kept my mouth shut. If you're happy, I'm happy."

"Well, that's good, because I'm happy." Still, I feel a heavy, disappointed feeling spread over me, which is strange. What did I want him to say?

"Sorry if I stepped over the line."

"No. You were just being honest. I appreciate your love advice, Doctor." I give a small laugh, and glance up at the clock. He's watching me, trying to see into my eyes, but I can't meet his gaze. "I have to go," I say. "Angus is waiting."

"You sure you're okay?"

I force my face into a smile. "I'm fine. Really. There's just a lot going on right now." I gather my purse and coat and walk toward the door. "Thanks for the coffee."

I can feel him watch me trudge through the snow to my car, but I don't look back.

CHAPTER TWENTY-THREE

Sophie

I wake slowly, my legs pinned to the bed, and kick out in panic. The weight moves and I hear Angus jump onto the floor with a loud thud, then sprawl across the carpet. I roll over and stare at the ceiling, blinking my eyes and yawning. Tonight is the party at Jared's. It's also the day my dad thinks I'm going over to his house. Why didn't I just tell him I wasn't going?

Because he didn't give me a chance.

In the end I decided not to say anything to Mom about how he admitted he left the CD. The cops will have to figure it out on their own. I'm not going to turn in my own dad. It's too weird and stressful. Maybe the party tonight will help. I need to blow off some steam. Or maybe the party is the problem. Jared and I have only been "together" for a few days. Is this like making it public? Will he want us to hang out with his friends all the time? I don't have anything in common with those girls. They're the beautiful happy crowd, where everyone lives in nice houses with two parents and they don't have to worry about anything.

I think about canceling and saying I'm sick, but then remember what happened in his bedroom the last time I was there, and feel warm all over. It makes me think of yellow ochre, or maybe deep cadmium yellow. Something bright and beautiful and golden.

I want to kiss him again, but I'm nervous he might want to have sex and I don't think I'm ready. It's not like I want to be a virgin forever, but Delaney said it really hurts the first time. Nothing about that sounds fun. My phone vibrates on my night table. Jared.

Want to come over early and help set up?

I'm relieved about the idea of going over before the party. This way I won't have to show up by myself—Delaney has gone skiing with her family.

K. What time?

Pick you up around 12?

This means we'll be spending almost the whole day together. I'm excited, but scared, too. What if we find out we don't like each other that much after all? I think it over, my thumb still hovering over the keyboard. Then I notice he's typing again.

Hey, don't leave a guy hanging!

I laugh and text, *OK, see you soon.*

Two hours later, Jared's sitting on my couch and looking around at our colorful living room with its mismatched furniture and paintings. It's strange seeing him here—like an actor who walked onto the wrong movie set and doesn't realize yet that he doesn't belong. We're like a box of Crayola crayons, and he's willow charcoal, all velvety shadow and interesting layers.

"This is nice," he says.

"Thanks. It must seem really small to you."

"No. It feels like a real home."

"I guess." Angus is bumping his head into Jared's legs and dropping his wet ball onto his lap. "Sorry," I say as I try to drag Angus away from him, which is kind of like trying to move a duffel bag full of cement blocks.

"I don't mind. I like dogs." He may not mind, but as far as I'm concerned, three's a crowd. I get a bone from the kitchen and Angus instantly loses all interest in Jared.

My cell phone rings. I glance at the call display—it's Andrew. I drop the phone on the coffee table—as if he can look through it and see me ignoring him.

"Who was that?" Jared says.

"My dad. He wants me to come over, but I'm not going."

"I thought you told him you didn't want to see him again?"

"I did, but I don't think my dad takes no for an answer."

Jared reaches out and holds my hand. "I'm sorry if I freaked you out the other day."

"It's okay," I say, feeling my face get hot. I was hoping he wouldn't bring it up.

"Did I do something wrong?"

"No. That's kind of the problem. I liked it."

"Oh." He looks happy, then shifts his weight and leans closer to me on the couch. Angus gets off his bed, rams his head between us, and whines for attention.

"I'll put him outside." Angus doesn't want to go and I have to bribe him with dog cookies. When I come back inside, my cell is ringing again. Jared hands me my phone.

"It's your dad. He texted."

I feel weird that he looked at my call display. Did he read my texts? Maybe he only glanced at them because he was curious—and concerned. I would probably do the same.

I shove my phone into my pocket without looking at the text and sit back down on the couch. I don't like thinking about my dad sitting at home waiting for me to call, but more than that, I'm angry. Why can't he give me some space? "I wish he'd leave me alone."

"You *sure* you don't want to see him? He seems upset. I can drive you."

I shake my head. "He promised to stay away from my mom, and then he went and put a present on her car window!"

"That's kind of romantic."

"It's freaky." I give him a look.

"Sorry. I guess I just understand how you can like someone that much."

"What if the person doesn't like you back?"

"Then he should definitely give up. But I wouldn't give you up that easily." I know he's just trying to flatter me, but why doesn't he get that what my dad is doing is *wrong*?

He holds my hand again, rubs small circles on my palm with his thumb. "I'm really glad you're coming tonight. It will be fun. There'll be booze and drugs going around, but you don't have to do anything you don't want, okay?"

"Your mom told my mom it's a dry party."

He laughs. "She tells all the parents that, but they leave us alone downstairs and we just do whatever we want."

"Wow."

He shrugs. "My parents don't care what I do as long as I don't make them look bad in front of their friends. My dad's been giving me beer since I was like thirteen."

"Seriously?"

"Yeah. He has lots of prescription pills and he knows I take them sometimes, but he never gives me shit. He just doesn't want me to tell my mom about all his affairs."

Holy crap. So his family isn't as perfect as I thought. I guess I'm not the only one who has a messed-up dad. I should probably feel bad for Jared, but for some reason I'm relieved.

"Doesn't that bother you?" I say. I'm a little freaked out to hear that Jared takes prescriptions, but it can't be anything too serious. He doesn't seem like he's a drug addict.

"Not really. I didn't like it when he was messing around with my babysitter. I walked in on them when they were doing it. He bought me my first camera after that."

I stare at him, stunned. "That's just so horrible."

"I haven't told any of my friends." He's looking at me intently. "But I trust you."

"I'll never tell anyone," I say. He leans closer, gives me a gentle kiss on the mouth. I relax into the couch and we kiss for a few minutes. This time he's slower, more cautious, and doesn't put his hand under my shirt. After a while, he raises his head and smiles down at me.

"You ready to go to my house?" He glances at his watch. "My mom is probably waiting."

"Sure. I just have to let my mom know." I fire off a quick text, get her reply almost instantly. *Don't forget the laundry!* Right. "I have to put some clothes in the dryer."

"Can I use your bathroom?"

When I'm finished with the laundry, Jared's not in the living room yet. I wait on the couch until he comes down the hall, then I say, "I have to grab my clothes for later."

"Okay. I'll warm up my car."

I walk down the hall to my bedroom, noticing that my mom left her door open. She's been trying to keep it closed so Angus doesn't climb onto her bed. I shut the door.

I pack my things and grab my makeup from the bathroom. I'm not sure how the other girls are going to dress, so I bring a few options, my favorite black tunic I always wear with purple leggings, couple of skirts. Before I leave the house, I set the alarm and lock the door.

Jared's car is running, but he's not inside. I wait by the passenger door, confused. Finally he comes around from behind the house. "Sorry," he says with a sheepish smile. "I had to pee."

"Again?"

"Nerves." He's looking really embarrassed now.

"What are *you* nervous about?"

"You," he says. "I want you to have fun tonight."

I've never had anyone my age care so much about what I think. It makes me feel excited and pleased and confident. I smile. "Then I guess you better be really nice to me."

"I plan on it."

He opens my door with a flourish and I slide behind the seat, ignoring my phone, which is ringing in my pocket again. I'm not going to let my dad ruin this night for me.

CHAPTER TWENTY-FOUR

Lindsey

I slowly push my cart around the produce section at the grocery store, my shoulders and hands aching after cleaning two houses. They're both having parties tonight and were willing to pay extra. I'd rather have gone straight home, but we ran out of milk and coffee this morning. I drank almost a whole pot trying to wake up from a restless night. Why was Marcus asking about Greg? It was as though he was trying to find out if we were going to break up, but that shouldn't matter to him—unless he has feelings for me. The idea makes me pause in the middle of the aisle, staring at a row of salad dressings. Do I *want* him to have feelings for me?

I think about calling Jenny, but part of me is afraid to hear what she has to say. She might tell me that I'm way off base, or encourage me, and I'm not sure I'm ready for that. I know she likes Greg—she thinks he's a fun guy who doesn't take himself, or life, too seriously—but she also likes Marcus. She told me once after a meeting that some very lucky woman was going to end up with him one day. I'd said I'd be happy for him, and she gave me a look.

I really don't feel like going to the New Year's Eve party at the church tonight when I'm so confused about my conversation with Marcus. I wish I hadn't agreed to bring an appetizer. I planned on making an artichoke dip, but when I wheel past a display case of assorted spreads and dips, I toss a couple into my cart and add a bag of chips and a tray of vegetables. Screw it. I'll put them in a nice dish and no one will ever know the difference.

My arms full of grocery bags, I walk into my house and dump them on the counter. Angus usually meets me at the door. Maybe he's sleeping in Sophie's bed.

"Angus?" I call out. "I'm home!" Silence. I walk down the hallway. He still doesn't come running. Did Sophie leave him outside? Tentacles of fear begin to wind their way around my ankles, pulling me faster into the house. Finally I find him sprawled on the couch in the living room, his legs hanging over the edge and his head on the pillow. "There you are!"

He doesn't open his eyes or lift his head. I rush over to him—and step in something wet. Vomit. Now I notice the other piles of vomit on the rug. I place my hand on Angus's rib cage, and feel a surge of relief when his chest rises. I press my fingertips under his armpit, remembering something about that being where you check for a dog's pulse. It seems really fast, but I'm not sure what a normal heart rate is for dogs.

"Angus?" I give him a gentle shake. When he still doesn't wake up, I grab my cell out of my pocket, look up the number for the emergency vet clinic, and describe his symptoms. "He's thrown up everywhere." I take a closer look at one of the piles. "There are hunks of meat." I crouch down and notice a tiny white fragment. "I think he ate some pills."

"Better bring him in right away—and the vet will want to see the pills."

"He's huge. I don't know how I'm going to get him into my car."

"Can you make a stretcher on a blanket? Or ask a neighbor for help?"

"I'll try a blanket." I run into the kitchen, grab a plastic bag, and collect a few spoonfuls of vomit. Then I take a quick check around the house. What did he get into? No cupboards are open. Someone had to have drugged him. Not *someone*. Andrew.

It takes all my strength to slide Angus onto my homemade stretcher and drag him outside, then down the stairs. I wrench my back trying to lift him into the car. I sprint to my neighbor's house through the woods. I'm hot and sweaty and frantic. I imagine poison spreading through Angus's body every second, flowing into his liver and kidneys and brain. I can't let him die.

My neighbor, a retired schoolteacher named Tom, has a passion for fishing and is thankfully outside installing downriggers on his boat. When he looks up, I shout, "I need help!" over the noise of his tools. He follows me back to my house and we load Angus into my car.

I drive fast on the snowy roads, too fast, but we make it to the clinic ten minutes later. Dr. Langelier checks Angus over, gently opening his mouth, examining his gums, lifting his eyelids. There was a different doctor when I brought Angus in for his post-adoption checkup. I'd felt like she was too young, too unsure of herself, but I'm soothed by this doctor's snow-white hair, his calm manner and deep voice. My pulse settles and I take some breaths. It's okay. Angus is in good hands. I glance down at his sweet face. *Just get through this, buddy, and I'll take you for all the walks and swims and car rides you want for the rest of your doggie life.*

"Do you know what he got into?" the veterinarian says.

"I saw bits of pills in his vomit." I hand him my little bag and he surveys the contents. "My daughter and I don't take prescriptions—and we don't have any pills like this. He also had hunks of wieners or sausages in his vomit. I think someone tossed them into our backyard."

"How long ago do you think that might have been?"

"I don't know. My daughter was home until around one."

"Did she notice anything wrong with his behavior?"

"I haven't had a chance to talk to her yet, but she would have told me."

"He probably ingested the substance in the last couple of hours—it would've hit his bloodstream fast. Let's get this guy in the back right away and get him on an IV and run some tests. We'll give him activated charcoal to bind what's in his bowels so it gets passed out." He picks up the plastic bag. "We'll see if we can figure out what he was given."

"Will he be okay?"

"Hopefully you found him in time, but we're going to have to monitor his kidney and liver function to make sure they aren't damaged. We'll give him IV fluids to flush his body and treat his symptoms as they appear. I want to run a CBC—complete blood count—to see if it affected red to white cells, and monitor clotting time."

I look down at Angus, stroke the soft fur around his neck. "I hate leaving him."

"We'll take good care of him. Someone will be in the clinic all night."

I fight back tears. "He's such a great dog. He doesn't deserve this."

He gives me a sympathetic smile. "Try to go home and get some rest. We'll call as soon as we know what he was given, and then you can report it to the police."

"Thanks." I lean over, whisper in Angus's ear. "I'll come back and get you really soon."

When I get home, I call Parker and tell her what happened. "I know it was Andrew. He's angry because Sophie isn't seeing him anymore."

"I'll do a trace on his phone and see if he was near your house today. Did you keep any samples from the vomit? Any of the meat pieces?" Parker sounds just as furious as me, her voice tight, but her thoughts are more focused. I feel my grip on the phone loosen. She believes me.

"He threw up everywhere in the house, but I haven't looked in the yard yet."

"I'll come over and check it out."

While I wait for Parker, I take a walk around the house to make sure Angus didn't throw up anywhere else. When I enter my room, I take a quick stock of everything. Have the books on my nightstand been moved? My bedding is slightly rumpled, but that could have been from this morning.

I walk over to my desk. Nothing seems out of place, but I have that sick roll in my stomach. I try to think it through logically. The alarm was still set when I got home and the doors were locked. When Greg installed the dog door for Angus we changed the alarm to the pet setting. Anyone taller would've tripped the alarm. *It's impossible. I'm just scaring myself.*

When Parker arrives she doesn't find any remnants of food in the yard, but I'm not surprised. Angus would gulp down anything Andrew threw over the fence.

"I'll find out what his cell records tell us," she says. "We'll know if he was in the area."

"Can't you arrest him?"

"We still have to prove he was the one who did it, and that will be a lot harder if there are no prints or other evidence. Let's see how this plays out. I'll keep you posted."

After she's gone, I grab my supplies and clean up the mess. I feel so bad that Angus was suffering all alone in the house, probably scared out of his mind—and I hate Andrew like never before. After I'm finished cleaning, I take a shower to wash off the medicinal smell of the clinic and the lingering scent of dog vomit. I stand under the warm spray for a long time.

Sophie said she called him this week, but she was vague about how he took the news that she wasn't going to see him anymore. I wonder what else was said during that conversation. I assume she left some things out, to protect me. I would do the same.

I'm toweling off in my bedroom when my cell rings. Marcus. In the panic I forgot to text him that I wasn't coming to the party. I answer on the second ring.

"Sorry! I meant to call," I say.

"Everything okay? You didn't show up tonight."

"When I got home, I found Angus really sick and I had to take him to the clinic."

"Is he okay? What happened?"

"I think Andrew threw some meat laced with drugs into the yard."

"Jesus. What an asshole. Is Angus going to be okay?"

"They have to keep him overnight and check that his liver and kidneys aren't damaged. He's so sick, Marcus—he threw up all over the house, and he couldn't move. It was terrifying seeing him like that."

"I'll come over."

"It's late. You don't have to." But I'm relieved at his offer. I don't want to be alone.

"I'm already out the door. The party is lame without you anyway."

He arrives fifteen minutes later, carrying a bottle of wine and a Styrofoam plate of snacks. He sets them down on the counter, then pulls me in for a hug. It's the first time we've embraced, and for a second it's awkward, my nose bumping into his jaw, but then we fit together for a perfect moment before parting. Now I feel cold, bereft. His body had felt so solid and real.

"You okay?" he says.

"Not really." I walk back into the living room, curl up on the couch. He grabs some glasses in the kitchen, pours the wine, then sets a glass and the plate of snacks in front of me.

"Here. I stole these for you." He flops down beside me.

"Thanks." I take a mini-cheese-quiche, pick at the edges. "I'm so worried about Angus. I never should have brought him into my messed-up life. He was better off in the shelter."

"You didn't know this was going to happen. Have you told Sophie?"

"Not yet. I'll talk to her when she gets home. Jared's parents have rides arranged. We agreed that she'd come home by one." I check my phone, notice it's almost nine already.

"Did you call the police?"

"They're going to trace Andrew's cell and see if he was near our house. And the vet will try to figure out what kind of pills he was given."

"How long does Angus have to stay at the clinic?"

"I'll find out in the morning. I don't know how I'm going to afford all this. The emergency fee is going to be even more expensive because of the holidays, and—"

"Don't worry about that right now. I'll take care of it."

"I don't borrow money from friends."

"Well, you're going to from this one." He holds up a hand to stop me from speaking. "I have lots of investments and no one to spend it on. Let me help, please."

"I'll pay you back as soon as I can."

"I'm not worried about that, but I am worried about you. Andrew is escalating."

"I know. I think he was punishing me because Sophie cut him off. When I tell her what happened to Angus, she's going to be so upset."

"Yes, but she's strong and she has a great support system."

I rest my head on the back of the couch, think over his words. I hope he's right. I give him a small smile. "Thanks for coming over tonight. It helps."

"Of course." He leans over and squeezes my hand. "I just want to be a good friend. I still feel bad about what I said the other day. I had no right to interfere in your relationship."

I study his face, searching out any hidden meaning in the words. Does he realize he's still holding my hand? His skin is so hot. We're so close. I could lean over and kiss him, which is a crazy thought and one I really shouldn't be having. I shouldn't even be on this couch with him.

"It's okay," I say. "Friends should be honest." I hold his gaze.

"Yes, but I went too far. My timing sucked." He releases my hand, takes a sip of his wine, and I wonder if he's gathering courage to say more. What does he mean about his timing? He hesitates for another second, but then, as though he's decided something, he gives his head a small shake and picks up the remote. "Should we watch the ball drop in New York?"

"Sounds good." I focus on the merriment on TV, the noisy crowd, and the lively cohosts. If there had ever been a window into his thoughts, even a small one, he'd just slammed it shut.

When Sophie walks through the door a few minutes after one, she's smiling, her cheeks red from the cold, and singing under her breath. Sophie *never* sings. Has she been drinking? Jared's parents said it would be a dry party, but it wouldn't surprise me if some of the kids snuck booze. I watch as she takes off her coat and boots. She isn't stumbling or wobbly. She notices Marcus and me sitting in the living room and comes over to flop down in the other chair.

"Happy New Year," I say. "How was the party?"

"Good." She yawns, one of her hands reaching up to twirl a chunk of her hair, the violet hue catching the soft light in the living room. "How about yours?" Before I can answer she looks around, a confused expression on her face. "Where's Angus?"

"I had to take him to the clinic." There's no way to soften this. I have to spit it out. "When I got home from work tonight, I found him in the house and he was really sick. I think Andrew threw meat over the fence with some sort of pills in it, but he's going to be okay."

She looks stunned, her hand still holding a chunk of her hair. "You sure it was him?"

"He's the only person who's angry at me. I hurt him, so now he has to hurt me."

Her eyes are shiny now and I know she's close to tears. "I think it's my fault, Mom. He wanted me to come over today, but I ignored all his calls. That's probably why he did it."

"It's not your fault," Marcus says in a kind voice. "You didn't create this."

"He knows where we live because he followed me home from school one day. I never should have written him. . . ." Even though I'd suspected Andrew had been following the both of us, it still scares the crap out of me to hear it said aloud. I hate the thought of him stalking her.

"You just wanted a relationship with your father," Marcus says. "The only crime here is that he screwed up the chance to get to know an amazing kid."

Their eyes meet and he gives her a smile. "I mean, from what your mom has told me anyway. You could be a total pain in the ass, for all I know."

She cracks a small smile, but then it falters and she looks at me. "He admitted he left the CD, but I was scared that if I told you, he'd be arrested and then he'd hate me. Are you mad?"

"Oh, honey. No. But I'm sorry he put you in that position. That was really unfair."

She takes a breath and leans over and picks up one of Angus's toys from the floor, squishes it a few times, letting the air out in a slow squeak. "Poor Angus."

"You can come with me when I visit him tomorrow."

"Okay." Her phone vibrates and she glances down at the display. "It's Jared checking to make sure I got home okay. Can I go to my room and call him?"

"Sure, baby. We can talk more in the morning."

"Good night." She gets up from the chair, then looks at Marcus. "I appreciate what you said." He nods.

After she's gone, I say, "Do you want to stay in the spare room? There might be a lot of idiots out on the road tonight."

He glances at his wineglass. "That would probably be wise. If you don't mind?"

"Not at all. I should probably go to bed myself." I feel shy, uncertain of how to handle this. I can't count the times we've sat at the same table or beside each other, but sitting in the dark on this couch feels way more intimate.

I stand up. "I'm going to check the doors."

"You need help?" He clicks off the TV.

"No, I've got it. Do you remember where the spare room is?"

"I think I can find it." Now he stands up.

"Okay." We're two feet from each other. I think about giving him a hug but wonder where that would lead. Then I think about Greg. "Well, good night." I spin around. When I've finished checking all the doors and windows, Marcus has disappeared into the spare room.

My phone ring wakes me up the next morning. Greg calling to wish me a Happy New Year. "Sorry I didn't call last night," he says. "There was no reception at the chalet."

"That's okay, but I had a crappy night." I tell him about

Angus. "I'm hoping he's better this morning." I glance at the clock, wonder when the clinic opens.

"You and Sophie have to stay with me so I can protect you," Greg says, his voice firm. "I'm taking the early ferry home. I can meet you at my house around noon."

"You sure you want that?"

"You know I'm ready." He leaves the rest unsaid. I'm the one who has doubts, and we both know it. I think about Marcus sleeping in the spare room. It feels good to be talking to Greg, reminds me how comfortable and easy it is to be around him. I don't worry about what I'm saying or how I'm saying it. Maybe this will be a good test for us as a couple.

"Okay," I say. "We'll pack some things." I'll tell Sophie when she wakes. She might not be thrilled about staying with Greg, but at least we'll still be in Dogwood Bay.

I take a quick shower, pull on some leggings and a sweater. When I walk out into the kitchen, Marcus is already sitting at the table with a cup of coffee. His clothes and hair are rumpled and he has a dark shadow on his jaw, but it just makes him look even more attractive. I have a twinge of doubt about agreeing to stay with Greg. Too late now.

"Good morning," Marcus says. "Hope you don't mind I made coffee."

"Of course not." I pour myself a cup. "Want to stay for breakfast?"

"I should probably get out of your hair, unless you want me to go to the clinic with you?"

"We'll be okay. I don't want to take up all your time." We're being so polite, which is odd. You'd think him spending the night would have made us closer as friends. Instead we're tiptoeing around each other like complete strangers.

"It's really no problem," he says.

"If Angus is allowed to go home, we'll probably take him straight to Greg's."

He looks up from his mug. "He's back?"

"On his way. We're going to stay at his house for a few days."

"Oh." He's staring at me, but then he jolts his head as though snapping himself out of something, and says, "That's good. I feel better knowing you're safe."

"Do you?" The words are out before I have a chance to think about them.

We're looking at each other, his expression uncertain, as though he's not sure what I'm really asking. I hold his gaze steady. His lips part. He's going to say something. Then shuffling footsteps behind us. He looks over my shoulder. Sophie wanders into the kitchen. I take a step back, as though she caught us kissing. She gives me an odd look, then yawns.

"Can we go get Angus now?" she says.

"I'll call the clinic soon."

Marcus stands up. "I better get going."

"I'll walk you out." At the door, I say, "Thanks for coming over last night."

"Sure." He steps out, then turns. "You tell Greg that if he lets anything happen to you, he'll have to answer to me." He's smiling, but there's tension around his eyes. Is it worry for me, or something else? I feel awkward, off balance, like the porch is tilting under my feet.

"I will." I watch him drive away, then close the door.

CHAPTER TWENTY-FIVE

SOPHIE

JANUARY 2017

"Your room has a great view," Greg says. "You'll see in a minute."

I nod and try to look pleased, but I don't like the way he says "your" room, as though I'm going to be staying here for long. He's showing me around his house and Mom is along for the tour, but I know she's been over to his place lots. I'm trying not to think about that. I mean, I'm happy she has a boyfriend, but the thought of my mom having sex is just too weird. This is the first time we've all spent the night in the same house. I'm really hoping the spare room is far away from his room or I'm going to have to keep earbuds in all night, just in case.

His house is in an older subdivision, two stories, with a robin's-egg-blue bathroom, orange countertops in the kitchen, and an almond-colored fridge and stove, like it's all out of some movie from the seventies. It smells like lemon polish and Windex and the carpet has vacuum lines. He must've cleaned up before we got here. Above the fireplace there's a painting of a surfer standing with his board watching the waves, and he has some framed photographs of his family on the mantel. I drift past, glance at their faces. They look happy.

I'll be sleeping upstairs at the end of the hall. The room is big, with a queen bed and windows that look out over his backyard. I wish Angus was with us—he'd love digging holes in all that snow—but he's stuck at the clinic for another night. The bedding looks new, a deep purple duvet cover and pillowcases, and smells like fresh laundry detergent. I wonder if he bought it today and washed it already. There's also a small TV on the dresser.

"I set that up before you came over," he says. "Thought you might want some privacy."

I turn to look at him. He's standing in the doorway, Mom beside him, and I know she wants me to say something nice, but I'm realizing, for the first time, how they don't really fit together. Mom is kind of preppy, wholesome, like one of those women who go back to school in their forties and becomes a doctor or something. Greg looks like one of those guys who never really grows up. I instantly feel bad for the thought. "Thanks for letting us stay here."

"No problem. I want you to feel at home. If you guys end up staying longer, you can paint the room whatever color you want."

"We're going to be *living* here?" Mom didn't say anything like that. When we went to visit Angus, she just said we were going to Greg's until the police find out if Dad was in our neighborhood yesterday afternoon. The vet figured out Angus was drugged with Ambien. Mom freaked when she heard that.

Greg's face kind of turns red and he looks at Mom. Her face is also flushing. "We don't know yet what's going to happen," she says. "Let's take one day at a time for now."

I give her a how-can-you-do-this-to-me look. She smiles brightly and says, "So should we order pizza for dinner? Greg says there's a really good restaurant nearby."

"I'm not hungry." After we saw Angus, Mom and I went to Tim Hortons, then home to pack up. My sandwich is still sitting like a lump in my stomach.

"We'll order a couple types," Greg says. "You can decide later."

I sit down on the bed. "Okay if I hang out in here for a little bit and watch some TV?" I make my eyes big and sad. "I'm just really upset about Angus."

Mom narrows her eyes at me, making it clear she knows I'm playing her, but I know she won't say anything in front of Greg. I *am* upset about Angus and what my dad did to him, but mostly I want to be alone so I can call Jared.

"Sure," she says. "Come out whenever you're ready."

After they're gone, I close the door behind them, then settle on the bed and turn on the TV. I don't plan on watching anything, but I want the background noise. I flip to the music channel and it's playing one of the songs we listened to at Jared's party last night. I smile at the memory. The party was fun, and Jared was right, his friends were nice. Even the girls—one of them said she loved my hair. Jared was also right about his parents leaving us alone. I only saw them once at the door, then we hung out downstairs for the rest of the time. A few kids had brought bottles of booze and Jared rolled a couple of joints. I wasn't going to smoke any, but then he blew some in my mouth and it was kind of sexy and fun and I ended up getting high.

We snuck upstairs to his room and made out for a while. We even took our shirts off and it was amazing, feeling his skin next to mine. I almost wanted to go all the way with him, had made up my mind to just get it over with, but when his hands started going down my pants, I panicked and said no. He rolled over and stared up at the ceiling for a while, his chest heaving.

"I thought you were into it?"

"I am, but that doesn't mean I want to do everything."

He turned and looked at me. "Are you a virgin?"

I felt the heat in my cheeks. "Screw you." I started to get up.

He grabbed my hand. "No, sorry. Stay. I didn't know. I'll slow things down, okay?" I settled back down beside him and he rolled closer. "I wish you could stay here forever."

"You'd get bored of me."

"No," he said firmly. "I'll never get bored of you."

We texted all night after I got home, and a few times today. He knows we're staying at Greg's. My phone vibrates now. *How's it going?*

Okay.

Heard from your dad?

No. He's such an asshole. I can't believe he tried to kill Angus!

Want to get something to eat?

Greg and my mom are ordering pizza.

So?

I'll ask.

Twenty minutes later, Jared picks me up. I thought Mom would insist I stay home with them, but I think she feels bad about everything and only asked me to be back by ten. When Jared comes to the door she walks us out. "Be careful on the roads."

"Sure thing, Lindsey." My mom smiles, but it looks fake, then she closes the door. Sometimes I get the feeling she might not really like Jared, but I'm not sure why. It probably doesn't help when he calls her by her first name, which is pretty bold. We get in his car.

"Why do you call my mom Lindsey?"

He looks surprised. "I don't know her last name. I mean, yours is Nash, but she's divorced. I've always called her Lindsey at my house, so I thought it was okay."

"I don't think she likes it."

"Whatever." He shrugs. "I'll stop." He's staring out the window, so I can't tell if he's embarrassed, but I decide to move on. I've got bigger things to worry about.

We drive around town for a bit, stop at my house so I can grab a few things that I forgot to pack earlier, then decide to go to the Muddy Bean because they have free Wi-Fi and their food is good and lots of kids from our school hang out there. We're sitting at a table, scrolling through our phones and sipping our coffee, when I feel someone standing behind me. I look up. Andrew.

I make a little noise and drop my phone onto the table. Before I can say anything or move, he pulls over a chair and sits down between us.

"What's going on, Sophie?" His eyes are angry, his voice almost vibrating, as if he's trying to hold everything inside. I want to run away, but I'm blocked by his body, the force of his energy. It makes me feel like a little kid who's gotten caught doing something horrible.

"I don't want to talk to you." I shoot a look at Jared. His eyes are wide as he stares back at me.

"You said you would come over. I sat around waiting."

"I *never* said I would come over. You just assumed I would."

He flinches, then shakes his head. "Okay, maybe you're right. But why are you ignoring my calls?"

"I told you I couldn't see you anymore. You broke our deal."

"So now we can't even talk?"

"I *know* what you did," I say. "I *know* you drugged Angus."

He looks stunned, completely, absolutely stunned—and confused. He blinks for a couple of seconds, like he's still trying to figure out what I said. "Who's Angus?"

"I think you should get out of here," Jared says. "She doesn't want to talk to you." My dad holds up a hand, stopping him from talking.

"Who *the fuck* is Angus?"

"Our dog! I told you about him."

He makes an angry sort of laugh. "You think I drugged your damn dog?"

"It was you. He ate pills. The vet said it was Ambien. You tossed them over the fence in meat. He's still in the clinic—he almost died."

"Why would I do that, Sophie?" His voice is upset, almost pleading, but angry too. I want to stop talking to him, want to get up and leave, but I'm too far gone.

"Because you're so mad at Mom for not falling for your stupid present."

"Yeah, I can see how killing her dog would make her want to be with me again."

"You're sick and twisted," I say, tears running down my eyes. "You aren't better at all."

He rocks backward, closes his eyes like he's absorbing the blow, then shakes his head and leans closer across the table.

"I did *not* drug your dog. But if someone did, then you have big problems, little girl."

"*You're* my problem," I say. "How did you even know I was here?" When he doesn't answer, I say, "You were following me again." He must have been sitting outside our house, waiting. I never should have stopped there.

"I'm your father. I'm worried about you."

I stand up. "Just leave me alone!" Jared also stands up on the other side of the table.

Andrew grabs my forearm. "Listen to me, Sophie. Someone is screwing around with you and your mom. Maybe you should stay with me for a few days. I can protect you."

I laugh. "You've *never* protected me."

"I was there for the first seven years of your life and I made sure no one ever hurt you. I was the one who taught you to swim, to ride a bike, everything."

"*You* hurt me," I say, my voice breaking. I can feel people watching us, but I don't care anymore. "Don't you get it? You're the one who hurt me—and now you're stalking me!"

"Come on, Sophie," Jared says. He's standing behind me now. "Let's go."

I stare down at my dad's hand on my arm, and he slowly lets go, drops it in his lap. He looks sad now. It doesn't make me feel guilty anymore. Mom was right. It's all an act.

"Stay away from me," I say, then walk away with Jared. When we climb into his car, I see Andrew still watching from inside the coffee shop. I turn to Jared. "I want to go back to Greg's. Drive fast. I don't want him to see where we're going."

CHAPTER TWENTY-SIX

Lindsey

I squirt soap into the sink until the suds rise, then dump our plates, salad bowls, and cutlery into the water and scrub at the melted cheese and tomato sauce. I can see out of the window into the dark of Greg's side yard. I reach up and tug the blinds down. Greg is moving around behind me, putting away the leftover pizza. I've been to his house many times, but I'm uncomfortable tonight and not sure why. It could be because he keeps telling me to "make yourself at home," or because of the look on Sophie's face when Greg implied we might stay indefinitely. I glance over at him as he shoves the pizza box into the recycling.

"You okay?" he says, catching me watching.

"Yes, just thinking about Sophie." I give him a smile. "Thanks for all this."

"It's my pleasure." He stands straight. "So, what would you like to do now? Watch TV?" He's uncomfortable too, I realize. Whenever we spend time together, it's a "date," or we go straight to bed. Neither of us knows how to just be around each other. We've never had weekends puttering at home or evenings spent doing our own thing under the same roof.

"Sure, TV sounds great." It will come, in time, I tell myself. But I still have an itchy wanting-to-run feeling. I'm not ready for this. Not ready to play house with him.

Greg finds an action movie and I say it sounds good, but I don't really care what we watch and would have agreed to anything. I'm distracted, wondering about Sophie and Jared. Maybe I should have told her to stay home, but I wanted to see her smile again.

Headlights pull in the driveway and cast streaks of light on the wall. I stand to look out the window and recognize Jared's car.

"Sophie's home," I say. My relief is short-lived when I see the silhouette of their two heads coming together for a kiss. I move away from the window.

Downstairs I hear Sophie softly closing the front door, unzipping her coat, pulling off her boots, then light steps as she walks up the stairs. She leans against the entranceway of the living room, wraps a strand of her hair around her finger.

"What are you guys watching?"

"*Iron Man*," I say. "Want to join us?"

"Thanks, but I'm tired." She gives us a small wave and disappears down the hall.

I try to focus on the movie, but I can't get into the plot. "I'm pretty tired too. Think maybe I'll just go to bed."

"Yeah? You want me to—"

"No, no, stay and enjoy your movie." I get ready for bed, washing my face and applying cream, brushing my teeth. When I'm done, I hesitate for a moment about whether to place my toothbrush beside Greg's in his holder. In the end, I tucked it into my overnight bag.

I walk down the hall to Sophie's room, knock gently, but she doesn't answer. I want to go in and talk to her but decide to give her some space.

When Greg comes to bed an hour later, I'm still awake, staring at the ceiling. I hear the rustle of clothes as he moves around the bedroom, the water running in the bathroom, his electric toothbrush. I should feel happy about these domestic noises, maybe even comforted, but I miss my bed at home, miss the weight of Angus on my feet. Greg slides into bed beside me and drapes his hand across my stomach. I slowly roll onto my side, away from him. His hand drifts over my hip, pulls me against his body while he kisses the back of my neck.

"Not when Sophie is in the house," I whisper.

"She can't hear from her room."

"That's not the point."

He lets his breath out in a sigh as he rolls onto his back. "It's not about Sophie."

I roll over too. "What do you mean?"

He props himself up on his elbow and turns to face me. "This isn't going to happen for us, is it?"

"It just feels strange with Sophie in the house. I'm sure after a few days—"

"That's not what I'm saying."

I'm quiet, looking up at his face in the shadows. "I don't know," I finally say.

"Yes, you do," he says. "I can tell when a woman is crazy about me and when she isn't."

"I like you a lot, but—"

"It's okay, Lindsey. I've been around the block a few times. You don't have to give me the speech." He doesn't sound angry, more resigned.

"Do you really want this either?" I say. "Are you ready to be a stepfather to a teen girl? She'll always be part of our lives. She'll come home on weekends, vacations."

"I like Sophie."

"I know."

"But I was also hoping we could start our own family in time."

"I'm almost forty years old."

"Lots of women have babies in their forties."

"I have a daughter who's turning eighteen in weeks. I just don't think I can start back at the beginning again." Why didn't I tell him that when we first started dating? Probably because I knew it would be the end of things. "We should have had this conversation before. I'm sorry."

"I didn't want to ask because then I'd have to hear it out loud. I guess maybe I was hoping in time . . ." So I wasn't the only one who'd been avoiding reality.

We lapse into silence. I feel like I should say something, but any words of comfort or attempts to explain further would just be patronizing.

"I'll call Jenny in the morning," I say. "We can stay with her."

"What about your brother?"

"It's the first place Andrew might look. He doesn't know where Jenny lives."

"Do you want me to sleep on the couch?"

"Of course not. It's your bed." I pause. "Should I sleep on the couch?"

"Stay here," he says. "We might as well be comfortable."

"I'm really sorry."

"Me too." He rolls closer. "We can still cuddle, right? Gets cold in here. . . ."

I laugh. "Sure."

When I wake, Greg is already showered and sitting in the kitchen. He's friendly over coffee, though maybe a little overly polite as he offers me cream and sugar twice and asks if I want anything to eat. I glance at my phone, check my e-mails. When I look up, he's watching me.

"I'm waiting to hear back from Jenny," I say.

"If you can't get hold of her, I'm sure we can work something out for a few days."

"Thanks. I really appreciate that."

"Hey, just because it's not Lindsey and Greg forever doesn't mean we can't be friends." But his smile isn't meeting his eyes and he keeps taking sips of his coffee, like his mouth is dry, or he's trying to keep his hands busy. I'm definitely leaving his house, even if Sophie and I have to get a hotel. His cell rings and his face tenses when he sees the number. "I better take this."

"Problem?"

He shakes his head. "Just work stuff." But he answers his phone abruptly, then walks downstairs as though he doesn't want me to hear the conversation.

Sophie's still in her room and I decide to wake her while Greg is busy so I can tell her the change of plans in private. I knock on her door. "Sophie, honey, can I speak with you?"

"Yeah."

She's still in bed, her sketchpad braced against her legs as she works on a drawing.

"Everything okay? Why aren't you getting ready for school?"

"I wanted to finish this."

I look at her drawing, the dark strokes of leaves and gossamer butterfly wings taking flight into an upward spiral, reaching for something out of sight. I remember what she'd said weeks ago, about the butterfly effect, and the coffee burns in my stomach.

"So there's been a change of plans," I say. "We're going to stay with Jenny for a few days. We'll pick up Angus and take the ferry down to Vancouver after your last class."

She stops drawing, looks at me. "Why are we leaving Greg's already?"

"We talked last night and realized things aren't going to work out between us."

"You *broke up*? But why?"

"We're just very different people. We should've figured that out sooner, but I guess we were both hoping . . . I'm sorry to drag you through this, honey."

Now she looks annoyed. "Yeah. You're making me leave again."

I'm not sure if she means when she was a kid or when we left our house yesterday, but either way, she's right. For years I never even brought a date home until Greg. After living all over the place when we were hiding from Andrew, I hadn't wanted to put her through more upheaval. Now I can't seem to stop shaking up her world. Each day is a new earthquake.

"I know," I say. "I'm sorry. We'll talk about it later, okay? I'll help you pack."

"I have school this week. I can't go to Jenny's."

"It's just until the police can talk to your father and hopefully arrest him. I'm sure your teachers will understand and we might be able to get your lessons e-mailed."

"What if they can't prove it was him? Will we have to stay in Vancouver?" She's getting more upset, her face red and splotchy, her hand wrapping around a strand of hair.

"I don't know. If your father finds us at Jenny's, we'll have to go somewhere else."

She sets her drawing to the side, tosses her pen on top as though she's giving up. "He came into the coffee shop last night when I was there with Jared. He sat down with us."

My eyes widen before I can stop them. That's why she went straight to her room. I'm upset she didn't tell me, but I don't want to scold her. Not now.

"What did he say?"

"He was angry because I've been ignoring him. He *followed* me there, Mom." She looks really scared. "I don't know how to make him leave me alone."

"That is exactly why we have to get out of Dogwood."

"What about Jared?"

"You can call, Skype. Maybe he can come visit on the weekend, but I don't know, honey. Your dad could use him to follow us."

"He kept insisting he wouldn't hurt Angus—and he sounded so convincing. It was like he even believed *himself.* " She leans toward me. "I don't want to ever see him again."

"You won't. I'll make sure of it." I stand up from the bed. "Why don't you shower, and I'll drive you to school. I'll talk to your principal and we'll work it all out."

"Can I at least tell Delaney and Jared where we're going?"

"Tell them we have to leave, but don't mention Vancouver."

"Do you think we'll be back for my birthday?"

"I hope so, baby."

"This is so surreal."

"I know, but it's going to be okay. I promise."

I pour myself another cup of coffee and listen to the water running in the shower. I wonder what my daughter is thinking. I can't imagine what this must be like for her—scared of her father, unsure of her future. I promised her everything was going to be okay, but I don't know how I'm going to deliver on that promise. I just have to get her away from here.

Greg has been outside for a long time. I check the bedroom, but he's not there. I walk down the stairs, noticing a cold draft. The front door is open. "Greg?" I almost trip over him sitting on the front steps. He's holding his hand to the side of his head, his fingers red with blood.

"Greg! What happened? Are you okay?"

He looks up at me, wincing. "I was shoveling the top of the driveway, bending over, you know? And I heard a vehicle coming up fast. I tried to move out of the way, but it hit me, in the shoulder—must have been the side mirror." He takes his hand away, looks at the blood. "I smacked my head on a rock when I fell."

"Come inside and let me look." I help him to his feet and we slowly walk upstairs, where I sit him at the table, grab some ice from the freezer, and wrap it in a towel. He flinches as I gently press it to the wound. "I think you're going to need stitches," I say. "Did you see the car?"

"Sounded like a truck. By the time I looked up it was already around the corner."

Sophie comes into the kitchen, dressed in school clothes and with her hair wet. She stops abruptly when she sees us. "What's going on?"

"A truck hit Greg when he was shoveling the driveway, but it took off."

"Do you think it was Andrew?" she says, and I nod.

"It could have been an accident," Greg says. "It's hard to see through the trees at the end of the property. I should have been wearing my reflective vest."

I give him a look. "You have to talk to the police—and we're taking you to the hospital."

"I just need some Tylenol." He stands up and walks toward the bathroom, but he looks unsteady, his face pale. I follow after him, Sophie close behind.

"You definitely need stitches," I say. "I'll drive you to the hospital."

He's looking in the mirror, gingerly touching the wound. "I can take my truck."

"That's crazy. You can't drive right now."

"You should let her drive you," Sophie says. "At least that way blood will get all over our car, not your truck."

"She has a point," Greg says. He's smiling, but he's not meeting my eyes, and I wonder if it has something to do with our talk last night. I can't do anything about that, but I'm getting Sophie out of this house and far away from Dogwood before Andrew can make his next move.

CHAPTER TWENTY-SEVEN

LINDSEY

On the way to the emergency room, I call Corporal Parker, who comes to the hospital right away. She speaks with Greg while Sophie and I go for coffee in the cafeteria, then comes down and meets us. I wait while she stirs sugar into her coffee. She licks the spoon with a little smile of satisfaction before setting it to the side. She catches my surprised expression.

"It's an old habit," she says. "My mother never let me have sweets, so I always licked her spoon when she wasn't looking." I smile out of politeness. I'm too anxious to enjoy any childhood stories. She straightens her body as though ready to get down to business.

"It will take another day to get Andrew's phone records. In the meantime, I'll ask him to come in for an interview. He probably won't tell me much, but he might slip on something and we'll see if he lets us examine the truck without a warrant, which will take longer to get. If he's parked it on a street or in a public area we can have a look without his permission."

"We're going to stay with my friend in Vancouver," I say.

Jenny called back while we were waiting for the doctor, insisted we stay with her. *I'm making up the beds now.*

"I think that's a good idea," Parker says. "I'll keep you updated on the investigation."

"He might go to my house. He'll try to find out where I've gone."

"I'll do some drive-bys."

"Excuse me." Sophie stands and walks over to get another coffee.

I lean closer to Parker. "Please tell me you'll arrest Andrew."

"If we have enough evidence to prove he's the one responsible, then yes."

"Who else could it be?"

"We just need to make sure." There's something in her eyes, something she's holding back, and I wonder what Greg told her. I glance at Sophie. She's staring out the window as she waits for her coffee, one of her hands tugging at her hair, winding it around and around.

Greg's quiet on the way home and doesn't say much when we drop him off, either. The doctor said Greg is going to be okay, but he has multiple stitches, a bruised shoulder, and he might be out of work for a day or two. He has painkillers, but I still feel like the worst girlfriend—*ex-girlfriend*—in the world when I tell him we want to catch the afternoon ferry. "Do you mind?" I say. "Do you want me to call anyone for you?"

"I'll just watch TV," he says. "I'll be fine, but you guys should get to Vancouver." He grabs my hand. "Take care of yourself, okay? You need anything, you call me."

"Thanks." I smile, blinking back tears. Why does he have to be so damn nice?

After we say good-bye, we go by Sophie's school, speak to

her principal, and pick up her lesson plans, which Sophie would have been more than happy to leave behind. Then we get Angus from the clinic. Though Marcus offered to pay for the vet bill, I put the whole amount on my credit card, wincing when I see the balance. Angus was so excited to see us he nearly dragged Sophie out of the clinic and leapt into the backseat.

Parker meets us at our house—she offered to escort us while we closed up the house and got some more belongings. When I shut off the last light and lock the door, I pause on the porch, looking back in the window. Our Christmas tree is still standing there, alone in the shadows. Our life has stalled, just like it did eleven years ago.

I can feel Parker and Sophie behind me. Sophie shifts her weight, moves closer and gently touches the back of my arm. "Let's go, Mom."

The terminal is lit up and the ferry—almost the size of a cruise ship—looms in the water. Headlights bounce up and down as cars unload, and the metal ramp makes a hollow *whoomp* as each vehicle passes over. I watch the workers in their reflective vests direct the traffic, their hands moving in a well-choreographed dance. We'll be loading soon.

We didn't travel often to Vancouver when I was a child—the ferry tickets cost a lot for a family of four—but Andrew and I took Sophie over a few times, a concert, a school trip to the science museum, a visit to the aquarium. Sophie loved all the names of the boats: *Queen of Coquitlam, Queen of Cowichan, Queen of Oak Bay*. For her it was a wonderful adventure. She wanted to ride the elevator, walk outside on the decks and look for orcas and humpback whales, eat burgers and fish and chips and chicken fingers with fries and thick gravy in the cafeteria.

I rarely ate on the ferry. My stomach was unsettled on the

choppy water, but more from the turmoil in my life, my fear of Andrew as wide and vast as the ocean out the window.

I glance in my side mirrors now and out my back window, looking for a white pickup truck. We've been waiting in the car for an hour, hoping to catch the five o'clock boat, only getting out to walk Angus a couple of times.

Sophie's worried Andrew will try to contact her again—"He was so mad when I walked out on him, Mom"—but so far she hasn't gotten any texts or voice mails. I watch her playing on her phone for a moment, thinking about how her cell is always with her wherever she goes.

"Was your father ever alone with your phone?"

She looks sideways at me. "No. Why?"

"I wondered if he could have set it up so he can track us."

She stares down at her phone as if it had turned into a mass of snakes. "You mean like one of those find-a-phone apps?"

"Yes, but he'd have to set it up, right?"

Her face calms as she thinks it through. "It was always in my pocket when I was around him." She looks at me. "Could he put something on the car?"

"God. I don't know. Maybe we should check." We get out and peer underneath my car. "Look for anything small and square," I say. "Like those boxes people hide their keys inside."

We use our phones as flashlights and feel with our hands, which get grimy from dried road salt and cold with crusted snow. People in the line of cars behind us are probably wondering what the hell we're doing, but I don't care. I'm just relieved we don't find anything. Back in the car, Angus whines and licks my neck frantically like I've been gone for five days, not five minutes. Then he shoves his head between us, using the console as a pillow, and closes his eyes. Sophie's phone chirps with a few texts. One after another. Her fingers tap out a response.

"Did you tell Jared we're going to Vancouver?"

She shakes her head. "Just that we're going away for the week but I can't tell anyone where we're going. He's worried about us too."

It's strange for me to think of this boy worrying about my daughter's safety, let alone mine. "Things seem to be getting pretty serious between you two."

Her fingers pause and she turns to look at me with her eyebrows raised. "Really, Mom? This is when we're going to have a heart-to-heart?"

"We're not doing anything else."

"We're running away from my psycho father."

"You can joke all you want, but I know you're upset."

She puts down her phone. "Why couldn't he be normal? He didn't have to be perfect, you know? I just wanted a dad."

"I'm really sorry it didn't work out like you hoped. I wanted that for you too. It's one of the reasons I stayed with him for so long."

She lets out her breath in a heavy sigh and leans back against the seat. "You must think I'm really stupid for falling for his lies."

"Not at all." I touch her hand so that she turns to face me. "I know how charming he can be. I married him, remember?"

"Yeah, what were *you* thinking?" She gives me a look.

"I was thinking I might get a great daughter out of the deal." I smile.

She stares out the window and fiddles with her phone case. "What are we going to do tomorrow? I don't want to sit around being scared all day."

"How about we visit some art galleries?"

"Okay, and maybe we can go downtown."

"Sure. Whatever you want."

The parking lights flash from a car at the beginning of the line. Finally we're loading. We wait on the vehicle deck until the ferry pulls away from the terminal, then we weave between

260 · Chevy Stevens

the cars and walk to the side of the boat, hanging our heads out the large open windows. The salty wind plays with our hair as we watch the harbor lights grow smaller behind us, then disappear.

We arrive at Jenny's exhausted from the stress of the day and the boat ride. Chris called when we were unloading from the ferry—I'd left him a message earlier, but he was working late. His girlfriend said he's been putting in some extra hours, trying to save up before the baby comes. When I told him about Greg being injured, I had to hold the phone away from my ear, he was swearing so much. After a bit he calmed down and said, "Come stay with us."

"It would be too much for Maddie. You need to focus on your family."

"You *are* my family, dumbass."

"I'll be fine in Vancouver. I promise."

"You better be."

The words sounded ominous, but I know the threat isn't aimed at me. I'm glad Chris has Maddie and the baby in his life, or I would be worried about him confronting Andrew. I called most of my clients while we were waiting in the ferry lineup and explained that a sudden emergency has come up and rearranged the schedule so Rachelle could cover my jobs.

I wasn't sure how things were between me and Marcus since our awkward good-bye the other morning, so I texted him: *Have to get out of town. Will call you later and explain.*

He texted back. *Everything okay?*

Not really but we're all right. I'll fill you in soon.

Sophie goes to bed with her phone, and Jenny and I stay up late, talking over wine while Angus keeps us company. We're in our comfy clothes—leggings and slouchy sweater for me, yoga pants and a NAMASTE T-shirt for her. She's been teaching yoga and her arms are sinewy, her movements almost ballet-languid. I'm enjoying the time with my friend, if not the reason for the visit. We've had a few glasses of wine and my face feels warm. Jenny's is also flushed, her eyes brighter, her voice louder. Our serious conversation turns to bawdy jokes and black humor about the state of our love lives. She's been trying Tinder, shows me how to swipe right, and I help her pick out some new photos for her profile. After midnight she urges me to get some rest.

"This mess will all still be here tomorrow and you need some sleep," she says. "I'll make breakfast. You're starting to look like a bag of bones."

"Gee. Thanks a lot."

She gives me a wink. "I'd still jump you."

I laugh. "Times that tough, huh?"

Her expression turns serious. "I'm sorry he's putting you through all of this again."

I lean over and give her a hug. "Thank you."

It's only six in the morning, but I've been tossing and turning for the last hour and finally decide to get up and make coffee. I pour a cup, pause for a moment, then add two heaping tablespoons of sugar. I need the jolt. My eyes feel puffy and I'm sure I look like hell. Sophie is still sleeping, but Jenny will probably bounce out of her room soon and offer to make me a spinach power smoothie, or a flaxseed pancake, or something else guaranteed to give me energy. I scroll through my Facebook news feed, mindlessly reading celebrity gossip.

A text pops up from Marcus. *Give me a call when you can. Worried about you!*

You up now?

Yes!

I grab another cup of coffee and dial his number. He answers immediately. "You okay?"

"Yeah, sorry I didn't call last night," I say. "I was exhausted."

"What happened?"

"A truck hit Greg when he was shoveling the driveway. He didn't see who did it, but I think it was Andrew."

"Oh, shit. Was he hurt badly?"

"He has a minor concussion and stitches, but he's going to be all right." I hoped this was still true. I texted him last night letting him know we arrived safely in Vancouver and asking how he was feeling. He never answered.

"Where are you?"

"In Vancouver. We're going to stay with Jenny until they arrest Andrew for drugging Angus. They're also checking his phone records to see if he was around Greg's house."

"They haven't arrested him yet?" He sounds as shocked as I feel.

"They have to interview him first and look at his truck." I glance at the clock. "I'll call Dana soon. She's the officer who's been working our case."

"How is Sophie handling all this?"

"She's shook up, seems to be wrestling with a lot of guilt, but I'm the one who let her down. It was hard enough on her with my dragging her over to Greg's, then we break up, and now we're in Vancouver—miles away from her best friend and her boyfriend. The poor kid has been through so much. What the hell am I going to do?"

"Whoa. Back everything up. What happened with you and Greg?"

"We realized we don't have a future so there's no sense pushing things." I wait for him to say something about how he knew this was going to happen, but he's just quiet. The seconds stretch out and I have to fight the urge to fill in the empty space with chatter.

"That's a big change," he finally says. "You okay?"

"Yes." I look around Jenny's tidy kitchen, feeling a pang for my home, my normal routine. I'd be getting up and heading over to train with Marcus at his house, then we'd visit over coffee. I'm disappointed that I won't be seeing him today. I've come to rely on those workouts, the endorphin high, then sitting and having deep talks about life or laughing about nothing.

"I won't be able to work out with you today," I say. "You going to miss me?" I'm trying for a joking friendliness, to ease the stress and brutal reality of my current situation, but maybe I am a little curious. *Will* he miss me?

"It's definitely not going to be the same. The time goes a lot faster when I'm torturing you." His tone is also friendly and teasing. Nothing more.

"Maybe I'll do a few push-ups and get Jenny to yell at me."

He breaks out into a laugh. I lean into the phone, intrigued by the sound. He seems different, lighter. I'm not sure what's changed.

Then I think about Andrew again. He probably knows I go to Marcus's house. He may have even watched us through the window as we talked and drank coffee. I feel another surge of anger, hate how he's invaded my life. "Be careful today," I say. "He might be looking for me."

"I hope he shows up here. I'd like to have a few words with him."

"Please don't do anything crazy. If you see him just call the police, okay?"

Silence for a moment, then, "Okay. Give me a call as soon as you know what's happening. If you need anything from your house, I can bring it over on the ferry."

"I really appreciate that."

"Stay safe, okay?"

"Always." We're both silent now. I think of him standing in his kitchen, or maybe he's sitting on the side of his bed and looking out the window at the ocean. I wonder what he wears in the morning. The black robe I've seen hanging on his bathroom door? Boxer shorts?

"I should go," I say. "It was nice to hear your voice." My own voice is softer and more revealing than I meant it to be. I hang up the phone before he can respond.

My next call is to Corporal Parker, who tells me she interviewed Andrew last night.

"He's been very accommodating and insisting it isn't him, of course," she says. "I'm still recommending charges and we'll be arresting him later today, but I have to warn you that if the Crown doesn't feel we have enough for a case, he'll be out within twenty-four hours."

"What about the phone records?"

"They don't show him around Greg's house in the morning, but he admits he followed Sophie home from the coffee shop last night, which isn't a violation because Greg's address isn't on the bond, just yours."

"Why did he follow Sophie? He had to be looking for me."

"He said he didn't know that you were staying there. He thinks someone is stalking you and Sophie and he wanted to make sure no one was following her."

"This is the most ridiculous thing I've ever heard. You don't believe him, do you?"

"It's about what we can prove, and right now we don't have evidence he hit Greg with his truck. There aren't any marks or dents, not even a scratch. It could've been someone angry at

Greg. He mentioned he's had a few problems lately, but I can't go into that with you."

"Problems? He's never . . ." I remember the call he got the morning he was attacked. And his joke about needing to borrow money. Maybe there's some trouble in his life I don't know about. I'm upset that he didn't confide in me, but then again, I haven't exactly been open to listening lately. "It doesn't matter," I say. "I *know* this was Andrew."

"My gut says it was Andrew too, but the Crown doesn't care much about instinct."

"I'm going to have to live in hiding for the rest of my life."

I hear her take a breath, then let it out through her teeth. "I'm going to keep a close eye on him. I promise, Lindsey."

"Thanks. I appreciate that." I glance down the hall. I can hear Jenny moving around in her bedroom and Sophie will be awake soon. "I have to go."

She's quiet for a couple of beats, then says, "Be careful."

"I will."

I end the call and stare down into my coffee. A fruit fly has landed on top and drowned. Its little body floats in a circle. When I stab at it with my fingertip, it keeps drifting away.

CHAPTER TWENTY-EIGHT

Sophie

Jared's face is a shadowed blur on my laptop screen, going in and out of focus, his smile frozen for a moment, his voice delayed like in a foreign movie. The walls of his bedroom come clear, then the rest of him. He leans closer, his black eyes inches from the screen. I feel like I could reach out and touch his wide bottom lip, have the urge to press my lips against his like I might have done to a teen movie star poster when I was a kid. I glance at the little thumbnail shot of my image in the bottom corner and try to turn my head in a way that makes my hair look the best and shows a little bit of my collarbone and the hollow at the top of my cleavage.

"Where are you?" he says.

"I'm in the spare bedroom. It's nice." The room is fresh, with pale turquoise-blue walls, and a white bedspread with crisp dark-colored tree branches and a splash of teal sky at the top. When I woke up this morning, I felt like I was in a summery sea of cool blue, which was soothing until I heard Mom talking in the kitchen, until I remembered we're on the run again.

"Why are you speaking so quietly?" he says.

"I don't want my mom to hear." Okay, so it was a little bit of a white lie when I told her that Jared didn't know where we were going. He didn't know the *exact* address. I just didn't see any reason to hide anything else from him. It's not like he's going to tell my dad.

He leans closer. "School sucked without you today."

"I wish I was there too. My mom and I drove around and visited some art galleries." Mom's face was tense as she negotiated the Vancouver traffic, her smile fragile, though she kept it plastered on—as if I don't know she's upset. She insisted we stop at Starbucks for a treat when normally she complains about how expensive everything is there, so I knew we were going to have another "talk." I ordered a peppermint tea. My stomach couldn't handle anything else.

"What's going on with your dad?"

"He got arrested today. My mom's trying to make it sound like he'll leave us alone now, but I can tell she doesn't really believe it." She drank her coffee in record time while she talked, her fingers shredding the empty package of sugar into a million little pieces of confetti, her reassuring smile still in place, but I've seen it too many times for it to be any comfort.

"So when are you coming home?"

"I don't know. I think she's worried my dad will get away with everything and she might want us to stay living here. Jenny has extra bedrooms and Mom doesn't own our house anyway."

"What about your mom's business?" His dark eyes look worried, and he's leaning really close to the screen. I like that his voice sounds upset and he's not trying to hide it. If he acted like he didn't care, that would make this whole thing suck even more. If that's possible.

"I heard her talking to Jenny in the kitchen before you and I started Skyping. Jenny was telling my mom that she could get her lots of new clients in the city, and rates are higher."

"I don't want you to move."

His words fling a little hope into my heart, a delicious exhale of happiness and warmth. "I don't want to move either, but we'll be going to university together in September." We've both been accepted to UBC in Vancouver. Different programs, but we'll be on the same campus.

"That's like nine months away."

The way he says it makes it seem like an even longer time. Like an *impossibly* long time.

"I don't know what to do," I say. "I don't want to live here."

"Can you stay with Delaney?"

"I mentioned it to my mom, but she's too freaked out." I tried to slip it in. *You know, Delaney's parents have an extra room. . . .* But I shut up as soon as I saw the look on her face.

"Does she think he's going to hurt you?" Jared's propped on his elbows on his bed, and it's making his muscles bunch in his arms. I remember how firm his body had felt against mine when we were making out, how much stronger he was than I thought.

"I wasn't scared of him in that way. But I think he'd hurt my mom. Did you know he followed us home that night?"

"Are you serious? I drove all over the place." He'd taken different roads, up and down the neighborhood, while I'd watched my side mirror for Andrew's truck headlights.

"I know."

"Maybe I should go watch his place and see what he's doing."

"Oh, my God. No! Don't do that."

"Okay, but you just say the word and I'll tell him to fuck off."

I love how protective he's being, but he looked scared when my dad sat down with us. I glance at my door. I can hear the rattles of pots and pans, and smell food cooking, something with garlic and onions. "I should go. Dinner's almost ready."

"Skype later? We can watch TV together."

I slide sideways on the bed so it's like I'm lying next to him. "I really miss you."

He shifts his body so he's lying on his side too. "I like looking at you like this," he says. "I wish I could touch you." He raises his hand and touches the screen.

"I've been thinking about that," I say, the distance making me feel brave, safe to say what I'm really feeling. "Like what would have happened if I hadn't said no. . . ."

"I'm glad you said no. It wasn't the right time. I want you to feel good about it and trust me. So you know this is a real thing."

That breathless hiccup is back in my chest again. "Is this a real thing?"

"It is to me. I hope you come back to Dogwood soon. I'm having a party this weekend and I can't believe you're not going to be here."

I roll over onto my stomach. "Party? What party?"

"My parents said I could have some people over, just the usual suspects."

"Sounds like fun."

"It would be more fun if you were here." His phone chirps, and he picks it up, reads the text with a smile, then quickly taps out his reply. I'm surprised. He doesn't usually check his phone when we are talking—and he never replies to anyone that fast, except me.

"Who's that?"

He finishes sending his reply, then looks back at me. "Just Taylor."

Taylor. The pretty blond girl he used to date last year. The one he broke up with because he thought she was too flirty. She's popular, athletic, always wears trendy clothes, and actually seems nice. I remember when they were dating. They looked like the perfect couple.

"You still talk to her?"

"Sometimes." He shrugs. "She had a fight with her parents and wanted to know if I could go for coffee."

"What did you say?"

"I told her I was busy."

It doesn't sound like he mentioned my name. Does she know I'm his girlfriend? All my happy feelings start to evaporate. "Is she coming to your party?"

"I don't know. Maybe." He gives me a funny look. "What's the problem?"

"Nothing. I just don't have time for games." My eyes sting and my face feels all hot and I know I look upset. "Maybe you should go for coffee with Taylor. She obviously still likes you, and I have a lot going on in my life. I can't even come to your party." The whole conversation is spiraling out of control, but I can't stop my runaway thoughts.

"Wait, stop. I won't invite her, okay?"

"It's not like that." But it is like that, and now he probably thinks I'm some deranged jealous girl, and none of this is really important because my *real* life is so messed up, and now he's angry, his face pulled into this expression I've never seen before. He looks older.

"This is because of your dad, right?" he says. "You're stuck in Vancouver and you think I'm going to dump you because I don't want to deal with it?"

I'm silent. He's cut right through to the bone, and I don't like how it sounds.

"I don't care where you live," he says. "You're the only girl I want, and I can get through anything with you, okay? But I wish your dad would go away."

Everything in me settles down, a quiet sort of calm spreading through my body, like how sometimes during a winter storm the wind just *stops*. He understands.

"It's like he's taken over everything, you know? He's gone crazy."

"Yeah. Someone needs to show him what crazy really looks like."

I frown at him. "What does that mean?"

"Depends on what you think is crazy?" He's smiling, but it's a different kind of smile than I've seen on him before. I don't like it. I hear footsteps coming down the hall. "My mom's coming, I have to go. I'll sign on later." I end the call, then stare at the screen with my heart thudding hard in my chest. What if he goes and talks to my dad? What if they get in a fight?

My fingers hover over my keyboard. My mom is getting closer. She stops outside my door. "Dinner's ready, Sophie."

"Okay. I'm just finishing up my homework." Her steps fade back down the hall. Jared's icon still shows him online. I should call him back and make sure he stays away from my dad. My phone rings and I grab it, glancing at the call display. I don't recognize the number. Andrew?

I press the phone against my stomach, muffling the sound for a moment while I think. I don't know what to do. Turn my phone off? Call my mom? Talk to him?

Before I can think any more, I answer the call. "Who is this?"

"It's Andrew. We need to talk."

"I told you to leave me alone." My blood is rushing so fast through my body and my head that it feels like I'm in a tunnel, everything dark and closed in and loud.

"Sophie, this is serious. I'm in jail."

"Yeah, for hurting Greg."

"I didn't have anything to do with that."

"You keep saying that none of this is your fault and I still don't believe—"

"Shut up for a minute. I'm trying to help you."

I'm so stunned by his words that everything else I wanted to say dies in my throat.

"Who has your mom been hanging out with? Has she pissed someone off?" he says. "Someone is trying to get to her and screw me up. When are you going to listen?"

I stare at the calm blue walls, my ears ringing. The way he's talking to me. It's all familiar now. I've heard this voice. I've heard him talking to my mom like this.

"When are you going to stop *lying*?" I say. "Mom is right. The only person you care about is yourself, and now my whole life is fucked up. Because of *you*. I wish you'd disappear."

"I'm not going to let anyone hurt you, Sophie." The way he's speaking scares me more than I've ever been in my life. It feels like I'm standing in the middle of a road and a big truck is coming straight at me. He's angry, but there's something else in his voice that I don't understand. It's like he's making some strange sort of promise, and I'm terrified of what that means.

I open my mouth, my throat so tight I have to strain to speak. "I have to go." I end the call, pressing my finger down hard on the keyboard, and then throw my cell onto the bed with so much force, it bounces off and clatters onto the floor.

"You okay?" my mom's voice floats down the hall.

"Yeah, just dropped my phone."

"Your dinner is getting cold."

"Be there in a second." I open my sketchpad and rip out every picture that had anything to do with Andrew. Then I sneak outside into Jenny's backyard, the pictures clutched in my hand, and shove them under the metal grate over her fire pit. I light the corner of one sketch with a match. The flames leap and crawl over the drawings, eating everything in their path, turning the paper black. I watch until the fire has destroyed every last page and it's all crumbled into ash.

Gone is the drawing of our fishing day at the river. Gone is the drawing of his new house with its ocean view. Gone is the drawing of his work boots with melting snow. Gone is the sketch of his hands next to mine. They're all gone.

CHAPTER TWENTY-NINE

LINDSEY

"Do you want to stop for coffee?" Jenny asks. We're walking in the park near the beach, where we've been taking Angus every night after dinner.

"Better not. The caffeine will just put me more on edge." It's been four days since we left Dogwood and Parker just called a couple of hours ago to let me know Andrew is out on bail. Unless the police find more evidence that he hurt Greg, they'll drop the charges. I need to make some decisions soon if Sophie and I are going to move, but I keep faltering when I pick up the phone to call my landlord. This is the most important year in Sophie's life. She should be graduating with her friends, obsessing over prom dresses, not having her life ripped to pieces.

Jenny glances over. "What are you thinking?"

"I don't know when this nightmare will end. Even after Sophie moves out, Andrew can still get to me through her. What do I do? We're living like fugitives."

"I wish I had the answers." She gives me a sympathetic look.

The wind is whipping off the ocean and she stops to tie her hair back, her eyes squinted in concentration. We're the same height and our shoulders bump together as we start walking down the path again.

"I feel like a rat in a labyrinth and I keep scurrying around looking for the exit. We're not even safe in Vancouver with you. He could easily hire a private investigator."

"So what would you like to do?"

"I don't know. I really don't. Do we just move back to our house and stop running?"

"He won't leave you alone."

I watch Angus chase a seagull into the water and give a whistle, calling him back to my side. He returns with a lopsided grin, his fur wet, then bounces down the trail in front of us. It's stormy today, the waves hitting hard on the shore with a *smack*. The rocks are slippery and covered with kelp, and the occasional eagle circles above our heads, riding the wind up and down.

"I think all the time about how much I wish Andrew had died in the accident that night," I say. "I hate feeling like that about the father of my child."

"You're human. I try to forgive my ex-husband, but when he messes with our kids' heads, I wish he was dead too." Both of Jenny's kids are in university, old enough to understand their father's mental games, but he still has a way of sucking them into his web of lies, getting them mad at their mother for some imagined slight, then spitting them back out when he's finished.

"I used to have fantasies about buying a gun," Jenny says. "I came close once."

"Really?" I'm startled, can't imagine my petite friend walking into a gun store, smacking her hand down on the counter, and asking for a weapon. Though, come to think of it, maybe I could see her at a shooting range, her steely eyes focused onto a target as she bangs off shots.

"I know. I'm supposed to be so Zen, but trust me, that man had me thinking some murderous thoughts many nights. It felt like the only way out sometimes."

"Sophie was telling me about the butterfly effect, how one small decision changes everything. She asked me if I have any regrets."

"Do you?" She glances sideways at me.

I wonder if I could confide in Jenny about how I drugged Andrew so I could escape with Sophie. I know she would understand and if anything would probably give me a high-five, but I've been holding on to my secret, and my guilt, for too long.

"It doesn't matter," I say. "We can't go back in time."

"That's true. We can only move forward. Maybe you should run away to the States. Andrew has a police record. They wouldn't let him into the country."

"What about Sophie? I can't leave her here."

"Do you think Andrew would hurt her?"

I think for a moment. "When she was younger, I worried about him disappearing with her, or driving when he was drunk, but I didn't think he would ever deliberately hurt her. Now I don't know. If he sees he can't control her, I don't know what he might do, you know?"

"I know. It's terrifying. It's like there's a ticking bomb sitting right next to our children, but there's nothing we can do about it." She looks frustrated, her face red from wind and anger. She picks up a rock and throws it into the water as hard as she can. Then another.

I watch for a moment. I understand what she's doing, trying to find some small way to alleviate the stress, the trapped feeling. I pick up a rock too and throw it into the water. Angus bounds in after it. Jenny and I both stand still now, our hands tucked into our pockets.

"When I go back to Dogwood tomorrow for the girls'

paychecks, I could ask Andrew to meet me and have Parker waiting outside. Then I'll provoke him. If he attacks me, they'll have to arrest him." I'd forgotten about payday until Rachelle called a couple of hours ago asking for hers.

Jenny turns. "Are you insane? He could *kill* you."

"Not if Parker gets him first."

"That's too big of a gamble, Lindsey—she'll never go for it."

"You're right. It was a stupid idea. I'm just desperate."

We keep walking, both lost in thought, our feet slipping and sliding on the uneven beach trail. Angus's collar jingles as he runs ahead, then comes back to check on us.

Jenny stops again, this time so suddenly I think she's going to fall. I reach out to grab her arm, but she's perfectly still, looking me straight in the eyes.

"Don't go back. I have a bad feeling."

"The girls need their checks and everything is saved on my home computer. I'll ask Marcus to meet me at my house, okay?"

"Okay, but I still don't like it."

I step closer and grab her for a hug. She squeezes hard, her cheek cold against mine. I can smell her lavender lotion. She makes it herself, adds sage and avocado. I tell her that she shouldn't put food on her face. She always laughs.

"Please don't get yourself killed," she says as we pull apart. "I don't want to raise another daughter. Mine are trouble enough." Her mouth turns up in a smile, but her eyes are scared.

"I won't." I try to sound confident, but my head is filled with the memory of Andrew's hands tight around my throat, his face twisted into a grimace that almost looked like a smile.

Sophie is in her bedroom, Skyping with Delaney, who's helping her with an assignment. She hasn't mentioned Jared, but her cell has been chirping with texts constantly and she raced back to her room to Skype after dinner last night.

"Come in," she calls out when I knock softly on her door. She's sitting on the window seat, staring out. I sit near her feet and follow her gaze. In the distance there's a glimpse of ocean lit by moonlight. The sky is clear this evening and full of stars. I remember how Andrew used to point all their shapes out to Sophie and my breath hitches in my throat.

"What are you doing?" I say. She has a sketchpad in her lap, but the page is blank. On the bed her notebooks and binder are spread out. Her laptop is open, the screen dark.

"Just thinking." She straightens her legs so they run alongside mine. When she was little we often sat on the couch like this, our heads at the pillows at either end, our legs tangled. We'd read our books or watch movies, just happy to be with each other. "I miss our house," she says.

"I want to talk to you about something."

She narrows her eyes. "I hate when you start a conversation like that."

"It's nothing bad. I just have to go home for a day. I need to pay the girls."

Her whole face lifts. "You're going to Dogwood? I want to come."

"You should stay here."

"No way. I want to see Jared and Delaney and get some clothes from the house." She tugs at her purple sweater. "I'm sick of wearing the same things."

"You can make me a list. I just don't think it's safe."

She leans closer. "Mom, if you don't take me, I'm going to get a city bus and go back myself." She looks determined, and I'm shot with a memory of her as a little girl. How I caught her packing one day because she wanted to meet Emily Carr, the beloved Canadian artist. It was horrible to have to tell her that the artist had died many years ago. She insisted on visiting her grave on Vancouver Island and bringing her flowers, because, "Even dead people like pretty things."

She reaches out and holds my hand. "Mom. I'm scared for you. I want to be with you."

I think it over, imagine her pacing Jenny's house, alone and worried about me. "Okay. But we're just going back for the day, all right?"

She's already picking up her laptop. "I'm going to tell Jared now." Her Skype is ringing. He'll be online soon. I stand up. "We'll take the early ferry."

"Sure." She's smiling, excited about going back. I stand at the door for a moment, watching her face brighten when Jared answers her call.

"Hi, babe," he says. "Did you get my texts? You didn't answer."

"Sorry, I was talking to my mom." She looks up at me, clearly wanting me to leave. I close her door, trying to ignore the uneasy feeling in the pit of my stomach. I don't like the way he asked about his text messages, and how much it reminds me of my life with Andrew. It's not the same, I remind myself. Sophie isn't me, and Jared isn't Andrew.

We take the first ferry over, both of us groggy and clutching at our coffees. Sophie's cell vibrates with a new text every five minutes, and I pretend to read a book while remembering how simple things used to be when she was young and told me all her secrets, when I was her greatest confidante. Now she's a mystery to me, and this relationship with Jared is uncharted territory.

Marcus is waiting on the front steps when we pull into the driveway, our car tires crunching on the snow. Most of it has been shoveled away. Piles of snow line either side, and he's even scraped off the front steps. He waves and walks toward the car, opens my door.

I climb out. "Thanks for clearing the driveway."

"I got here a little early."

"You must have been a lot early."

He shrugs. "I like the exercise."

Sophie comes around to the front, her hands shoved deep into her pockets. "Hi, Marcus."

"Sophie." He gives her a quick hug and I can see her relax, her hands coming out of her pockets. I'm grateful he's here today.

Angus jumps out of the car, runs to greet Marcus, then starts doing zoomies all over the yard, burying his nose in the snow and leaping into the air. Sophie laughs.

While she's distracted by Angus, I glance around the yard, looking for boot tracks, but it's snowed overnight and the ground is covered with a fresh layer.

As we move up the front steps, Marcus says, "I checked your outside tap and made sure it's turned off. It's been cold this week."

I'd left the heat on low in the house, but I'm still hit with an icy draft when we walk inside, and a scent I can't identify, something rotten. Marcus looks at me.

"You smell that?" he says.

"I must have left garbage under the sink." I flip open the panel for the alarm. Angus bounds into the foyer, finds one of his balls that has rolled into the corner, and wiggles around our legs, squeaking it madly. Sophie brushes past me and heads into the house.

The red light on the alarm isn't blinking. I stop, my fingers over the keypad.

"Something's wrong. The alarm is off." Angus chases after Sophie, his toenails scrabbling on the floor. Seconds later I hear him barking. I spin around. I've never heard him bark like that—so deep and frantic it vibrates inside my own chest. Now Sophie is screaming.

I drop my purse and keys and sprint toward her voice, Marcus close behind. When we come around the corner, Sophie is backed against the wall, still screaming and gasping some words I can't understand. Her face is a flash of panicky white in the dim hallway. Angus is yelping and circling something on the floor. The smell is worse. So much worse.

I flip on the switch beside me and the hall is bathed in light. It's Andrew.

CHAPTER THIRTY

I recognize this room at the police station. The fake wood table, the pale green cement walls, the color of hospitals. Nothing good ever happens in rooms this color. This is where I sat with Corporal Parker and filled out the paperwork for the peace bond. It feels like months ago.

Sophie and Marcus are in other rooms, giving their statements. I hate that Sophie has to go through this alone, begged and argued with the police to let me stay with her, but they insisted they had to speak with us individually. I keep replaying the sound of her scream when she found Andrew, that terrible anguished look in her eyes. She hadn't knelt down or touched him. She was frozen in the hallway, staring at his body with her hand pressed over her mouth. I wrapped my arms around her, held her close. I wished I could have stopped her from seeing him like that.

The congealed blood around his head had soaked into the oak hardwood and dried almost black in spots. One of his arms was outstretched as though he were reaching for something, his hand so white it looked like a leftover Halloween prop. His right leg was at an odd angle—was it broken? I wanted to walk over and pull it straight, but I just closed my eyes, held Sophie tighter.

Marcus called 911 and the police arrived in minutes. We waited outside, shivering in the cold, none of us talking. Marcus kept reaching out to touch my hand, or wrap his arm around Sophie's shoulders. Angus sat beside her, making a soft whine.

On the way to the station Sophie stared out the window, her expression blank, her body shaking. She was in shock, cocooned from the horror for a little bit longer, I hope. I remember when my mother and father died, how everything felt distant and unreal, until it became very, very real. I have to get her home, have to be there for her when she breaks.

"You okay?" Parker says. She's wearing a pale blue blouse today with a slim-fitting black pencil skirt and high heels, but she doesn't look any less official.

"Yes. I think so. It's cold in here." I rub at my arms. When I get Sophie home and settled, I'll have a hot bath, or drink a rum, or both, but then I realize we don't have a home anymore. There's no way either of us can ever spend a night under that roof again. And we probably won't be able to go back to our house to get our things for days, maybe weeks, while the police finish their investigation. The thought hits me hard in my stomach. Where are we going to go?

"You're in shock." She already offered me a coffee or tea, which I declined, not sure my stomach could handle it.

"I don't know what he was doing in there." I shake my head, still trying to process everything that's happened. I guess she's right. I'm in shock too. How can he be *dead*? A sudden image: Andrew at twenty-seven, standing at my cash register, his smile and blond hair lighting up my world. "I can't believe he fell down the stairs. I wonder how long he was in there. . . ." A horrible new thought scurries through my mind. What if he didn't die right away?

"You were going to drive past the house," I say. "Did you see anything?"

"I didn't get a chance—I worked double shifts all this week." Her gaze flicks away, over to a corner of the room, and I wonder if there is a camera or something set up. She mentioned that our interview might be recorded. Maybe she wasn't supposed to offer to drive past. "You said the alarm was off when you entered the house. So who else has the code?"

I try to focus on the question, but her voice is tinny and distant-sounding. I'm surprised at the ache of grief in my chest, the desire to set my head down on the table and cry. *Why do I care? I shouldn't care. He hurt me. But I loved him once. God, I loved him so much.*

"Lindsey? You okay?"

"Sorry. What did you say?"

"The code?"

"Right. Just me, Sophie, my brother too."

"What about . . ." She looks down at her notes. "Greg?"

"I never gave him the password."

"Did he ever see you setting the alarm?"

I hesitate, remembering all the times he stood beside me in the foyer, waiting for me to shut the alarm off when we came home from a date, then I realize why she's asking.

"You think Greg did something to Andrew? That's absurd." Greg might look tough, but he's the least violent person I know. He's the kind of guy who breaks up fights. Not starts them.

"Forensics still need to process the scene and there'll be an autopsy, but right now we're treating his death as suspicious. When is the last time you spoke to Greg?"

Forensics. Autopsy. Suspicious. I want to write down the words and stare at them, because they can't be right. She's watching my face. What is she looking for?

I think of Sophie in another room, with some police officer she's never met asking all these excruciating questions. Is she crying? Is she asking for me? I have to get this interview over with and get her the hell out of this place before I go ballistic.

"Greg and I broke up."

"How did your brother feel about Andrew?" The question is past tense. It throws me again, this realization that Andrew is gone. He was a presence in my life for almost twenty years. Good or bad, he was always there. In my thoughts, my memories. In my daughter.

"They don't talk."

"It must have been hard for him to see how Andrew treated you and Sophie."

We hold gazes and I feel a trickle of unease. "The same as any brother, I suppose. He has a girlfriend. She's pregnant. They're very happy." I'm rambling, telling her things she hasn't even asked about, but I can't seem to stop. I hope that Chris hasn't been telling any of his friends how he should have gotten rid of Andrew years ago. It won't look good. He'd been *so angry* when I told him about Greg getting hit with a truck. The trickle of unease swells to a river.

"So what do you think happened to Andrew?"

"He broke into my house so he could figure out where I'd gone—he was probably checking my e-mails again. Then he tripped on something. Angus always had bones and toys at the top of the stairs. He piles them outside my bedroom like gifts." I feel more confident now, sure this is right. She will see the truth in this explanation and stop asking ridiculous questions.

"My alarm code—it was the date of my divorce. He could have guessed." I pause, thinking. "He worked in construction. Maybe he knew how to disable it."

"Would Sophie have ever met him at the house or given him the code?"

"God, no." I think about Jared and wonder if Sophie has given him the code or if he'd ever seen her press in the numbers. I almost mention it, then decide not to. It's too unlikely.

"And your friend can verify you've been in Vancouver all week?"

"You think I had something to do with it?" I'm incredulous, though my face infuses with guilty heat when I remember the conversation I'd had with Jenny.

She looks at me evenly. "You were very angry with him."

"Of course I was angry, but I didn't *kill* him."

"Was Sophie with you the whole time?"

"I can't believe you're asking these questions." Panic digs sharp teeth into the base of my neck. Sophie is alone with a police officer. Should she have a lawyer?

"I know this is upsetting, but I wouldn't be doing my job if I didn't ask." She leans forward. "We just need to rule you both out, okay? It will help us know where we should focus."

That may be true, but I still resent her, even if she does look sympathetic. It's probably a ploy to make me think she's on my side so I let down my guard. Is the other cop twisting and turning Sophie's words? What if she tells them how angry she was at her father?

"Sophie was alone at Jenny's house for a few hours sometimes, but *that's it*. She didn't have any way back to the island. We only came back this morning because I have to pay my employees—they're still waiting." I sit back in the seat, exhausted and overwhelmed and close to tears. "I was supposed to meet one of my girls an hour ago."

"Once the officers have finished and his body has been removed, you can go back in for your belongings. Someone will accompany you because it's an active crime scene."

"I want to see Sophie. If you keep her any longer, I'm going to sue." I don't have a clue what I would sue for, but the threat feels good. I meet her eyes, and for the first time I notice she looks really tired, her skin pale with puffy circles under her eyes. She said she was working double shifts all week, but she still came in today. Did they bring her in just to interview me because we've been working together? Maybe they thought I'd trust her more. They were wrong.

"I'll check if they're finished." She stands up, then pauses with her hand on her chair. "I'm sorry things had to end this way. I really hoped he'd leave you alone."

I look up at her, startled by her words. Then I'm angry.

"You *hoped* he'd leave me alone? You knew that was never going to happen. You were going to keep an eye on him. You should've checked on my house. He might still be alive."

We're staring at each other. Her face is flushed and I realize what I've just said. I've placed the blame at her feet, and I don't know why. I just know I didn't want Andrew dead, and that might be the most terrifying thought of all. I'm remembering the night of the accident, the pills in my hand, and then getting that phone call from my brother. My first thought had been dizzying relief. Andrew was alive. I've never admitted that to anyone. Not even myself.

Her face changes, turns harder, and I see the cop side of her. "Whatever happened to Andrew," she says, "he brought it upon himself. Just remember that."

The door closes behind her and I'm left looking around the barren room thinking about what she said. I know she's right, but I've never heard her talk like that. Like this was personal. I still don't understand why she didn't drive by my house— she'd done it every other time. But what does it matter now? She probably wouldn't have seen him hiding inside anyway.

He brought it upon himself.

"Why haven't they closed the case yet?" I say to Marcus. "It's been almost a week. I feel like they know something they aren't telling me." We're sitting at a corner table at the Muddy Bean, having spent the day looking at rentals for Sophie and me.

The café is crowded, people clustered at tables or in the leather chairs, surfing their laptops and iPads, their heads close together in conversation. Normally I love the scent of roasted coffee beans and fresh baked goods, but today the air smells too sweet, cloying. "I drove by the house yesterday and there's still yellow crime scene tape across the front."

"It takes time," he says. "They have to wait for autopsy results and follow up on every detail, and the coroner has to make the final ruling, but it's just protocol."

"I want to move on with our lives." Mostly I want to stop waking up in the middle of the night thinking about Andrew. I want to still be angry—*furious*—at him, but instead I'm being haunted by memories of our early days, how sweet he had been. Then I remember how tender he was to Sophie when she was a baby and I can almost grab on to the anger again, especially when I see her drifting around the house, sadness exuding from her like a perfume. How could he do this? He's broken her heart all over again and I don't know how to put her back together.

Marcus reaches over and holds my hand. "I know it's frustrating. This will be over soon. I promise. Then Sophie and you can begin to heal." His hand is warm on top of mine, his fingertip pressing against my pulse. I wonder if he can feel it racing, then calming at his touch.

"Thanks for letting us stay at your place."

"Of course, and don't rush into signing any rental agreements. You can stay as long as you need. Timing is everything."

"Isn't that the truth?" Our eyes meet. We're sitting here,

holding hands, but I don't know what any of it means. I don't know what I *want* it to mean. It just feels comforting.

He gives my hand another squeeze and reaches for his coffee mug, takes a sip. "How do you think Sophie is doing? She seems really quiet."

"I know." Somehow it seems even worse that he's noticed. "The only person she wants to talk to is Jared. They never stop texting. He was waiting outside school this morning when I dropped her off." I pause, remembering that moment, how he took her backpack from her and tossed it over his shoulder, then put his arm around her lower back and pulled her close. "I should be relieved that she has someone in her life who can support her, and he seems to be treating her well, but something about the way he was holding her this morning . . . it felt protective."

"And that's a bad thing?"

"Maybe *protective* is the wrong word. It was more possessive, you know?"

"Hmm. I can see why that might make you nervous."

I grip the handle on my mug as I gather my thoughts. "Maybe I'm being paranoid because I'm worried she'll fall into the same kind of relationship I had with Andrew. Or I'm worried about how she's handling Andrew's death and I'm fixating on this instead."

"Good diagnosis," he says. "But it's okay to listen to your instincts about Jared. They might be trying to tell you something."

I look up and meet his eyes. "He was watching my car drive away. He didn't look at the school, or the other kids, or even Sophie. He was watching *me*."

Marcus frowns. "I don't like the sound of that."

"He calls me by my first name, and he has this aura about him . . . I can't describe it, but it's almost too confident, bordering on arrogant."

"You said his parents are wealthy, right? Do they work a lot?"

"The father, definitely. They leave him on his own all the time."

"He's probably been treated as an adult most of his life."

"Maybe. I just don't like the hold he seems to have over Sophie. She doesn't spend much time with Delaney anymore. It's all Jared."

"I think that's normal for a teenaged girl. Katie had a few boyfriends in high school and she would obsess about them."

"Was it different, though, when she met . . . him?" Marcus has never told me his daughter's murderer's name. He won't say it out loud.

He stares down into his coffee, his expression reflective. "I wish I could say I noticed, but we didn't speak as much after she moved out and started university. I was busy with my practice and she had her studies. I don't really know what happened between them."

"I just don't want Sophie to lose herself, and it would be easy for her to cling to Jared right now because of everything that's happened with her father."

"Why don't you talk to her?"

I mull it over for a few seconds. "If it sounds like I don't approve of Jared, I know she'll pull away from me. She needs to feel like I'm on her side—especially right now."

"But she also needs to know you care."

I think about what he said, tap my fingernail against the rim of my cup. "I know things are getting serious between them. Maybe I'll talk to her and see if I can find out *how* serious." It might also be a way for me to find out more about how she's coping with everything. I'd suggested we could find her a grief counselor—we could even go together if she wanted—but she shut down that idea with an eye roll and a snarky comment: "You can't afford it."

"Good idea. You don't want to regret keeping your fears to yourself."

We meet eyes. "You have regrets?"

"More than I can count." He looks around the room, gestures to all the people, smiles at a child. "But this is life," he says. "This moment now. Sometimes all you can do is breathe." He meets my eyes, nudges my mug toward me. "Drink up. It's getting cold."

Sophie's picking at her salad while she surfs Facebook with her other hand. She catches my look and pushes her phone to the side. "Sorry."

Marcus is in his office, working on his book. He often retreats after dinner, but I suspect it's to give Sophie and me some space. I've been thinking for two days about how to talk to Sophie about Jared, but there haven't been many opportunities. She comes home from school and goes straight into her room for hours. She emerges for dinner, then disappears again. I can hear her talking on the phone late into the night. She knows her father's death is still under investigation, but I haven't told her that they think his death is suspicious—and that I'm probably their prime suspect. That's the last thing I want her to worry about.

It's been weeks since she's taken one of her early morning walks, and I haven't noticed her painting or drawing since we came back from Vancouver. It's as though the light has been turned off in my beautiful, colorful daughter.

She frowns. "Why are you staring at me?"

"We haven't talked much lately. I was wondering how you're feeling. Please tell me how to help you. I'm so sorry you are having to deal with this."

"I'm fine, Mom."

"I hear you on your phone at night."

"You're eavesdropping? That's kind of rude."

I'm surprised by her tone, the anger in her face. "*That's* rude. I don't hear what you're saying, just that you're up late. I assume you're talking to Jared?"

"Yeah." Her expression is guarded now, suspicious. She knows I'm going somewhere with these questions and is already bracing herself. I might as well get to the point.

"How serious are you two? I mean, should we talk about you going on the birth control pill?" Then I realize she might already be on it.

She drops her fork onto her plate with a clatter. "You're not serious?"

"I just want you to know you can talk to me about anything."

"We haven't had sex, but thanks."

"Oh, I see."

"You don't have to look so relieved."

"I'm just worried about how intense things are with you two. In new relationships it's easy to get caught up in the excitement. You give up on your own interests, then your friends. It can happen so subtly you don't even notice until it's too late and they're your entire world."

"I'm not stupid, Mom. I know you're worried Jared is like Andrew, but he's not, okay? He's totally different. He'd *never* hurt me." Her voice cracks a little, and I'm not sure if it's from saying Andrew's name or the reality that her father had hurt me.

"In the beginning, I didn't think your dad would hurt me either." I lean over. "We talk about this at my support group. Guys who get very serious very fast are often possessive—"

"Just because you made a mistake doesn't mean I will."

"Sophie." I give her a look. "Stop that. Anything I say is only because I care about you. Disregard whatever you want, but my job is to take care of you."

She's staring at me. Her mouth a hard line. She looks so much like Andrew in this moment that I falter, but then I press on. "I'm just suggesting you might want to slow things down a little. This is your last year of school. Spend time with friends, have fun."

She stands up. "Can I go? I'm not hungry."

"Sure." I pull her plate in front of me and pick at her salad, but I'm not very hungry anymore either. I botched that one well and truly. I hear a chirp, and realize she left her phone on the table. I stare at it for a moment, then slide it closer and look at the text.

I can't stop thinking about you. Your body, your lips . . .

My face infuses with heat. I push the phone away just as Sophie comes back into the kitchen and snatches it up. She flicks a look at me and I stare down at the plates.

CHAPTER THIRTY-ONE

SOPHIE

I should be happy. It's my birthday and Mom took me out for pizza, gave me a beautiful silver snowflake necklace, and didn't make me feel bad about wanting to spend the rest of the evening with my friends, but I keep thinking about my dad.

The coroner ruled his death an accident. He died of a broken neck. Mom says it would have been very fast. But I still think about him falling, how he might have tried to stop himself as he tumbled down. I could tell by the questions the cops asked in the first interview that they were suspicious that he was pushed, but I guess in the end they didn't find anything unusual.

I don't know what's wrong with me lately. When I try to draw, I can't get into it, and I failed a chemistry test this week. It's like everything went out of my head. My mom got a call from a lawyer who handled my dad's business and I'm supposed to be getting some money when I turn twenty-five and all my schooling will be paid for. Dad left Mom money too, but she refuses to take it and asked the estate to give it to me. I don't know if I even want the money. I haven't told Jared or Delaney. I could go to any school I want now. But only because my dad is dead.

I told him to disappear. That's the part that bothers me the most.

Jared hands me another drink. I'm not sure how many I've had now. We've also smoked a joint, blowing puffs into each other's mouths. The room bends and spins, the music pulses, and now I'm thinking maybe none of it matters. I should take the money. I could buy a car, a house, and have my friends over all the time. Why shouldn't I have fun?

I'm giggling, but I can't remember who told the joke. Delaney is making out with Matthew on the other couch. Jared is holding my hand. "Come on, let's go," he says. I follow him down the hall to his bedroom. Laughing as I bump into his back and against the walls.

I flop down on his bed, feel the mattress shift when he lies down beside me. My stomach spins. I sit up to take some breaths. He pushes the hair out of my face, caresses my cheek. I turn to face him and he presses his mouth against mine. He tastes like rum, and something bitter. I'm holding the bottle in my hands. I take a swill from it straight and he laughs. I feel strong, brave, and I laugh too. I can be this girl. I can be this wild reckless girl.

Our clothes are off, but I don't really remember when it happens. I'm naked and I think I should be shy, but I don't feel shy. I'm brave! I'm flying. I'm numb. His body is rolling on top of mine and his hand is reaching for something in his drawer. Right. A condom. I'm laughing, thinking how funny this all is. I'm going to lose my virginity. On my birthday!

Two days after my dad's funeral. I don't want to laugh now.

Everything feels all restless and hot in my head and my body. I keep thinking about my dad. Why was he in our house?

Jared is on top of me, his mouth nipping at my neck and his hands on my hips. He thinks we're going to have sex. I haven't said I wanted to do it. But I haven't said I don't want to.

I don't know what I want. I feel like I should say something, but his mouth is over mine and it's kind of hard to breathe and I can't lift my arms and my legs feel all wobbly and I just want to close my eyes and sleep and listen to the music and it feels good not to think about anything. He pauses and whispers against my lips, "Do you want to?"

I don't want him to talk. I want to listen to the music. I pull him down on top of me. Then I feel him pushing up between my legs and there's pain, a burning, and I whimper and try to get away from the pain but I can't really move, and he's panting in my ears and saying he loves me and tears are leaking out of my eyes.

When it's over we lie still in the dark. His skin is sticky against mine and he's nestled against my side, kissing my shoulder and my neck, his hand stroking my hair.

"You okay?" he whispers.

I nod because I don't think I can speak. It's done. We've had sex now. I guess I must have wanted it, but I don't remember. I close my eyes, take some deep breaths. I just need to sleep. My body is so heavy. I let myself sink into the darkness. I disappear.

I open my eyes, roll onto my side, and the room spins. I think I might be sick and press the heel of my hand over my mouth, choking back the bile. He's asleep beside me, the sheet down around his waist. His chest is white, his ribs bony. When he's sleeping, his mouth is slack and he doesn't look so handsome. I look around the room. The half-empty bottle of rum on the dresser. My clothes beside the bed. The condom wrapper on the night table. I turn away.

Delaney. She has her car. She must be in the living room. We have to get out of here. I reach over the side of the bed, pull my clothes closer. My cell is in my pocket.

Five missed calls from my mom, then I see the time. Three-thirty.

I get dressed, pausing each time the room spins, then find the bathroom, bumping into the door in the dark. I have to grip the counter to hold myself up. I let the water run slow. My lips feel bruised, the area between my legs tender. I wince, press a cool cloth against my skin.

I tiptoe out of the room and down the hallway to the living room. The walls squish toward me and beads of sweat break out on my upper lip. I brace against the wall, close my eyes, and wait for the moment to pass. The living room is empty. Just glasses left on the table.

I'm confused. I spin around. Could she be in one of the rooms with Matthew? I don't know. I don't know how I'm going to get home. I sit on the couch. Maybe I should wake Jared.

Bits of the night are coming back to me in broken images, but I can't remember so much. I'm scared about what I might have said, the things I did.

I see his face hovering over mine, his lips moist, and feel my stomach shudder. Then I remember him saying something. I think harder, bring the moment back into focus.

I'd do anything for you. That's what he said. What does that mean? I don't know.

It's cold outside. I was dressed for being in a warm car, not walking, but the air feels good. Clean. I want to roll in the snow like when I was a kid and made snow angels, but then I remember making them with my dad and my eyes sting. The driveway is slippery, ice crunching under my boots, and the road is still a long way off. Delaney's car is gone. She's left me, and I think that maybe we argued, that maybe she was trying to get me to leave earlier, that I may have even shouted at her, but everything is muddled. I hate the thick sludge in my brain.

I hold my coat tighter against me, my cell clutched in my hand. When I get to the road, I'll call a cab. That's what I'll do. But when I reach the top of the driveway and rummage through my purse, I don't have any cash. Then the rest comes back. Delaney and I stopping at the store on our way to Jared's. She needed gas and I gave her the money.

I look back down the road toward Jared's house, but I keep smelling his bedroom, it clings to my clothes, the booze, his sweat, our sex smell. I turn and dry-heave into the snow.

I slide my finger across the screen on my cell. All those missed calls. She's going to be so upset. So disappointed. I scroll through my phone, search the numbers, and call Marcus's cell.

We've been driving for a few minutes, but he doesn't say anything. He didn't even ask any questions when I called, just told me that he'd get me as soon as possible and I should wait inside the house where it was warm, but I sat on the front steps. His car is hot, the vents blasting at my face, and the heat makes me more nauseated. I'm still shivering and have my arms wrapped around my body. He's pulled over twice so I can throw up, stopped at the gas station to buy me Gatorade, and passed me a couple of Tylenol out of his glove box.

"Is she really mad?" I say.

"She's worried."

"She's going to freak out."

"She may sound upset, but mostly she's just going to be relieved you're okay."

"She can't baby me all the time. I'm moving out soon."

"She's still going to be your mother. And we worry about people we love."

"You used to be a shrink."

"Yes." He glances over at me.

"How am I supposed to be feeling about my dad being dead?"

"You'll probably feel all kinds of different emotions. Sometimes all at once."

"I did something stupid."

"Feel like talking about it?"

I can't tell him about the sex. No way in hell. "I got really drunk."

"We've all done that. Are you hurt?"

The way he says it makes me think he knows. He sounds like a doctor at a hospital. My head is fuzzy. I want to talk to him more, ask questions about his daughter. I'm staring out the window, but my eyes feel heavy again, so I let them drift closed.

The car stops. I hear his door opening and shutting. Now my door is opening, cold air nipping at me. Reluctantly I open my eyes. Marcus is reaching for my hand, helping me out. Mom's waiting at the front door and I brace myself, but she just steps forward and hugs me tight. She's crying. I put my head into the crook of her neck. I'm home.

The scent of coffee drifts under my nose. I turn my head to the side, cover my nose and mouth with my arm. Angus snuffles across my face, his snout jabbing at my ear, thrusting under my arm as he whines and grunts at me.

"Stop it!" I give him a shove, but he pounces on me again,

his weight pressing into my belly. I squint my eyes. Mom is sitting at the foot of my bed. She looks amused. Sun streams in from the window—she's opened my blinds wide.

I groan and pull the pillow over my head. "It's too early." I've never had a headache like this before in my life. It's like my skull has been ripped open and someone is pounding at it with knives and hammers, maybe an entire tool kit. The image makes me think of my dad and I feel sad and nauseated again. I'm going to sleep all day. I'll just stay in bed until tomorrow.

"It's almost noon. Jared's been calling all morning."

Images tumble through my mind in a hot rush of shame and disgust at myself. I'd waited so many years for *that*? It wasn't romantic or sweet or even a little bit fun. I was just another stupid girl who got drunk and lost her virginity to her high school boyfriend.

This is *real*, he said.

I blink at the tears filling my eyes and try to sniff quietly so Mom can't tell I'm crying. She lifts the pillow from my face, touches my check, then lies down beside me.

"Do you want to tell me why you were walking home by yourself in the middle of the night? Were you trying to turn yourself into a snow queen?"

I shake my head. "It's complicated."

"You can tell me anything."

Right. As if I can tell her about this. I can't stop remembering what we did. He knew I was drunk, but so was he. So is it my fault? I got in bed with him. I took off my clothes, didn't I?

"Delaney called too. She's worried about you."

I wish I'd gone home with her, wish I could do the whole night over again. Maybe the whole year. "I just got too drunk and acted like an idiot. Guess I'm like my dad."

She rolls me back over, looks me in the face.

"No, Sophie. You're *not*. You could never be."

"He's gone," I say. "He was here and now he's not."

"I know." Her expression is sad, but I know she's not sad he's gone. She's sad for me, and that makes it all seem worse, makes me feel all jagged inside.

"Sometimes I feel relieved because we don't have to be scared anymore, Mom. But that's such an awful thing to say. Then other times I just feel really angry at him. I'm never going to have a dad. I think about my graduation, my wedding, all kinds of stuff like that."

"I know it's hard. It will probably hurt for a while, then it will get easier. Different times in your life you may miss him more, but you will have lots of wonderful people who will be there for you during all those special events. You'll always have me."

"I think I should give away all his money. It never made him happy."

"You don't have to decide anything right now."

I sigh and rest my head on her shoulder. "I'm sorry I didn't call. I was a jerk."

"I was really scared, but I know you're dealing with a lot of emotions right now." I feel her hesitate, notice the caution in her voice as she says, "I don't like that you were drinking last night, especially when you were upset. Alcohol lowers your inhibitions, it makes people do different things, reckless things, but it doesn't make the problem go away."

"I know. I acted like an idiot."

"Everyone makes mistakes. But being an adult means learning from them, apologizing for our actions if we hurt someone, and moving on. Today is a new day."

I think about Jared again. But now I'm not feeling so ashamed, I'm feeling bad. How would I have felt if he just walked out on me? I need to text him.

"I should call Jared."

She looks startled, like that wasn't what she expected to hear. Maybe she wanted me to say that Jared was the mistake. Maybe she was hoping that I was going to break up with him. I feel a roll of anger in my stomach and brace for another lecture, but then she just sits up.

"I brought you coffee. Drink lots of water too. It will help." She passes me my phone. "Come downstairs whenever you're ready."

After she leaves, I hold the phone in my hand for a few minutes. I don't know what to say. How am I going to face Jared at school on Monday? Is he going to want to have sex all the time now? I read the text messages he sent this morning. *You pissed off? What's wrong? Call me!* I press in his number, hold my breath as it rings. He sounds relieved when he answers.

"You okay?" he says. "I've been freaking out."

"Yeah." I lean back against the pillow and take a sip of the coffee, feel my stomach lurch. That was a mistake.

"You sure?"

"I guess. I don't know."

He's quiet for a minute. "Do you regret doing it?"

I don't know how to answer. I wonder if my dad woke up like this all the time when he was drinking. Did he ever feel ashamed? Maybe I would have made different choices if he wasn't dead. Maybe last night wouldn't have happened. Then I feel angry again

"I'm just confused. Everything feels weird now."

"Maybe we should have waited." He sounds worried.

I think it over. Would anything have been different? Maybe it would have sucked no matter when we did it. "I don't think anyone's first time is great." Delaney's first time had been horrible. She didn't even like the guy she did it with and doesn't talk to him.

"Can we hang out?" he says. "I'll pick up pho and come over."

I pause, thinking.

"Please, Sophie?" The way he says it gives me a strange happy feeling, like something inside is bending toward him, softening.

He seems so desperate to fix everything. Maybe if he came over with lunch it would help things with my mom. She'll see that he's caring and sweet.

"Okay," I say. "My mom really likes those deep-fried wonton things."

"Great. I'll get some of those too."

I take a quick shower and down a few mouthfuls of Pepto-Bismol. I'm feeling halfway human when I walk into the kitchen, where Mom is sitting at the island reading the newspaper. Marcus is at the other end with his laptop.

"Jared is coming over. He's bringing lunch."

Mom looks up. "Oh." She pauses. "That's nice of him." But I see how her mouth thins, how she's tapping her fingernail on the rim of her mug.

Maybe I'm still drunk, because I can't just brush it off this time, can't tell myself that it doesn't matter what she thinks.

"Why don't you like him?" I say. "He likes you."

"I've never said I don't like him." Her cheeks are turning pink and I can feel my own getting hot too. Marcus is frozen, watching both of us.

"Can't you just give him a chance?"

She lays her newspaper down, glances at Marcus. "Do you mind giving us a minute?"

"Not at all. I'll be in my office." He picks up his laptop and heads down the hall.

Mom looks back at me. I can see different expressions crossing over her face like she's not sure exactly what to say. "It's just, are you sure you want to date anyone right now? You've been through so much. Look what happened last night, and now he's coming over already?"

"See. That's what I'm talking about. If you liked him, you'd be fine with it."

"That's not true."

"Isn't it?"

We hold gazes for a minute, and she lets out her breath in a long sigh. "Maybe I've been a little overprotective when it comes to Jared." She gets up and walks around the counter, gives me a hug. "I'll try to make more of an effort to get to know him, okay?"

I rest my head in the corner of her neck. "Good, or I'm going to throw up on you."

She laughs, her breath tickling my hair. "I'm sorry, baby. You shouldn't have to be dealing with any of this." Her voice is serious-sounding now, and I know she's not talking about Jared anymore. I close my eyes, blink a few times.

"It will get better, right?"

"Just give it a few months," she says. "By spring break, everything will feel different."

PART THREE

CHAPTER THIRTY-TWO

LINDSEY

MARCH 2017

I stand in front of the wide picture window and stare out at the lake. It's dark, but I can see the dock and the wharf below in the lights from the house. The wind has picked up, heralding that we're in for a stormy night. The water is choppy, and white-tipped waves slap against the shore and the side of the dock, the wind pushing at the ramp, which sways and bounces.

We can't see any neighbors' houses, though Marcus mentioned a few cabins around the lake. Across the water some lights glow in the distance. The only signs of life. I smile at the scene reflected behind me. Marcus is building a fire, the kindling crackling as the blaze catches.

"The house will heat up soon," he says. I look over my shoulder, already feeling warmed by the cozy sight. Marcus sitting on the hearth and poking at the logs, his faced outlined in amber. Our damp coats are hanging by the fire, boots placed in front in a neat row.

We had to park on the road, then walk down the narrow steps to his lake house, which was built on a steep hillside, while the rain lashed against us. Angus kept his nose to the ground, inhaling all the new scents in big chuffs, almost yanking Sophie off her feet. He's on a blanket by the fire now, his nose tucked under his tail while Sophie idly strokes the fur around his neck.

I can't read her expression, but she's barely said a word since Marcus picked us up at our house in Dogwood Bay. We'd moved out of Marcus's place at the end of January and into a rental. I still remember how lost I felt that first weekend, wandering around our new home. It was cold and lonely, and I missed Marcus. The next week I invited him over for dinner while Sophie was out with her friends. We sat on the couch and polished off a bottle of wine, getting closer and closer with each glass. The feel of his leg against mine, his chest so close, his arm grazing against mine every time he reached for his glass, was driving me crazy. I couldn't stop watching his mouth, how his lips quirked to the side when he smiled or laughed. A couple of times I caught him watching me, a warm look in his eyes, and his hand lingered on my leg a little too long when he was making a point in his story. He had to be feeling the chemistry.

Finally I got bold and said, "Are you ever going to kiss me?"

He looked surprised. "You want me to?"

"Do *you* want to?" Okay, so it wasn't my best line, but I was more than a little drunk and out of practice. I've never had to make the moves before. It worked anyway. He smiled and leaned over and kissed me, his mouth warm and tasting of sweet red wine and chocolate cake.

We kissed on the couch for a while, then I took his hand and led him to my bedroom. My body felt drugged with endorphins, my legs wobbly and my heart beating fast. He left before Sophie came home, murmured against my lips, "I'll call you."

I woke up daydreaming about the scent of his skin, his touch, the taste of his lips, his deep laugh that made his chest vibrate, how good his shoulder muscles felt under my hands. I could still smell his cologne on my sheets and wrapped them tight around me. Then I had the panicky thought that it might have been impulse on his part. What if he had regrets? I rolled over and checked my cell and saw his text message. *Good morning, Sleeping Beauty. Last night was amazing, but let's do this right. I want to take you out for dinner. Is tonight too soon?*

We've been dating for two months now. During the day we text or FaceTime, and the nights we don't stay together, he always calls before bed. I don't know where we're going—we haven't discussed our future, it's too early, but we agreed to live in the moment. Each weekend is an adventure—a new hiking trail, rock climbing, a bike ride in the mountains, shopping the local market and cooking together, or maybe just an all-day movie marathon.

We were sitting on the couch at my place one night, legs entangled while we talked about spring break, when I said, "The three of us should go away somewhere." With any other man, I would have waited, but Sophie didn't seem to mind when I stayed over at Marcus's place or when he came to our home—probably because we'd already lived with him for a few weeks.

"Yeah? Have any ideas?"

I studied his face while I thought it over. His hair had gotten a bit long, falling across his forehead. I brushed it away, smoothed my thumb over the lines on his forehead, marveling that I can do that now. It still amazed me that I'd known this wonderful man for over a year and had no idea our friendship could turn into something so special.

"Maybe skiing? The mountain is still open."

He paused for a moment, then said, "What about my lake house? I just have to call the caretaker and check that it's ready. It hasn't been rented for a few months."

"Are you sure? Would that be hard for you?"

"The lake is beautiful at this time of year. I'd like to show it to you. What do you say? Want to give it a try?" He leaned closer and whispered, "I need *you* there."

I cuddled closer. "It sounds lovely."

I was still a little nervous about how it would be for Marcus, with all his family memories, but we would build new ones together. I imagined early morning walks, a cozy fireplace, making meals together, playing board games. When I told Sophie, she asked if she could bring Jared. After discussing the ground rules—separate bedrooms, no sneaking around—I agreed, but then Friday she announced that he was going away with his friends. She said it was no big deal. "Everything's fine, Mom." But I think she's more upset than she's letting on.

I move to the couch near where she's sitting and pull the cream-colored afghan over my shoulders. "Why don't you check out some of the movies?"

Marcus looks up from the fire. "Help yourself."

Sophie opens the entertainment center under the flat-screen TV, but her movements are listless, her shoulders slumped. She pulls out a few DVDs and puts them to the side. She slides in a music CD instead, then lies on the floor, arms behind her head and eyes closed.

The music is soft, romantic. I think of Marcus's ex-wife, Kathryn, their shared history in this cabin, all the memories they must have made here with their daughter. Did they listen to this CD? Above the fireplace there's a painting of a couple in a boat, just their backs visible, and I wonder if it might be Marcus and Kathryn, then I shake off the thought. He would've taken that down—even if it doesn't seem as though he's changed much else. The house is friendly and inviting, but definitely feminine, with a large sprawling couch, overstuffed chair, and ottoman in a floral pattern, and antiques like the mahogany dining room set that separates the living room and kitchen. None of it looks like Marcus's taste, which is more modern.

On the main floor, there's a small bathroom down the hall leading to the master bedroom with its own bathroom, a laundry room, and a spare bedroom at the back of the house. Upstairs there are two more bedrooms. Marcus pointed out which one was Katie's—the door was closed. Sophie picked the other upstairs bedroom because she liked the view of the forest.

Earlier I noticed a framed photo of Katie on the dresser in the master bedroom. It was a shot of her sitting on a beach, which I assumed was on the lake. Her chin rested on her knees as she gazed out at the water. I wanted to ask Marcus when the photo was taken, but I decided to wait. This is hard enough for him, I'm sure.

In the living room knickknacks are spread around like happy little treasures, quaint owls and woodland creatures, a rustic paddle hanging on the wall. I touch the sterling silver shell jewelry box on the side table, run my fingers over the edges. It's exquisite, shaped like a large clamshell, and obviously an antique. I pick it up and gently open it. In the center a tiny silver pearl is melded to the bottom. The metal is cool under my fingertips. Curious if the shell might be engraved, I turn it over, but the bottom is unmarked except for a small scratch.

He must have left these things so it looked homier when he was renting the house. Or maybe he had someone decorate. I'm not going to ask. I haven't thought about Kathryn much at all since we've been dating—he rarely speaks about her, though I know he checks in with her sometimes to make sure she's doing okay, especially around holidays. I've never felt jealous before, but something about this house makes me feel as though I'm intruding.

The lights flicker. I look up at the ceiling, hold my breath and wait for them to go out, but they stay on. We'll probably lose power soon, though.

"Do you have any candles?"

Marcus glances up from the fire. "Good idea. Check the drawer by the phone."

I rummage through the drawer, full of odds and ends, pens, a pack of cards, some twine, a bottle of glue, batteries, and pull out a couple of white candlesticks. I place them in the porcelain candelabra on the kitchen table, light the pillars on the coffee table. The flames weave and dance.

The warm wax smells strongly of vanilla and reminds me of the first time I had dinner over at Greg's house—he burned the meal and sprayed vanilla everywhere to try to cover it up. I smile at the thought and wonder how he's doing. I heard a rumor that his brother-in-law got into trouble with bad debts and Greg helped him get back on his feet. Maybe that's why he was so distracted those last days of our relationship. He never did return my texts. I'm sure he knows I'm dating Marcus now. I wish I could explain everything to him, but what can I say?

It's only been a couple of months, but it feels like a lifetime ago that my life was upside down and I was talking to the police almost every day. I saw Corporal Parker once at the Muddy Bean. I was picking up coffees for Marcus and me, when she came through the door. I was surprised to see her in a white Windbreaker and black running pants, her hair braided.

We chatted while we waited for our coffees. I told her about Marcus and the lake house. I felt that I was speaking too much, but something in me wanted to let her know that I was okay. When I asked if she had any plans for spring break, she said, "Just working," and ordered two lattes. I watched as she left the shop and got into a car with a blond woman behind the wheel. I wondered if she was another cop. Then the woman smoothed a strand of hair off Parker's face. The gesture was tender, affectionate. Parker glanced toward the coffee shop and I spun around, feeling awkward for staring. I guess Parker kept her life private for a reason.

Sophie and I are washing dishes after dinner when the power goes out. She screams and grabs at my arm, then laughs at her overreaction, but it sounds forced.

"You okay, sweetie?"

"Of course." She turns away and says to Marcus, "Do you have a deck of cards?"

We play poker by candlelight, then Sophie says she's tired and gives me a kiss on the cheek as she leaves the room. I hold her close to me for a moment, then let her go.

Marcus and I have another glass of wine by the fireplace. Finally we stumble to our room and he holds me in his arms while the wind blusters outside. His breath deepens, his warm chest rising and falling under my cheek. I match my breathing with his and fight sleep for a little longer, luxuriating in the delicious feeling of being drowsy. I let my eyelashes flutter closed, and slide my hand down the side of Marcus's body until I reach his hand. I entwine his fingers with mine. He nuzzles my neck and pulls me tight against the length of his body.

Let the storm rage all it wants, my fight is over.

CHAPTER THIRTY-THREE

SOPHIE

I can hear them speaking in low voices downstairs, but I can't make out any words, just the muted sound of Marcus's deep voice and Mom's soft laughter. I know they must talk about me sometimes. It's weird thinking about Marcus analyzing me, so I don't tell Mom much about my feelings anymore. Especially not about the nightmares where I keep finding Andrew's body and how sometimes he opens his eyes and smiles, or how I feel all relieved until I wake up and remember that he's actually dead. I don't need a shrink to tell me what that's about.

It's easier to just let Mom think I'm okay.

My room is dark and the lantern casts strange shadows on the wall. I told Mom I was going to bed because I wanted to listen to music on my phone and draw, but when I flip through my sketchbook, I see one of my sketches of the beach and remember sitting on the picnic table with Jared—he brushed off the top with his hand, fir needles flying through the air. We sat for a while, my hands tucked into his warm pocket. Then he photographed seagulls spiraling in the wind, white frothy waves, and dogs chasing sticks, his camera constantly in motion while I worked on my drawing, but I never finished it. It was more interesting to watch him.

I pick up my phone and check to see if he texted, even though I don't have cell service. Even though he said he wasn't going to message me. Even though I tell myself I don't care.

I still don't know how the fight started. Well, I guess I started it, but I don't know *why*. It was just two days ago that Jared was messing around on his computer—trying to find a song to play for me while I lay on his bed. We'd been at his house for an hour and he hadn't noticed that I wasn't talking much. Maybe it was always like that. Maybe it was always him telling me stuff about his friends or photography while I listened. I don't know anymore. The months are blurred, the days running into each other. After Andrew died I couldn't sleep, so Jared gave me his dad's leftover sleeping pills from when he had knee surgery. He told me not to take them every night, so I cut them in half and tried to make them last longer. They helped but gave me a constant hungover feeling. This week I stopped taking them and now I can't sleep again.

Jared and I spent almost every weekend together since my birthday and it was great at first. When I was with him, I didn't have to think about my dad or how he died, and having sex was kind of like getting high, but in the last couple of weeks it hasn't worked the same anymore.

It had been raining heavy all day and I felt restless and bored. All we ever did was hang out in Jared's bedroom and watch movies or have sex. We'd skip school early and go to his house before his parents got home. Sex had gotten better now. I felt different. More grown up.

"Delaney doesn't call me anymore," I blurted out.

"It's because you have a boyfriend and she's still single."

Maybe he was right. She'd been hanging out with some other girls at school and I was glad she made new friends, but I missed going to movies and coffee, or coloring our hair and hanging out. Then I wondered if it was my fault. Maybe I was the one who stopped calling *her*.

The other day I saw her in the parking lot at school and tried to talk to her, but she was in a rush to meet with her friends. They were going swimming at the pool. We used to love to go swimming. We'd stay in the sauna so long it would feel like our skin was melting off.

It wasn't just Delaney who was drifting away. I never had time to draw anymore. Last weekend I was going to hang out at home, but Jared needed my help editing the pictures we'd taken down at the harbor. That was fun at first too, helping him on his photo shoots, but then I got tired of spending hours outside in crappy weather just so he could get the perfect shot.

He turned away from the computer. "What's wrong?"

"Nothing. I'm just tired."

He climbed into bed with me. "I've been looking at apartments online for when we go to UBC. If we find something great now, we can sign a lease before anyone else takes it."

I looked at him, confused. "You mean for you?"

"For you and me. We'll get a nice place—maybe something with a view downtown."

"I told you Delaney and I are getting a place together." We hadn't talked about it lately, but that's always been our plan. I hope it hasn't changed because I've been thinking that it might be good for Jared and me when we go to university. This summer he'll be traveling with his family, and when we start school, we'll have even less time to hang out. Then I wondered why I wanted less time for him and added it to the pile of things that I didn't want to think about.

"Yeah, but that was before," he said. "I thought you'd want to live with me now."

"We're only eighteen."

"So?"

"Don't you want to live with your friends?"

"They're slobs. I want to live with you."

"Why? Because you think I'll clean up after you? Can you even cook? Or do you want me to do all the cleaning and cooking and shopping?"

"Whoa. Where is that coming from? I can learn to do all that stuff." Of course. He had to learn to do something that I'd been doing for years. He'd had everything easy.

"I'm not ready to think about next year. I just want to get through graduation."

"We can talk about it again in the summer. I'll put a deposit on something." He looked unruffled, like he was so sure I'd come around to his way of thinking.

I sat up, crossed my legs, and faced him. "I don't know if I want to live with you *ever*. My mom got with my dad when she was only nineteen and she missed out on all kinds of stuff."

"I'm not like your dad." Now he was starting to look annoyed, but it didn't make me want to back away, it made me want to dig a little deeper.

"You're kind of acting like him."

"That's a shitty thing to say." His face was flushed.

"Every time I want to stay home, you act like you are all bummed out, then I feel bad."

"You kidding me? You're always depressed, so I've been trying to keep *you* busy."

Everything was lurching and scrambling inside me and I just wanted to get up and go home and hide in my bedroom with my earbuds and loud music. I'd stay in there for days. Maybe weeks. I'd never come out again. "Sometimes I want to be alone. I need space."

We stared at each other. I could feel the truth crumbling inside me, the horrible aching yearning to be on my own, to not have to discuss my feelings, or wonder what he was thinking, or try to make him happy, or be Jared *and* Sophie. I just wanted to be Sophie again.

He sat up. "You need *space?*" His face was pale, his eyebrows a dark slash. His lips even seemed pale, as though I'd stabbed him and all the color had bled out.

"Not forever, just a small break." I couldn't believe I'd said it, but now the words were out and I watched them fall like bombs onto his face. His eyes widened, then his mouth drooped.

"Seriously?" He sounded winded.

"I've been thinking lately that maybe I haven't really dealt with my dad dying. Maybe I just dove into everything with you because I was avoiding it."

"I tried to get you to talk about it."

"That's the problem. I don't want to talk about it. I just want to work it out in my own head. I was thinking that maybe we shouldn't see each other over spring break."

"I don't get it. Yesterday you were telling me how much fun we're going to have."

"I just want one week alone. Why is that such a problem?"

"You're *making* it a problem."

I got off the bed and grabbed my backpack and coat. "I'm going home."

He grabbed my arm. "Stop it," he said. "We need to talk."

"There's nothing to talk about. I already told you I wanted a break, but now I think we should make that permanent." I'm a runaway train, smashing through mountains.

He was gripping my arm hard and he looked desperate. "I won't let you do this."

"You won't *let* me?" I pulled free, his fingertips digging into my skin.

"Just don't decide right now." His voice was hoarse and his eyes black and shiny like pools of ink. I could dip my pen in and draw his heart breaking all over a page in my sketchbook, then I could tear it out, or put it back together again.

"Please?" he said. "I'll give you space—just don't end everything."

I hesitated. Was this really happening? Were we really breaking up? "I don't know. I have to go." I moved through the house, frantic to get outside, to breathe the fresh air.

He followed me out to the front steps, still in his socks even though it was pouring rain. "Wait. I'll drive you home. Don't be stupid. You'll get soaked."

I looked at him standing there in his T-shirt, his shoulders up near his ears, and the rain falling down around us. I remembered my father pulling up beside me in his truck. *Get in.*

"I'll call Delaney," I shouted through the torrent. Then I was running. My feet plunged through cold puddles that splashed water up my calves. Running, running, running.

He texted me a bunch of times that night, my phone lighting up in the dark. *Why can't we talk? Why are you doing this? What did I do wrong?*

I didn't have any answers, couldn't explain the panicked feeling inside of me, and I finally had to turn my phone off. In the morning, I saw his car in the distance when I walked to the bus stop, but I didn't wave to him and he drove off. I spotted him a few times in between classes and he was always with his friends, staring at me. After school he was waiting by my locker.

"You can't just ignore me," he said.

I shoved my books into my backpack. "I told you I needed to be alone."

"Something changed and I want to know what. Did you meet someone else? Is that it?"

"No," I hissed at him. "Do you really want to have this conversation right *now*?" Other kids were giving us curious glances as they walked past.

"Can we go to my house and talk? I want to fix this."

"There's nothing to fix." I thought about how to explain my feelings. "You didn't do anything wrong. Something inside me just shut off, okay? I don't know why, but it's like I can't get back to my happy feelings. The more you push and push at me, the further it goes away."

"Just come over to my house for a little while."

"I have to pack."

"You can't leave like this."

"Well, I'm not going to your house. So what are you going to do? Kidnap me?" I slammed my locker and walked away. When I looked back, he'd disappeared.

Delaney drove me home. I told her I'd had a fight with Jared and we'd broken up.

"Why did you do that?" she said. "I thought you guys were in love."

"I don't know." I was crying because I was sad, but I was confused too. "I can't explain it," I said. "It was all too much and I couldn't breathe. I just couldn't breathe."

She gave me a sympathetic look. "I'm really sorry. Do you want to go for coffee?"

"Okay." I stared out the window, watching the trees whipping past. I was shaking, my hands and body so cold. I tucked my hands under my legs to hold them still. Coffee would be good. We'd talk and Delaney would help me understand why I just blew up my life.

An hour later Delaney dropped me off. I watched as she sped up the driveway and turned back onto the road. There was the sound of tires on wet pavement, then silence. I half wished I were still with her so we could talk more, but it wouldn't have helped. She'd asked me a bunch of questions about my feelings (stuff her therapist asked when her parents divorced), but all I could say was, "I don't know what happened," which somehow made everything feel worse.

Angus jumped all over me when I opened the front door and almost knocked me over while I tried to get my shoes off. "Cut it out!" I said, pushing him out of the way when he licked my ear. He needed a walk, but all I could think about was how good it would feel to crawl into my bed. I'd take him later if I got the energy. I just needed to shut everything out.

I stopped at the doorway to my room. A box was in the middle of my bed. I walked over slowly. It was things I'd left at Jared's house. One of my scarves, a couple of books, a pair of earrings— and the photo he'd taken of me. I glanced at the window, noticed the footprints on the sill. Jared had snuck in a few times to spend the night with me and I guess I never locked it again.

I sat on my bed beside Angus and texted Jared, my fingers hitting the screen so hard that Angus lifted his head and stared at me. *You broke into my house????*

I was giving you back your stuff.

That's so immature.

Right, and you're being so grown up.

I just wanted to think. You're smothering me.

You wanted to be with me all the time!

I did, but then it was like I stopped being ME.

He didn't answer for a few moments. I stared down at my phone and waited for the bubble to pop up. Finally I saw that he was typing.

You're just scared. We were really happy and that freaked you out. You think I'm going to leave you like your dad did so you pushed me away, but it doesn't matter anymore. I'm done.

He never wrote anything else. I even woke up in the middle of the night and checked my phone, then first thing this morning before we left town, but there was nothing. When we were on the ferry, Delaney texted that she heard Jared was going camping on the island with his friends for spring break. He's only about an hour away.

I pull my phone out of my pocket now and read the message again. The last two words roll around in my head like sticks of dynamite, blowing up every time they touch something.

Done. Done. Done.

It's what I wanted, right? So why does everything inside me feel like it's ripping apart in different directions? Why can't I stop thinking about how empty everything feels now?

I hear a scratching sound near the window. I look up, waiting for the sound again. When Jared used to sneak into my bedroom at night, he'd tap softly on the glass to get my attention. I hold my breath, until I realize it's just branches. Of course it's not Jared. Even if he did remember the address and came out to the lake to find me, he doesn't know which room is mine.

I roll into a ball under the thick quilt and tuck my legs tight against my chest. The sheets are cold against my skin. I think about my dad walking through our old house. Did he sit on Mom's bed? I wonder if he went into my room. Everyone thinks he fell by accident, but I worry sometimes that he did it on purpose. He wanted us to find him like that.

I get out of bed, rummage through my makeup bag, where I've hidden the sleeping pills Jared gave me. I take one, rinse away the bitter taste with a handful of water from the tap. Then I stare in the mirror. Mom said everything would feel different by spring break. She was wrong.

CHAPTER THIRTY-FOUR

LINDSEY

Marcus and I have been hiking in the woods for an hour. It's stopped raining, but the trees are still wet and cold drops of water land on my head or drip down the back of my neck. The damp brush slaps at me as we push our way through the trail. We haven't seen anybody else, not even a deer or a rabbit, and the forest is quiet. I'm careful where I put my feet, but I still slip a couple of times and have to reach out to Marcus or grab a branch to steady myself. We've been climbing uphill for the last few miles. Marcus wants to show me the view from the lookout.

"Trust me, it's worth it. You can see all the way to the ocean."

It better be amazing. My leg muscles are aching, and I'm so hot from the exertion I've had to take off my coat and wrap it around my waist. Angus is running ahead, his tongue lolling, and his fur gathering bits of twigs and leaves. There's mud all the way up to his shoulders.

This morning the power was back and Marcus cheerfully made eggs, bacon, and pancakes while I showered. When I came into the kitchen, he already had a pitcher of orange juice, plates, cutlery, and a bundle of napkins set out on the table.

"Where's Sophie?" I said.

"Still sleeping."

"I'll wake her."

"Let her sleep. This house is meant for relaxing."

I sat down at the table, pulled the plate closer, and inhaled the scent of bacon. "Yum." I took a crunchy bite—he'd cooked it exactly how I like it. "Do you think she's sleeping too much?"

He sat down across from me and shook pepper over his eggs. "Teens always sleep."

"I worry that she's depressed."

"Would you like me to talk with her?"

"Maybe. I don't know. That might make her resent you." They seemed to get along well, at least she was always polite and friendly to him and said she was happy for me, but she'd pulled away so much now that she was dating Jared, it was hard to be sure.

"How about we give it some time? It's only been a couple of months since Andrew died, and grief can come and go for many years. Trust me, I've been there. Sometimes sleep is the only peace you can get, the only time where you don't hurt. It's okay for a little while."

I reached across and held his hand. "Thank you for always saying the right thing."

"Oh, I say the wrong thing lots of times, but I feel pretty confident about this. Sophie's going to come through just fine. Now eat your breakfast, I'm taking you for a hike."

We finally reach the summit, and I flop down on a rock, not caring that the seat of my jeans gets wet. I wipe at my forehead and blow my breath out. "Wow. That was steep."

Marcus is standing in front of me, almost at the cliff's edge, and surveying the view. He spreads his arms out wide. "Isn't this incredible?" he says. "Nature at its finest."

The view is stunning, stretching for miles, with sleepy mountains bathed in misty clouds. Nestled in the middle I can see the lake, and far into the distance the long dark blue stretch of ocean. He turns to look back at me, beckons with his hand. "Come see."

"I can see just fine from here."

He laughs. "Get up, lazy bones. You need to feel the breeze on your face."

I stand beside him, resting my cheek on his shoulder, enjoying the scent of rain and forest on him. "You're right. That breeze is lovely." I notice a pretty fern on the edge of the cliff, lean over to take a look, and feel my shoes slip on the rock. Marcus grabs my hand, yanks me back.

"Careful. It's a long way down." He wraps his arm around my shoulder, holds me tight against him. "I don't want to lose you."

"You just don't want to have to climb down to get me." I laugh, but my heart is beating fast at the near-miss. I glance over the edge at the dark trees far below, the jagged rocks.

"That's true." He nuzzles the hair at my temple.

I nestle into his warmth, remembering that long-ago day when Andrew pretended to throw me into a hole at his job site.

We stand in silence for a few minutes, taking in the view. His hand is warm around mine. I think about the rest of our day with pleasure. We'll linger in front of a fire and read our books, stopping once in a while to share something that made us laugh, then we'll make dinner together, drink wine, and watch a movie. The idea feels cozy and warm and perfect.

"I wish we could stay here forever," I say.

"Maybe we can."

I look at him. "What do you mean?"

"After Sophie goes to school we could move out to the lake. You could find work around here, go back to school. Whatever you want."

I'm pleased and surprised by the suggestion. I hadn't realized he was thinking about our future already. "What will you be doing while I work?" I tease. "Fishing every day?"

"Writing my book and then selling it for a million bucks, of course."

"I like the sound of that." I cock my head. "You getting serious about me, Doctor? I thought I was just a fling."

He laughs. "I wouldn't have brought you up here if I wasn't serious about you, but you just moved to your new place. You needed time. I didn't want to scare you off by getting too serious and moaning about how much I missed you and Sophie at my house."

I smile at him, feeling a swell of affection. Of course he understood exactly what I needed back then—and what I need to hear now. He's Marcus.

He cups the side of my face, his thumb caressing my face. "So? Do you need more convincing?" For a moment I wonder if he's going to tell me he loves me. We haven't said the words yet, but I've been so close so many times. Then Angus nudges Marcus's hip with his nose and he looks down with a laugh and pats his head. I glare at Angus. *Thanks a lot, buddy.*

I watch Marcus for a moment, his natural easy way, his handsome smile. Could I move to the lake and let go of my house and business and everything? Do I really want to start over? I look out at the mountains, breathe in the sweet air. Marcus is right. This place is special.

"Yes," I say. "Let's do it."

"Really?"

"I'm already in love with you. I might as well jump in with both feet."

He's staring at me in a stunned sort of silence, and now my

face is hot and I wish I could take back the words. What was I thinking? I watch him mutely. The seconds tick past until it feels like we've been standing there forever. He still hasn't said it back. He's just looking at me.

"Well, we should probably head back," I say, and begin to walk away.

"Lindsey, come here." He grabs my hand, pulls me around. "I love you too—but I have to admit it scared the hell out of me at first. I tried to fight it for a long time."

I lean my body against his chest. "You tried to fight it? Really? Tell me more."

"You're not going to stop until you get every last detail, huh?"

I rub my cold nose against his collarbone. "I'll torture it out of you."

He laughs. "Okay. True confession time. When I walked into that first meeting and saw you sitting under those fluorescent lights, your hair glowing like you were some sort of Swedish goddess, I thought, *Wow, she is one beautiful woman, I better stay away from her. She'll break my heart.* It didn't matter how kind, or loving, and funny, you were, I wasn't going to risk getting hurt again, but I lost the battle." He smiles. "Is that all right? Think you can handle me?"

I give him a cheeky grin. "I'll give it a shot."

He presses his mouth against mine. The rain is hitting hard now, trickling down our faces and over our lips, but we don't stop. I'm going to kiss this man for the rest of my life.

CHAPTER THIRTY-FIVE

SOPHIE

Mom's hair is plastered onto her head and her eyelashes are all spiky, but she's laughing as she pulls off her boots and says, "Don't believe Marcus if he tells you he's taking you on a short hike. I feel like we climbed Mount Everest." Marcus is also laughing as he helps her take off her wet coat. She pretends to shake her hair like a dog and he jumps back.

"Hey! Stop that or I'll leave you outside with Angus!"

I'm glad someone is having a nice time. I spent all morning scrolling through my saved text messages on my phone, thinking about Jared.

"Can you grab some towels, Sophie?" Mom says.

"There are some old ones under the sink for Angus," Marcus says.

I find the towels in the washroom and bring them out. They're both sitting on the hearth now, so close that their shoulders are touching. I towel off Angus and he trots into the house.

Mom and Marcus are holding hands. Jared always holds my hands when we drive. Sometimes he blows on my fingers when they're cold. I touch my phone in my pocket, wish I could pull it out and read his texts again, but Mom will wonder what I'm doing. I glance at her and catch her looking at Marcus. She's got this silly sort of smile on her face.

"What's up?" I say. "You're acting weird."

"Nothing. I'm just happy we're all here together. I love this place."

"Yeah, it's nice. It would be fun to come every summer."

Mom flicks another glance at Marcus and he squeezes her hand. She looks back at me. "We were just talking about maybe moving to the lake next year."

"Oh." I'm looking at them and they're looking at me, and I swear even Angus is looking at me like he's waiting for me to say something really profound. I can see the tiny lines around Mom's eyes, and I'm wondering when she got those and it feels like maybe it just happened in the last couple of months, and it seems as though every one of those lines is pointing to the hopeful excited expression in her eyes, saying, *See how happy I am! Please be happy for me!*

I don't know why, but suddenly I am thinking of my dad's face when he used to talk about Mom, how it was different for him. He wasn't excited, it was like something deeper, like he needed her to *breathe.* Now my eyes are blurry and I quickly make my lips move into a smile.

"That's cool," I say. "I'm only home a few more months anyway. Then it will just be weekends." I smile at Marcus. "Don't let her clean my room."

I'll have to travel over to the island now. I might not get to see Mom as much, but I can't be selfish and tell her any of that. I have to be happy for her. Maybe they'll even get married.

I glance at her hand, try to imagine what kind of ring Marcus would buy her. Something big, probably. I liked the simple set she wore when she was married to my dad. When we cuddled, I would roll it around on her finger, playing with it, and sometimes she'd slide it onto my finger, and I'd pretend we were married. She'd tucked that ring away and said I could have it one day. When is one day? When I get married? Will I want it? I think about my dad, shopping for her, and how she was only nineteen. How did she know she wanted to marry him? How come she didn't know what was going to happen? I think about Jared. Done. Done. Done.

"We won't make any changes for a while," Marcus says. "We want you to be comfortable with everything. We know this has been a tough year."

A tough year. Is that how he describes it? He has a kind expression and he looks concerned like he wants to make sure I'm okay. If they get married, he'll be my stepfather. He'll be at every Christmas dinner, every holiday. He'll come to my graduation.

Not my father. It will never be my father.

And then I want to talk to Jared so bad I can taste my want, like this bitter aching thing in my mouth. I want to spit it out, but it's too late, I've already swallowed it.

They're waiting for me to say something. "This is big news. Should we do a toast?" I get up and head into the kitchen. "Let's have some wine." I have my hand on the bottle.

Mom is following behind me. "Whoa," she says.

"I'm almost nineteen. Come on. Let me celebrate with you."

"You just turned eighteen a couple months ago." But she's hesitating and I can see that she wants to do it, wants to do anything that will prove to her that I'm really okay with this.

"Maybe just this once." She reaches up to grab the glasses from the cupboard.

They've gone to bed. I'm sitting in my room, looking out the window. Angus is with me. He doesn't sleep with them as much anymore. I guess he knows three is a crowd.

I can hear the low hum of their voices traveling through the walls, or maybe it's through the vent. I wonder what they're talking about. Maybe they are making plans, talking about how much they love each other. I wonder if Mom even thinks about my dad anymore.

Marcus is nice. He treats Mom well. He doesn't get drunk, he doesn't hurt her—and he doesn't make her cry. So why do I feel angry at him? I dig deep through my thoughts, try to isolate the feeling, but it keeps scampering back into the corner, hiding from me.

Then I put my finger on it. There'd been a sneaky little part of my heart that hoped my father and mother would get back together again. All those times I told my father that he needed to let go and accept that she had moved on, it was really me who needed to move on.

I take a sip of wine. After Mom and Marcus went to bed, I snuck back out and grabbed the last of the bottle. She won't remember. I was the one who kept filling their glasses.

Now I feel warm and hot and sleepy drunk, but it's not cheering me up. I pick up my phone, scroll through my messages, read Jared's messages again and again.

Hours later, I wake with Angus's head on the pillow next to me. He yawns noisily and blasts me with a waft of doggie breath. I roll over, wait for the spins to settle down. The clock says three in the morning. The empty wine bottle is sitting on my night table.

I pick up my phone and squint at the screen. I have a vague memory of texting someone, but that can't be right. I don't have cell service. Then I see what I wrote Jared.

Okay. Maybe I am scared. Because I love you too much. You might leave me like my dad, and then I would die twice. I thought this would be easier. But it's not. I miss you.

Oh, shit. Thank God that didn't go through. I stare at the blue bubble. All I would have to do is drive where we have service and it would fly off my phone and land on his. But I don't want that. Those were just my drunk words. They don't mean anything. I have plans. I'm going to be single and focus on finishing school, then move to the city and meet new people.

My fingers hover over my phone, then I open up my photos. Jared and me, selfies on the beach, in his bed, making crazy faces, kissing. I stare at his face, his dark eyes. I think about how he always seemed to know when I was upset, and how he'd find new places to take me, how he'd drag me outside for walks when I didn't feel like doing anything.

He was right. He'd just been trying to help me. It's not his fault I stopped drawing. He used to even tell me to bring my sketchpad with me. I stopped hanging out with Delaney because we just didn't have as much to talk about anymore and having sex with Jared was more fun. That wasn't his fault. I made all those choices. I look at Angus. "I really screwed up, didn't I?"

He wiggles closer, licks and snuffles at my face until I have to push him away. At least he still loves me. I sneak out to the living room, pull open the fridge, and search for the bottles of water Mom brought. I drop one as I take it out and it rolls across the floor. Angus pounces after it nosily and I shush him. Too late, I hear footsteps behind me, then Marcus's voice.

"Thought I heard you coming down the stairs. You okay?"

"Yeah, just can't sleep." I open the water and guzzle half of it without stopping to breathe. I feel as though I've just woken up with a mouthful of sand.

"Hungover, huh?" He's leaning on the counter, wearing a white robe like he's at the spa. His hair is all messed up. I'm not going to think about how it might have gotten like that.

"I'm just not used to wine." As if I'm used to so many other things.

"You know, if something is bothering you, you can tell me. We can keep it between us."

He has that understanding therapist expression on his face again. The one that makes him look like he wants to sit down with a pad of paper and talk about all my deepest fears. I'm surprised he'd keep anything from my mom. Maybe he's just saying that so I'll trust him.

"I'm okay."

"You sure? Seeing your mom move on in a new relationship must be hard. Especially when your father just died. It would be natural for you to feel some anger."

Jesus. I thought shrinks were supposed to be sensitive. I feel the room spin a little again. I take a breath. It's just the wine. I fiddle with the lid on my bottle. "It's not that. It's Jared."

He cocks his head. "I wondered why he canceled last-minute."

"I broke up with him, but I think I made a mistake."

"Is it too late to fix?"

"I don't know. He's on the island too, but I'm not sure if he wants to see me."

"Well, maybe the time apart will be a good thing. We're only here for the week. You can talk when we get back to town. Like they say, absence makes the heart grow fonder."

"Yeah, maybe. What's a week, right?"

"Exactly." He looks relieved, like he thinks he's just scored some big parenting win and now everything is cool and he can tell Mom how we bonded over my broken heart in the kitchen.

We say our good-nights and I go back to bed with Angus and my bottle of water. Good thing Marcus isn't a shrink anymore, because he's really not all that smart about teenagers.

There's no way I'm waiting for a week.

CHAPTER THIRTY-SIX

LINDSEY

I wake abruptly as though someone reached over and shook me. I blink in the dim room, unfamiliar shapes coming into focus. Right. We're at the lake house. Marcus is breathing softly beside me. It's eight in the morning, according to the clock, which projects the time onto the ceiling. What was I dreaming about? I think back. Snow-covered roads, a sense of urgency. The night I ran away from Andrew? It's been a long time since I dreamt about that. It must be some sort of subconscious anxiety about moving in with Marcus, which is silly. This time I'm doing it right.

I let my eyes drift closed, imagine living at the lake with him, our love growing stronger as we build a life together. We'll redecorate the house, get to know the neighbors and the community. Maybe I'll take some evening classes in town. I can do homework while he writes at a desk in front of a window. We'll take breaks and talk. I see Marcus smile, his hand reaching for me. But then there's a knock on the door. Corporal Parker is standing there.

We know about the pills, Lindsey.

Now I see Marcus's face change from confusion to horror and finally to anger. *What did you do? Why did you lie to me?* And then I know it's over. It's all over.

I open my eyes. Why did I have *that* thought? Marcus wouldn't judge me for what I did that night. But now I can't stop thinking about how I watched those pills fall into Andrew's glass of whiskey, how I swirled the spoon around and around until they dissolved.

I glance over at Marcus, the shadowed outline of his shoulder. *Should* I tell him? How do I explain that I drugged my ex-husband? Would it change his feelings for me? Jenny would probably tell me to keep it to myself. There's no reason he needs to know.

I leave Marcus to sleep and go into the living room. The fire has gone out, leaving the air chilly. I wrap one of the throw blankets around me like a shawl, then hunt through the cupboards for the coffee beans and brew a pot, gazing out the window at the lake while I wait for it to finish. I can't help but wonder if Marcus's ex-wife ever stood like this. When I walk over to the fridge for milk, I'm surprised to see a note from Sophie stuck under a magnet.

Went into town. Borrowed Marcus's car. Sorry, didn't want to wake you. Back soon. XO

What the hell is she thinking? The roads will be a mess and she's not used to driving a big SUV. I imagine her hitting potholes and sliding on the loose gravel. I reach for my phone to tell her to come back, then I remember we don't have cell service. I check the landline. It's dead. Of course. That's probably why she went into town. She wanted to call Jared or Delaney.

I hear footsteps behind me and spin around. Marcus is wearing jeans and a T-shirt, his hair rumpled and his face shadowed after two days with no shaving. He gives me a sleepy smile.

"Sorry," I say. "I didn't mean to wake you."

He wraps his arm around my waist. "You're worth getting out of bed for." He notices the note in my hand. "What's that?"

"Sophie took your car and went into town."

He steps back, raises his eyebrows. "I found her in the kitchen last night getting water and we talked about Jared—they broke up. I suggested she wait to talk to him, but she must have decided to take matters into her own hands. I forgot about the impulsiveness of teenagers."

I'm startled to hear that Sophie and Jared broke up. Why hadn't she said anything? Obviously that's why she's been moping around. I'm glad she confided in Marcus, but am hurt that she kept it from me. "I can't believe she just ran off. I'll speak to her when she gets back."

"She might not be long." He looks out the window. "I wouldn't be surprised if the roads aren't still blocked with trees."

"I hope she doesn't get stuck."

"If she does, she can walk back. It's not that far."

I nod and tell myself he's right. "I guess I need to get used to this feeling. Once she goes away to school, she'll have her own life."

"And so will you." He presses his mouth against mine for a kiss, but I can't relax into it. He raises his head, gives me a look. "What's up? I brushed my teeth." He smiles.

"I just need my coffee. I'm still half asleep." I gently pull out of his arms and busy myself with pouring two cups. "Let's go into the living room."

He sits on the couch and I settle beside him. The lake is calm outside the window, the surface smooth as glass. The trees are still. If I want to tell him about the night of the accident, this is a good time, but I falter inside. I look over at him, his kind eyes and his reassuring smile. He's a wonderful person, I remind myself. I can trust him.

"I woke up thinking about something I did in the past," I

say. "A mistake that I made when I was married. It happened a long time ago, but it still bothers me sometimes."

"And you aren't sure whether you should tell me?"

"I'm just worried, I guess, that it might change things."

"Lindsey, whatever it is, it can't be that bad." He reaches out and holds my free hand. "Nothing will change. I promise."

I stare into my coffee. I've gone too far now, can't pull back and laugh this one off. I take a breath. "The night I ran away, I gave Andrew something so he'd sleep. I was just so scared he'd wake up, you know?" I've told Marcus how Andrew had choked me the first time I tried to leave and I'm glad I don't have to go into that now. This is hard enough.

"You mean like sleeping pills?"

I nod. "My brother got them for me because I was too scared to get a prescription. Andrew had started tracking my finances even closer after he discovered I was secretly taking birth control pills. I didn't tell you about that either. . . ." I look up at his face, waiting to see how he reacts to this new revelation, but his expression is still understanding.

"I'm not surprised," he says. "Of course you didn't want to get pregnant when you were in an abusive marriage." He gives my hand a squeeze.

My body relaxes. I didn't realize how these secrets had been eating at me, how much it means to be able to finally share them with Marcus.

"I was going to give him a few of the sleeping pills, but he'd been drinking a lot that night and I was worried if I gave him too many, he'd die. So I only dropped two into his glass."

"That seems smart. You had to get out of that house."

"Yes, but he must have woken up—maybe he got sick from the mixture. I don't know what happened. Later, I realized I might have left the cotton from the bottle on the counter. All these years, I wasn't sure, but when Andrew approached me outside the bank, he said something that made me realize he *did* know I drugged him. That's why he was so angry that night."

"You blame yourself for the accident?"

"I know logically that he was the one who chose to get behind the wheel, but the thing about Andrew was that even when he was drinking, he could still drive okay. He was usually *more* careful. Sometimes I couldn't even tell. I think the pills changed his coordination. After the accident I read online that some people sleepwalk when they drink and take sleeping pills."

Marcus is just watching me, his eyes intense.

"Can you say something?"

"Sorry. I was waiting for you to finish. It sounds like you've been torturing yourself over this for a long time, and I understand. Trust me, I understand, but you need to forgive yourself."

"Even though it's my fault that woman died?"

"Elizabeth," he says.

I pause, surprised to hear him say her name.

He catches my look. "You mentioned it once."

I nod. "Right. Elizabeth. I just can't help thinking if I hadn't drugged him, he wouldn't have lost control of the truck. Or if I'd just given him more pills. . . ."

"You'd probably be in prison right now and Sophie wouldn't have a mother. You can imagine a thousand different scenarios, Lindsey, but you aren't responsible for his choices. The chances of it being a sleepwalking situation are pretty rare. He knew what he was doing."

I lean back against the couch. "I've told myself that so many times, but I don't think I've ever believed it until now. I was so scared you'd think I was a terrible monster."

"Not even close. We're all capable of doing things we never thought possible." He gives my hand a squeeze, reaches for his coffee mug, and takes a sip.

I smile at him. "What have you ever done that's so bad?"

He smiles back. "Well, apparently I'm dating a monster."

I lightly punch his shoulder. "That's not nice!"

He winces and pretends to rub at the spot. "See? She's a dangerous woman."

I laugh, lean forward, and give his arm a kiss. "You're right, I'm *very* dangerous." I take the mug out of his hand, and set it on the table, then slide my hand up his my forearm, to the sensitive spot at his elbow, where I rub a slow circle with my thumb. He gives me a look.

"How about we take advantage of our alone time?" I say.

He hesitates. "I was hoping to get out on the lake soon."

"This won't take long." I stand up and straddle his body, kiss him until his mouth opens. We stumble to the bedroom, toss our clothes onto the floor, and collapse onto the bed. We make love, our hands entwined over his head, our breaths mingling. I can't see his eyes, his face buried in my neck, but I can feel his desperate need for release, our bodies rocking together. Every time I slow, his hands sink into my flesh, urging me on.

CHAPTER THIRTY-SEVEN

Sophie

The house is quiet when I tiptoe down the stairs. I move extra slowly, waiting for a moment in between each step. I don't want to wake Marcus this time. Angus's toenails tap on the floor as he follows me and I stop to take off his collar so it doesn't jingle. I put my finger to my lips. "Shush!" He looks at me as though he understands. I let Angus out for a pee and quickly scrawl a note, debate about where to leave it, and finally settle for on the fridge. I'll get a coffee in town. When Angus comes back in, I coax him onto his blanket with a bone stuffed with peanut butter, then sneak out of the house before he catches on that we're not going for a walk.

I feel bad about using Marcus's Cherokee without asking— and a little freaked out. It's brand-new, without a single scratch. I drive slowly, my hands tight on the wheel. I'll be extra-careful. I won't park by any other cars and I'll wash it after our trip. Hopefully he'll just be so happy he and Mom are getting married that he'll let my auto theft slide. Every kid gets one get-out-of-jail-free card, right? Though maybe that's for real parents. *Real* fathers. I think about my dad. He would have let me use his truck. He was even going to buy me my own car.

No. I'm not going to think about that anymore. Andrew is gone and I can't make anything up to him, but Jared is still alive and I'm not letting him go this time.

The road is rough, the tires slogging through deep puddles. I fumble with different buttons until I think I've put the Cherokee in four-wheel drive. Isn't there something about speed? You can't use four-wheel drive on a highway? I don't know, I don't know. What was I thinking? I don't want to kill his transmission. Some of the branches scattered across the road are so big I can feel them scrape against the undercarriage. I hope I don't rip off the muffler.

When I come to a junction, I slow down and try to think which way to turn. There are no direction signs and nothing looks familiar. I'd been sitting in the back the whole drive, playing on my phone. All I remember is Marcus saying something about all the logging roads in the area.

I turn right, but twenty minutes later, when I still haven't hit the highway and the road is getting bumpier and narrower, I realize I've made a mistake. I find a small clearing in the woods where I can turn around, and head back. This time when I reach the junction, I go the other way.

Five minutes later, I notice a sign. I'm almost at the turnoff to the highway. The road should get better soon—thank God. I haven't passed any cabins for a while and the forest is thinner. Light breaks through the trees.

I glance at my cell on the passenger seat, wondering if I have service yet. I stretch over to the side, my rib cage pressing into the leather console, and pick up my phone. I press my password in, while taking quick peeks at the road, and hold the wheel with one hand.

Success. I have cell service! I wonder if I've gotten more text messages. I glance down and open the app with my thumb, and hear a distinctive whoosh as my text to Jared leaves my phone. Shit! I'd wanted to look over it again and make sure it didn't sound stupid.

I look up—and in a quick flash of panic, I see the tree lying across the road. I slam on the brakes, the seat belt cutting sharply into my stomach and across my chest. The back end of the Cherokee is sliding and I'm trying to turn the wheel, but the front is pointed toward the edge of the road. The Cherokee bounces into the ditch, rockets forward, and smashes into a tree.

So much noise, like the world is coming apart. Metal screaming, glass shattering. A branch stabs into the windshield and scrapes against my face in a sharp slap. The driver's-side air bag blows up with a loud bang, then the passenger one. I'm surrounded by white balloon material.

It's stopped. Everything is quiet, just the hissing of the engine. I'm scared to move. I cautiously move my legs and feet. Everything seems to work, but I'm shaking hard. The engine is making a weird noise, like a high-pitched whine underneath the hissing.

I reach out and turn the key. The engine shudders off. I fumble for my seat belt and press the button, but it doesn't release right away. I have to yank and tug and finally it comes free.

I look for my cell phone, but I can't see anything with the air bags filling the front seats. It's not on the console. I push and shove the driver's-side air bag out of the way, and feel around with my feet until I spot my bright pink cell case.

I reach down, wiggle it out with a finger, and slide it closer. The rectangle plastic shape is solid and familiar in my hand, comforting. *Please, please, let me still have cell service.*

Three bars. It should be enough, but who do I call? I hesitate, staring at my screensaver photo—Delaney and me, making a funny face. Jared took the photo. I don't know if the lake house has phone service yet, but it doesn't matter—I don't know the number anyway.

Should I call 911? I think about the text leaving my phone. Can cops look up that stuff? They'll see I was using my cell while driving. I'll be charged. I don't want to lose my license. My phone vibrates in my hand, startling me so much that I almost drop it. It's a text from Jared.

Can we talk? I miss you.

I had an accident. I need help!

WTF? Call me!

He answers right away. "You okay? Did you get hurt?"

"My head hurts a little . . . and my neck. My mom is going to be so pissed."

"What happened?"

"I borrowed Marcus's Cherokee. I was so stupid—I looked at my cell when I was driving. I slid off the road and hit a tree. Should I call the cops? I'm scared I'll get in trouble."

"Just stay there. I'll come get you."

I wait, hunched over in the Cherokee with my arms wrapped around my legs, shivering and staring at my phone while worrying that he'll get lost, or that some other driver will come along and see the Cherokee in the ditch and then they'll call the cops. Forty-five excruciating minutes later, I finally hear a car door slamming, then his voice calling.

"Sophie?"

I push open the door, climb out, my legs cramped and stiff. "I'm over here!" I push my way through the brush and slide down into the ditch, try to get to my feet.

Footsteps on gravel—sounds like he's running. Then he's standing in front of me, his face pale and his hand reaching to help me out of the ditch. I grab at it.

"I'm sorry," I say. "I'm so sorry for everything. I was such a bitch. I just—"

"Don't worry about that right now." He pulls me up until we are face-to-face, brushes glass out of my hair, then cups my cheek. "Don't ever scare me like that again."

"I didn't mean to have an accident."

"That's not what I mean." He steps closer, presses his cold lips against mine. His mouth is warm, soft, and we kiss desperately. Finally we separate, but keep our hands gripped together.

"The tree is still covering the road," he says. "How far away is the lake house?"

"I'm not sure. I got lost."

"Can you walk?"

I nod. He tucks my hand into his pocket and we make our way back up the hill. I don't care if it takes two hours to walk back. I don't care if Mom and Marcus yell at me. I have Jared.

CHAPTER THIRTY-EIGHT

LINDSEY

It's almost ten and Sophie still isn't back. Marcus is fishing on the lake—he wants to catch some trout for dinner. I had planned on reading my book and enjoying another cup of coffee, but I'm watching Marcus from the window, the bright red of his life jacket, the flick of his wrist as he casts the line. He hasn't acted any different since my confession, just in a hurry to get out on the lake before he "missed the bite," but I still feel exposed, vulnerable.

I walk back to my book, which is still open on the couch where I was sitting. I pick it up, put it down again. Listen for the sound of Sophie parking the Cherokee, her boots coming down the stairs, think how she'll burst through the door with flushed cheeks and apologies, but there's only silence. If she doesn't come home soon, we may have to borrow a neighbor's car.

I get up and hunt for cleaning supplies under the kitchen sink, wash every surface, including the floors, the cupboard doors, and the inside of the fridge. Why is she taking so long?

If something happened to her, would anybody know where to find us? I head into the master bedroom. When I reach up to dust the top of the dresser, I accidentally knock into Katie's photo and the frame hits the floor with a smash. I quickly crouch and check the damage.

The wood is split and glass fragments cover the floor like slivers of ice. I feel terrible and hope the frame didn't hold any sentimental value for Marcus. Thank God the picture doesn't seem to be harmed. When I remove the back piece and take the photo out, I realize it's on photo paper—I can see the brand name. Marcus must have printed it from his computer.

I flip the photo over and look at Katie's face. She was so beautiful. Everything in the photo is perfect, the wind in her hair, her makeup, the woven blanket spread perfectly straight on the sand, which I now realize now looks fine-grained, and lighter-colored than the sand on the beach I can see from the front window. The vegetation in the photo isn't like what we have on the West Coast either. They must have been on vacation somewhere, which would explain the glass of wine in her hand. But Marcus told me his daughter never drank. It could just be water, but now that I'm looking closer, something about the photo doesn't seem natural. It seems staged. They probably had a photographer take the shot. Come to think of it, most of the photos I've seen of Katie in Marcus's house all look like they have been taken by a photographer. There aren't any candid shots of her—and none of them together. He must have packed those away.

After I sweep up the glass and dump it into the recycling so Angus doesn't cut his paws, I walk upstairs to clean Sophie's room. I stop outside Katie's door. When's the last time anyone dusted in there? Marcus hasn't said her room is off-limits, and I'm curious about her. The daughter of the man I love. I want to know her in some way. I'm sure he wouldn't mind. I try the door, but it's locked. He probably just didn't want any renters using her room. Downstairs, I find a few keys hanging on the rack and try them in the door. One fits.

I walk in, sniffing the stale air. It doesn't seem like a young woman's bedroom and I wonder when she stayed here last, if it's been redecorated. It's more like a master bedroom, with a painting of a sunrise on a snow-covered lake hanging over the wrought-iron bed, and a luxurious-looking silver faux-fur duvet cover. It's much bigger than the bedroom downstairs.

I walk over to the window to let in some fresh air. The window is stiff, clearly hasn't been opened for years, and I have to struggle to slide it up. When I turn back around, I notice a wooden wardrobe at the side of the room. I pull it open. There's women's clothing inside. I flip through a few shirts, a cashmere sweater, and a pair of black dress pants. A girl in her early twenties wouldn't wear clothes like this. They must have belonged to Kathryn. I notice a white silk kimono, which makes me cringe when I think about her wearing it for Marcus. I close the door.

I step back and look around again, taking in every detail. There are no photos on the nightstands—*two* nightstands, with lamps on each side. Could this have actually been the bedroom Marcus shared with his wife? That doesn't make sense. He told me he bought a new mattress and bedding for the room downstairs so I wouldn't feel uncomfortable about anything.

To the right is another door. I push it open and discover a bathroom. I walk in slowly. I'm definitely snooping now but unable to turn around. I pull open one of the drawers. Women's makeup, odds and ends of samples, things she left behind. I can't stop my fingers from pulling out more drawers, taking inventory. Q-tips, cotton balls, a dried-out perfume bottle, travel-sized shampoo, and a bar of scented soap still in Christmas paper. I turn it over, read the tag.

Love from Marcus.

Why didn't he clean out this room? I don't understand. Is

he still in love with Kathryn? I grab at the counter, feeling woozy. I have to talk to him. I have to find out what this all means. I blink at my reflected image in the mirror. I look pale. I have to get out of here.

I'm passing the left side of the bed when I notice the bright yellow and red cover of a book on the bottom of the nightstand. I tilt my head, read the title.

Nursing Leadership and Management in Canada.

I drop to my knees and pick up the book, skim through some pages. Marcus said his ex-wife was an accountant—and Katie was going to university to be an accountant. Maybe Kathryn had been thinking about a career change. The book flips open to the title page and I see the label, neatly filled out in bright blue ink: *This book belongs to Elizabeth Kathryn Sanders.*

CHAPTER THIRTY-NINE

It can't be right. It can't be the same woman Andrew killed. How is that even possible? I spin around and walk over to the small bookshelf under the window. I pull books out, one by one, slowly at first, then faster and faster. Mystery novels, romance novels. So many romance novels. They all have a label on the inside page. I read her name over and over again.

Elizabeth Kathryn Sanders. Elizabeth Kathryn Sanders. Elizabeth Kathryn Sanders.

I shove the books back onto the shelf, trying to make sure they are all lined up again, lock the door, and run down the stairs. Before I do anything else, I check out the front window. Marcus's boat is near the shoreline, his back toward the house. He's still fishing.

In our room, I rummage through his suitcase, run my hands through his coat pockets, peer under the bed, and dig into the nightstand drawer. I don't know what I'm searching for, but something deep inside is spurring me on. *Look, just keep looking.* My hands are moving fast, lifting, feeling. The floorboards are cold on my feet. I've let the fire go out, but I'm hot, sweaty. Angus is following me, nudging me with his nose, his tail wagging. He thinks this is a game.

I yank open the medicine cabinet, rifle through bottles of mouthwash, disposable razors, bottles of heartburn medicine, Tylenol, Advil, cold remedies. No prescription bottles.

His shaving kit is on the side of the counter. I look through his grooming tools, his electric razor. When I lift out his plastic soap holder, something inside makes a soft rattling sound. I fumble with the lid, my hands heavy as though they're frozen. Finally I get it off.

I'm staring at a handful of white pills. I've seen these before. Ambien. The same pills someone gave Angus. I look down beside me where Angus is sitting. His tail thumps.

I'm remembering how Marcus drove me home that time when my tire suddenly went flat, how he stood nearby when I turned off my alarm. I blamed Andrew for everything, for hurting Greg, for sneaking around in my house. Was it really Marcus? He said his ex-wife's name was Kathryn. There never was a daughter. There never was a Katie.

Elizabeth was his wife.

The answer comes loud and clear and I realize that I already knew. As soon as I saw the books, I knew. That's why I was looking for the pills. I slide to my knees, still holding the soap container. No. This is wrong. I'm jumping to conclusions. Andrew *died* in my house.

They'd ruled it an accident, but Corporal Parker had questions, so many questions, about me, Greg, and Chris. She said lots of people were angry with Andrew, but maybe she missed one. The most important one. I think back to what I know of Elizabeth Sanders. The newspapers had mentioned a husband but nothing else. The family had asked for privacy.

Each new thought hits harder. Marcus volunteered at my support group, he became my friend. Had he just been waiting for Andrew to get out of jail? He probably knew Andrew would come looking for me one day. And now he knows I drugged Andrew that night. I sat here and told him all about it, then we made *love*.

What kind of game is this? What does he want with me?

As soon as Sophie is back with the Cherokee we have to leave, but what do I say to Marcus? Do I confront him? No. We have to get to a safe place. I'll have to come up with some sort of emergency that means we need to go back to town. Then I'll call the police.

I stand up on shaky legs, carefully put the pills back into his shaving kit. I look at his razor. I need a weapon in case he tries to attack me. Maybe a knife.

I move cautiously out of the bedroom, peer into the living room. It's empty, the fire is dying. I check the window again, keeping my body in the shadows, and grip the curtain tight when I see his boat tied up on the dock. I press closer to the window, check the beach, the path.

He's not down at the lake anymore.

CHAPTER FORTY

Marcus is standing by the front door, unlacing his boots. I'm struck with an image of Andrew and how he'd loosen the top laces first on each boot, starting with the right. Then he'd straighten and use his left foot against his right heel, while bracing his hand on the wall. I never realized before that they move the same way. Marcus looks up at me with a smile.

"I was getting lonely out there."

I smile, but my lips feel stiff, fake. He's going to sense something is wrong if I don't find some way to pretend everything is okay. I've done this before. I did this for *years*.

"Catch anything?"

"No luck today."

"Want some coffee?"

"That'd be great." As I pull down a mug from the cupboard, he comes up behind me and wraps his arms around my waist. His skin is cold against the flesh at my belly where my shirt has risen. When he brushes his lips across the nape of my neck, I almost can't breathe. I concentrate on lifting the decanter.

"God, you're freezing," I say "Why don't you have a hot bath?"

"Maybe." He pulls away, takes the coffee. "Where's Sophie?"

"She's not back yet. I might take Angus for a walk and see if any of the neighbors are home. Someone might have a car I could borrow."

"It's a long way around the lake. Let's just give it a little more time, okay? It's getting stormy outside again. There'll be branches falling from the trees. I don't want you hurt."

"Okay." I hide my face behind my coffee mug. *Who are you? What have you done?* His handsome face is so familiar. I just kissed his lips hours ago, but now he's a stranger. I want Sophie to come back soon so we can get out of here, but the other part of me wants her to stay where she's safe. If Marcus realizes something's wrong, I don't know what he's going to do.

He looks around. "Do I smell cleaner?"

"I did some tidying, but I accidentally broke the photo frame in your bedroom—the one with Katie's photo." I watch his face, waiting to see how he reacts, and keep a tight grip on my mug. If I have to run, I'll throw the hot coffee in his face.

"That's okay," he says calmly. "I can replace it. Was the photo damaged?" He's probably wondering if I've noticed anything amiss. I have to keep my own voice calm, but I've never been so deadly afraid in my entire life. Not even with Andrew.

"I didn't remove it. I was worried about scratches."

"Well, don't worry about it," he says. "Accidents happen."

But it wasn't an accident that we met. Just like it's not an accident that we're at the lake house with him right now. He'd been so convincing, weaving his spell. I *need* you, he'd said.

"Why don't you have a bath with me?" he says. We'd done that before, when I stayed over at his place. He'd lit candles, dribbled champagne over my body, teased me with his mouth, made me twist and moan and beg for his touch. I fell in love with a man who hated me.

I glance at the front door. "I don't know. . . . Sophie—"

"Is a big girl. I don't think she'll be traumatized. She knows about the birds and the bees." He smiles. "You can help me warm up."

"I'm just not in the mood for a bath."

"Okay." He gives me a quizzical look. My tone was too short, my voice tight.

"I'll come and sit with you. Let me just freshen my coffee."

The sound of running water floats down the hall. I think of the bathtub upstairs. Did Elizabeth sit with him? Does he still bathe in there sometimes and think of her? I wonder if he's ever actually rented this house out or if that's just another lie. I fill my coffee cup.

When I enter the bathroom he's already got the tub half full, bubbles covering his body up to his hard stomach. His feet are braced against the spout, and he uses one to tighten the tap.

"Sure you won't join me?"

I shake my head and perch on the side of the tub. He lifts a wet hand, trails a finger down my arm, following a bead of water. I want to scratch at it. Maybe I should just leave now, when he's in the bath. I might get a few miles down the road before he catches on, but he's fast—I've seen him on the treadmill. If he chases me down, I won't be able to intercept Sophie.

"I was thinking I might want to cook something different tonight," I say. "When Sophie comes back, mind if I run to the grocery store and pick up a few things?"

"Want me to come with you?"

"No, that's okay." I can't meet his eyes, so I stare down at my coffee, rubbing at an imaginary spot on the handle with my thumb.

I hear a noise, the front door opening, then Angus barking excitedly. I don't look at Marcus. I just rush out of the bathroom—and stop when I see Jared with Sophie in the kitchen. He's kneeling down and petting Angus. Jared looks up at me, gives a friendly smile. I can't stop staring at him. I feel as though I've slammed into a wall, my thoughts scattered. Jared can't be here. Now he's in danger too. I have to get them out of here. Noise in the bathroom. Marcus is draining the tub. I only have moments. His keys, Sophie must still have his keys.

I meet Sophie's eyes, trying to figure out how I can signal that we have to leave without alarming her and setting off panic. "Sophie, we need to get to town. We—"

"Mom, I crashed the Cherokee."

"You *what?*" She's pale, I realize now, her hair messy, and her arms wrapped around her body as though she's freezing cold. I hadn't noticed. I'd been too scared. I walk closer. "Are you injured?" I search her face, notice a red mark by her temple. I graze my fingers across the spot.

"I'm okay," she says. "But the Cherokee is wrecked." Her voice is quavering and I can tell she's trying not to break down in front of Jared. "There was a tree and I tried to stop, but the Cherokee slid everywhere, and I went off the road." Marcus comes up beside me with a robe wrapped around him and she looks at him, her face pleading. "I'm *really* sorry."

His face is calm as he looks at her, almost reassuring. If this was yesterday, I would've been grateful for how he was always so thoughtful about everything, how he'd take a beat or two before responding—he was so centered. So in control. He'd never lose his temper like Andrew. Now I see something else. I see *anger*. I'd never noticed before, how his eyes could go so flat and cold. I hadn't seen it for what it really was, deep-seated hatred and rage.

"I'm just glad you're all right, Sophie," he says. "I'll get you some ice." He heads over to the fridge, says casually over his shoulder, "Have you called the police?"

I feel a tiny leap of hope. The police. If they come to take an accident report, I might be able to signal that we need help. I look at Sophie. *Say yes. Please say you've called them.*

"No." Her face flushes. "It was my fault. I glanced at my phone. . . ."

She's watching me. She's expecting me to be angry, to lecture her about driving while distracted, but it's as though the roof has collapsed onto my head and I'm still trying to dig out from the rubble. Marcus is listening. I have to say something.

"Sophie!" I finally manage. "What were you thinking? You could have been really hurt."

"I'm sorry, Mom." She looks so ashamed, and I want to hug her and reassure her, but I can't think past the next few minutes and how I'm going to keep myself together.

"We'll talk about this later."

"We'll have to call a tow truck when the phone lines are fixed," Marcus says. "And I'll have to contact my insurance company and make a report, but we should be able to keep the police out of it." His voice is still smooth, assured. He's so confident. Why wouldn't he be? He's played the game for months.

"You need to get checked at the hospital, Sophie," I say. "You could have tissue damage or torn ligaments." While Marcus is distracted by taking care of the Cherokee, I'll get Sophie and Jared out of here and call Corporal Parker as soon as I have cell service.

"The road is blocked, Mom. Jared had to park on the other side—we walked here."

I hold on to the edge of the counter, feel the world tilt for a moment. It's all coming back. The night we ran away from Andrew. The storm. Trudging through the snow with Sophie.

Marcus is turning from the fridge, giving me a curious look.

"Okay, well, we'll just walk back." I sound cheerful, upbeat. It's as though I'm standing on the other side of myself, pulling my strings like a puppet, making my mouth move.

Sophie is looking at me like I'm insane. "It's freezing cold and super-windy. I don't want to go back out." I glance at the window. The trees are swaying wildly and I can hear the wind whistling down the chimney. Darkness and fear, pressing tighter and tighter around me.

"Where was the tree?" Marcus hands Sophie an ice pack wrapped in a towel.

"Close to the turnoff," Jared says. "We walked like forty minutes."

"You should probably just rest while we wait out the storm," Marcus says to Sophie. "If you're sore tomorrow, one of us can walk to the car in the morning."

The morning. We'll have to spend the night.

"What about your parents?" I say to Jared. Maybe they'll be worried. They'll call the police, someone will see his car parked on the side of the road and come investigate.

"They know I'm with Sophie. I texted them that I'm spending the night."

That was it, our last chance. I want to grab him by the shoulders and shake him. *Do you know what you've done?* But he's not the one I want to hurt. It's Marcus. And now we're trapped with him.

Jared and Sophie are sitting on the couch, Sophie holding ice to the side of her head. Marcus has gone to get dressed. I watch as Jared picks up Sophie's free hand and holds it. I'd thought he was a risk. I'd worried about him being with my daughter and now I want to scream at him to run away with her. I have to warn them, but I can hear drawers sliding open and shut. Marcus is too close. If he comes out and sees their shocked expressions, he'll know something is wrong. So far I don't think he's caught on. Before he went into the bedroom, he looked relaxed, even happy when he said, "Looks like we're having an afternoon of board games!"

I look at the clock. It's not even twelve. How are we going to make it through the rest of the day? I've been trying to come up with a plan so we can sneak out after Marcus goes to sleep, but three people and a dog might make a lot of noise—especially the dog. We have to make sure Marcus stays asleep. I could drug him. I've done it before. Why not again?

Sophie and Jared are talking. Jared is saying how scared he was when she called. Sophie rests her head on his shoulder. Something has happened between them, but I realize this in a distant, unfocused way. I'm too busy thinking about how I can get the pills.

Marcus comes out wearing a thick sweater and jeans, walks into the kitchen, and grabs a bottle of Baileys liqueur from the cupboard. "Irish Cream in your coffee, Lindsey?"

"That would be lovely." I stand. "I'm just going to get a sweater."

"Cold?"

"A little."

"I'll build a fire."

"Great." We're so civilized, so polite. Both liars now. I move swiftly down the hall. I only have moments. I skip the sweater and go straight into the bathroom and lock the door. Marcus's shaving kit is still on the counter. I fumble with the zipper. It's stiff, like it's caught inside on something, and won't open. I tug harder, knocking his shaving cream onto the floor.

"Lindsey? I've got your coffee." He's in the bedroom, walking closer. He's standing outside the door. He'll hear me rummaging around. I can't open it now.

I stare into the mirror at my wild eyes, press my hand over my mouth, trying to hold in the scream I can feel building in my throat.

"Out in a minute!" I take some breaths, splash cold water on my face, and open the door.

He's sitting on the edge of the bed. "Feel okay?" he says. "You look pale."

"I'm just hungry. I'll make us all some chicken soup."

"Need help?"

"You can help by keeping the kids occupied." I laugh. "Maybe you can watch a movie or play cards." I'm babbling, throwing out ideas, but I have to keep him out of the kitchen. I might be able to write a note for Sophie or hide a knife. I can come back to the bathroom later.

He holds out the mug. "Here you go."

I take the warm drink, grip it tight in my hand. "Thanks."

"It will help. I know you're upset about Sophie's accident, but she's handling it fine." His mouth is curved into an understanding smile. I used to love that smile. It made me want to share my heart and soul with him. It made me tell him *everything*.

I give him a grateful smile back, then take a small sip, and make a satisfied sound. "Yum." It doesn't taste strange, and I don't think he'd drug me—not when the kids are still in the living room—but just in case, I'll find a way to dump it out when he's not looking.

"I better start on that soup." I head for the door.

"Lindsey? You forgot something."

I turn around, fear thick in my throat. This is it.

He's holding out my white wool cardigan. I come closer and he stands, wraps it around my shoulders, and brushes his lips against mine. When I step back, he holds my hip in place and whispers into my ear. "This morning was fun. Maybe later?"

My face is burning hot with anger and shame, remembering how I'd straddled him, how I'd felt so powerful. The entire time he must have been laughing at me, but now I'm the one laughing in a low, husky voice. "Maybe. If you're good."

I walk out, give him a wink over my shoulder, then turn away so he can't see the hatred in my face. I'm going to kill him. I'm going to kill him for what he's done.

I'm in the kitchen, stirring the soup while keeping an eye on the living room. They're playing cards and seem to be having fun. Marcus is joking with the kids, his teeth flashing white each time he wins a hand. Sophie is also in good spirits, obviously happy that Jared is with us now. She offered to help me, but I declined. She's too sensitive. She'll pick up on my fear.

I was going to pass her a note, but now it feels too risky. There's too much chance of error or interception by Marcus. Better to wait until he goes to the bathroom, then I'll tell them my plan. I'll suggest we watch an action movie later. The noise will cover our voices.

I glance at Angus, who is begging at my feet for scraps. I stroke his head. I'll keep him with me, but he might alert Marcus to Sophie and Jared sneaking out. I *have* to find a way to drug Marcus. I'm not going to make the same mistake I did with Andrew. I'll give Marcus a few pills.

I open the cutlery drawer for spoons and notice the paring knife in a sheath. It might not do much damage, but anything bigger would be noticeable on my body. I pretend to drop a spoon, then lean down and tuck the knife inside the top band of my sock under my jeans.

I stand back up. "Lunch is ready!"

We've been playing card games for hours. I make mistakes, count the cards wrong, and fumble with my chips. My laugh is too high-pitched, my face warm from the fire and nerves. Sophie is giving me strange looks, almost exasperated. I'm hoping she just thinks I'm tipsy. Marcus is affectionate, his arm around my lower back. He hasn't noticed that I switched my drink for a plain coffee. Since lunch, I've made sure I'm the one mixing our drinks, while waiting for a chance to go back to the bathroom. Finally, Marcus decides to make popcorn.

"Good timing," I say. "I have to go to the ladies' room."

This time I'm able to open his shaving kit and remove a few of the pills, which I quickly pocket. I'm careful to put the container back in the same spot. When I come out the air smells of butter and popcorn. Marcus has set out a couple of bowls and the kids are digging in.

I walk into the kitchen. "Another drink, Marcus?"

"I know what you're up to, Lindsey. Getting me drunk," he says. I look at him, startled, then realize he's joking when he says, "I'm switching to water before your daughter robs me blind." Sophie tries to steal his stack of poker chips and he laughingly blocks her.

"Darn. You figured us out," I say, with a tinny laugh. I'm so frustrated, my anxiety through the roof. Now I'll have to wait until dinner, when he usually drinks wine.

But through dinner—he grills salmon and vegetables, all of which taste like ashes in my mouth—he keeps pouring his own glass. I never get a chance. The pills sit heavy as stones in my pocket. He hasn't gone to the bathroom for hours. I used to tease him about his iron bladder.

He helps me clean up. Each time he touches me, his shoulder brushing against mine as he reaches for a plate, his fingers tangling with my hand in the dishwater, I feel my shell crack. I'm not going to be able to hide my fear much longer. When he leans down to kiss me, I almost sob into his mouth. I'd loved him. I'd truly fallen in love with him, and the hurt and betrayal is so raw in my throat I can't breathe. I pull away, hide my face in his chest, and he holds me tight.

I think about him out on the lake fishing. He'd come back in happy. Is there a chance he's forgiven me? Maybe he really meant all those reassuring words. Or maybe he'd been out there planning his revenge. Would he shoot us while we slept? Did he just want to kill me?

Please. Let it just be me. If I can't stop him, just take me.

We sit back down in the living room. The kids are on the couch, so thankfully I'm given a little space from Marcus when we take different armchairs. He *has* to go to the bathroom soon.

Jared is looking at the fire. "Do you think we need more wood, Marcus?"

Marcus turns and checks the stack. "We should probably load up before the night."

I hold my breath, my hands clenched so tight my nails dig into my palm. The woodpile is around the back of the house. If Marcus goes alone, I'll have time to talk to the kids.

"I can do it." Jared's face is hopeful, eager. He wants to impress us. Sophie is gazing up at him proudly. I want to shout at him to sit down.

Marcus rises to his feet. "You can help cut some kindling."

"Bring lots. It's going to be cold tonight," I say. Marcus gives me a wink and I know what he's thinking. *I'll keep you warm.* I dig my fingernails harder into my palm.

While they get their coats and boots on, I flip through the movies as if I'm picking one for us to watch tonight. The titles blur. Sophie sits nearby reading a magazine. Finally I hear the door close. I wait a few beats for them to get around the side of the house, then quickly move closer to Sophie and grip her arms. She's startled, almost jerks back, but I hold her in place.

"Honey, listen to me. Marcus isn't who he says he is. He was Elizabeth Sanders's husband. I went into that room upstairs and her things are still there. Books, clothes, and—"

"Mom, that's nuts!" She tries to tug free, looking at me like I'm drunk or insane.

"It's the truth." I raise my voice to a firm whisper. "I saw her *name* in the books and I found pills—the same kind that almost killed Angus. I think he wants to hurt us. You and Jared have to sneak out tonight and get help."

Her face is stunned, her green eyes staring into mine. Her expression changes from surprise to horror. "He heard me on the stairs last night. He'll catch me."

"I have a plan. We can do this, just listen. After the movie, say you're tired and want to go to bed. Tie sheets together, climb out the window. Then you have to get Jared out his window downstairs." I pause, glance at the door. "Once you have cell service, call the police."

Even as I'm talking, she's already shaking her head. "I don't want to leave you behind."

"You *have* to. I need to keep him distracted." I glance at the door again. I can hear chopping sounds outside, but that could be Jared. I decide not to tell her that I think Marcus killed Andrew. If she's too upset, she won't be able to think straight. She's already in shock. Her skin is pale, her nostrils flaring. Her hands balled into fists.

"You have to try to act normal, okay?" I say. "He can't suspect *anything*."

She nods, but she still looks petrified. "What if he figures it out?"

Before I can answer, the door swings open with a bang and my heart jolts in my chest. I sit back on my heels. Marcus and Jared come in carrying armloads of wood. Sophie hurriedly picks up her magazine. I try to give her a comforting smile, but she's not looking at me. I can feel her frantic thoughts, see her eyelids blinking rapidly.

I get to my feet and sit beside her, slide my hand into hers, and give it squeeze. *It's going to be okay. We can do this.* She squeezes my hand back. Marcus and Jared stack the wood beside the fire, complaining about the wind and the rain and joking about how we're lucky to be inside beside the warm fire. I laugh and tell them to hurry up. Sophie is smiling too, but I know she's working hard at it. Her body feels stiff. I have to get her to calm down before Jared or Marcus senses something has changed. When they go outside for another load, Sophie and I talk more and work through the plan until her voice sounds stronger, more confident.

The guys come in with their final loads and stack them beside the fire, then take off their coats and boots. Marcus goes into the bathroom and comes out with a couple of towels for him and Jared. They ruffle their hair and dry their faces, then hang the towels by the fire.

"We'll be lucky if we have power for much longer," Marcus says.

Sophie flicks a sideways glance at me. I know she's thinking about our plan.

Marcus collapses down into the armchair and Jared perches on the hearth. Jared's fiddling with the metal screen, trying to close it across the fire. Marcus glances at him. "It's broken." He looks back at me. "Did you pick out a movie? Something with lots of action, I hope."

"Of course." I point to the one I'd set aside on the floor. "*Point Break.*"

"Great choice." As he slides the movie in, I stare at the back of his head and keep my daughter's hand tight in mine.

CHAPTER FORTY-ONE

SOPHIE

The credits are rolling on the movie. The warmth of Mom's body against my side is solid and real. I don't want to leave her, but I can feel her tension, see it in her face when she glances at me with a small smile that doesn't reach her eyes. It's probably meant to be reassuring. My insides are churning and I feel like my voice is going to come out all strangled when I try to speak. Jared is sprawled on the floor with Angus. I have to get him to leave with me. I look over at Mom. She's staring at the TV as if she's totally interested in finding out the names of all the actors and stunt doubles. She presses her leg against mine. *Do it. Do it now.*

I yawn slowly and stretch my arms. "I'm tired."

Jared rolls over, looks up. "You going to bed?"

"Yeah. Come with me for a minute? I want to show you a new drawing." I hope my voice sounds natural, but it sounds fake to me. Like the worst actress in the world.

"Leave the door open," Mom says. "Or I'm coming up." I

know she's only saying it because she wants Marcus to think everything's normal, but I still have to act annoyed.

"God, Mom. We're just talking." I roll my eyes.

"Humor me, please."

"Fine." I get up and walk toward the stairs, then slow as I near the kitchen counter, and glance back at Jared, who's taking forever to get to his feet. I try not to look at Marcus to see if he's watching. I hated sitting in the living room with him for the last two hours. I kept wanting to stare at him, like somehow his face might look different now that I know the truth. I don't remember a second of the movie. My head was filled with memories of conversations I'd had with Marcus, how nice he's always been. I've been alone with him so many times. I never knew anything was wrong. I keep seeing the newspaper photos of Elizabeth Sanders, the mangled wreck of her car, the tarp over the side so photographers couldn't take pictures of the blood.

Jared is finally leaving. I hear the jingle of Angus's collar as he gets up to follow, then a whine. He wants to go outside. I turn around. Jared is opening the door. Angus darts out.

Jared looks at my mom. "Sorry. He ran down to the lake."

"It's okay. I'll bring him back in."

She sounds calm, but I know she must be upset. We didn't want Angus outside—he might bark if he hears me climbing off the roof, but there's nothing we can do about it now. I've reached the bottom of the stairs. Jared is right behind me. I look back at Mom and Marcus. He's getting up as though he's going to sit on the couch with her. I feel a lurch in my stomach.

"Get some rest, kids," Marcus says with a smile. "We'll go out on the lake tomorrow."

"Cool." Everything he's told us is a lie. Everything. This is just another one. Or maybe it's not. Maybe he plans to tip the boat or do something horrible out there.

"Good night, honey," Mom says. "I'll see you in the morning." Our eyes hold for a moment, and then I have to turn away.

The roof is slick. Water spills out of the gutters and rushes down over the wood shakes, which are slimy with old leaves and moss. The wind throws rain in my face, tugs at my body. I tread carefully in bare feet, crab-walk down to the edge. I glance up. I can't see anything in the window. The lights are off. The bedsheet stretches out from my hand.

Once I'm on the ground, I'll hide in the bushes and wait for Jared. I hope he gets out through his window soon. I wasn't sure if he was going to believe me when I whispered everything to him upstairs, but he caught on quickly. We grabbed the sheets off my bed, knotted them together with the duvet cover, and tied them to the leg of the iron bedframe. Jared waited until I was on the roof, then went downstairs to distract Marcus in the living room in case I made any noise.

I'm over the edge of the roof, the hard edge scraping against my stomach and breasts, then I'm free and hanging in the air. The wind catches me. I spin around, bumping into the side of the house. I kick off with my legs, lower myself hand over hand. My feet finally hit earth.

I run a few feet from the house and crouch in the bushes. My hair is soaked and the water runs down my neck. I couldn't get my coat from downstairs, so I layered shirts under my hoodie, but they're already wet. *Soaked through to the bone*, is what Mom would say. I slide my slippers on—they were stuffed into my hoodie pocket. I figured bare feet would have more traction on the roof, but my toes are freezing. My runners are by the front door. Jared didn't have any extra clothes with him, so I gave him a pair of my socks and a sweatshirt.

I can't tell what's going on inside the house. The only thing I can hear is the wind roaring and trees snapping back and forth in the forest. I want to peek through the window of the kitchen and make sure Mom is all right, but if Marcus sees me, everything will be ruined.

Something nudges my back and I let out a little cry and spin around—hands out, ready to block a blow. It's Angus, soaking wet and jumping all over me and whining. "Shush!" I grab his collar to hold him still. "Calm down, boy!"

A soft thump from the back of the house. Footsteps. Angus's body stiffens, a rumbling growl starting in his throat. I wrap my hand around his snout. Then stare into the dark shadows.

"Sophie?" Jared's voice.

"Over here!"

We run down the center of the gravel road, mud splashing up our legs. My slippers are saturated. The wind is pushing against us, scattering branches and leaves and broken bits of wood across the road. We dodge and leap. Our breath is ragged, our feet thudding. I falter and stumble, my legs wobbly, and Jared presses his hand into my lower back, pushing me on.

"You can do it!"

I keep running. His feet must hurt, with just socks for protection, but he doesn't say anything. Angus lopes beside us, his collar jingling and his breath chuffing. I tried to make him stay behind at the house so he could protect Mom, but he followed us anyway. I hope Marcus doesn't go searching outside for him and notice the sheets hanging from the window.

We round a corner and I finally see the dark shape of the tree across the road. It looks like a fallen giant, branches reaching up to the sky as though begging for help. Jared's car is just on the other side. Almost there. We slow to a jog, catching our breath, and check our phones. My fingers are wet and cold and slip as I press in my password. The screen lights up.

"I have service!" I quickly dial 911. Still out of breath, I stumble over my words as I explain that Mom is trapped in a house with a man who's trying to kill her. "You have to come quick!"

The operator is asking questions that I can't answer, wants details and facts, but I just want them to get here. What if Marcus has realized we're gone? "I don't know the address!" I shout into the phone. "It's the one with the green mailbox, but there's a tree blocking the road. It blew down in the storm." They're going to take too long. I think about Mom, all alone with Marcus. The operator is saying something about officers on the way. I hang up and look at Jared.

"We can't leave her. We have to go back."

"Let's go." We turn and sprint back down the middle of the road.

Hang on, Mom. Please, just hang on. We're coming.

CHAPTER FORTY-TWO

Lindsey

"Looks like it's just us," Marcus says.

He's putting more wood on the fire, stoking it to a roaring blaze. The orange flames make the side of his face glow. It must be so hot, but he doesn't move. He's the devil.

I have to get him to the bedroom so the kids have a chance to escape. If Sophie can't get off the roof, she'll have to come through the living room. I need to keep him distracted.

"Why don't we watch the TV in the bedroom?"

"Sure," he says. "I'll just lock up."

"I'll do it. I have to call Angus back anyway." While Marcus walks to the bedroom, I open the front door and whistle for Angus, but there's no sign of him. If he starts barking at the kids, I'll have to bring him in right away before Marcus gets suspicious. I close the door.

Marcus likes to keep a glass of water on his night table. It's my last chance to drug him, but I have to cover the taste of the pills. Maybe lemon. In the kitchen, I cut up a wedge and squeeze some into the water, then look up and listen. He's still in the bedroom. I drop all of the pills into the water and mix it quickly, take a sip. My mouth fills with tart lemon. I remember the night I drugged Andrew, the burning taste of whiskey in my mouth.

I walk into the bedroom, glass in hand. Running water in the bathroom, sounds of him brushing his teeth. I put the glass on his table, move around to my side of the bed, and swiftly pull the knife out of my sock and slide it under my pillow.

I hesitate, thinking about what to wear. Then change into the T-shirt and pajama bottoms I wore last night. I turn on the TV. Marcus comes out wearing his boxer shorts. His chest is defined, his arms like ripped steel. I think of his obsessive working out. I'd believed it to be his way of coping with grief. I guess it was, but grief for his wife, not a daughter. I wonder where he was all those years after she died. He couldn't have been looking for me all that time.

"Do you mind if I watch the news?" I say. "I'd like to hear the weather report."

"Sure." He looks around. "Where's Angus?"

"He must be chasing something. I'll call him in a while."

He climbs onto the other side of the bed, slides closer to me, and rests his head against my shoulder, his lips cool on my bare skin. I feel as though spiders are crawling on me. We watch the news together, but it's just flickering images. I can't take in the information. I'm listening to every sound and waiting for him to drink his water, but he hasn't moved toward it.

"I brought you water. I thought after all that wine . . ."

"Thanks, honey," but he's still watching the TV. Like he actually cares what's happening in the world. Like it's just any other night of the week. Finally he turns and takes a sip of his water, then makes a quizzical face.

"I put lemon in it," I say.

"Doesn't really go with toothpaste." He puts the glass down.

I stare at the TV, despair and panic chasing each other in an endless loop. How much did he swallow? One mouthful? That won't even make him drowsy. I try to think how long it's been since Sophie and Jared went to bed. Fifteen or twenty minutes? Not enough time.

Ten more minutes pass. I try not to look at the clock too often, pretend to fiddle with the alarm. Marcus slides down, rests his head on the pillow. I keep glancing at his face to see if his eyes are closed, but he seems fascinated by the news—and not the least bit tired. I can't wait any longer. I have to see if the kids are gone. I might be able to sneak out while he's engrossed.

"I'm going to call Angus."

"Okay." He doesn't look over. I ease to the edge of the bed, walk out, and close the door behind me. I pause, listening. I can still hear the TV.

I creep down the hall toward the back of the house and push Jared's door open, peer into the dark room. The window looks like it's closed. I stare at the bed, wait for my eyes to adjust. A huddled shape. What went wrong? I have to get him out of here.

I move quickly inside, touch Jared's shoulder, and feel softness. I push again, and almost sag in relief. It's a pillow. I close the door and move down the hall, holding my breath as I cross in front of the bedroom door, then head up the stairs to Sophie's room. I smell fresh rain, shiver in the cold air. The bed is near her open window, a sheet still tied to it. They made it.

I'm halfway back down when my shoulder brushes against a frame on the wall, pushing it with a loud scrape. I stop, wait in silence. Did he hear? The wind is loud outside, gusts making the house shake and moan. I start moving again, set my feet down lightly on each step.

"Everything okay?"

I jerk back with a startled gasp. Marcus is standing in the shadows at the bottom of the stairs. How long has he been there?

"I heard something, but it was just the wind," I whisper. "Kids are fine." I take the rest of the steps, pause in front of him.

"One of the windows might've broken in the storm," he says. "I feel a draft." I don't like the way he's peering up the stairs with a frown, like he's thinking about going to check.

"Everything looks okay. Sophie's under a few blankets."

"You find Angus?" He's facing me now. I hope this means he's decided to leave the windows alone, but I'm not in the clear yet. He'll be suspicious if I don't want to search for Angus. Then it comes to me. That's exactly how I can escape.

"Not yet. I'm going to look around outside. He must be hiding from the storm." I walk toward the bedroom, praying that Marcus follows. I have to get him away from the stairs.

"It's blowing pretty hard. I'll come with you."

I grit my teeth, glad he can't see my face. He's just being polite. I can still get out of this.

"I'll be fine. One of us might as well stay dry."

"I can't let you go out there alone."

We're in the bedroom now. I can't protest anymore or he'll catch on. I grab a sweater from the drawer, pull it over my shirt, and slide on some jeans. I delay for a few moments as I rummage for socks. What if Angus is waiting at the front door? We'll have to come back inside. Maybe I can break away, run into the forest, hide somewhere. I'll have the element of surprise.

Marcus picks up his silver flashlight from the night table. "Ready?"

The wind almost yanks the door out of my hand as I open it, snatches at my coat. I press my hood tight to my head, glance around. I don't see Angus. He's never disappeared like this before. He must be with Sophie and Jared. Marcus is behind me. I need him to walk ahead.

"Angus!" I shout into the wind.

Marcus whistles loudly, the noise piercing through the storm. I stiffen, count my breaths. *Stay away, Angus. Stay away.* Each moment drags into the next. I can hear the rustle of Marcus's rain gear as he shifts his weight, the rain beating against my shoulders.

"Let's check the woodshed," I say.

Marcus nods, his face shadowed under his baseball cap, gestures for me to go first. He shines a beam of light ahead. The concrete stairs are slippery, wet with rain and leaves. I scan the forest as though I'm searching for Angus. Where would be a good place to take off? The land is rugged, steep with cliffs.

"I need to fix my boot." I bend over to lace my hiking boots, wondering how fast I can run in them. Marcus is standing behind me on the narrow stairs, the light aimed at my feet. I'd hoped he would pass, but he's still playing at being a gentleman. I scour the ground, looking for a rock, a branch, something I can grab fast, but there's nothing, only a river of rainwater.

I start to stand up. Something slams into the back of my head and I pitch forward, land hard on my hands and knees. Pain ricochets through the back of my skull, down my spine in a sharp jolt. I try to get to my feet, but my arms sway, the steps rush toward me, and my face smacks into the edge of the concrete. My teeth snap together, my cheekbone throbs. I taste blood.

Beside me, Marcus's boots. Black tips, shiny with rain.

"Lindsey?" His voice sounds far away, floating in and out like I'm underwater. "Can you hear me?" The world is crumbling at the edges, darkness pulling me down. I need to stay awake, need to protect myself. I try to crawl, reach for the step below. I slide down on my torso, topple to the side, and land in the mud, the river of rain flooding my legs. I'm looking up at Marcus.

He's raising his arm, the flashlight coming toward my head.

CHAPTER FORTY-THREE

I blink slowly as I wake up. The ceiling blurs. I blink some more until it comes into focus. I try to raise my hand to feel the side of my head, but there's something sticking to my wrists. Duct tape. More across my mouth, pulling at the skin. My legs won't move either. My ankles are taped together. I'm soaking wet, and cold. So cold. I'm just wearing my shirt and jeans; my coat and boots are gone.

I look to the side, and the world shifts and distorts and spins. My stomach rises into my mouth, bitter acid. I can't see Marcus, but I hear movement, rustling. I slowly lift my head.

He's at the other end of the room, hunched over in front of the dresser. He's changed into a camouflaged coat. I've never seen it before. He looks like a hunter.

My body starts shaking hard, my muscles clenched as I yank and twist my wrists. It's no use. The knife under the pillow. I bring my hands up. Too late. He's turning around.

"You're awake." As he moves toward the bed, I push my bound feet against the mattress, use my stomach muscles to pull myself up, press my back against the headboard. I'm breathing hard behind my gag, taking quick rushes of air in and out through my nose. I'll kick him. I'll lift my legs and kick him in the stomach. I'll use my fists like a club. I'll stab my fingers into his eyes.

He stops at the bottom of the bed, slides some shirts into a duffel bag. He didn't have a bag when we arrived—he had a suitcase. This is army-green, wilderness survival style. Now he's at the closet, pulling clothes off the hanger. He folds the shirts, places them carefully in the bag.

What's his plan? He doesn't look angry, or even upset. His movements are quick and efficient. Not rushed.

He didn't kill me. He could have, but he hasn't yet. That has to mean something. He's taking me with him? Like a captive? I listen for sirens, but I can only hear wind outside.

Now he's in the bathroom. I reach for the knife, feel around with my fingers. Where did it go? He's coming out. I pull my hands back in front of me. He goes down to the bottom of the bed with his shaving kit, unzips it, brings out the container with the pills, and pushes them around with his finger. Counting. Then he glances at the water glass, meets my eyes.

"You were going to drug me, just like you did with Andrew."

I grunt behind the tape, hold my hands out in a plea, then point them toward my mouth, beg him with my eyes. *Take the tape off! Let me talk, please! I can explain!*

He drops the shaving kit into the duffel bag. "We both know if I take off the tape, you'll scream." He still thinks the kids are in the house. He hasn't checked the bedrooms, that's why he's moving so unhurriedly. He thinks he has time. What will he do if he hears sirens?

His hand is in his pocket, something jingles as he takes it out. Keys. Now he's crouching in front of the chest. I can only see the top of his baseball cap, hear the snick of the lock, then things being moved around. When he stands back up, he's gripping a gun.

I press myself harder against the headboard, hold my hands out in front of me. I'm shaking my head, making animal noises as I choke on my strangled breath.

He doesn't look at me, just slides the gun into his pocket, then bends over again and takes something else out of the chest. It's a photo album, white satin.

"Elizabeth loved this house." He slowly flips through the album. "We came here almost every weekend." He touches one of the photos, almost reverently, his hand grazing over the surface. "I heard that women glow when they're pregnant, and I always thought that was a myth, but when we found out she was finally pregnant, it's like she was lit with a hundred candles."

Elizabeth was pregnant? No, how could this be? There wasn't anything in the papers, nothing came out at the trial. Wouldn't the police have known?

"I didn't tell them she was three months along. They might've given him a longer sentence." He puts the album back inside the chest, closes the lid, and rests his hand on top. "Her ashes are in here, with her wedding dress, the baby shoes she bought— pink ones. She was so sure it was a girl." He looks up at me. "I was notified when Andrew was released. I could've shot him as he walked out of the prison, but that would have been too easy. He had to feel like he was getting everything back, his freedom, his family, then I was going to take it all away."

He's studying my face, his expression satisfied as he notices my tears. He's enjoying this, revealing his clever plan, gloating over his brilliance. "You told me everything. You told me about your marriage, and I used it all. You even let me watch as you typed in your alarm password. Sophie's letters told me everything else. She kept them under her dresser, you know."

He'd been through every inch of my house. He knew everything about my daughter, our home, had been through our
drawers. And I was the one who let him in.

"I'd drive down and watch him in Victoria, going about his
day, laughing with guys on the job site, enjoying *his life*." He
spits out the last words. "Then I saw him buy his plane ticket.
He was coming to Dogwood Bay. It was time. You believed he
was stalking you, eventually even Sophie believed it. The police would've blamed him for your deaths."

I stop straining at my bindings, this final truth wrapping
tighter around me than the tape. All this time, as the months
and days sped past, he'd been planning to kill me and Sophie.
I sag backward, reeling from the blow, the knowledge. I'm shaking again, my body in blind panic.

"You trusted me so much by then. I could have made it look
like he'd tracked you down in Vancouver and killed you there,
but then he followed me into your house."

The rest comes clear. I see him and Andrew standing at the
top of the stairs. I see them fighting. I see how much Andrew
loved Sophie. How much he loved me.

"I was still so *fucking* angry." It's the first time I've ever heard
him swear, the harshness adding to my terror. "What was the
point of his death? I had nothing left. I still thought about Elizabeth every second of every day. Then you needed a place to
stay, and it seemed right, like some sort of message. Why
shouldn't I take his family? He destroyed mine. I almost started
believing I could have some sort of life again. But then you told
me about the pills. . . ." He meets my eyes, stares into them. It's
all in there. His despair, his rage. It was never about me.

I twist my body, roll up onto my knees, my hands in front of
my heart in the prayer position. I'm crying hard now, trying
to moan and grunt. *Sorry. Sorry. Sorry.*

He looks around the room, takes a deep breath, as though
savoring the very scent of the walls, the air. "I'm going to miss

this house, but it's time. I have to start over. It's the only answer." In one smooth motion, he lifts the duffel bag over his shoulder and meets my eyes again. "I'm going to burn the house down now. It will go fast—the smoke will kill you first."

I slide off the edge of the bed, drop to my knees. He's already walking out of the room in quick strides. I crawl after him, an awkward shimmy on knees and elbows. I have to get out the door, wedge it with my body. But he's moving too fast, I can't keep up.

The door is opening. I have a quick glimpse of the dark living room, the table, chairs. He doesn't look back as he closes the door. I'm a few feet behind, still crawling. Scraping sounds, something being dragged in front of the door. The bookshelf.

He's trapped me in the bedroom.

CHAPTER FORTY-FOUR

SOPHIE

I don't hear sirens. Our feet thud on the road in tandem. I've lost one of my slippers, but I don't slow down. We've been gone too long. Angus stops suddenly, ears pricked, then he plunges into the darkness beside the road.

"Angus!" I turn and peer through the trees. Should we wait for him? Jared grabs my arm and I start running again. He'll be okay, I tell myself. He'll catch up. I keep hoping to hear the jingle of his collar, but there's nothing, just the sound of the heavy rain and screaming wind and our gasping breaths.

"What are we going to do?" I pant.

"There's an ax by the woodshed." Jared's eyes are squinted against the rain, his hair slicked back, his arms tight to his side. "We'll jump him."

We're going to attack someone with an ax. Not just someone. Marcus.

I look down the road. We've started to see some lake houses but I'm not sure how close we are now. The trees all look the same, the curve of the road that never seems to end.

I pick up a familiar scent, growing stronger. "You smell smoke?"

"Probably from the chimney. We're close."

Then we round the bend and see the lake house. Thick smoke hovers around it in a hazy cloud. It's coming from the chimney, the windows, crawling over the roof.

"Mom!" I sprint toward the house, reckless now, my feet and arms wild. Jared's yelling something behind me, but I can't hear him. All I see is the smoke.

CHAPTER FORTY-FIVE

Lindsey

I can hear Marcus moving around the living room, his quick footsteps. He's not going to come back and check on me now. I can smell smoke already. I have to get out. I swing my body around until my legs are curled under me, then roll onto my hip, and use my core to pull myself up onto my feet. I hop back to the bed, my arms straight out in front for balance. This time when I reach under the pillow, I find the knife where it had slid next to the headboard.

I pause, listening. Boot steps, walking away. The front door slams. Now there's only silence. Sitting on the floor, I use my fingers to carefully slide the knife out of the sheath, then brace it between my knees, and cut the tape. With my hands free, my ankles go faster. It's only been minutes, but the smoke is stronger now. It hangs in the air, seeps under the door.

I peel the tape from my mouth, cry out as it takes off some skin. I suck in air. The only way out is the window. It won't open. Something is wrong with the lock. I slam the lamp against the glass. It bounces back, flies out of my hands, shatters at my feet. I take one of the pillowcases and wrap it around my hand, then hit the window, but I'm not strong enough. Maybe there's something in the bathroom I can use. The shower rod, the back of the ceramic toilet.

A noise. Someone shouting, loud and frantic. Two voices. Sophie and Jared. Coming closer, running footsteps. Yelling for me. They're in the house.

"I'm in here!" I sprint to the door, pound my fists on it.

"Stand back!" Jared's voice. Something is hitting against the door, splitting wood. The head of an ax, slicing through. Kicking sounds, and the door flies open.

"Mom! Come on!" Sophie grabs my hand, pulls me out. We run for the front door, but the living room is filling with smoke. The curtains are already in flames, curling higher.

"Stop!" Jared grabs our shoulders from behind. "The back door."

We follow him down the hall, pressed together. I wrap my fingers around the back of Sophie's sweatshirt, the cold wet fabric. We have our arms over our faces, coughing. My eyes are watering. I squint through the smoke, follow their shapes. Jared is leading, then Sophie. I grip her shirt harder. Jared opens the back door. I see the dark night, smell the rain.

A sharp cracking sound. I lose my balance as I jerk my body to the side, and bounce hard into the wall. Through the smoke, Marcus, running after us. He's pointing the gun at me.

Another cracking sound. Loud, close.

Something hits the wall beside my head. I duck, drop to my knees. Sophie's on the other side of the doorway, her face a white mask as she reaches for me, rain pouring down on her, heavy strands of violet hair splayed across her cheeks. She's in the open, outlined by light.

A perfect target.

Jared's behind her, pulling her arm, yelling something I can't hear, the shot still ringing in my head. His mouth is open, panicked, his face terrified. I sprawl forward, hook my finger onto the bottom of the door, and slam it shut. More shots. Hitting the closed door.

I scramble into the laundry room on my hands and knees, searching. The box of cleaning supplies is on the shelf. I dump it on the floor, grab at the lemon polish, the spray bottle of cleaner. The door crashes open. He hits me from behind, knocking me onto the floor.

I flip around, kick up hard with my heel, connect between his legs. He doubles over and crashes into the washing machine. The gun hits the floor and spins behind the laundry tub, out of reach. I spray the cleaner wildly, coating Marcus's body and head. He screams, claws at his eyes.

I shove past him and sprint toward the front door. The living room is ablaze. Heat hits me, almost pushes me backward. I drop to the floor, slide like a snake. Hands, knees.

He's gripping my shirt, pulling me back. I grab one of the table legs, still holding the spray with my other hand. He's trying to wrestle the bottle free, bending my fingers backward. The door is open. Fresh air. There's a roar behind me as flames greedily suck on the oxygen.

He's too strong. I can't hold on. My fingers loosen. But then, a large shape moving past me. Angus, leaping through air, snarling and barking. Marcus lets go, yells out something.

I twist my body around while fumbling with the nozzle on the bottle. Angus has Marcus's leg in his mouth and is growling and biting him. The couch beside them is engulfed in flames.

I get to my feet, arm over my mouth, stumble toward them. Aim, don't think. Hold breath.

I press down hard, blast the spray into Marcus's face, his torso. It ignites in the air. He falls against the couch, and the fire devours him, the cleaning fluid acting as an accelerant. Burning hair, flesh. His body twists, a dark shape, an arm clawing. I hear screaming.

I drop the bottle, stumbled backward, fall to my knees. Heat scorches my skin, sears my lungs. I can't breathe. Smoke and flames everywhere. Angus is barking and tugging on me. I crawl to the door, but I can't see anymore. Then there are hands.

"Mom. Mom!"

Someone is picking me up, dragging me, urging me to stay awake, and the air is sweet and the rain is coming down. I turn my face up to it, gasping for breath. My throat burns. Ash washes into my eyes, down my face, mixes with tears. I don't hear the screaming anymore.

CHAPTER FORTY-SIX

August 2017

I carry the box up the stairs, my shoes tapping on the hard-wood, and navigate the maze of boxes stacked in the center of the living room. The late August sun is warm as it spills through the floor-to-ceiling windows, covering everything with a sheen of gold. The furniture is mismatched, mostly secondhand items, but it goes together in an interesting, if eclectic, way and suits the loft-style apartment, which is the converted top floor of an old department store.

When Sophie, Delaney, and I first toured the place a couple of months ago, we stood by the windows, admiring the city view and pointing out buildings and landmarks we recognized. I'd watched Sophie's face in the reflection, looking for a hint of joy, excitement, anything, but I couldn't tell how she was feeling. Then Sophie and Delaney wandered around, poking into the bedrooms, opening closets, cupboards. Finally Sophie stopped in the living room and stared at the sun splashing across the wall. She turned and looked at me. "I want to live here."

It wasn't a smile. But it was something.

She's already hung some paintings on the wall and propped a large canvas with abstract flowers on the mantel. She's making it a home. Her first one without me. I feel a pang, but quickly shove it away. This is her time. I never had my own place, never went to university. Sometimes I feel like I was never young. I'm glad Sophie's following a different path.

I set the box on the kitchen counter. "How's it coming?"

Sophie stands up from the fridge, a sponge in hand, and twists her face into a disgusted expression. "I think someone was creating a science experiment in there." She's wearing a pink bandanna over her own hair, which she's dyed back to a light honey, almost her natural shade. It makes her look even more like Andrew, but the thought doesn't sting anymore, doesn't bring with it the memory of fear. It's just Sophie. Not Andrew, not anyone but my lovely daughter.

"You sure you don't want help?"

"Thanks, Mom, but you've done enough already." She notices the box and peeks inside. I've stuffed it with organic bread, trail mix, several types of vegetarian soup, canned spaghetti sauce, and various kinds of pasta. She gives me a look. "You know I can buy food, right?"

"I wanted to get you a few more basics."

"Basics? I don't think we even have enough cupboards for all this. You already filled most of them yesterday."

I give her a sheepish smile. "What can I say? I'm your mother. I don't want you living on french fries. Jared will probably eat most of it anyway."

"True." She glances at her watch. "He's coming over tonight."

"Is he all moved into his place?"

"Yeah. It looks really good." Jared found a house downtown and is sharing it with a few friends. Even though I'm no longer concerned that Jared is anything like Andrew, I still worried that he and Sophie might get a place together. I wanted Sophie to have the freedom to enjoy her first year of school. I was relieved when she told me they were getting separate places.

Sophie begins putting away the groceries. I want to help, but I make myself sit down at our old kitchen table that I gave her when I moved out of our temporary rental and into a small but cheerful two-bedroom house near the ocean. Angus and I walk on the beach every morning. In the beginning, when I was still working through the deep hurt of Marcus's betrayal and lies, I'd walk for hours at a time.

Corporal Parker kept in touch daily during the investigation and told us what she knew. Marcus and Elizabeth had been married for five years. He was a psychiatrist—that part was true—and he worked at a hospital, where they met when she was a volunteer. They wanted children so badly they'd mortgaged their house for fertility treatments. She hadn't even had a chance to tell her parents or her sister that she was finally pregnant. I grieved for a long time about that, imagined how excited she must have been, how happy.

After Elizabeth died, Marcus stopped communicating with his family and friends. When he was fired from the hospital for stealing painkillers, he sold off everything he owned except the lake house, took the accident insurance money, and drifted all over the world, moving from country to country, until he turned his rage into a plan for revenge.

The police think he always intended to kill us at the lake house—he'd invited me to stay there *twice*, suggested it as somewhere we'd be safe. They found a motorbike stored under the house, some other supplies, which is probably why he came outside and hit me with his flashlight instead of waiting for us all to fall asleep. He couldn't let me find his escape plan.

When they searched his home, they found passports, thousands of dollars in cash, and detailed notes in his laptop on me and Sophie and Andrew. He'd been watching me for months before he started volunteering at my support group. It still horrifies me, thinking how I'd let him into our lives. How I really thought I was in love with him. Corporal Parker tried to reassure me and told me that Marcus was very intelligent, but I still struggle with lingering anger and post-traumatic stress. At any point in all those months, he could have ended our lives.

I never told the police what triggered his attack that night. I wondered sometimes what would've happened if I hadn't told Marcus about the pills. We could have been together for years without my knowing he was a murderer. But then I realized that something else would have sent him over the edge when I couldn't fill the void, couldn't erase his grief.

I've been seeing a therapist and Sophie has come to a few sessions with me. For weeks after the fire she slept in my bed, reaching out in her sleep for my hand. I did the same thing.

I watch her now as she neatly arranges the cupboards. She looks tired, but her face is relaxed, not as tense around her eyes and mouth. It's been agonizing, seeing her struggle these last couple of months. On top of finding out that her father was killed by the man her mother was dating, she's had to deal with all the media and public scrutiny that's come with that. We were hounded for weeks, our entire lives ripped open for the world to see and judge and comment on.

She still drifts into quiet moods, but she seems a little happier. There's a new sensitivity to her art, a maturity that wasn't there before. I am hoping that a different environment, with school and friends, will pull her the rest of the way out of the dark.

"I found a car," Sophie says, glancing over her shoulder at me. "One of Greg's friends is selling his Acura. It's ten years old, but doesn't have much mileage on it. Greg said he'd check it over and teach me how to change the oil and tire pressure and stuff like that. Nice, eh?"

"Greg?" I'm startled at hearing his name. I've thought of him a few times over this summer, saw his truck once or twice around town. He doesn't do my delivery route now.

"I bumped into him in line at the Muddy Bean. He was asking how you're doing. Maybe you should give him a call. I think he's still single."

"How about you worry about school, and I'll worry about my own life, okay?" I keep my voice teasing. I've spent months sure that I would never date again. But lately, with the help of my therapist, I've been feeling hopeful that one day I'll be able to trust someone again.

Right now I'm focused on planning an upcoming vacation with Jenny—we're going to Palm Springs for a meditation retreat—and turning my spare bedroom into an oasis for any women from my group who need a place to stay while they recover. I'll be their safe house.

"I'm worried that you don't have a life!" Sophie says.

I laugh. "I have Angus, remember? But he's waiting at home, so I better get going."

She nods and walks with me toward the door. We hug, and as I pull away, she meets my eyes. "You going to be okay?" I know what she's really saying. *Will you be okay without me? Is it okay that I'm spreading my wings and flying away? Will you always love me?*

"I'm going to be just fine, honey. It's a new beginning for both of us. I'm actually even a little excited. Hey, maybe I'll go back to school and take some classes."

"Whoa." She holds up a hand. "This campus isn't big enough for the both of us."

I laugh. "Don't worry. I was thinking about the local college. Women's studies, or design. I don't know." I shrug. "The future is wide open."

"That's really cool, Mom." She reaches out and squeezes my hand. Feeling her smooth fingers in mine reminds me of something.

"I almost forgot. I brought you these," I say, taking a small velvet box out of my purse and passing it to her. "It's my engagement and wedding rings. I thought you might want them."

"Really?" Her voice is awed as she opens the box. "I wasn't sure if you kept them."

"Of course." I reach out and touch the engagement ring. I had the rings cleaned and they look shiny against the black velvet. "I was so happy when he gave me this."

She looks at me. "Do you still hate him?"

"No." I smile at her. "I don't hate him." I touch her face, tuck a strand of her hair behind her ear like I used to when she was little. "How could I? He gave me you."

"That's true. I am pretty awesome." Her voice is teasing, but her eyes are overly bright, like she's trying not to cry.

"Well, you have a pretty awesome mom—and a dad who loved you a lot."

Her face turns sad. "He wasn't lying, Mom. He was trying to protect us."

"I know, honey. I think about what might have happened if I'd just given him a chance to explain. But he'd be happy to know the truth came out in the end. He never let you down. It was important to him that you knew how much he loved you— and it's okay that *you* loved him. I really loved him once too. Your father wasn't evil. He was just broken."

She closes the box and holds it against her heart with a smile. I pull her closer and rest my cheek against hers, inhale her fresh scent. I think about that night so many years ago when I leaned over her bed, whispered in her ear, and stole her away from her father. I think about how she asked me if I would have done anything differently, and I finally know the answer. No. I had to take that risk. I had to run away. If I'd lost Sophie, I'd have lost everything. I'm truly at peace now, I realize, remembering Andrew. He was searching so hard to find forgiveness, and so was I. But I've found it. It was with me all along.

CHAPTER FORTY-SEVEN

Sophie

December 2017

Dear Mom,

Okay, so you're probably wondering why I'm writing you an actual letter and not an e-mail, or maybe you're thinking, "Why didn't she just pick up the phone? She doesn't call home enough!" I do! I call all the time but you're never there. Seriously, Mom. Stay home once in a while. You're having more fun than me. Don't you know you're supposed to be spending all your nights making healthy food for my freezer? Just kidding. I'm glad you're happy.

Time for the real stuff. When I sent that letter to Dad last year, I didn't lie. It really was a school project. It was supposed to be to someone who had the most impact on us. But I should have written it to you. You did so much for me, raising me all on your own. I always knew you loved me, more than anything, no matter what. Maybe that's why I was a smartass sometimes. Okay, okay. More than a few times. I just knew you wouldn't leave me.

When anything happens, bad or good, you're the first person I want to tell. I want you to be proud of me, proud of my choices, proud that I'm your daughter. Because I'm so proud that you're my mother. You're the bravest woman I know, which kind of sucks sometimes because you're a lot to live up to. But I'm going to try my best.

Mostly I just want you to know that I'm okay. I really am!! I know sometimes I've said I was and maybe I wasn't all the way there yet, but it's different now. It's like the air and everything feels better, lighter or something. Even my food tastes better (send more!).

I know that you feel bad sometimes, guilty or whatever, like maybe you think you messed me up or damaged me somehow, but you didn't. I think all my best, strongest parts have come from you. I might look like Dad on the outside, but on the inside, I'm all you.

Thank you, Mom. Thank you a million times over for loving me and letting me love my dad and for telling me how much you used to love him too. It helps, knowing that when you had me, you were truly happy. I didn't want to be a mistake! Ha. Thank you for pushing me and encouraging me and letting me explore the world. Thank you for being so cool about Jared. But, and this is my BIG secret, don't let me go just yet, okay? I still need you. Like water.

Love always and always,

Sophie

ACKNOWLEDGMENTS

As usual, I have so many people to thank, but I'd like to start with two wonderful friends who held me together during the process of writing this book, Carla Buckley and Robin Spano. You ladies make me laugh on the good days and understand on the bad days, and I really couldn't have done it without you.

Jen Enderlin, my editor at St. Martin's Press, who teaches me something new about writing, and about life, with every book. The fantastic Sally Richardson, Lisa Senz, Nancy Trypuc, Kim Ludlam, Brant Janeway, Elizabeth Catalano, Katie Bassel, Kristopher Kam, Caitlin Dareff, and the entire Broadway and Fifth Avenue sales force. Thanks again to Dave Cole and Ervin Serrano. In Canada, many thanks to Jamie Broadhurst, Fleur Mathewson, and the wonderful group at Raincoast.

Mel Berger, my agent now for over eight years, and the first person in the publishing world to believe in me. I can't imagine ever working with anyone else. My gratitude also to David Hinds, Simon Trewin, Anna DeRoy, Erin Conroy, Tracy Fisher, Laura Bonner, Raffaella DeAngelis, Annemarie Blumenhagen,

Covey Crolius, and the rest of the team at William Morris Endeavor Entertainment in New York and L.A.

Constable J. Moffat, Virginia Reimer, Dr. Ken Langelier, Renni Browne, Shannon Roberts, Bert King, Doug Torrie, Joanne Campbell, and BJ Brown for their professional advice. BJ, I hope we get to meet one day so I can thank you in person.

My husband, Connel, and my daughter, Piper, who hopefully won't write a book about me someday. Thank you for filling my life with so much love and laughter. You are the best kind of adventure.